The Violin Maker's Wife

DODIE BISHOP

You would sound me from my lowest note to the top of my compass; and there is much music, excellent voice, in this little organ, yet cannot you make it speak.

WILLIAM SHAKESPEARE - HAMLET: ACT 3,
SCENE 2

Prelude

AN UNFORMED THING

One

THE PARISH OF SAN MATTEO, CREMONA,
ITALY. AUGUST 1714

'GIUSEPPE?' THE OLD MAN'S VOICE BOOMED IN THE
cluttered shop with its wall of small wooden drawers behind the
ware-bench, all neatly labelled with their mysterious contents.
Rosin. Peg Dope. Peg Drop. Peg Pins. Cat Gut-assort. Whirling
Chalk. And many more, some so faded Katarina could not read
them.

'Giuseppe,' he called again over his shoulder. 'I've need of
you, lad. *Fräulein* Rota here wishes a violin played for her.'
Andrea Guarneri turned back to her. 'My fat fingers be too
clumsy now to do 'em justice.' He looked down at the offending
digits with obvious distaste.

How Giuseppe had reacted to his father's summons Katarina
did not know, for it was the violin that held her gaze when he
cradled it like a golden, newborn infant bringing it out from the
workshop. And when his fingers danced on the fingerboard, she
marvelled how the bow seemed to belong in his other hand like
an extension of his flesh. Yes, she was entranced, but she did
not look at his face.

Later, it made her laugh – and it was much discussed
between them over the years – to have no clear picture of him at

3

that first encounter when she remembered his grey-haired papà so clearly (and, in truth, he had not been so very old then). How could she not have noticed Giuseppe's unruly black curls for they were the single most striking thing about him? Never mind his beauty. He always claimed to remember his first sight of her clearly, though his wildly differing descriptions led her to believe otherwise. To put it bluntly, she had been a colourless, unformed sort of creature then. A plain child, (and what is worse for a child than to know it?).

And the sound the violin made that morning seemed to her otherworldly, like singing beyond the top of any possible human range before plunging down to a bass deep and rich as molasses … down into darkness. One word filled her thoughts. *Heartbreaking*. To her surprise, she saw Leda brush away a tear. Leda was not one for displays of emotion either in herself or others. Especially not in Katarina. Yet her appearance belied her nature, being soft and fair with a pillowy bosom and a child's dimples. Her eyes, the innocent blue of a china doll's, were full of fiery steel when caning her charge's hand for forgetting her Latin declensions.

Might it be the contrast with the playing Katarina had heard the Sunday before in the cathedral that had so moved her? While that sound had led her to the violin district to find out more about the instrument, she had not anticipated the extent of the difference. And violins in a church service? Who would have imagined it? Not John Calvin. In Katarina's church the only music came from the human voice. And that was often discordant.

Though it could be claimed she had arrived there in the Guarneri workshop in a way that seemed preordained, it had been a random choice made to silence Leda's complaints, walking the cobbled streets around the Basilica of San Domenico.

She really had no idea which workshop to enter yet opened

that fateful door as though it had been the one she searched for and, indeed, she had wished Leda to think it was. (She had told her that she looked for sheet music for the pianoforte.) Whilst her eyes adjusted to the gloom after the dazzle outside, the pungent smell assailed her, though she had no idea what made it then. But it smelt exotic and so somewhere she ought not to be. That thought had made her smile. Though, in truth, she held no truck with predestination especially when proselytised by her father's Calvinism. Even then she thought of it as her father's and not hers for she had already decided the idea of God held little interest for her, and most certainly not that one.

So, on the previous Sunday with her father laid low by a summer ague, she had joined some of the officers' families whose religion took them to Cremona's magnificent *Cattedrale di Santa Maria Assunta* with its great rose window over the portal, its octagonal baptistry, and the *Torrazzo* towering above. She had explored it many times, overawed by the weight of whispers and echoes lost in the great height of its vaulted ceiling, disappearing into gloom. The scent of beeswax and candle smoke, incense and flowers, and the sweetness of their decay, seemed embedded in its ancient stone. She had gaped in awe at bright frescoes telling the stories of Abraham and Isaac, Jacob and Joseph. The Passion of Christ. Jesus with the doctors. Every time she visited, she found something new to marvel at … the inlaid wooden choir screen, the great altar cross crafted from silver and gold … but she had never experienced a Mass there. Needless to say, her father knew nothing of this and would not have approved, being especially censorious of everything papist.

It did cross her mind that should there truly be a God, would he not prefer the glory of a cathedral laboured over for centuries in his name to the little wooden church close by the banks of the Po, which the Calvinists seemed to believe would please him more? And, of course, she had not expected violins to fill the pauses in the Mass which it turned out, had been a poor introduction to what this astonishing instrument could do.

It was some time before she learnt about a violin's tonal range and later still what Giuseppe had played for her that day. A concerto by Tomaso Albinoni, one of the earliest compositions for the violin virtuoso. There would be many simpler pieces for her to master before she was ready for that.

When she told Signor Guarneri her intentions, he had shown no reservations that a girl, small for her thirteen years, should be so much in command of her own life that she could say with confidence that her father would purchase the three-quarter-size violin he had suggested for her and pay for the lessons she would need. Katarina never doubted it then, and neither did Andrea, he told her later, which was why he had not asked Leda for conformation. It seemed they were both good judges of character. Why had Leda not interfered in the exchange? Might she have believed Katarina's father had truly given his permission or did she hope her charge would be humiliated by his angry refusal?

Several days later, when Anja fetched Katarina to the morning salon, she could honestly say it was the first time she had looked at Giuseppe. She found him gazing around the room with undisguised admiration. That it was filled with sunlight showed it to best advantage with its gilded marble fireplace and bright frescoed ceiling appropriately depicting the muses, and all its polished mahogany furniture with silk upholstery gleaming. The floor-length casement windows were open to the garden as it was already hot though early still, and the scent of roses in full bloom filled the room.

'*Palazzo Poli* is where the Austrian commandant lives.' He smiled a little uncertainly. 'Is he your papà?'

'His deputy. We have this apartment because he is.'

'Ah.' Giuseppe nodded.

She took a few moments more to study him surreptitiously while he surveyed his surroundings still. He was tall and broad-shouldered with dark-lashed eyes the colour of honey, and wild black curls already escaping the leather throng at his neck, and Katarina unexpectedly found she had no idea what to say to him. 'You have it, I see.' She gestured towards the violin case he carried, quickly feeling heat on her face at the absurdity of such a remark. He would hardly arrive to give her a lesson without the means to do so.

'Er, yes.' He held it up as though to prove it.

She realised then he was likely feeling just as awkward. Katarina turned to the maid who was openly grinning at their mutual discomfiture. 'That will be all, Anja.' The girl bobbed a curtsy and left.

With that, he seemed to gather himself. 'Shall we start, then?' He placed the case down on a side table and brought out the violin, smiling as he handed it to her.

When she took it, she let out a small gasp for it was so much lighter than she had expected. She stroked its rich amber patina which glowed in the sunlight as though lit from within. 'How can it weigh so little?'

He laughed. 'Like lifting a hen, no?'

She had never held a hen but understood what he meant. While it looked a large bird, it was very feathery. 'I suppose this is not full size, so—'

'Makes little difference.' He rubbed the bow with a piece of a clear yellowish substance before placing the instrument beneath his chin to play a scale.

'What was that you rubbed on it?'

'Rosin. Without it, the strings wouldn't sound.'

He dropped it into her hand, and she frowned sniffing it. 'It smells like pine. What's it made from?'

'Pine resin.'

Again, she blushed. A stupid question.

Giuseppe played the scale again before handing her the instrument and positioning it with the chinguard against her neck and the bow clasped firmly in her right hand. When he stood behind her to place her fingers on the fingerboard, she felt his heat and noticed the same odour that permeated his workshop. She began tentatively and the noise she made, even with his clever fingers guiding hers, was not pretty. Finally, she thrust the violin back at him, mortified. 'I didn't expect to sound quite so bad.'

'Everyone does when they start.'

'Even you?'

'I'm sure I did but I can't remember it. I can't even remember when it was. I must have been just a young lad.' He shrugged. 'Maybe three or so. What age are you, Katarina?

'Thirteen.'

He tilted his head, studying her. 'You look younger.'

Katarina felt herself redden again, knowing it would be all too obvious on her pale cheeks. White as milk and treacherous (blushes, and ugly freckles with the sun's slightest touch). Not to mention lank brown hair. And worst of all she was ridiculously small and completely unremarkable. She eyed his tawney skin and those wild black curls. Unremarkable he most definitely was not. 'Can you really teach me to play? Perhaps it will be beyond me?' She felt close to tears even thinking of such a failure.

He lifted her chin gently, his eyes soft with kindness. 'No. You love the violin's voice. I saw it when you listened to me play. When you felt it like that, well, I've no worries about you learning.' He demonstrated the scale once more describing the fingering as he did, before handing it back.

Katarina tried her best to master it over and over that morning and before Giuseppe left, he insisted she had already improved though she could hear little difference herself. She walked with him to the stables through gardens heavy with the scent of hot flowers,

'You speak Italian without much of an accent.'

Katarina bristled. 'I haven't got an accent. I've lived in Cremona for seven years.'

'I expect this lot speak German quite a bit though, don't they? I can hear you have a touch of it.'

She shrugged. Perhaps it was so? And it was a little disconcerting to think everyone knew she was Austrian the moment she opened her mouth. *One of the conquerors.* In the stables, she watched him mount his horse. A rather fine chestnut mare which for some reason surprised her. 'She's lovely.'

He seemed to read it on her face. 'Bella. And she's not mine she belongs to Antonio.' He grinned. 'He won't mind I borrowed her.' He turned the horse and began to move away. 'I hope,' he called back over his shoulder. And with that he cantered across the paddock towards the road.

She watched until he was out of sight. Who was Antonio?

Two

CREMONA, SEPTEMBER 1714

THE FOLLOWING WEEK, KATARINA'S LESSON WAS HELD
at number 5 Piazza San Domenico, for she had not been alone in
finding the sounds she made hard on the ears, though it was her
father who suggested the change of venue.

She had discovered her bedchamber seemed the only place
she could practice without any complaints but could hardly
invite Giuseppe there, Leda insisted. So, they set off together in
one of the carriages kept for the officers' use.

Leda made her feelings plain about accompanying her
charge. 'Surely Anja would be an adequate chaperone for you. I
fail to see why I must be the one tortured by your horrible
noise.'

Katarina shrugged. 'Not my idea for you to come. Why do I
even need a chaperone?'

The governess looked her up and down with a frown. 'Well,
quite.'

Katarina was not entirely sure what she meant by that but
felt certain it was not complementary. They did not speak again
for the rest of the journey from San Pantaleone, passing the
curved wall of Basilica San Domenico's side chapel before

arriving at the piazza in San Matteo, the heart of the luthiers' isle made up of the streets around the basilica and the cathedral, including the parishes of San Faustino and Giovita.

When Katarina walked into the shop, it was as though she had never been inside before finding no memory of it beyond a tidy ware-bench and the drawers behind, and the smell of the place. There was an old lady behind the counter that morning who beamed at her, obviously knowing who she was and why she had come. 'Giuseppe,' she called behind her. 'Your little signorina is here. Well, aren't you a pretty one. You'll be a beauty when you're grown, that's for sure.'

Katarina smiled dutifully, thinking her sight must be failing for she did appear extremely ancient. 'I'm here for my lesson,' she said, unnecessarily.' And she blushed. Of course, she did.

Giuseppe came out from the workshop, wiping his hands on a rag before removing his leather apron. 'You're an early bird, Katarina.' His gaze moved behind her to Leda who smiled her pretty, deceiving smile, fluttering her lashes over her button eyes. She had blatantly ignored the old woman who, to be fair, had not given her a glance either.

Giuseppe put his arm around the old lady. 'This is my nonna, Barbara Franchi. My mamma's mamma. We call her Nonna Barb.' He saw her eyes were still fixed on Katarina and grinned. 'I think she's taken with you.' He kissed his grandmother's wrinkled cheek before gesturing to the workshop. 'Come. We must go through there to get to the parlour. Your maid can come too if she wants.'

Katarina heard Leda's hiss as she followed Giuseppe. Leda saw herself as very much the superior in their relationship. How could Katarina help but grin?

'I'll take a turn or two around the square,' she called, haughtily.

The workshop looked like an Aladdin's cave to Katarina. There was a large window with a workbench set beneath it where a man and two boys in canvas aprons worked on instruments in various stages of completion. The walls were hung with racks holding tools and others for instruments, with more hanging from bars suspended from the ceiling. She wanted to stop and ask him about everything she saw, but he hurried her through dropping his apron on the bench beside a partially completed violin as they passed. 'Where's your papá?'

'Privy,' he said opening a door to a small bright room with a further door open onto a sunny courtyard lined with terracotta pots full of scarlet geraniums and a table and benches set beneath a grape vine trained over a fame to give shade. And grapes. Heavy bunches of them ripe and ready for picking.

She blushed again. What could she say to that? Nothing. 'How long does it take to make one?' She gasped, which sounded like a hiccough. 'A violin, I mean.' Her face burned on and on.

'Depends on the luthier—'

'Luthier?'

'Maker. I try for six a year. Antonio makes four, though he's an old man now. He wastes too much time prettifying them in my opinion, but they sell very well.' He shrugged and watched his father cross the court from the outhouse. 'I'm more interested in their voices.'

'It is possible to do both, lad. Do you think Antonio Stradivari's instruments don't sound good too?'

It was clearly a conversation often revisited.

Giuseppe threw his arm around his father's shoulders. 'Here he is again, my papá. His name is Giuseppe too by the way, but everyone calls him Andrea after his papá, even though my real first name is Bartolomeo.'

Andrea harumphed going through into the workshop.

Katarina watched the door close behind him. They seemed to have made it all unnecessarily complicated for themselves.

Giuseppe took the case from her and removed the violin,

playing a few notes before tuning it for a moment or two. 'You've been practising, I'm sure.'

She nodded, marvelling that he could hear when each string sounded as it should. 'Until my fingers almost bleed and I'm still terrible. How long will it take until I'm not?'

He held out his own fingers. 'You'll soon have calluses. Play for me.'

She plodded through the three scales he had taught her, sliding her fingers noisily up the strings. 'See. Have you ever found anyone who truly can't do it?'

'I've never taught before.'

She could not hide her surprise. 'So, why are you teaching me?'

He grinned. 'Your father pays well, and I like you.'

She did wonder for a moment if he could be teasing her. 'But why?'

'I've already told you. The way you listened ... the way you *heard* me when I played.'

As they continued that morning, Katarina became more and more conscious of where she was. This was the heart of the luthiers' district and the hideous sound escaping from the open casement must be echoing all around, forcing knowing ears to be covered and work disrupted. Needless to say, these thoughts did not help her, and her fingers stumbled again and again until she stopped.

'What's wrong?'

She shook her head and tried again, keeping the notes as quiet as possible.

'What are you doing?' He took the violin from her and played the scale at the correct volume.

She refused to take it when he tried to hand it back. 'I can't do this here. Everyone can hear me. The noise I make is shameful.' It was not difficult to see how her words vexed him.

'It's the sound of someone learning to play. What do you expect?' He started to replace her violin in its case. 'But if you want to give up it's your choice—' He gave her a hard stare. 'Are you really so full of yourself you can't take a little failure so you might learn?'

Heat flamed on her face, again. Was that what he thought this was about? And then she wondered if, perhaps, he was right. She lifted her chin. 'Not at all. I'm merely thinking of peoples' ears.'

'Well, don't.'

He handed her the instrument, and she began again as loudly as she could. When he chuckled, she glared at him. Though he stopped, his eyes were full of laughter.

Finally, he took the violin from her again and played a simple tune that seemed to use no more notes than she had already learnt ... or tried to. Then he stood behind her, placing her fingers on the fingerboard and guiding her bow hand to play the same tune. And it was wonderful to get some idea of the sound she could make if she worked hard enough. She turned to face him, and they smiled at each other. 'Thank you.' She thought they both knew then that she would not give up. It was at that moment a sudden cramp in her belly made her gasp and she clutched herself. 'Forgive me, I don't feel ...'

He guided her to a worn armchair, looking alarmed. 'Sit—'

'No. No. I can't. I—' She fled out of the door and across the yard to the outhouse. When she lowered herself onto the earth closet and found blood, she almost fainted. Was she about to die here in a privy where her corpse would be found by strangers? But after several moments waiting for the bloody flux that did not come, and finding herself very much alive, she clenched her jaw trying not to weep though tears blurred her vision for she was now completely at a loss what to do. A light tap on the door startled her. Sweet Jesu, someone wished to use the privy. 'A moment.' She dried her face on her sleeve as she stood.

'What's wrong, child. Are you unwell?' Signora Franchi called.

Her eyes brimmed with tears again at the sound of such gentle concern. 'I think I'm dying.'

'May I come in?' She did not wait for an answer and pulled Katarina into her arms, patting her back as she sobbed. Then she took her hand leading her out to the table beneath the grapevine, sitting her down and fetching her a dipper of water from the well bucket.

Katarina gulped it down.

The Signora sat beside her. 'Tell me what's happened, little chick.'

So, haltingly, she did. 'Am I going to die?'

Nonna Barb patted her hand. 'Not at all. Pray God, not for a very long time. 'It's just your monthly courses beginning. Has no one told you of it?'

Katarina shook her head, rubbing her belly where cramps still gripped her. 'But why? What purpose does it serve?'

Nonna Barb tutted and stroked her cheek. 'I know someone who can help you with the pains.' She stood. 'Come with me.'

Katarina rose and looked back towards the house with some trepidation.

The old woman understood at once. 'There's a gate into the alley. We'll go that way.' She grasped Katarina's hand to lead her. 'You'll like Merla Bianchi. She's a fine apothecary.'

Katarina walked with the old lady past the Basilica of San Domenico with its three great entrance doors. That there was no sign of Leda was a great relief. 'My governess will be back for me soon—'

'Don't you worry about her, my chick, I'll leave you with Merla so I can send her on her way. We'll get you home when you're feeling better.'

Katarina was not too sure she wished to be left with this unknown woman. Could a woman even be an apothecary? She pictured someone of Signora Franchi's age though rather more witch-like. In truth, she pictured an actual witch (well, one from a fairy tale). With warts. And a broomstick. And a black cat.

The small shop was little different to the others in the street, with a painted sign hanging from a bracket showing various cordials and botanicals used in physic – similar to the bottles and dried bunches hanging in the window – as a border around the name *Alberto Bianchi, Apothecary*, in large black letters. Katarina stopped and stared at it.

Signora Franchi turned to her. 'Merla's papà, God rest him. We'll get you inside and soon have you feeling better.'

The woman behind the ware-bench could not have been further from her imaginings, though there was indeed a black cat sitting close beside her on the counter, its emerald eyes viewing Katarina with studied indifference. Merla Bianchi was about the same age as Leda, Katarina thought, though where Leda was plump and fair, she was slender but womanly too, with hair like a stream of black silk down her back, a startling white streak coming from her right temple cutting through its mass like a blackbird with a single white feather. Her hand swept through it pushing it back from a face that was pointed rather like her cat's, though her large eyes were the grey of winter storms.

Katarina thought her the most beautiful woman she had ever seen, and so stunned was she by her appearance that she barely heard what Signora Franchi said or noticed her leaving.

The apothecary stood looking down at her, black brows raised, hands on hips. 'Well, you are a poor little scrap, aren't you? Come with me, I'll make you comfortable in the parlour and brew some willow bark tea for those cramps.'

Katarina could think of nothing to say, so followed her meekly through her pungent workroom where bunches of dried herbs hung from hooks beside shelves of assorted canisters and flagons of coloured liquids. The long narrow layout of the place appeared almost identical to the Guarneris'. In the kitchen parlour the open garden door led to a large walled space laid out as a physic garden, most of the plants were unknown to her but their spicy scents filled the air.

'Let's get you seen to first.' She led Katarina though another door to the cooking kitchen where she showed her how to make what looked like an infant's clout out of cloths until, eventually, she sat at the table and drank her tea which had enough honey stirred into it to mask its bitter taste.

When she had finished, Merla Bianchi sat beside her taking her hand in hers. 'So, no one told you about this.' She stroked Katarina's palm with her thumb. 'It must have been very frightening. Have you no mamma, little one?'

Katarina shook my head 'She died when I was born.'

'Then I'm sad for you. Who cares for you now? Barb said there was a woman with you earlier.'

Katarina frowned and repeated Leda's own words. 'She's my governess, not my nursemaid.'

'If she teaches you, she should have taught you about this, no?' Merla smiled. 'But no matter, I can tell you all you need to know.'

And that is what she did, including some things Katarina probably did not need quite then, but she imagined the apothecary thought that if she could get a child then she should at least know of the basic process in order to avoid it. Though, in truth, Katarina could not imagine ever wanting to perform such a disgusting act.

After walking her back to the Piazza San Domenico along streets more or less deserted in the noon heat, they stopped outside the door to the Guarneris' shop and Merla held Katarina's face, gently. 'Don't worry. They'll be kind.'

Yet how could she not feel mortified by the nature of her

complaint? Though the more she thought of it all, the angrier she became that she had been left in such ignorance. She lifted her chin. 'I shall speak to my father about Leda.'

'Good, little one. You do that.'

Merla Bianchi opened the door leaving Katarina no choice but to go in. 'Come and see me again.'

Katarina nodded and stepped inside. That Signora Franchi was alone in the shop was surely not an accident?

The old woman hurried around the ware-bench to take Katarina in her arms. 'How are you now, my chick?'

Katarina managed a smile. 'Better ... much better. Thank you for being so kind to me.'

'I gave that maidservant of yours a piece of my mind. Hoity miss waited outside for your carriage after that.'

Katarina managed a somewhat broader smile then which, in truth, was closer to a grin. 'I shall speak to my papá about her.' *Maidservant.* How she wished Leda could have heard it again.

'Quite right too. Now we'd better see about getting you home.' She handed her a parasol lifted from beneath the bench. 'You'll need this.'

Giuseppe came out from the workshop then, holding her violin case. 'Pietro's gone to fetch the pony cart. Sorry it won't be as comfortable as you're used to—'

'I shan't mind it. I'm very grateful to you.' She could not bring herself to look at him. How she hated her face flaming. She so wished to appear nonchalant, but her glowing cheeks refused to cooperate. She prayed he would not question her.

The Signora hugged her again at the sound of hooves outside. 'We'll see you next week, yes?'

Katarina nodded and followed Giuseppe out to the street. The cart waiting there appeared abandoned.

Giuseppe scanned the empty square, frowning. 'Why the hell would he just leave it like this?'

The sturdy piebald pony contentedly resting one hind leg

atop its hoof looked more ready for a doze than an escape attempt. 'Who's Pietro?'

'My brother. He's been working with Gianni Gabrieli for the last few weeks.'

Katarina turned to him, wondering why she had not heard a brother mentioned before, but Giuseppe said nothing further before climbing up onto the driving bench and reaching down to pull her up beside him. Seeing how the sun gleamed off the cream stone of San Domenico's on the corner, she was glad the cart was in the shade. 'Sorry you must come out in the heat.'

He grunted, frowning, and shook the reins sending the pony plodding forward.

'And for keeping you from your work,' she added in a small voice.

He turned to her with a sigh followed by a slow smile. 'Don't worry yourself. I'm glad to get away from Pietro and Papá's bickering.'

Something in his expression told her she should not comment, and she knew she was right when he changed the subject as they clopped across the Piazza Maggiore through a scattering of people keeping to the shade of the *Duomo*, the slow hoofbeats echoing against the sound of midday Mass.

'Do you read music, Katarina?'

She nodded. 'I play the pianoforte a little.' She blushed. 'I mean I play badly.' She turned to look at him. 'There seems to be a pattern emerging.' As soon as she said it, she wished she had not. *Does he think I'm fishing for compliments?*

He shook his head smiling. 'Hogwash. That's hogwash and you know it. Anyway, I'd hoped you would sight read. I've put some sheets in your case that you might like to try when you practice. And some diagrams for the fingering.'

Now it seemed important to explain. 'I do prefer the violin. Or I will when I can play it. The pianoforte seems so limited in comparison.'

'Well, of course it does. Because it is.'

When they both laughed, just like that, they were at ease with each other again. Giuseppe kept the cart in shade where he could, and Katarina raised the parasol where he could not, until they arrived at the gates in the high stucco walls surrounding *Palazzo Poli*.

Giuseppe climbed down to help her alight and gave her a quick hug. 'I'll see you next week, Katarina.' He stepped away to clang the rusty bell fixed to the gatepost, summoning the gate-keeper, and waited beside her until they opened revealing the shady courtyard. She watched him climb onto the cart and move away before going inside.

Three

~~~

CREMONA, SEPTEMBER 1714

WITH THE PONY STABLED AND THE CART SECURED IN the yard, Giuseppe felt no urgency – or indeed wish – to return to the workshop so, instead, settled for wandering the streets aimlessly, keeping to the dusty shadows in the stifling afternoon heat.

His father and brother's arguments were becoming more and more bitter and spiteful with his work being disapproved of by both, though for different reasons, damn them, so he found himself being pulled in against his will. Pietro's insistence that a violin's appearance was of equal value to its sound was horse-shit, of course.

When a stumble on the curb brought him out of his reverie, he spotted Merla Bianchi's apothecary shop a short way along the street and decided to speak to her about Katarina. He had felt sorry for her that morning when belly cramps had struck so suddenly. The shits he had supposed until Nonna Barb said not and cautioned him not to speak of it. Though she had seemed recovered on their journey to her home, he now felt a vague sense of unease about her. He had intended to press his nonna on it, but Signora Bianchi seemed a better bet. He sighed. At least this problem had an easy solution.

The bell sounded over the door when he opened it to step inside the deserted shop, hit by the sharp scent of herbs. With the shutters closed, it took a few moments for his eyes to adjust to the gloom before he saw the black cat curled up sleeping on the ware-bench, snoring softly. When Merla did not appear, Giuseppe realised she must be resting in the heat of the afternoon. What was he thinking? Of course she was. He was turning to leave when she emerged from the back dressed in a jade green banyan, her hair a cloak around her. Giuseppe swallowed, seeing how the silk of her robe clung to the contours of her body, her breasts swinging slightly as she moved around the counter to stand before him.

'What can I do for you, Giuseppe?' She glanced at the shop door. 'I thought I'd locked it for *riposo*.'

Giuseppe took another step towards it. 'Forgive me, I wasn't thinking. I'll come back later.' She caught his arm to stop him and again he was acutely aware of her nakedness beneath the thin fabric.

'No. You're here now. Tell me what you need.'

When she swept her mass of hair back from her forehead, her banyan parted showing the rounded top of one heavy breast, Giuseppe's face burned, and he knew his blushes would be as crimson as Katarina's had his skin been so fair. But worst of all, he found himself quite unable to utter a word. With his face on fire and his cock painfully hard, he managed a small prayer of thanks that the shadows would hide him.

Merla tilted her head, staring at him intently, and then she laughed. 'You desire me.' She moved closer and placed her cool hand onto his hot face. 'I'm flattered … and you should not be ashamed of such feelings. They're quite natural. How old are you now, Giuseppe?'

'Sixteen,' he croaked.

'Hmm. Come with me.'

She grasped his damp hand in hers and led him through the workroom to a kitchen parlour the mirror image of his. When she opened the door to the staircase, he found his heart beating so fast he could barely breathe.

She turned to look at him and laughed again. 'Don't look so terrified, I'm not going to eat you.'

Later, when he lay beside her on her featherbed, the window shutters open and the thin curtains billowing in the gusty breeze, their naked bodies slick with sweat, he was scarcely able to make sense of what had happened between them. Christ. The first time he had not even made it on top of her before … he closed his eyes trying to block out the memory. But she had been kind … and gentle. And he had got better. Much better. He grinned, raising himself up on his elbow to look down at her. 'Why? Why would you take me to your bed like this?' How could he ever forget his first sight of her body when she had slipped out of her robe and stood before him naked? Or the feel of her flesh beneath his hands. That salty sweetness of her skin.

She reached up to cup his face. 'You're a beautiful boy, and I find beauty hard to resist.'

'Have there been others like me? Boys, I mean?'

She laughed. 'One or two, though a long time ago when I was just a girl myself.'

'So, why me now?'

'Why not?' She raised her heavy dark eyebrows. 'Do you wish it otherwise?'

He chuckled. 'What do you think?'

Merla joined him in more laughter until his mouth found hers and conversation took a back seat once again until he rolled away trying to recover his breath.

She moved onto her side to watch him, and their eyes met.

'You should be on your way now, sweet one. I must open the shop.'

The question felt awkward, but he could not resist asking it. 'Have you enjoyed this … being with me like this?'

She smiled. 'Did it seem to you that I hadn't?'

He grinned. 'No. It felt like you did. You showed me how to please you, I just …' He chewed his lip. 'I hoped you weren't pretending … to not hurt my feelings.'

Merla ran her fingers through his hair, teasing out the curls. 'Women do that sometimes, but I wasn't doing it with you.'

'So, we can do it again?' The raw eagerness in his voice shamed him. He sounded like a needy kid.

'We'll see,' she said as though answering that child as she swung her legs down to the floor.

He dressed silently, trying to hide his humiliation.

In the shop with the shutters opened, she turned to him placing her palm on his face. 'Of course I want you again, but it can't be too often or people will talk. And you should keep company with girls your own age. You—'

He laughed. 'But not in their beds.'

'No. Not that.' She tilted her head studying him. 'You never told me why you came here?'

'I was worried about Katarina. I know Nonna Barb brought her to you when she had a bellyache this morning.' His own belly chose that moment to rumble, reminding him it was a long time since he ate breakfast.

'Come. I'll feed you and explain about Katarina.' She led him back to the kitchen parlour where she cut bread at the table and sliced mozzarella, tomatoes and basil onto a plate before dousing them with olive oil. After pouring two glasses of wine, she sat watching him eat, dipping the wedges of bread into the green oil.

When he was done, she refilled their glasses. 'Now to Katarina. You must understand this is not something I would ever do under normal circumstances but in this case.' She shrugged. 'I don't want you questioning her ... asking her how she is. Anything like that. She's horribly embarrassed about it, poor little thing.' Merla explained it all to him succinctly, stressing how Katarina's lack of knowledge had been the real cause of her distress. 'Looking at you, I think you know something of this already?'

He stared down at his hands. 'Only some friend's jeering about their sisters. They laughed about it. I joined in.' He closed his eyes for a moment. 'But it felt mean ... it didn't seem like something they could help.' He looked up and met Merla's gaze. 'I never knew it was about getting a kid ... and that it happens every month.' He swallowed. 'Sounds fucking grim.'

'It's part of a woman's life.' She gave him a hard stare. 'And it's why men should not spill their seed carelessly.'

Giuseppe walked home through streets filling with people again as the air cooled and shops opened their shutters. He had not understood that a woman could enjoy lying with a man just as much as the man did. Well, Merla certainly seemed to have. And how ready a woman's body was to get a child, which explained why she had taught him what to do to try and prevent it. He felt a sudden wave of tenderness for Katarina. How frightened she must have been. Why in the name of holy hell had her family allowed that to happen to her?

Katarina closed the door to her bedchamber, leaning against it with a sigh of relief. There was a great deal to think about. She crossed to her window and looked out over the garden, the roses appearing hot and dusty in the heat, much like her. She spun around at the sound of a knock and watched the door fly open before she had time to respond.

Anja scurried in. 'You's back.'

'Yes. I do believe I am.' Dressed in her usual simple grey gown and white apron, which her womanly shape somehow managed to make attractive, with her large hazel eyes and cheerful expression, Anja turned heads and knew it.

The maid giggled and sat down on Katarina's bed, auburn curls escaping from her coif as always. 'I've been waiting for you. The countess has been in to see your father, complaining about them violin people.'

Katarina's fury was instantaneous. 'How dare she when she's the one at fault, and I shall tell him so.' She sat beside her maid. 'And don't call her the countess. She'd enjoy it however much you mean it unkindly.'

Anja laughed. 'Very well. Now, tell me what's 'appened.'

So, that is what she did and, unexpectedly, it helped her make more sense of it.

'Why didn't you ask me about all that? I could 'ave put you right.'

Katarina tutted in exasperation. 'How could I when I didn't know there was anything to ask about?'

A frown appeared between Anja's brows. 'I sees what you mean. Well, I can tell you a good deal more about what 'appens with a man and a woman than what that wise wife did.'

And, indeed, she could – and did – in the most explicit detail. Did Katarina need to know how men and women pleasured each other? And how to prevent a child when they did? Probably not. But after knowing nothing it felt no bad thing to know too much. 'Might it not have occurred to you that Signora Bianchi chose not to tell me all this because I have no need of it yet?'

'Pah. How do you knows when you'll need it?'

'I'm thirteen, Anja.'

She tapped her nose. 'I were but a year older when I 'ad need of such. How glad I were my sister had already told me what I just told you.'

Katarina tried so hard not to ask. But how could she not? Though she had a strong notion she would find Anja's answer distasteful. 'Very well then, what happened.'

Somehow, she managed not to cover her ears though she shuddered when the maid's tale finally came to an end. '*Really? He put that in your mouth?*' She felt sick at the thought of such a thing. 'How could you let him?'

Anja laughed. 'I wanted to. He done me first see, so it were only polite. And I liked it. I liked how it gave me power over him, if you sees what I mean. He were that desperate for what I were giving him.'

'Well, I shall never do that under any circumstances. Or let anyone do such a thing to me.'

Anja giggled. 'You will. You'll see.' She stood. 'Now, you'll want to bathe. I'll have 'em bring water up.' She went to the armoire to select fresh clothing, for Katarina's gown was dusty and sweat-stained after her ride in the open cart. Anja laid them out on the bed beside her. 'This'll do for dinner, too. I'll wash your hair. You've plenty of time for it to dry afore you must go down.'

After dinner, when Katarina took her father's arm for their customary stroll around the gardens in the cool of the evening, she knew he would raise Leda's complaint against Signora Franchi now they were alone.

'After what I heard today, I think we must find another violin teacher for you.' He looked down at her. 'If you are determined to carry on with it, of course?' He was tall and broad with a soldier's bearing, still. And she wondered, not for the first time, how she was his daughter when she was such a meagre creature.

'I am quite determined, Father.' She stopped and moved away from him, trying to hold his gaze in the twilight. 'And

Giuseppe must remain my teacher.'

He frowned, appearing quite taken aback by her unusual defiance. 'No, Katarina. You will not visit a household where your governess can be spoken to with such disrespect. Surely you must have heard what was said to her?'

'I did not.' And when she told him exactly where she was and why, she saw many emotions chase each other across his face. Would he tell her that such things should not be spoken of between a father and daughter?

He took her hand then and led her to a stone bench in the rose garden where they sat, and he cupped her face staring at her intently in the fast-fading light. 'You truly are so like your mother. I should have noticed you were growing up. Can you forgive me for it, Katarina? It tears at my heart to think of you so distressed.'

I don't seem to grow any taller, Father, so there is little to notice.'

'You have your mother's stature.' He sighed. 'I'm glad this family were kind to you. I shall write to the grandmother and thank her myself … er … can she read, do you know?'

'Of course she can,' Katarina hoped. 'They're not peasants.'

He stood and hugged her. 'Perhaps you would find Leda for me and instruct her to come to my office.'

'What will you say to her?'

He tilted his head. 'Maybe this was just thoughtlessness on her part. Though I did make it clear from the start she must be more than a governess to you when you had no mother to guide you. Tell me, is she kind to you, my daughter?'

Katarina shook her head. 'I don't think she likes me. She thinks me stupid.'

'My dear girl, that is the last thing you are.' He sighed. 'Then I think we must let her go. I shall make other arrangements to continue your—'

'Not another governess, I beg you.'

He laughed. 'Let me give it some thought.'

Katarina took a deep breath for she knew precisely what she wanted instead. 'There are officers who have tutors for their sons. Erwin and Gerhart Hartmann have one. Might I not join them? I would very much like the chance to learn Latin properly … and Greek, too.'

He laughed again, softly. 'Well, my Katarina, knowing you as I do, I'm sure you'll quickly become proficient. I'll speak to Captain Hartmann.'

Her eyes widened in disbelief that such a thing might be possible, and she flung her arms around him. 'Oh, Father, I promise I shall.'

First Movement

❧

THE LUTHIERS' ISLE

Four

CREMONA, OCTOBER 1717

KATARINA CONTINUED HER WEEKLY VISITS TO PIAZZA San Domenico, though no longer for the lessons her father still paid for. When Giuseppe had claimed there was nothing more he could teach her – her playing had already gone beyond his – she was not entirely sure she believed him, though he would not budge on it. How could she not think he had simply grown tired of her, and the thought of not seeing him anymore left her feeling sick and shaky and on the verge of tears?

When she spoke of this to Anja, she pushed Katarina to make Giuseppe jealous by showing interest in Pietro.

'He won't even notice. He's not interested in me in that way.' Might it be possible she loved him? Jesu, it was hard to know. But one thing she was certain of, she could not bear to think of a life without him in it.

Anja shrugged. 'Bet he'll be up for it if he thinks his brother's after you. I have brothers. I know these things.'

Katarina said nothing but decided to practise her violin more diligently than ever and, after a flash of inspiration, to start composing her own pieces, which she would somehow contrive to play for him … if they were any good, of course. Interest in

33

her as a violinist was better than no interest at all. So, she would not stop going to the workshop. And as it turned out, no one objected, especially as they were still being paid. Katarina did not really wish to deceive her father but as he never asked how her lessons were going, it was more a sin of omission than commission. Or so she told herself. Her time there was now spent in the workshop, watching, asking questions, and helping out in any way they would allow.

That following Anja's suggestion to spend time with Pietro had no noticeable effect upon Giuseppe – it certainly did not provoke any discernible jealousy on his part – did not surprise her in the least, though it left her with the not inconsiderable reward of Pietro's friendship.

Anja accompanied her each week and would disappear off with Nonna Barb helping her with household tasks, while they chattered to each other non-stop. Anja's Italian remained a work in progress and even after three years, still liberally strewn with German. Nonna now had passable German too, which Katarina imagined was not something she had foreseen in her future.

One afternoon, Katarina sat beside Pietro at his bench as usual, watching him working an elaborate tracery pattern onto a violin's ribs 'It's beautiful.'

'Antonio designed it for me.'

Giuseppe made a derogatory sound through his teeth. 'Stradivari. What a surprise,' he murmured.

Pietro flung down his chisel. 'We're doing this again, are we?'

'Let's not.' Katarina said, provoking dirty looks from both brothers, confirming that they enjoyed revisiting this often gone-over ground. She lifted her chin. Well, she did not enjoy it. She took a breath. 'Let me summarise for you to save you the trouble. Giuseppe sees no point in patterning at all and thinks Pietro prioritises prettifying over an instrument's voice. He believes

Pietro takes a … and I quote, "a foolish amount of time sanding away tool marks as though a violin was not man-made."' She gestured at Giuseppe, who watched her through narrowed eyes. 'He, of course, likes his to show some signs of the work that went into them – that display of the labour needed to reach such perfection. But Pietro follows Antonio in all things because he is the one who makes the money. And all the aristocrats and wealthy merchants want a Stradivarius, after all.'

Katarina watched them stare daggers at each other now. They did not really look alike the way some brothers did but there was a hint of it in their high cheekbones and aquiline noses. The faces of Roman statues. Though three years older, Pietro was smaller and slighter than Giuseppe, with their papá's straight hair and mahogany eyes. Had Giuseppe's curls come from their mother? She had died in childbed just as hers had. Did Pietro remember her? She hoped he did, at least a little, for it seemed a particular cruelty for a mother not to be remembered by either of her sons.

Giuseppe set down his violin on the bench with his thumb plane beside it. 'Kat, didn't you have something you wished to play for me?'

She turned to him, surprised. She had not been sure he'd heard her earlier, for he had not replied. 'I have, if you're not too busy.'

He took off his leather apron and stood for a moment staring at her with a strange expression on his face. 'Come. We'll go upstairs to the parlour.' At that moment, his papá arrived back with a cask of varnish tucked beneath his arm. He raised his eyebrows but said nothing as he took it into the storeroom. 'Come,' Giuseppe said, again.

Katarina picked up her violin case and followed him through the kitchen parlour where Anja and his grandmother were sitting at the table chatting while they chopped vegetables.

Again, eyes followed them across to the narrow stairs in the corner, but nothing was said.

This room was full of sunlight. Giuseppe sat on a padded armchair and waited for her to begin. She took a deep breath, suddenly a touch afraid by how much she needed his approval. She placed her violin beneath her chin and began to tune it. How could she not think of the very first time she had heard him do this and how she had wondered at the skill of it? Though when she began to play, as always, she felt herself move into another realm, eyes closed, swaying as the music moved through her, seeming to come from within as though already there inside her waiting to be released. It took her some moments to find herself after lowering her instrument to her side.

He stood. 'You wrote this?

She nodded, feeling heat on her cheeks. 'What do you think?'

'Kat, it's ...' He shook his head. 'I've no words.'

Her heart swooped. 'In a good way or a bad way?'

His eyes widened. 'In a good way, you goose.' There's such sorrow there and when the relief finally comes there's a magical lightness to it. You do know if you were a boy you'd be learning from a *maestro* in Rome or Venice and be well on your way to making your name.' He sighed and shrugged. 'As it is, you play for me. And I can do nothing. Only applaud.'

And that is what he did before taking her into his arms for a hug and planting a kiss on her burning cheek. 'Did you like it, Giuseppe? Truly?' she asked sounding needy and foolish. Had not he already said so?

'It's wonderful. We should print it. Sell it in the shop. But who would have the skill to play it like you do?'

'Katarina,' Anja called from below. 'The carriage is come for us.'

She replaced her violin in its case. He had made the instrument for her himself earlier that year, knowing the voice he wanted for her. He gave it no embellishments, as she knew he would not, and for the first time she had truly understood how little such things mattered. 'I'll see you next week.' She saw him looking at her violin. 'Every time I play, I thank you for it and wonder how you knew what would be right for me.'

He smiled. I'm glad you feel like that.'

Jesu, she felt so much more than he knew.

Giuseppe told himself he would not visit Merla that evening knowing, of course, that he would. Watching Katarina play earlier had left him strangely agitated ... angry even, and uncertain why. Was it because he hated to see her talent wasted? He hoped it was not envy of it. He would talk these feelings over with Merla and she would help him to make sense of them as she always seemed to.

Later, walking into her workshop he told himself he would not go to her bed though with about as much conviction as he had felt earlier about seeing her. He found her at her pestle and mortar grinding dried herbs, and beside her a young woman he had never seen before, tying them inside small muslin bags. And that was the first time he set eyes on Sancia Estes.

'Sancia has not long come from Mantua to live here with her uncle and aunt. You'll know them, I'm sure. The Estes.'

'You live with Salvatore and Maria?' Salvatore was known for his viola da gambas and that he would not consider making cellos, which were now the more popular instrument ... and his filthy temper. Perhaps the two were connected?

She nodded, smiling shyly. Yet she did not look the sort of girl to be shy. She was very like Merla to look at, though much younger. He glanced at the apothecary feeling guilty for recognising it, despite its truth. Merla could easily have been this girl's mother. 'When did you arrive in the city?' It could not be long ago for his more idle friends would surely have reported on her many attributes already. That wide, full-lipped mouth and the tops of her full breasts rising tantalisingly above the tight fabric of her bodice.

'Last week.' He watched her eyes brim with tears. 'My Mamma—'

Merla put her arm around Sancia's waist and pulled her close. 'She's an orphan now, poor dear. Maria told me she has some knowledge of herbs, so I've asked her to help me out in here.'

The smile returned. 'I'm so grateful, Signora. It's better to be occupied.'

Watching her still, Giuseppe saw something calculating in her gaze, her large eyes still glittering with unshed tears. A gaze that met his with no suggestion of shyness now. Though he could not know it then, Sancia had already decided he would be hers and would use all of her considerable charms to make it so.

Giuseppe crossed his arms behind his head on the pillow, looking out at the great swathe of cold stars filling the sky. 'I was in awe of her. That she had written such music and could play it the way she did.'

She moved closer and kissed his shoulder. 'You taught her, *amore*.'

He snorted. 'Her talent is nothing to do with me. She should be able to share it with the world, but she can never do that—'

'Because she's a girl.'

'Exactly.' And that was what had made him angry. But what of those other confused feelings? He found himself comparing Katarina with the girl he had met earlier. That they were the same age shocked him. Kat was so childlike still … in appearance anyway. Chocolate coloured hair that she called mouse. Grey eyes. A small, shapely mouth. More than anything she resembled a figure in a medieval religious painting. He smiled at the thought, thinking of Kat with a golden halo circling her head as she played.

'What amuses you, *carissima?*'

'I was thinking about Katarina.'

'You care about her.' It was not a question.

'I care about what she is and what she should be.'

'You're a sweet boy, Giuseppe.'

'Boy, is it? You think me a lad?' He rolled over her. 'Do I feel like a lad to you now?'

Her hands moved down his muscled back. 'Now you feel like a lover.'

The following week when Katarina arrived in the workshop, Pietro was there alone, so she sat quietly on a stool beside him trying not to disturb his concentration while he gouged a back-board. After some moments, he stopped and turned to her, his expression inexplicably hostile.

Katarina leaned back, startled. 'Forgive me. I didn't mean to interrupt you.'

'When did you start seeing Giuseppe away from here? Does he come to your place?'

Now she was even more surprised. 'What are you talking about?' She saw uncertainty now.

His eyes narrowed. 'The way he looked at you before you left last week—'

'*What?*' She hoped he could not tell what those words did to her. The idea that Giuseppe might look at her in a way that would make Pietro jealous. Her face flamed. Of course it did. She tried to appear angry. 'I've not seen him since then. Why would I?'

He sighed. 'Forgive me, then. When he didn't sleep here, I thought … well, I thought he was with you. I thought—'

Giuseppe stormed in, clearly having overheard the last part of their conversation. 'Just what did you think, Pietro?'

He glared at his brother. 'You were with a woman. I could smell it on you. If it wasn't Kat, then who was it ... some doxie?'

Smell it on him? What? Giuseppe looked angrier than she had ever seen him.

'Kat is just a child and I've no need of doxies.' He grinned, unpleasantly. 'Perhaps you'd care to tell me about *your* needs?'

Pietro leapt from his stool lunging towards Giuseppe. 'You cunt—'

Their father marched in then, standing between them, a pastry in his hand. 'I can hear you from the kitchen. What are you thinking brawling like this in front of Katarina? Using such base words?'

Though it was not that word which offended her, but the one Giuseppe had said earlier. *Child.* She was just a child. So whatever Pietro had thought he read in the way his brother looked at her, he had been quite mistaken. *Jesu.* Just a child, indeed. She would show him she was a woman, as Pietro had said. If he saw her as one, then so would others.

As the morning wore on, an uneasy peace seemed to have been restored until Pietro put down his sandpaper. 'I need to get a colour wash on this one then I'll go out for a bit. It should dry while I'm gone, and I can get the ground on later.'

Why had he so carefully sanded away the little stepped indentations in the spruce, those artifacts of its making Giuseppe valued so much? He really had persuaded her. How could she not agree when the marks of his work on her own instrument meant so much to her? To see the magnitude of his labour for her felt special. And Pietro was erasing himself from it.

'Where are you off to, brother?'

Pietro turned to look at him, defiance in his hard stare. 'Fishing with Gianni. We need a break. We've worked too hard lately.'

Andrea frowned. 'What?'

Pietro began to wash a small amount of natural pigment onto his instrument to get a touch of colour started, readying it like preparing a canvas for paint.

'Pietro?'

He did not move his eyes away from his task. 'I don't believe I need your permission to take a few hours off, Papá.'

'Go fishing as often as you wish, just not with him.'

Pietro stood, placing his violin carefully down onto the workbench, glaring now. 'And why might that be, Papà?'

His father stood too and faced him. 'He's a sodomite—'

'Is he really? And how is it you know this?'

'Everyone knows it.'

'I don't.' He shrugged. 'What is this? He's a *finocchio* so I must be, too. Is that it?' He took a step closer to his papá. '*Really*? Is that it?'

Katarina realised that once again they had forgotten she was there. Was she such a mousey presence? She cleared her throat loudly, but it made no difference, though Giuseppe did finally glance at her.

He frowned. 'Don't do this in front of—'

The child. She added in her head.

'Christ's holy wounds. I told you. Everyone knows what he is. Do you wish 'em to think you're one like that?'

Pietro's voice rose. 'I don't give a poxy fuck what people think. Gianni's my friend. If I spend time with him, it's no one's business but mine and his.'

'And if Monsignor Gardi decides to visit San Domenico's again, poking his snout in, eh? What then? Father Paulo is too drunk to care most of the time—'

Giuseppe raised his eyebrows, seeming to forget Katarina again himself now. 'Monsignor Gardi definitely has a snout for pederasts. Don't really know why but I've got my—'

'Go fuck yourself.'

Giuseppe sighed. 'We know you're not a *finocchio*, Pietro. But surely you can see a time might come when even a suspicion of it might harm us.' He gestured around himself. 'Harm this workshop. We're not Stradivari. We have to scramble for every poxy scudo, here.'

Pietro's voice was full of scorn. 'You think I don't fucking know this, Giuseppe. I'm the one who works with Antonio. I know what he rakes in.' He turned to look at his father. 'Perhaps if Giuseppe could make the occasional instrument that didn't look just right for a farmer playing in a tavern, our fortunes might be on the up.'

Giuseppe laughed, unpleasantly. This argument was an old and tired one and neither of them would ever convince the other they were right.

'Yet they sound fit for St Peter's in Rome.'

Pietro shook his head, a scornful smile fixed on his face, and left without another word.

Andrea's eyes followed him until the shop door closed behind him. 'Is he a *finocchio*, do you think?'

'*What?* Course not!' Giuseppe tilted his head. 'But what would you do if he were, Papà?'

Andrea scowled but had no answer.

The following week Katarina learnt from Giuseppe that Pietro was gone. He had taken all his possessions and unsold violins. She wondered how he had slipped away in the night without waking Giuseppe in their shared bedchamber but, somehow, he had. When she asked him about it, he had seemed cagey, shrugging and saying he had no explanation.

'I must have slept deep.' He had said not meeting her gaze. Could he have been elsewhere again? But where? She found herself reluctant to contemplate it.

And Pietro had left no word of where he had gone. When Andrea made to storm off to the Gabrieli workshop on Becharie Vecchie, Giuseppe persuaded him it would be more circumspect for him to go.

'I could go with you, if you like?' His nod of agreement took Katarina by surprise.

He saw it had. 'You thought I'd say no?'

She smiled as winningly as she could in case he should change his mind. 'I thought you might need a little more persuasion.

'We'll seem friendlier together ...'

'Less confrontational,' she finished for him.

He grinned. 'That.'

It was only a short walk from the Piazza San Domenico to Becharie Vecchie and Katarina was grateful for it when they hurried along the street and across the basilica concourse beneath a sullen sky, the chilly wind whipping leaves from the trees with those already underfoot a mosaic of red and gold, treacherous from an earlier downpour.

Gianni was alone in the shop when they arrived and unsurprised to see them.

He kissed Katarina on both cheeks, seeming genuinely pleased to see her. She had felt the warmth of his charm when she first met him, introduced by Pietro. He truly was one of those people who it was difficult not to like.

'I really did try to persuade him to leave a letter for his papà, but he was adamant.'

Pietro had been enraged about Andrea's objections to their friendship and his refusal to follow Antoni Stradivari's methods. Gianni had shrugged and smiled at Giuseppe. 'He wants your papà to stop you from working the way you do. But I'm sure you know that.'

'Indeed, I do. More than I wish to.' He sighed. 'I don't suppose you know where he's gone?

'Venice. He took a riverboat. He thinks his work will flourish there.

Giuseppe smiled scornfully at that. 'Perhaps he thinks he can become the Stradivari of Venice.'

Katarina shrugged. 'Well, maybe he can.'

Five

⸺

CREMONA, SEPTEMBER 1721

KATARINA'S EDUCATION WITH THE HARTMANNS HAD finally come to an end when Gerhart joined Erwin at the university in Vienna. No university for her, alas. For a time, she had thought herself in love with their tutor, red-haired handsome Gustav Weimar, as young girls were wont to do. (Especially those who hoped such a state would drive jealousy in another, though at the time she denied any such motive.)

Gustav was thirty years old and a man of the world, and later Katarina came to understand it was what he knew, what he was able to pass on to her, that was the true enchantment. Socrates. Plato. Aristotle. Homer. Virgil. Her mind had soared. Yet she had always known it must end. So, when Gerhart moved on, so did Gustav, and Katerina turned her full attention onto number 5 Piazza San Domenico, and it had taken up a large part of her life ever since.

Pietro's absence had allowed her to carve out a niche for herself in the workshop almost by stealth over the years until she had become genuinely useful taking on tasks which freed up more time for Andrea and Giuseppe to make their instruments. She had even started finishing some of Giuseppe's rougher makes, prettifying the purfling and adding a touch of patterning to the ribs, and carving the scroll a little finer.

The first time he realised what she was doing, for he was engrossed in the early stages of gluing ribs to a violin's back plate, she thought he would be angry. And he had scowled, demanding to know what the hell she thought she was doing. But when he saw her skill, he was only astonished, wondering how she knew the techniques. That Katarina had watched them done for so long did not seem sufficient explanation. All he could do was repeat, 'But how, though? How? In the end, he left her to it especially when these violins began to attract a wider selection of patrons.

How had a mind that had so recently soared on The Iliad and The Aeneid settled so readily to carving maple and spruce? Yet, for Katarina, when those instruments were finished, and she watched Giuseppe examine them before handing them to her to play, this time it was her heart that soared at the sound of their voices. All subtly different. All beautiful.

Katarina soon took on other tasks too, such as sanding catgut (made from sheep intestines not cats, she had been pleased to discover) to craft strings of the thickness the luthiers needed for each instrument. Someone had to do it, and she did make excellent strings even though she said it herself. And it was this that occupied her when Giuseppe suddenly seemed to notice her, appearing surprised to find her there.

He put down his work and stretched. 'Why are you not away home?'

She had already told him why, though she had suspected he had not heard her even after his grunted acknowledgement. Not an uncommon occurrence. 'I'm staying with Anja so I can join you all at Niccolo's.' She tossed her head, failing to hide her impatience. 'I did tell you earlier.'

He laughed. 'Yes. I remember now. Which also means you can come with us to the river tomorrow.' He walked over to her, looking down. 'I'm glad you can join us for once at these … things.' He shrugged. 'Entertainments?'

Katerina grinned. 'Why do you think I persuaded Anja to marry Carlo Moretti?' In truth, Anja had been giddy with love for the handsome instrument case maker and lived blissfully over his shop with their first child already on the way. She had another motive for this overnight stay too, and one Anja knew all about, for Katarina thought herself in love with a young luthier, Claudio Rugeri, (the evening feast was to be held at his family home) and this time she believed she had found someone who felt the same about her. Was it too much to hope that one of these gatherings might be his chance to tell her so?

Was there still an element of attracting Giuseppe's attention by telling him of her interest in other men? For she always kept him fully informed, though, in truth, sensing his full attention only when she played her violin.

Giuseppe snatched the sandpaper from her fingers and pulled her to her feet. 'Well then, we should be on our way. Come on.'

Katarina took off her apron and shook out her skirts before removing the kerchief from her hair. 'I need to wash my hands. And have you a hairbrush I might borrow?'

She followed him into the kitchen and filled a bowl from the well bucket, enjoying the cool water on her hands hot from the friction of the rough paper, while Giuseppe fetched a brush from his bedchamber. He washed his hands in the same water while she brushed her hair. After pausing a moment noticing her lighter hairs beside the tangle of his black ones caught in the bristles, and with no idea why she did it, she moved to him and undid the string tying his at his neck, watching it fall in wild curls around his shoulders. After damping the bush, she was able to tease out some of the tangles. 'You have wonderfully exuberant hair.'

He reached out and ran his fingers down Katarina's. 'Yours is like a cloak of silk.'

'A mouse cloak.' They held each other's gaze for a few moments before stepping back. 'We should go.'

He sighed. 'We should.' He handed Katarina her violin case before picking up his own.

The gathering to celebrate the feast day of *Santa Cecilia* – patron saint of luthiers and musicians – was hosted by a different family each year with the left-over food eaten at the river picnic the next day, augmented by fish caught and cooked over a fire.

In the almond orchard behind the Rugeri house, loaded trestles were set out beneath trees strung with candles in coloured glass jars adding their scent to that of earth and foliage still warm from the day's heat, and rich aromas from the spectacular array of food. Each family had brought their own platters: Mutton sausages. *Gran bollito Cremonese. Risotto alla Milanese.* Pumpkin *tortelli* and *Casoncelli. Pizzoccheri della Valtellina.* Sardines. Poached whole fish. Fruits. Breads. Cheeses. And many plates and dishes of pastries and sweetmeats.

Nonna Barb had been there most of the day with Anja and many of the other women helping Maria Rugeri with the baking while the men had fetched tables and benches and built a small stage where music would be played later.

Giuseppe placed his hand on Katarina's back, guiding her to the table where a large bowl of punch and wooden cups were set out. He dipped a cup to fill it. 'Watch how much you drink. It's got a bigger kick than it tastes like.'

Katarina took a sip and gasped as heat flooded her throat. 'It tastes strong enough to me.' Her eyes darted around those gathered beneath the trees in the fading light, hoping to see Claudio,

Niccolo's youngest son. And there he was, a little way from the main throng talking with Gianni Gabrieli. Katarina turned back to Giuseppe and found him watching her, a slight frown between his dark brows. 'What?'

His eyes moved to look behind her. 'Here's Anja.'

She dashed past him and flung her arms around Katarina, though her swollen belly prevented them embracing closely. 'We've put up a pallet for you in the kiddie's room.' She patted her belly. 'We can test out it's comfort for our little lad when he's big enough for a room of his own,' she said in German.

When Katarina linked her arm through Anja's, she realised Giuseppe had moved away and was now standing beside Merla, talking quite intently. She wondered what that was about.

Anja grinned. 'Have you seen him yet?'

Katarina nodded, glancing across to where he had been but moments ago, but was no longer. 'He was with Gianni and Ricardo.' She could not see them either. 'They all seem to have disappeared.'

Carlo arrived at Anja's side then, slipping his arm around her waist or where it would be had she still had one. 'Come, wife. Sit. Sit. I'll fetch food for you both.'

She giggled. 'I'm not a dog, husband.' But she sat down heavily onto a vacant bench, showing relief to do so.

Katarina lowered herself beside her friend, watching Carlo hurry away weaving through the crowd. He was short and slight with a soft flop of hair falling over his forehead. A smile never seemed far away from his lips, which was unsurprising when he was just as besotted with Anja as she was with him. 'How lucky it was that Leda was such a bitch and father sent her packing otherwise you'd never have found each other.'

Anja crossed herself, having taken to Carlo's religion with the sort of relish sometimes seen in reluctant former Calvinists. 'She were such a cunt, though, weren't she.' Anja giggled.

Katarina laughed too, despite herself, even while trying to

look disapproving. Speaking in German had its uses. 'Well, I can't really argue with that.' Carlo arrived then with heaped plates, assisted by two of the many children eager to help for a coin or two, carrying loaded wooden trenchers with insouciant skill. The friends switched back to Italian and moderated their language.

Katarina spotted Giuseppe sitting with Sancia Estes not far from the little stage. Claudio was now with his family and Gianni was at the next table with his wife, Mia, who was clearly some years older than he. Though her complexion was rather sallow, her high cheekbones and large dark eyes made her handsome. She was handsome while Gianni was beautiful. Katarina wondered how that made her feel.

For some reason she found her eyes drawn more to Giuseppe than to Claudio, amused by his obvious discomfort with Sancia's flirting, hiding her grin behind her hand. Though each time she glanced at Claudio, she was disappointed to see he showed no interest in her.

When most had finished eating (though not drinking, of course) men began to assemble on the platform, one with a bass viol and two with violins, Giuseppe joined them. He took the role of first violin and Katarina closed her eyes listening to them play some old Monteverdi pieces beloved in Cremona, his birthplace. Soon, she knew, others would take over to play more lively tunes for those who wished to dance on the little piece of open ground in front of the stage.

'Katarina.'

She opened her eyes. Giuseppe was now alone on the stage and smiling down at her, pointing at his violin.

'Come up and play for us.'

He had told her she needed her instrument to join in at the end when those still sober enough played together as a finale for the celebration. He had not prepared her for this. She was glad her senses were a little dulled by the punch and hoped her high colour would be put down to such overindulgence. Katarina stepped up onto the platform beside Giuseppe. 'What should I play?' she whispered.

'Something of your own.'

'Will you join in?'

He touched her arm. 'If I can.' He grinned. 'If it's not too tricky for me.'

She began with a piece she had played for him many times, closing her eyes and losing herself in it, Giuseppe only joining in from time to time to pick up the central melody and to double-up on pizzicato and tremolo. She finished on a solo flourish and lowered her violin, bowing to the audience. When she looked up, all eyes seemed fixed on her, even those appearing to have difficulty focusing. The silence was absolute, even the children had gone quiet, until the clapping and cheering started. Katarina stepped off the platform and felt her face hotter than ever when Claudio pulled her into his arms and kissed her on the lips.

Sitting on the narrow bed while Katarina perched on a stool beside it in the room where she would sleep, Anja's eyes sparkled in the candlelight. 'What did he say, though? What did he say when he kissed you?'

Katarina sighed. 'He didn't say anything, really. Only about my playing.'

Anja patted her shoulder, commiserating. 'Well, at least he kissed you.'

Katarina chewed her lip. 'In truth, it was a rather chaste kiss.'

'What else could he do in front of all them people. He could hardly stick his tongue down your bleedin' throat, now could he? You need to find a way to have some time alone with him tomorrow.'

Katarina shivered, surprisingly unsettled by the thought. 'If I can shake off Giuseppe.' But was that what she truly wanted?

'Make sure you keep Sancia Estes close. She'll see to the rest. He can't keep his eyes of her tits.'

'I think he finds her more annoying than attractive—'

'He's a man. It don't matter how annoying she is with them tits. Then you can get up to whatever takes your fancy with Claudio.'

Katarina's heart began to race a little at the thought of it, though she wasn't sure it was in a good way. 'What if he wants—'

'Holy cows, Kat. Don't let him do that.'

Holy cows? What? 'Really, Anja. What do you take me for?'

Katarina had to listen to many tales of Anja's courtship with Carlo then, all of which she had heard before, many with explicit description of intimate acts between them before they married. This always ended with a detailed description of their wedding night as, once more, Katarina wondered what Carlo would say if he knew.

Six

CREMONA, SEPTEMBER 1721

KATARINA HAD FOUND SLEEP ELUSIVE – EVEN IN THAT unexpectedly comfortable little bed – caught-up in the events of the evening. Some of it amusing, thinking of Giuseppe dealing with Sancia's tiresome presence, all heaving bosom (he had shown no sign of being won over by it) silly prattle, giggles, and fluttering eyelashes. And then her thoughts had drifted to how supported she felt when he stood beside her while she played.

She understood now that he had joined in only when sensing it would help both her confidence and highlight her skill. It was a reminder of how well he understood both her strengths and weaknesses. Again, she felt herself swaying to the sound, eyes closed, whilst the music inhabited her completely. She wondered if he understood what it felt like to be in that kind of thrall. She would ask him. Yet did he not lose himself in his making when there was nothing but the scent of the wood and the feel of it under his fingers and through his tools? He was certainly oblivious to those around him then.

She remembered he had told her once of a sense that the instrument was already there within the wood just waiting for him to release it, like a sculptor uncovering the figure hidden inside the marble block. Was the music there inside her too, just waiting for her violin to find it? It was not the first time this had occurred to her.

Katarina had awoken – certain she had barely slept – just as dawn was breaking, so in good time for the trip out to the River Po. She knew the men needed an early start if they wanted a good catch, for the carp would rise only when the insects warmed enough to fly across the water but once the sun rose higher, they would retreat to denser wooded shade until their evening return. And she had no intention of missing any of it.

The night before, Giuseppe together with Francesco and Vincenzo Rugeri, had loaded their pony cart with the rods, nets, boxes of hooks, and bate; maggots, squats, and bloodworm boilies they would need for their fishing. He had explained them all to her, so she now knew rather more about carp bait than she wished to. This morning they would add the remaining food tightly wrapped in linen cloths.

Katarina had dressed carefully with Claudio in mind and left the house as quietly as she could so as not to wake anyone. Anja and Carlo would join them later. As promised, she found Giuseppe and his companions waiting for her there on the corner beside the curved wall of San Domenico's side chapel, so they were soon on their way to the Piazza Maggiore where the other two carts would join them carrying those coming for the fishing ahead of the picnic, all sitting on rugs in the cart beds with sleeping children curled up around them.

Once they had left the deserted streets, with gable ends and roof lines just catching the first spark of sunlight, they moved along grass tracks beside ground shrouded in mist, lifting here and there to reveal rice fields irrigated by ditches fed from the river. The men knew exactly where they headed, for it was the same destination each year.

Fishing from the high banks of the Po could be problematic Katarina knew, as here they were often covered with impenetrable bush. Their destination lay where a wide stream flowed into the river, the bank falling away down to a small sandy beach. Giuseppe had told her his father, and his before him, had fished there. Unsurprisingly, it was a place the families of the isle kept to themselves.

When their cart arrived on a track along the steep bank, the fog had stolen the river away. To the east a streak of pale citrine looked like a brush stroke on a pristine canvas. As soon as the wagons had been positioned beneath a stand of hornbeams, Giuseppe and Katarina led the ponies down to the little beach to let them drink, their heads seeming to vanish into the mist as though the river had washed them away. When the beasts were done, they hobbled them beneath the trees for shade when the sun finally burnt off the mist, and they were soon cropping the lush grass.

The men and women unloading the carts spoke in whispers. And the swirling fog certainly felt otherworldly and not a little unnerving to Katarina. Who knew what their voices might awaken in the silence? She shook herself. A silly fancy. She almost laughed but that would have sounded most disturbing of all. Rugs were spread upon the dewy ground, and rods carried further along the beach to where branches overhung the still hidden water.

Women sat yawning while children slept on and those men not fishing went off to gather the firewood needed to cook the catch. Giuseppe stood beside Francesco Amati, hooking maggots onto his line ready to cast when the mist cleared, and the fly nymphs hatched. As the light grew, Katarina looked at the groups seated on the bank and quickly spotted Sancia Estes. As soon as she saw her, she realised hers was the voice she could now hear above the whispers of others and the gurgle of the shrouded water flowing by.

Katarina moved away to help women lift the wrapped platters of food from the cart beds and set them out on the trestle tables already set-up not far from the firepit. All the women acknowledged her with friendly smiles and soft touches on her shoulders. It was the first time she had truly felt included in their world and realised it was because of her playing at the Rugeris'. And for that, she had Giuseppe to thank. He had known what he was doing calling her up to play.

After depositing two baskets of bread onto a table, Katarina strolled along the bank to where the path led down to the beach. Though the water was invisible still, she could smell it. The earthy scent of silt here where the river ran slow and wide, carrying the run-off from the marshes and rice fields that served it in flood. She imaged it would smell different closer to its source in the Alps. Would its scent there be of ice and granite and mountain flowers?

She looked up hearing a fish eagle's cry, soon answered by one across the river in the distance. Were they sounding their frustration at the mist that stopped them feeding? Then, as the fog began to lift finally, the tweets and twitters of the little birds roosting in the woods began to fill the air.

Katarina watched Giuseppe and his companions cast their lines across the silt-dark water allowing the current to carry their baited hooks beneath the trees where their quarry carp, barbel and bream would loiter waiting to feed. Would she see one of the giant catfish – some the size of a child – she knew to inhabit this part of the river? These could only be caught from a boat ... but might she not at least see one? Giuseppe turned his head and smiled seeing her there. She waved to him and moved away to join a few newly arrived women sitting together on rugs, gossiping, and laughing quite raucously now the mist had cleared. Anja sat a little way beyond with a group of younger women, surprisingly quiet, smiles hidden behind hands. She patted the rug beside her, and a plump girl moved away a little to make a space for Katarina.

Anja leaned over to whisper into her ear. 'Have you heard what them old biddies is saying?'

Katarina shook her head, wondering why she should wish to.

'Secrets of the marriage bed.' Anja whispered.

Katarina raised her eyebrows. 'It would not be the first time I have heard such.'

Anja giggled. 'I only tell you, not a whole bunch.' She put her finger to her lips. 'Listen,' she hissed.

Katarina tried not to, but it was impossible not to hear random voices rising above the screeches of laughter. 'Two minutes then he farts and rolls away. More laughter. 'Touches my night gown, that's all it takes and bless the Holy Mother herself for it, I say.' Lots of the women crossed themselves. One woman groaned. 'Alf pounds on and on ... and on but I must pretend he pleases me or else he starts fiddling with me which I can't abide.' Here there was much nodding of heads and expressions of agreement. 'No that's the worst. They never know what they're doing, do they? Stupid buggers.' More agreement. And laughter.

Anja leaned towards Katarina's ear again. 'Don't you pity 'em? Getting no pleasure from it. That'll never be me.'

'What do I know of it,' Katarina murmured. 'Other than what you've told me.

It was then men began to arrive with their catches, and many of the older women rose to join them ready to gut and clean the fish for cooking on a frame over the fire, which had just been lit.

The next few hours were taken up with eating and drinking, followed for many by a doze in the shade. Katarina sat with Anja and Carlo, watching her sleep with her head on his lap while he gently stroked her hair, his face a picture of devotion.

She glanced around at the other groups, quickly spotting Giuseppe sitting with a cluster of young luthiers ... and Sancia, who was attempting to flirt with all of them. Though Katarina barely noticed her antics when one of them was Claudio. She saw him stand, looking towards a grove of crape myrtles down towards the stream, and followed his gaze. Gianni. They took off their sandals to cross the shallow water and walked off together along the riverbank. Where was Gianni's wife?

When Katarina looked back at the remaining men, she found Giuseppe's eyes on her, though he was soon distracted when the rest of the group rose, calling for him to join him at the swimming hole, which took them off in the opposite direction to that taken by Claudio and Gianni. Katarina had no real desire to sit down again with a sleeping Anja and besotted Carlo any more than she did with the mostly snoozing matrons. So, she began a desultory stroll along the path taken by Gianni and Claudio.

Had she been wrong in thinking he returned her interest? When a small voice suggested she might be manufacturing her feelings for him as a ploy to gain Giuseppe's attention once again, she quickly silenced it. She had drunk too much wine. That was where such a notion came from. She increased her pace.

Perhaps Gianni would return to find his wife when Katarina appeared, leaving her alone with Claudio. Her heart began to flutter unpleasantly at the prospect. She halted when she heard voices off to her left, quickly spotting a track through a covert of aromatic bay laurel. Well, it more resembled a tunnel, forcing her to stoop as she made her way through. The two men must have crawled. Katarina halted. If it was them? It could be anyone. Yet she had to continue for there was no means of turning round. After a few moments, she stuck her head out into a small sunlit clearing carpeted with emerald moss, with the river so close she could hear its gurgle. The voices had stopped, replaced by other sounds that she could make little sense of until she moved further out. They were at the far side, entirely naked, and ...

Katarina turned and blundered back through the tunnel as quietly as she could, praying they had not seen her. Surely they had not, for they had seemed completely lost in each other. She shook her head, hurrying along the track trying to dislodge the image from her mind. Jesu, how she wished she had never seen them. And what of Mia? That poor woman. That poor deceived woman.

She walked up towards the trees where the ponies were hobbled to avoid the townsfolk. Men sleeping. A group playing softly on violins. Wives watching their children splashing in the shallow water lapping the beach. Katarina carried on, uncertain what she would do. Could she walk back to Cremona and if she did, how would she get home to the *palazzo*?

Below she saw men dressed only in breeches, their wet hair dripping, making their way back from the swimming hole. Giuseppe was not amongst them. And quite suddenly, she was angry with him. He had watched her go after Claudio and Gianni, and she now felt sure he knew about them. Why the hell did he not stop her? She would find him. He needed to explain himself.

Giuseppe enjoyed the place best when he had it to himself, floating on the surface his eyes closed in cool, green shade dappled by beams of sunlight filtering through the tree canopy, his thoughts free to roam. Though he had tried to send them elsewhere, today they seemed set on finding Katarina. The sight of her on the stage the night before. A little girl in a soft blue gown, her back straight, her face serious and so determined. And when she played, swaying to the sounds she mined from somewhere deep inside her, a glow seemed to come from her as though she shone with some kind of inner light. He opened his eyes then, trying to drag his mind away from such fancies. How could a girl glow? He chuckled quietly and closed his eyes again.

Not possible, of course. Too much punch from the punch. He chuckled again.

His musings moved on ... and there was Katarina again, ambling off after Claudio and Gianni. He frowned. That might have been a mistake—' *Splashes.* His eyes flew open in time to see a small avalanche of pebbles sliding down the bank to land noisily in the water not far from his head. He moved upright, hiding himself in its brown murk. 'Katarina.' It appeared she had hoped to make her escape along the bank unseen.

'Damn it. Another naked man I have no wish to see.' She flung back at him over her shoulder, before halting and turning to face him. 'This is all your fault.'

'What the devil do you mean?' Even in the gloom, he could see her face blotched with embarrassment. 'Katarina?' He spoke gently now. 'What's happened?' But he had a bad feeling he already knew.

She flung her arms up in a wild gesture of dismissal and stomped off up to the track.

Giuseppe scrambled out of the water and pulled on his breeches, struggling to get them up over his wet skin before setting off after her.

When she heard his pursuit crashing through the under-growth, she halted and turned around to face him again. 'Did you think I was spying on you?'

'*What?* Why would I think that?' What on earth was she talking about? 'Do you have any idea where this path takes you? Why are you going this way?'

She shrugged. 'I'm taking a stroll. What does it look like? Why does it matter where I'm walking?'

'There's nothing along here. It ends in a blackthorn thicket. Have you ever seen one? You'll never get through—'

'Which is where I shall turn around and come back. Now if you'll excuse me—'

'What's wrong, Kat?' He reached out and grasped her hand

to stop her walking away. 'Has something happened?' he asked again, sure now of what she would say.

'Has something happened?' she repeated with about as much sarcasm as she could muster. 'Well, let me see now. I came across two men showing a disconcerting amount of affection for one another.' She laughed, mirthlessly. 'One of whom I have a certain fondness for, myself.'

'Christ. What were they thinking—' There it was, just as he had feared.

'Not much thinking involved it would seem.' She studied his face. 'You knew, didn't you? You knew about them and yet you let me go after them. You wanted me to. You … You cur! You wanted me to see Claudio doing … that.' She slapped his face, hard.

Giuseppe grabbed her shoulders and shook her, lightly. 'Why would I do such a thing, you imbecile? How would I ever think they might … out in the open where they could be seen.' But he had felt uneasy when she followed them.

Once more, Katarina seemed to read doubt in him, and pushing him away, she turned on her heel and strode off again without another word.

He watched her disappear into the trees, knowing he should let her go but seeming unable to. It took some time to find her, for she had left the path, but eventually, he came across her in the long grass, her back against the smooth bark of a white-beam, its leaves shuddering silver in the breeze, her face wet with tears. He knelt beside her. 'Forgive me.' He cupped her face, smearing away tears with his thumb. 'I was worried when you went after them, but I never dreamt for a moment they'd be so reckless—'

She looked at him at last. 'They weren't. They'd tried to hide.' She managed to find a wan smile from somewhere. 'I scrambled through the undergrowth when I heard voices.'

He sat down on the grass beside her and took her hand in

his. 'Oh, Kat.' Once again, he realised how young she was. No. More like young for her age. She was twenty now, far from being a child. Sancia Estes would never have made that mistake.

'I'm sorry I slapped you. I don't know what got into me ... I —' She laughed softly. 'I knew the rumours about Gianni.' She looked hard at him. 'But he's married. I didn't think ...'

'Oh, Kat,' he said again.

Something in his tone vexed her then. He still thought of her as a child and was pitying her for it. She stared hard at him, her eyes moving over his muscular arms and chest, the sun glinting off the damp black curls there. And seeing him like that stirred such a storm in her ... a racing heart ... throbbing heat between her thighs. Jesu, she knew what it was. What it meant. Anja had described such feelings to her often enough. How mortifying when he would never feel such things for her.

'You think I'm such an innocent, don't you? Well, I'm not (very far from it at that moment.) You're just a ... an oaf.' She rose to her feet in one fluid movement and hurried off towards the path back to the picnic place. Tears pricking her eyes, she would not look back fearing she would find him laughing at her. Even as she ran, she knew she was the fool and not him. He had done nothing more than show her kindness. Her feelings were not his fault. What was wrong with her?

Seven

CREMONA, SEPTEMBER 1721

KATARINA HAD PARTED FROM GIUSEPPE THAT evening without acknowledging him, mortified by her earlier behaviour, though she had noticed him watching her with a strange expression on his face. How could he not think less of her? When she left with Anja and Carlo, he was with the men gathering up fishing equipment and detritus of the day to load into the remaining cart.

After Anja had been dropped at home (Katarina wishing she could have told her all that had happened with Giuseppe), Carlo insisted on taking her out to the *palazzo*. On reaching the park surrounding it, she had asked to be put down there and refused to take no for an answer. He should get home to Anja. She could easily walk the rest of the way. While twilight was approaching, there was still plenty of light in the sky. After waving him off, she decided to cross the fields taking care to avoid the stables for the head groom would be sure to tell her father he had seen her.

With this in mind, she followed the stone wall intending to go through the gate into the apple orchard. When she heard hoofbeats approaching, she turned to look behind her. It was at that moment a horse soared over the wall from the far side, landing but feet away from her and reeling, she lost her balance, falling flat on her back.

The rider reined in his horse, gleaming black and impossibly large from her current viewpoint on the ground, calling out to her in poor Italian with a strong German accent, '*Signorina*, hurt are you?' He kicked his leg over the saddle's pommel and vaulted from his mount.

Katarina sat up, answering him in German. 'I'm a little winded, *Mein Herr*.'

He dropped to his knees beside her. 'Allow me to assist you. I never imagined there would be anyone on the other side of the wall. How very remiss—'

She struggled to her feet with his hand beneath her elbow to help her. 'There's no reason why you should expect it. You were not at fault.' Her laugh sounded shrill for she was more than a little shaken by how close she had come to disaster. 'You didn't land on me, so no harm done.'

They now stood facing each other, and she was able to appreciate the sincerity of his concern and just how very good-looking he was. Tall and slim. Thick, fair hair cut short. Large darklashed blue eyes. Yet she sensed he was unaware of the affect his appearance had. Just like Giuseppe, she realised. She looked away, noticing his horse had not moved far from where he had left it.

He followed her gaze and frowned slightly. 'Would be useful if they did that on the battlefield ... but unwise.' He smiled then, clearly with some relief, finally seeming to accept she was uninjured. May I assist you to your destination, *Fräulein*?' He glanced around at the empty fields with some puzzlement. 'Have you no companions nearby?'

Though she was dressed for the river picnic, her speech was sufficient to tell him she was no peasant girl, but he had shown no hesitation in rushing to her aid when that was what she must have appeared to be. She smiled, holding out her hand. 'I am Katarina Rota. My father is *Oberst* Rota, the deputy commandant. I live at *Palazzo Poli.*'

His smile broadened and he brought her hand to his lips. 'I have just visited him there.' He stepped back to bow. '*Hauptmann* Johannes Horak. Please allow me to see you safely home.' He was not in uniform, but his olive-green coat was of the finest wool and tailored to fit him perfectly, his cream silk stock pristine.

Horak led his horse to follow Katarina through the gate into the orchard where she then walked beside him through trees already heavy with ripening fruit, towards the rear of the Rotas' wing of the house. The sky was now showing great sweeping brushstrokes of indigo across the sapphire and gold of twilight. Johannes looked up, clearly appraising the remaining light. 'I should be on my way, I think. A ride back to barracks in the dark in unfamiliar country seems a touch foolhardy.' He grinned. 'Especially after having had one rather alarming mishap already.' He mounted his horse with athletic grace. 'Do you enjoy riding, *Fräulein* Rota?'

'I do, *Hauptmann* Horak. Very much so, though I get little opportunity.'

Katarina saw this puzzled him, but he did not question it. 'Then, if you're agreeable I will call on you tomorrow morning and perhaps we could ride out so you might show me the surrounding area?'

'I shall be happy to. Will nine o'clock suit? It is pleasant then before the heat builds too much later in the day.'

'It will suit admirably.'

He bowed and rode away at a canter. Katarina watched but he did not look back.

. . .

On their first outing together, Katarina had taken Johannes across the fields and on into Cremona. There, they explored the cathedral together and she had enjoyed showing it off to him, hoping it did not seem too provincial against the splendours of Vienna. At her request, they parted company there after he had agreed to come to *Palazzo Poli* for dinner that evening.

Katarina had gone then to visit Anja. She had much to tell her sitting at the table in her kitchen parlour, incongruous in her riding habit.

'Well, he sounds a real gallant, don't he? I like how he were keen to help even when he thought you was nobody. But what's he doing here, Kat?'

'On some sort of regimental secondment, I think.' She frowned a little uncertainly. 'Though his duties seem rather light.'

Anja tilted her head looking intently at Katarina. 'There's summit else, ain't there?'

'I ... I—'

'Did summit happen with Claudio?'

'You could say that, yes.' Katarina hesitated. She knew then she would not tell Anja the details. In truth, it was not something she ought to know herself. 'I caught him with someone else so that's that with him.' Why had she ever thought she loved him? She was seriously beginning to doubt her judgement in such matters. She looked down at her fingers. 'Then I sort of had a falling out with Giuseppe over it.'

'Why on earth would you fall out with 'im? Who was Claudio with, anyway?'

Katarina looked out of the window at Anja tiny kitchen garden dappled with sunlight. 'I didn't recognise her.' She could tell Anja did not believe her.

Anja sighed. 'So how did Giuseppe get tangled up in it?'

What could she say? 'I'm afraid I blamed him for it at first. For not stopping me following ... them.'

'He knew about Claudio?'

'I think he suspected.' Katarina shook her head. 'I knew I was being foolish but ...'

'But? But what, Kat?'

'He slighted me. He thinks me a child—'

'Well, I'm not bleedin' surprised when you act like one.'

'Anja!'

She grasped Katarina's hand in hers. 'Forget all this now. What about your 'andsome Austrian? When's you seeing 'im again?'

'Dinner tonight.' The conversation moved back to the more comfortable topic of Johannes Horak, though Katarina could not quite banish thoughts of Giuseppe. They parted company with Anja being helped upstairs by Carlo who had come in from the shop to assist his wife up the narrow staircase to rest on their bed for the *riposo*.

Katarina let herself out through the garden into the alley that ran behind the row of shops, all with living quarters above them, to make her way back to the livery stables and her horse. Walking out into Piazza San Domenico, she kept to the shadows in the afternoon heat. This time of day had a distinctive smell as though the very stones gave off a sun-baked odour under the white sky.

'Katarina.'

Startled to hear her name called, she whipped around to find Gianni Gabrieli hurrying to catch up with her. Her heart began to pound uncomfortably as she contemplated what he might want from her, but as he came closer his wide smile reassured her and she released the breath she had not been aware she held. Yet his first words made her anxious again.

'Katarina, I've been hoping to speak with you since the picnic.'

She had no idea what to say.

'Please don't be alarmed.' He patted her arm gently. 'There's no need.'

Now he stood before her she could see his smile masked his own anxiety. 'What can I do for you?'

The smile fell away, and his complexion darkened, his confidence seeming to fail him. 'I think you may have seen certain—'

She quickly took pity on him. 'You've nothing to fear. I've told no one about what I saw, nor shall I.' She gasped at the untruth. 'Well, I told Giuseppe Guarneri, but—'

'I know we can trust Giuseppe.' He touched her arm again.

Of course, the 'we' referred to him and Claudio. She wanted to ask about his wife, but it really was none of her business.

'I'm sorry that—'

'The fault was mine. I should not have …'

'No. We should not …' He flung his arms up, a broad grin breaking out on his face. 'What can I say. There truly is nothing.'

Katarina began to laugh. For what, indeed, could he say? Gianni soon joined in – he could not help himself either, it seemed – and they clasped each other for support as wild mirth overcame them both. After a time, once they had recovered sufficiently, she took his arm allowing him to see her to the stables and when she rode away, she knew she had made a true friend.

For the next three weeks, Katarina and Johannes spent a good part of each day together often riding or walking, Katarina showing him more of Cremona – though not the luthiers' isle – and much of the countryside bordering the river. They talked and talked and, pleasingly, found they laughed at many of the same things.

When one evening after their usual dinner with her father and other officers, Johannes unexpectedly joined the ladies in the salon, Katarina could not help but notice his unease with the decidedly female topics being discussed, so suggested they play chess.

'What made you leave the dining room?'

His embarrassment was plain. 'Your papa requested that I should. There was to be talk of regimental activities in Cremona that I could not to be privy too.'

'I see.' She gestured to the table which held a marquetry chess board with the intricately carved pieces already set out. 'I'll take white,' she said, seating herself.

When Johannes found they were evenly matched, Katarina saw it surprised him.

'I've never faced a woman opponent before. Who taught you?'

'I've always played.' She frowned. 'I suppose Father must have. I used to play with my tutor too and the boys I shared lessons with.'

Again, he looked uncomfortable. 'I should tell you, I knew Erwin Hartmann at the university—'

'You knew Erwin?' She watched a flush of colour sweep across his cheeks.

'He mentioned you. Forgive me. I should have told you before.'

'Mentioned me?'

He raised his eyebrows. 'He told me you'd had problems with your governess.'

She had to clench her jaw not to repeat problems. 'Let's just say she was not a success.'

Katarina was silent for a few moments, thinking of Leda's downfall – not something she could share with him, of course – while a maidservant lit the candles in the floor standing candelabra close beside them. She looked out from the large windows giving a view of the formal gardens, seeing the sky was already taking on the inky hues of approaching night. She grinned, eager to change the subject. 'I think I must beat you quickly if you are to leave before darkness falls.

He returned her grin. 'We'll see about that.'

Katarina called checkmate while light still streaked the sky.

Johannes studied the board in open disbelief for several moments, slowly shaking his head. 'How?'

'Perhaps it was a fluke, *Hauptmann?*' Her eyes danced as she teased him.

His lips curled in a self-deprecating grimace. 'Somehow I think not, *Fräulein.*'

'Well, we could try again tomorrow and find out?'

He stood, bowing formally before kissing her hand. 'Very well, I shall look forward to it.'

'So shall I, Johannes.'

Watching him take his leave of the remaining ladies and the gentlemen who had since joined them, she was struck again by his rather rigid Austrian formality, all heel clicks and staccato bows. Perhaps some Italian informality had brushed off on the officers who had been stationed in Cremona for some time? And that had to be a good thing, surely?

Johannes often seemed surprised by the breadth of Katarina's knowledge, and more noticeably, by her willingness to challenge his opinions. Not in an overtly disapproving way, she thought, but he certainly appeared disconcerted, as though he did not quite know what to make of it.

This time, they were walking along beside the Po not far from where the picnic had been held, having left their horses hobbled in shade. 'Do I make you uncomfortable? I can be a little too forthright in my views, I know.' Her father had drawn her attention to it more than once, though always with an edge of pride behind his words, which she knew he would deny if challenged.

He smiled almost shyly. 'It's just not something I'm used to.' He chuckled. 'You're certainly a most unusual young lady.'

She grinned. 'Is that good or bad?'

He stopped, grasping her hand, and bringing it to his lips. 'How can you even ask?'

Now Katarina was the one disconcerted. 'I had a rather singular education as you know.' Just how much had Erwin Hartmann told him? 'I learnt the rudiments of Latin with my governess.' With little success if the assaults upon her hands had been anything to judge by. 'But it was only with our tutor I was able to truly discover Latin and Greek Literature. And then on to the more arcane delights of theology.'

'You're a Calvinist though, I know—'

'You do?' She was not expecting it, for it was not common within the regimental families.

'Your father told me.'

'I must admit I think of it more as his choice than mine.' She wondered whether to go as far as revealing her doubts about the existence of a God. His next words confirmed she was right to hesitate.

'Then I take it you have no objection to Catholicism?'

'You're Catholic?' *Why would he ask such an odd question?* 'Many of our officers are, and they're well served with so many places to worship in Cremona, of course.' She remembered how they had both genuflected and crossed themselves after dipping fingers into the stoup of holy water at the entrance to the cathedral. She always performed this ritual, it seemed only polite, so had thought nothing of it when he had done the same.

It was time to change the subject. 'The Po is an interesting river.' Her description of its part in irrigation, and the luthier trade telling him how the spruce was washed in the river by the boatmen to remove excess resin making it especially good for instrument making. Not forgetting the huge catfish that inhabited it – which she had still not managed to see for herself – had held his attention until they arrived back at their horses.

After giving Katarina a leg up into the saddle, he mounted his own horse, and they rode two abreast along the track beside the paddy fields before joining the Cremona road. 'The river serves the city's instrument makers well, bringing them raw materials and access to other markets.' He turned to look at her. 'You're very well informed about that industry.'

'Yes. I learnt to play the violin here.'

'Is that so? Well, in that case might I hear you play before I return to Vienna?'

Tomorrow would be their last day together. 'I don't see why not. I'll need to have my instrument fetched from … a workshop. It needed re-stringing,' she lied, not wishing to explain why her violin was not kept at the *palazzo*. 'I'll send a note.'

That Giuseppe happened to be in the shop helping a customer with a replacement string – Nonna Barb had slipped out seeking a potion from Merla for some ailment she had thankfully kept to herself – meant that when the servant from *Palazzo Poli* arrived with Katarina's letter, he was the one to open it. He decided at once that he would take her violin there himself later that afternoon. He guessed that she would be playing for this Austrian *hauptmann* he had heard about from Anja and was curious to see the man for himself.

When he led the piebald pony with its feathered fetlocks, more used to pulling a cart than carrying a rider, into the *palazzo* stables he came across the man rather earlier than he had expected for he had just handed his fine horse to the head groom and was discussing how to cool him down after what appeared to have been a hard ride.

At the sound of the pony's hooves on the cobbles, both men turned to look. The *hauptmann* took a stride towards him, gesturing at the two violin cases attached to his saddle. 'Ah, Fräulein Rota's instruments. I can take them for you. Save you stabling your pony. I'll hand them to her myself.'

Giuseppe had dressed in his Sunday best, for he had every intention of being there when Katarina played, but the pony rather spoiled the impression he had hoped to make. He smiled doffing his extravagantly feathered (and borrowed hat) bowing as he did so. 'One instrument is Katarina's. Giuseppe Guarneri at your service, *Mein Herr*. I'm her music master. She will expect my accompaniment when she plays.' He hoped his less than top-drawer accent would not be obvious to a German speaker. Of course, the pony was unfortunate, damn it. Perhaps he should have borrowed a decent horse from Antonio? Too late now.

Unperturbed, the captain returned his smile, bowing and clicking the heels of his jackboots before holding out his hand to shake Giuseppe's. *Hauptmann* Johannes Horak. *Fräulein* Rota has invited me to hear her play. Allow me to accompany you inside, Signor Guarneri.'

Horak led the way to the large, elegantly furnished salon – a room Giuseppe had never seen – where other guests were already gathered, many of the women matronly, their uniformed husbands' silver haired and portly, all seated on rows of gilded chairs holding glasses of wine. The casement doors were thrown open to the evening air and the scent of roses took Giuseppe back with a jolt to his first visit to the *palazzo* when Katarina was yet to lift a violin.

His quick glance around the room told him that neither Katarina nor her father were yet there. He moved away towards the door, feeling apprehensive. Katarina had never played to such an audience before. Though there had been more people present at Santa Cecilia's feast-day, they had been luthiers and their families who knew how the violin should sound. What sort of a reception could she expect from people like these? Just then the doors behind him opened and Katarina followed her father inside. That he had never seen her so pale told him all he needed to know about her state of mind.

Oberst Rota took in Giuseppe's presence and, clearly, his daughter's relief at seeing him. 'Signor Guarneri. Ah, I see you have her instrument. We were getting a little worried. I'm sure you can give my daughter any assistance she might need.'

'Of course, *Oberst*.' They were both silent watching him walk away to greet his guests. Giuseppe held up both violin cases. 'I can join in if you need me to.' She clutched his arm, though his attention had momentarily wandered to take in Eduard Rota now in close conversation with Johannes Horak, both watching Katarina intently. What was it about such scrutiny that made him uneasy?

She tapped his arm lightly to reclaim his attention. 'Thank God you're here.' She gestured towards the rows of people. 'I hadn't expected this. I thought I was to play for Johannes alone.' She smiled, shakily. 'I had started to hope my violin would not arrive—'

'We'll play together to begin with, just like before. Then I'll support your solo again. You'll astound them, I promise you.' She nodded and he watched her begin to relax, putting her trust in him. He gave her a quick hug, blinking back the sudden prick of tears because of that unquestioning trust. 'Come. Let's get it done.' He led her to the space at the front before the assembled guests, and she stood beside him at the consul table while they lifted their violins from their cases. 'Both bows have been rosined.'

She nodded.

Then with backs to the audience, they began to tune their instruments before playing a few bars of a simple folk tune together and making final adjustments. He held her gaze for a moment, and they nodded to each other before turning back to the now silent audience and bowing.

Eduard Rota rose, joining them at the front. 'I give you Signor Giuseppe Guarneri and my daughter Katarina Rota.'

They began to play, Giuseppe taking on the harmonies and leaving the melody to Katarina, though sensing she was unable to abandon herself to it in quite the same way she had playing her favourite pieces by Monteverdi and Albinoni at the Rugeris' party. As then, she finished with her own composition, again finding its heady mix of texture and colour. Finally, after the sound soared to a sustained crescendo, she lowered her instrument to silence, quickly followed by thunderous applause.

As Katarina took her bows, Giuseppe was able to watch Johannes who had a look of wide-eyed amazement on his face which was remarkably similar to that on Eduard Rota's. Both men quickly came to join them.

Johannes stood before Katarina shaking his head. 'How in God's name did you learn to play like that?'

'Giuseppe Guarneri.' She gestured towards him. 'Now I hope to make an instrument all by myself, if they'll allow me to.' She turned to him and laughed. 'Not that I've dared to ask him yet.'

Giuseppe laughed, too. 'We'll see, Kat.' She had never mentioned this before. He knew she was interested but not that she wished to become a luthier herself. No woman had ever done that. He was unsure if it were even permitted.

Johannes frowned, glancing at Eduard Rota before speaking. 'You must spend a lot of time with Giuseppe?'

Giuseppe laughed again, though he sensed something pass between the *hauptmann* and the *oberst*. 'She certainly does. She—'

Katarina interrupted him. 'And I love it. Violins are part of my life. Playing them. Watching them made … helping a little in the workshop where I can.'

Giuseppe wondered how he had not known she felt this way. He should have seen it. How had he not?

'Well, how admirable,' Johannes said stiffly.

Those words vexed her, Giuseppe saw.

'It's hardly admirable to occupy oneself doing something one loves, now is it?'

Eduard Rota cleared his throat. 'I must say your skill has improved somewhat since I last heard you play.' He went on to describe in detail Katarina's early attempts and how many complaints there had been about the hideous racket she had made.

Both men laughed rather too heartily, Giuseppe thought.

'That is how one learns, Father,' she said primly. 'And that, of course, is how I first began spending time with the Guarneris.' She patted Giuseppe's arm. So, I'm extremely glad such a fuss was made for without it I would never have got to know them all.'

Eduard and Johannes looked at each other again. *Just what is going on?* Then, like a bolt from the blue, Giuseppe understood. He was a suitor. And why would that surprise him? Katarina was now twenty years old, never mind that she did not look it. More than old enough for marriage. Did she know? Looking at her, he thought not. How would she feel about it? Though girls like her must know this was their fate. And he was unsure what he felt himself. Should she marry Johannes Horak, she would go to Vienna. Well, he would miss her. That was one thing he *was* certain of.

Johannes watched this odd little girl who had just filled the room with the most astonishing sound and was now moving around the salon with Guarneri at her side, smiling and accepting all the praise with what seemed admirable humility.

He had heard much about her from the Hartmanns and secured his uncle's agreement to arrange this meeting. What was it about her that had so captivated him? She could not be called pretty, well not it any conventional sense of the word. Her face was too narrow … too sharp, her mouth small, and her light grey eyes disproportionally large. Her hair though was striking. Not its colour but the weight of it, and its lustre.

But none of this answered his question. Could part of it be that he could already sense his mother's disapproval, and he had never crossed her before? In truth, he had never needed to. And Katarina was so young, how could she hold her own against his formidable mother? There really would be no contest. His mother was a past master at overwhelming a person's misgivings with kindness backed by remorseless certainty.

Eight

CREMONA, OCTOBER 1721.

THE DAY AFTER JOHANNES LEFT FOR VIENNA, Katarina returned to number 5 Piazza San Domenico, and breathing in the familiar smells of spruce and varnish when she opened the door felt like coming home. Nonna Barb and Andrea were pleased to see her, but Giuseppe seemed oddly reserved if not downright unfriendly. She needed to ask him what was wrong but could not seem to snatch a moment alone with him.

Yet instead of ignoring him, as he was doing so successfully to her, Katarina inexplicably found herself trying to ingratiate herself. Smiling and asking his opinion on the quality of her final finishing on a scroll for Andrea or telling him snippets of gossip passed on by Nonna Barb, receiving little more than a grunt in reply. She felt she had reached the nadir when, after Andrea had gone to attend a customer in the shop, she asked Giuseppe if there was anything she could do to help him, instead of challenging his bad mood. How abject. How could she not blush because of it? He turned to stare at her then as though he had forgotten she was there at the bench beside him. Oh, he would, wouldn't he when her face was scarlet?

'Why would I need your help?'

It seemed unnecessarily cruel when he knew how much she had needed his at her recital. And, finally, her temper deserted her. 'For the same reason you have done before. To make your instruments a touch more saleable, perhaps?'

He tilted his head back, staring down his nose at her. 'So, *Hauptmann* Jackboots has gone home to Vienna and here you are again with nothing better to do,' he said, his voice dripping scorn. 'Well, you should probably know before you get any more foolish ideas, women aren't allowed to be luthiers.' He tilted his head. 'Perhaps you might see if Nonna Barb needs you in the kitchen?'

Katarina turned and walked away without another word, though had she seen his expression behind her back, she would have recognised self-disgust for he could not explain his spitefulness and was already deeply ashamed of it.

Nonna Barb, though, had gone to the market, so Katarina decided to visit Anja instead. She had not seen her since her first ride with Johannes, and she would be eager to hear all that had happened since. Katarina found her sitting on the armchair in her tiny kitchen parlour, her feet up on a stool looking decidedly larger in the belly since last she saw her. 'How long now?'

Anja gave her a lazy smile while Katarina fetched them cups of well water from the bucket by the back door. 'Merla thinks only days.' She placed her hand on the great dome of her abdomen and Katarina could see it lift as it was kicked from beneath. 'I think he's trying to fight his way out.'

'You're quite certain it's a boy now?'

'I believe so. Guido after Carlo's father and Karl after mine.'

'But what if it's a girl?'

She grinned. 'My ma and then his. Maisel Nessa.' She pulled herself higher in her chair, her eyes dancing with mischief. 'Now tell me about your Johannes. I want to know all the filthy details.'

'He's not mine. And there's very little to tell. Well, nothing that would interest you, anyway.' Katarina raised her eyebrows, trying to look stern. 'And certainly nothing filthy.'

'Really? I thought you said he were a looker.'

Katarina laughed. 'I did. He's rather sweet too. Kind—'

'Holy cows. Don't tell me you didn't even snog him?'

'I did not. We just enjoyed each other's company, that's all. We became friends.'

'A decent snog is very good way to enjoy a pretty man's company. Followed by a good shag, of course.'

Katarina summoned her sternest look. 'Now, what would Carlo say if he heard you talk like this.'

She cackled prettily. (And, yes, Anja really was able to do that.) 'Well, he wouldn't say a whole lot seeing as how he don't speak no German.'

Katarina had to concede her friend had a point.

'So what did you do with him then?'

Katarina cleared her throat, aware of how tame it would sound to Anja. 'We explored the countryside more on horseback. Walked. Played chess.' She tried not to join in with Anja's incredulous grin. 'We talked a lot—'

'Oh do tell, please?' She mimed a huge yawn.

Katarina tried to scowl. 'Philosophy. Religion. That sort of thing if you must know.'

'No wonder he's pissed off back to Vienna. You must have bored the drawers off 'im.'

'I'll have you know, they were exceedingly interesting conversations. We both enjoyed them very much.' Then they burst into peels of childish laughter for how could they not think of the Calvinist euphemism of fleshly conversation for sexual congress? The two young women gulped their water, trying not to choke.

'Well, there's still Claudio, I suppose. If you can get him back from whoever the bitch is.'

'She's welcome to him.' Katarina sighed. 'I don't know why I accused Giuseppe of knowing about them.' She told Anja about her recital at the *palazzo* then, and how kind Giuseppe had been, how much he had helped her. 'Now he seems so cold and distant. I don't know what I can have done to make him act like this.' She laughed with little mirth. 'You should have seen me trying to placate him, simpering and fluttering my eyelashes exactly like Sancia does, trying to get him to be friends again. He just looked through me.' Katarina shook her head quite forcefully. 'And why in God's name do I care?' Because she missed his encouragement. She missed their easy companionship. 'What's wrong with him?'

'It's all the time you spent with Johannes. He's jealous.'

Katarina laughed. 'Absolutely not. He has no interest in me in that way.' Yet the thought that he might stirred a tiny glimmer of hope in her that she had long believed abandoned. 'Nor have I in him,' she added, defiantly.

They were unable to discuss it further, for at that moment the door opened, and Merla came in, giving Katarina a quick hug before dropping to her knees beside Anja's chair and placing a hand on her belly. 'How are you both today?'

A week later Katarina's father told her she was to marry Johannes Horak. She had been called into his study and asked to sit before his desk. Though the formality of it had immediately made her anxious, she had not been prepared for what transpired.

When he told her, she could scarcely believe what she was hearing. The shock of it was made worse when it seemed it was all entirely settled. Johannes had wanted to meet her first to confirm that she would make a suitable future wife, before agreeing to an arrangement being made between the two families. *How good of him. How wise to make sure I was suitable.* So why had no one inquired whether she found him acceptable? It simply beggared belief. 'Well, Father, do I truly have no say in the matter?'

He smiled, appearing genuinely amused. '*Really*, Katarina? It was quite plain you had no objections to him whatsoever.'

She had stood then, more than a little vexed. 'Just because I enjoy his company doesn't mean I want to marry him. I barely know him.' She chewed her lip, trying to gather her spiralling thoughts. 'And how do we know we saw the real him? He wanted me to like him and for you to see him as an appropriate match.' Yet, surely, she had indeed seen his true character when he came to her aid after that encounter with his horse at the wall. He had not known who she was then, until she told him.

'His uncle is *Markgraf* von Croy, one of the biggest land-holders in Vienna province. I think we should be honoured they consider you a fitting match for him.'

Katarina sat. 'I see.' If that were the case, then her feelings about it truly were of no consequence. Perhaps she should just be grateful she liked him, for it would have made no difference had she not. Then she wondered why such an illustrious family had settled for her. 'Why me?'

'Let's just say that while his mother is a von Croy, the Horak lineage is not quite so impressive. I believe the man was an infantry sergeant, though he died before Johannes was born and his mother lives in a manner suitable to her own station rather than his father's, in the family schloss. He was bought up and educated as a von Croy.'

Katarina rose again, intending to leave, but thought of one final question. 'How on earth did such a family know of my existence?' Then she answered it herself. 'They didn't, but Johannes knew the Hartmanns at the university.'

Her father smiled. 'Indeed. He must have liked the sound of you.'

'What can they have said?' *And why?* Well, it seemed she would have plenty of time to find out.

. . .

It was odd returning to the isle the next day. Though the routine of it was exactly as it always was, everything had changed. When Katarina climbed down from her carriage outside number 5, she suddenly felt unready to face the Guarneris with her news. To face Giuseppe. So, she went instead to Merla, hoping to find her alone. She knew how Anja would react and was not ready for that, either. She needed Merla's pragmatism. Anja's would show too much emotion ... and Giuseppe too little.

She was at her ware-bench grinding something aromatic with her pestle and mortar and looked up smiling when Katarina came in. Her eyebrows rose immediately, clearly reading something on her face. There seemed little point in prevaricating. 'My father tells me I am to marry Johannes Horak.'

Merla took a long breath, putting down the pestle and wiping her hands on her apron. 'And how do you feel about it?'

'I think I'd prefer to have been asked rather than told ...'

'But?'

She managed a weak smile. 'It could be worse. Much worse.'

The apothecary came out from behind her counter to hug her. 'So tell me all about him.'

And that is what she did, sitting in Merla's kitchen parlour, including what she had just learnt about his family.

'So, he's been brought up by his mother. He must be very close to her.'

'He didn't mention her much.' She shook her head. 'There is a pleasing kind of symmetry to it, isn't there, though? Me with only a father and him a mother.'

'When is it to be? When must we lose you?' She slapped her forehead with the heel of her hand. 'Listen to me making it sound like a tragedy. What I mean is, when is the happy event?'

'Early next spring.' It seemed far enough away not to be real.

'He is to come back to Cremona soon on another short secondment.'

'That's good.' She gave Katarina a penetrating look. 'It will give you time to get used to the idea of him as a husband.'

'Yes, I hadn't thought of that.' She felt suddenly queasy.

Merla seemed to read her mind. 'Don't be afraid of it, Katarina.'

'I'm not. I—'

Merla grasped Katarina's hands across the table, holding her gaze. 'Let me offer you some advice before Anja does—'

'How do you know she hasn't done so already?'

She tilted her head. 'I know you. I'm the first you've told.'

She was right, of course. But how could she know? 'Very well. What do you wish to say to me?' Though Katarina already knew the territory as soon as Anja's name was spoken.

'Don't allow him any intimacy with you before you marry him. When a man asks to put his cock in a woman's hand that's not where he wants it and, believe me, it might not be where she wants it either. He'll say you're betrothed so it doesn't matter. But it does, Kat. Because once he has you, he can still change his mind. But you can't. Make sure you keep the option.'

When Katarina tried to imagine such an intimate scene with Johannes, she found she simply could not. She chewed her lip, not knowing what to say.

Merla placed her palm on Katarina's face 'Don't fret on it, little one. Now go and tell Giuseppe ... and Anja.'

Katarina was grateful to find Giuseppe alone this time. She wanted him to be the first to know and stood in front of him until he looked up from his work. He, too, seemed to read something on her face for he held her gaze, unsmiling. So, for the second time that morning, she spoke the words. 'I am to marry Johannes Horak.'

He was very still, and their eyes held for what seemed an age. How strange that she should suddenly appreciate again how beautiful his were. The colour of brandy held up to the light. Perhaps it was because they were focussed on her in a way she had never seen before. As though, at last, she truly was all he could see.

He blinked and shot to his feet, pulling her into his arms. 'Kat, I'm cock-a-hoop for you' He held her away, smiling. 'That's grand... I can't find the words.'

Well, perhaps she had not wished him to be quite so delighted. She sat then, telling him all about Johannes's illustrious family. How he lived in their *schloss* which was German for *palazzo*. Something he must know perfectly well but showed no signs of irritation to be told, which was unfortunate for she had hoped he would. He was just too damn happy about it.

'So, you'll be a great lady in your *palazzo* and can forget all about chisels and thumb planes.'

He knows full well I don't want to forget. Why would I want to? I use those tools because I love using them. I love what they do. She would not give him the satisfaction of hearing her tell him so.

When the door to the shop opened, Nonna Barb bustled in bringing a gust of the isle's heat with her, full of dust and scents of luthiers' labours.

'Katarina is to be married,' Giuseppe called.

So, there she was telling it all again and then to Andrea, of course. Nonna Barb shed many tears at the thought of losing her and even Andrea's eyes welled up a touch, while Giuseppe laughed and grinned and continued to look so damnably, damnably pleased about it.

But when they were alone again, his eyes focused on her once more. 'Shall we make a violin together before you leave, Kat?' he said, softly. 'Then every time I play it, I can think of you.'

So, he would miss her after all. And he was going to let her make an instrument, which was the best parting gift he could possibly give to her. She flung her arms around him. 'I can't think of anything I'd rather do.' She pulled away. 'I thought it wasn't permitted, though?'

'Er ... well, I'm not sure why I said that. I don't know if it's right. I don't think it's ever been considered—'

'Because a woman wouldn't be able to do it anyway? And I shall prove that wrong. There's so much time before I go to Vienna. I—' She did not like how relieved she sounded about it, but it was too late to change her tone. 'It will be a fine violin, Giuseppe. We'll make sure of it together.

'How will I bear it without you here.' Anja dabbed at her water-logged eyes with a tiny scrap of lace.

She was lolling in her armchair again. Carlo had employed a girl to help her with the household tasks, though it seemed to Katarina that meant she must already carry out all of them. Though she imagined this would be the case after the child came.

'You're to be the boy's Godmother, too. How can you not be here?'

'We shall visit Father often. And I'm sure you can visit us—'

She snorted. 'Like me and my sort would be welcome by his hoity lot. His ma's nose would be up at the very sight of us.'

'Don't be absurd. You can meet Johannes when he comes next time. You'll see he's not like that at all.' It did occur to her as she spoke that she had absolutely no evidence to base this on. Anja had been her servant as well as her friend. While Johannes was always perfectly pleasant to servants, she had no idea what he would make of her relationship with Anja now.

Anja smiled, happy to change the subject to Johannes. 'Now that is somefink to look forward to. If he's all you say he is, you won't be able to keep your hands off 'im for long. And you shouldn't. Take him into your bed next time he's here, and you've caught him hook line and sinker. Then you can drop him in your net.'

'He's a gentleman, Anja. He's hardly going to try and take advantage of me as a guest in my father's home, now is he?'

She laughed. 'Silly mare. It's you what'll be takin advantage. Don't matter where you do it just get it done. He gets your cherry, he gets you. No two ways about it. And if you gets a bun in the oven then the flash bugger'll marry you all the sooner, won't he.'

Though Katarina joined in with her friend's laughter, there was only one piece of advice on this that she intended to take, and it was not Anja's.

Merla looked up from the ware-bench when Giuseppe stepped inside the shop. 'I was just about to close-up for the day. Do the shutters for me, would you.'

He did as she asked. He had waited in a nearby doorway to see Sancia leave before coming in. With the shop now full of shadows, he followed Merla through her workshop and into the kitchen parlour where windows showed the sun already low in a sky slashed with red and gold.

She took two glasses and a bottle of wine from a cupboard and sat down at the table, pouring for them. 'I thought you'd come this evening.'

He lit the candles before joining her at the table. 'You know me too well.' There was something comforting about that.

'You're here to ask me what you should feel about Katarina's marriage.' It was not a question.

He grinned. 'Amongst other things.'

She blinked. 'We'll see.'

He did not react. She was well aware how that answer had made him feel since he first came to her bed as a sixteen-your-old lad. He refused to feel like a child now. He drained his glass and poured himself a refill.

Merla sighed. 'Sancia is thrilled that Kat will leave Cremona. I do believe she thinks you'll fall into her arms.'

He shrugged disparagingly. 'Kat's my friend that's all … and Sancia will never even be that.'

'You will miss her though, you do know—'

'Of course I do. We've known each other for eight years. Spent a lot of time together.' He placed both hands on the table, splaying his fingers. 'I've always known somewhere in the back of my mind she would have a marriage like this … arranged for her.' He raised his eyes to look hard at her. 'I must be pleased for her, mustn't I? Horak seems a decent enough sort and she'll have a comfortable life with him.'

'Yet you're finding it difficult to be pleased?'

He shook his head impatiently. 'When she first came back after he left … I don't know why I had to be so fucking unkind to her.' He drained his glass again, trying to push away the memory of her face when she had tried to please him … to bring him out of his foul mood. She should have clouted him one.

Merla placed her hand over his on the table. 'You don't like things changing. You didn't then, and you don't now. I don't think she does either, but you must both come to terms with it. You have no choice … but you do have a choice about being unkind.'

'I know. I know. I've already tried to make it up to her. She's going to make a violin before she goes. It's something she really wants to do.'

Merla smiled. 'Being cruel really isn't you, Giuseppe. I think, perhaps you wanted to hurt yourself too.'

He returned her smile. 'That sounds way too complicated for me.' He stood, holding out his hand, watching her smile widen until her hand found its way into his and he led her up the narrow staircase to her bedchamber. Clothes were quickly shed until his hands came to rest upon the familiar contours of her flesh. 'Christ, I need you, Merla,' he gasped as, at last, he plunged inside her and was able to forget everything else.

That night Anja gave birth to a daughter and the next day Katarina shed tears holding the tiny scrap in her arms because she would not now be there to watch her grow up.

Intermezzo

A MOTHER'S LOVE

Nine

VIENNA – SCHLOSS VON CLOY, MARCH 1722

BRIGHT CLOUDS SCUDDED ACROSS A CORNFLOWER SKY belying the frigid air when Katarina and Johannes finally set out for Vienna. The von Croy coach – just one of many she learnt – was by far the most luxurious she had ever seen with its gold studded panels, never mind ridden inside. The six matched greys harnessed to it were equally impressive, as were the liveried drivers and postillions.

She had a soft fur rug covering her knees as did Johannes who sat opposite on the butter-soft leather, sleeping, his head resting back against the squabs, lulled by the carriage's well-sprung motion along Italian roads made serviceable by Austrian expertise.

It was a sort of violation to watch him so closely, but hard to resist. His countenance seemed softer with a fine gold stubble on his jaw glinting in the early sunshine. Something stirred in her seeing him so vulnerable to her gaze ... so unguarded. She discovered a certain fondness for him ... a certain tenderness, and indeed a desire to protect him. Could this grow into love? She found she hoped it might.

They would stop several times along the way to change

horses, with teams already in place, and would be accommo-
dated by the Austrian army wherever possible and otherwise by
well-placed local people of sufficient standing to be acquain-
tances of the von Croy family.

For Katarina, it was a journey that for so long had seemed far
enough away in the future for it not to be real ... as though it
would never truly happen. She had seen Johannes three times in
the six months since she learned they would marry. The first
time he had come to the *palazzo* as their guest, he had asked her
to walk with him in the rose garden as dusk – the scent had
been almost too sickly sweet and cloying – where he had
formally asked her to be his wife. She, of course, had formally
consented and he had given her a ring which was obviously a
family heirloom and far too big and heavy for her small hand.
He had promised to have the fine diamonds and emeralds re-set
for her and, had she known it, blamed his mother for insisting it
would be entirely suitable.

And during his absences, Katarina had spent her time
making the violin with Giuseppe. It was a time she now felt
deeply grateful for, especially as she would never do any of it
again. They had even been able to collaborate in adding subtle
embellishments to achieve what Katarina wanted. A violin
which showed some tool marks and was also delicately
beautiful.

To start, Katarina chose her wood. Maple for the violin's
back, ribs, and neck, softer spruce for the top as it vibrated more
easily. Then she had assembled her tools, planes and chisels, a
backsaw, fret saw, purfling pick and many more. The mould was
surrounded by maple ribs, shaped by the hot bending iron, and
glued to the corners and end blocks. The plates were joined
ready for gouging and the surfaces smoothed with a scraper. F-
holes were cut, a base bar glued inside the spruce top plate, and
the finished plates glued to the rib assembly. She carved the
neck and scroll from maple before the peg box and fingerboard

were attached. The varnished violin was completed with a chin rest, tail piece, strings, bridge, and pegs. Giuseppe knowing when to support her and when to let her work alone (just as he did when she played) had made it an experience she could never forget.

The downside of this time-consuming labour of love had been the lack of preparation for her wedding. In the end, her trousseaux had been assembled at great speed with seamstresses working all hours to make sure the garments were ready for her journey to Vienna. Lilli Schneider, the wife of the regimental medical officer, had taken it all in hand having done the same for her daughter the year before. Katarina found it hard to believe she could possibly need such quantities, and that it all had to be embellished with quite so much lace and so many frills. And on undergarments. Nightgowns. *Really?*

It had been Merla who had reminded her of the time she would need for all this to be ready, horrified to find nothing had yet been done. Of course, it was not something she could have expected her father to organise, though she was uncertain why she was expected to know of it either. Anja had needed nothing like it before her marriage to Carlo.

Johannes's small snort woke him with a start. He blinked, clearing his throat, obviously disorientated. 'F-forgive me. I fell asleep.' He frowned. 'I trust I wasn't snoring?'

She nodded, feigning displeasure. 'Well, I suppose it's something I must learn to live with.'

He reddened. 'I've never been told such—' His colour deepened. 'Perhaps it's just as well we shall have separate bedchambers. I would hate to inflict—'

She moved across to sit beside him, clutching his arm. 'I'm teasing, Johannes. You weren't snoring. Will we really have separate bedchambers?' She was unsure what to make of that.

His smile returned. 'Adjoining rooms. It's a convention, nothing more.'

How strange. But, in truth, the only married couple whose sleeping arrangements she knew anything of were Anja and Carlo who happily shared their tiny bed. Not that they had any other choice. He moved his rug so it covered them both and she enjoyed his warmth pressed close. So there had been others to share his bed. After pondering this for a time, she decided it must be a good thing that one of them knew what they were doing in that department.

The journey took ten days in the end, and though the sunshine did not last beyond the first, there was no rain, which would have delayed them further when roads would likely have become mired in mud.

When, at last, the carriage pulled in through a suitably impressive arch in the gatehouse, it followed a fine gravelled driveway beneath tall trees forming a tunnel of skeletal branches above them. Katarina sat back, relieved to no longer be at the mercy of assorted hosts who had (giving some the benefit of the doubt) entertained them to the best of their abilities. However, she was tired of sleeping in a different bedchamber each night and it had to be said, in lodgings of varying comfort and quality. She often had to turn a blind eye when Johannes's accommodation had been rather more salubrious than her own, particularly when housed by the army.

The schloss would now offer some welcome stability, not least from days spent in a lurching coach. While she would still be subjected to avid scrutiny, from Johannes's mother in particular, at least they would be the same people each day and she might at some point feel able to relax with them. And this place would become her home. She watched from the window as the drive wound its way through trees and alongside pastures where sheep grazed. As the track widened the trees began to take on a more manicured look until they resembled clipped hedges, though far taller. Katarina wondered how this was achieved. It must be a precarious business.

The schloss itself took her breath away. Catching a first glimpse above the trees Katarina saw it was built from pale, buttery stone, its many upper floor windows gleaming in late afternoon sunshine that seemed returned in their honour. When, finally, the carriage rounded the last bend, they found the servants – from the youngest kitchen maid to the finest liveried footmen – arrayed at the bottom of a wide flight of stone steps to welcome them. When a silver-haired woman dressed in a fine velvet gown of deep sapphire blue, stepped forward as they alighted from the coach, Katarina believed she was about to meet her future mother-in-law, so the woman's deep curtsy to Johannes startled her.

Johannes's annoyance was obvious. 'Where the hell is Mother, Ida?'

'She was called away to the city. Your Aunt Brigit is unwell again. She asked me to offer her apologies.'

Johannes took Katarina's arm and pulled her close in the frigid air. 'Why must she be at her beck and call, she's nothing but a hypochondriac. Mother should stop indulging her.' He smiled down at Katarina then. 'This is Katarina Rota, Ida. My betrothed.' His smiling good humour had quickly returned. 'Ida is in charge of us all. I often wonder how we would fare without her.'

Ida glowed under his praise but said nothing to Katarina. 'Your rooms are ready for you, *Hauptmann* Johannes.' She clicked her fingers, and several footmen began unloading their boxes. Katarina shook her head slightly seeing again the extent of her luggage and wondering how she could possible need so much. When would she ever use it all?

Ida led them up the steps to the marble columned and grandly porticoed porch where great doors were already thrown open to receive them into the vast hall echoing with footsteps. A wide stone staircase with a balustrade ornately carved with foliage swept up from its centre to a gallery above.

After Ida had supervised the removal of their fur-lined cloaks, they followed her up to the first floor where, with her arm still held firmly in his, Johannes guided her into the salon. An extravagant fire blazed in a fireplace that looked large enough to roast a whole ox, not that such a thing would be done in so grand a chamber. There was much highly polished dark wood and gold embroidered brocades covering formal looking chairs and sofas which appeared to stand to attention. Certainly, none invited occupation.

Katarina stood beside Johannes at one of the triple height windows watching her breath mist before her, looking down over formal gardens with clipped hedges planted in complex swirling patterns alongside more fine gravel pathways. The grounds certainly required the extravagant use of shears.

Ida followed them in. 'May I have refreshments sent in for you, *Hauptmann?*'

'No. We'll take it upstairs.' He looked down at Katarina. I ... we have a suite of rooms on the floor above.' He gestured at the vast room with its distant though gloriously frescoed ceiling sporting brightly coloured cherubs and putti frolicking in the clouds above mythical beasts. 'Shall we say it's a touch cosier than this great mausoleum.'

After climbing a second flight of stone stairs, Katarina followed Johannes along a gallery with walls almost completely lost behind portraits of various shapes and sizes, some so blackened by time it was almost impossible to see a person depicted at all. At the end, a narrower corridor led to an oak doorway, which Johannes opened to reveal another smaller salon comfortably furnished with chairs and couches upholstered in bright velvets and silk florals. Here the fire blazed just as fiercely as below but in surroundings more conducive to warmth permeating the room.

They had not long been seated before its welcome warmth when Ida led a footman into the chamber, watching while he placed a large heavily laden tray of refreshments down onto a console table where he poured glasses of claret which Ida handed to them. Johannes first, of course. Katarina's glass was only half-full and presented without a word, and she realised then that this woman had not yet spoken to her. 'Thank you, Ida,' she said pointedly. But the woman had already returned her attention to Johannes, holding a platter of assorted pastries and sweetmeats, smiling encouragement as he made his selection. The platter was then offered to Katarina again without a word. She waved her hand to decline.

'That will be all now, Ida. Thank you.'

She curtsied before clicking her fingers at the footman, who left the room after a swift bow. 'Ring for hot water when you're ready to bathe and Gustav will attend to you, *Hauptmann*,' she said before closing the door behind her.

Katarina drained her glass. 'Perhaps I might use your water after you're done, *Hauptmann*?' she said with heavy emphasis on the title.

Johannes chuckled. 'I think we might manage to get you some of your own, at a stretch.' He stood to refill her glass this time to a more generous level and handed her a small plate of the sweetmeats. 'Eat them, they're good.'

Katarina did so, and greedily, before draining her wine glass once again. 'She doesn't like me, which seems a little presumptuous when she doesn't know me.'

'Take no heed of her. She doesn't enjoy change that's all. She—'

'Change? Surely she must have expected you would marry at some point?'

'Indeed. I believe she and Mother discussed such a possibility.' He grinned. 'On many, many occasions.'

'Ah.' Katarina began to understand. 'Perhaps you turned

down their suggestions?' And then chose her for reasons she had still not fully understood.

He finished chewing a pastry. 'Let's just say I was introduced to several quite lovely and sweet-natured young ladies who soon proved rather too vacuous for my taste.'

'So you chose me because I'm not vacuous?' Though probably not sweet-natured, and most definitely not lovely. Well, if his mother and Ida selected young ladies with such attributes it was hardly surprising she was not welcomed with open arms. 'Just who is Ida? Is she some sort of housekeeper?'

'Perhaps it would be more accurate to call her a companion. She was Mother's lady's maid when she was a girl and has become more and more indispensable to her. Running a household of this size is, shall we say, a little tiresome for someone of my mother's disposition, and Ida is able to lift some of the burden from her.'

'I see.' Katarina could not help wondering how Johannes's father had fitted into this arrangement. She knew he was long dead but nothing further about him. But now did not seem quite the time to ask.

After his valet had been summoned and bathing water arranged, Johannes showed Katarina into her bedchamber where a young maid was already unpacking her belongings. She stopped to curtsey. 'I'll leave you with … er?'

'Chiara, *Mein Herr*,' she said in a strong voice that belied her tiny stature, if not her youth, and her German had a strong Italian accent.

'Ah, yes. Chiara from Naples. How long have you been with us now,' Johannes asked in his stilted though well-intentioned Italian.

The maid smiled prettily. 'One year now, *Hauptmann*,' she replied in rather more accomplished German.

'You came with your brother into my uncle's service, if I recall?'

'Yes, *Mein Herr*. Your mother kindly fetched me here.' She looked down at her feet. 'I didn't settle in your uncle's household.'

'Ah, yes. Quite. Well, I'll leave you to it, then,' he said, again.

When the door closed behind him, Katarina stood surveying the room. Having now seen something of the schloss's magnificence, its proportions did not surprise her, nor its opulence. All gleaming dark wood and embossed emerald velvet drapes.

Chiara stood watching her.

'Are you going to speak to me, I wonder?' Dare she hope Chiara from Naples might be a touch friendlier than Ida?'

Chiara tilted her head, her gaze now startlingly direct. 'Why would I not, Madonna, unless you don't wish it, of course?' she said in Italian.

Katarina smiled. 'I do wish it. No one here has done so far, and I was becoming disconcerted by it.'

Chiara resumed lifting Katarina's trousseau from her trunks and laying each garment carefully onto shelves inside a walnut cabinet. 'Her, you mean?'

'Her?'

'Ida Schmidt. It don't surprise me none. She's a right baggage that one, though not as bad as the mistress herself.'

'You mean *Frau* Horak?' Surely this could not be so, for it did not match Johannes's description of his mother at all.

'She goes by *Gräfin* von Cloy. Don't get that wrong for gawd's sake. The *markgraf* is her brother, but he's got no heirs, nor likely to have if you knows what I mean?'

That Katarina did not, must have been conveyed by her expression.

'He's a *finocchio*. You know? Likes lads? He fetched us from Naples 'cause my brother were pretty. His *palazzo* were full of 'em running around bare-arsed, giggling like girls. Got on my tits, it did.' She grinned, patting her flat chest. 'Well, it would of if I had any you could notice.' Just then there was a tap on the door. 'It'll be your hot water. Bring it in, you daft culls, the mistress don't want it cold, now do she?'

Katarina thought perhaps she should have been the one to give permission but let it pass. The copper tub was carried in by footmen and placed before the fire. Chiara quickly lined it with towels before large cannisters of steaming water were poured in to fill it.

When the men had closed the door behind them, Chiara stood, arms on hips, surveying it. 'Well, don't that look inviting?'

It truly did. With the maid's help her clothing was quickly shed and she was able to climb into the warmth, feeling it penetrate her bones. It was only then she realised she had felt no embarrassment about her body in front of Chiara, which was clearly because it was the first time, she had a maid as slight as she was. And voluptuous Anja had been unable not to tease her about it.

'Shall I wash your hair, Madonna?'

Would there be time before dinner to dry it? She found she did not care. 'Please do. Now, what can you tell me about this Ida Schmidt and *Gräfin* von Cloy?'

Chiara poured a jug of water over Katarina's hair while she held a towel to her face. 'Ida is the *gräfin's* eyes and ears is the truth of it. The *gräfin*, she likes to show herself as kindly and like she can't say boo to no goose, but that ain't her at all. Ida's spite comes straight from her.' She poured some sweet-smelling liquid from a bottle onto her hand and began to work it through Katarina's hair.

'But how can you possibly know that?'

'I've heard 'em. The mistress tells her what to say and do. They's a pair of weasels.'

So, Chiara liked to eavesdrop. She must bear that in mind.

Could it be possible that Ida's silence had been an instruction from Johannes's mother? Surely not? 'What about the young ladies they chose for the captain to marry? Tell me about them.'

Chiara began to towel Katarina's hair. 'What you'd expect. Rich. Cows to servants. Braying voices. Big tits. The *gräfin* thinks he likes 'em.' She glanced at Katarina's clear lack of such attributes but said nothing. They both giggled.

The maid helped Katarina from the water and wrapped her in a towel already warmed before the fire. 'There's an old hunting lodge where he used to take women secretly. T'was afore my time, of course, but I heard tell of it off other servants. Regular stallion he were back then, so they say.'

There seemed nothing to say to that.

When she was dressed for dinner and sitting at the toilet table with her still slightly damp hair loose down her back, there was a light tap on the connecting door to Johannes's chamber. Katarina met Chiara's gaze in the mirror and gave a small nod. The maid moved to open it and curtsied.

Katarina stood to face him, getting a first glimpse of his room. That it was even more opulent than her own came as no surprise. 'I hope I haven't kept you waiting?'

'You look quite lovely, Katarina.'

She wore one of her new gowns with its fussy lace frills, but its rich damson colour suited her well enough. Johannes was not in uniform, although elegantly attired in a fashionable green satin coat liberally embroidered with swirls of silver thread. This was the first time she had dined with him when he had not worn his dress uniform. 'I rather like you in civilian clothes.'

'As Mother is away, we'll dine less formally.' He smiled taking her hand and bringing it up to his lips. 'I'm sure you're relieved to hear it on your first night here. Mother will inundate you with guests eager to meet you on her return.'

'I look forward to it.' That was about as far from the truth as it was possible to be, but she maintained her smile. 'When do you expect her?'

'Tomorrow, I'm reliably informed.'

Again, she met Chiara's eyes in the mirror, her dismayed expression summed up Katarina's true feelings rather well.

'At least we can have a few days all together before I must return to the regiment.'

What? How was this the first she had heard of it? Why had he brought her here now when their wedding was not until June if they were not to spend the time together? She had thought he understood how they needed to get to know each other a little more before they married but it seemed the time was designed more for her to get to know his mother. No, that was not it. For his mother to get to know her. 'Yes, that's good to know.' In truth, there was little good to be found.

Katarina and Johannes rode side by side across fields towards woodland where the ground rose steadily up into low hills burnished gold by Spanish gorse covering the slopes. They were heading out for *mittagessen* in a hunting lodge up in the higher slopes, which must be the place of assignation Chiara had told her of. Jesu. Was that what he had in mind for her? Her heart fluttered uncomfortably.

She had arrived to join him in the stables to find a pretty grey mare already prepared for her use fitted with a side-saddle. 'I can't use that. Take it off, please.' The groom appearing astonished, looked to Johannes for confirmation.

'You heard, Otto. Take it off and replace it.'

Otto did as asked but did not attempt to hide his disapproval, shaking his head and muttering to himself before leading the horse to the mounting block and tightening the girth strap after Katarina had lowered herself into the saddle.

The sour-faced man looked up at her still holding the horse's bridle. '*Mien Dame*, you should know Griselda here be trained to the side-saddle, you'll need to take care with her.'

Katarina nodded and touched the horse's sides gently with her heels, moving off to follow Johannes on his black stallion. Now, as they moved through the still dormant fields where the yellow grass was cropped short by sheep, she could not resist questioning him about the saddle choice.

'A side-addle is customary for ladies here, following the royal court I believe. But if you wish to ride astride there will be no objection, I'm sure. Why should there be?'

Katarina wondered if Johannes's mother would be quite so sanguine.

The ride took rather longer than Katarina had anticipated, taking them up through silent, deciduous woods – the horse's hooves quiet over leaf mould and moss – where bare branches were still rimed with frost. Then out onto ridges before descending once more into valleys where tumultuous streams gushed over green boulders, before climbing again up ever steeper slopes, the sky so heavy it hung exhausted like a pall over the treetops. Could it be they had not taken the most direct route?

At last, they arrived at the cabin set in a glade where another fierce steam flowed over mossy rocks, dropping in a short water-fall before flowing on into the trees beyond the clearing. The lodge had a substantial look about it clearly setting it apart from a simple shelter for hunters. That there was a thin stream of blue smoke rising straight up from the chimney showed the presence of servants. And, as there were no horses tied at the rail or loose in the small paddock, they had been and gone.

Johannes kicked his leg over the pommel of his saddle to vault from his horse before helping Katarina to dismount. 'Looks like we should be warm if nothing else.' He gestured at the smoke.

While Johannes tended to the horses and released them into

the paddock, Katarina looked around her, breathing air smelling of rotting vegetation and wood smoke. The sound of rushing water and the occasional bird cry were all she could hear.

Inside the cabin was simply yet comfortably furnished. Plane wooden chairs with heavy serviceable upholstery in browns and greys. A single door revealed the presence of an additional room off the rear of the building. A bedchamber, perhaps? Or a privy? Katarina took in the substantial sofa set close to the fire.

The sturdy oak table where a picnic was laid out, had been placed beneath a window looking out onto the glade. Rustic bread and assorted meats, poultry, sausage, and cheeses. A bowl of apples and dried apricots. A flagon of wine and two glasses. And somewhat incongruously, a large, iced cake.

'I trust you're hungry?'

After such the long ride, Katarina found she was indeed. Very much. They carried their loaded plates and glasses of wine to the couch in front of the fire, both setting their wine down onto a low table in front of them and holding their plates on their laps. They ate in silence until the serving platters were much depleted. Lifting a last chicken leg, Katarina pointed at the other door. 'What's in there?'

He took a gulp of wine before answering. 'All sorts. We call it the gun room, but guns aren't kept in there unless there's a shoot. There's plenty of fishing tackle. Other bits and pieces.'

So, no bed then. She cleared her plate and drained her glass before speaking again. 'I thought it might be a bedchamber.'

He barked a laugh. 'Why on earth would a hunting shack need a bedchamber?'

Katarina gestured around her. 'Hardly a shack.'

He shrugged. 'A cabin where men come to hunt and fish.'

'And women are entertained to picnic lunches.'

He smiled and moved closer to her. 'You could try your hand at fishing if you wish?'

Katarina laughed. 'Another time when the weather is a touch more clement, perhaps.'

'I'll hold you to it.' He pulled her close and cupping her face in his hands, he kissed her gently.

Though she had been expecting it, it still came as a surprise, somehow. She moved her hand to the back of his head, feeling the thick thatch of his hair as his tongue played over her lips. And then her mouth was open to him, and she quickly found herself beneath him on the sofa with her bodice lowered and his mouth upon her breasts as he began to lift her skirts.

Yet she felt strangely detached aware of his desire, his arousal obvious and pressed hard against her, and very much aware of the absence of her own. And then, suddenly, she was swept away by a vivid memory of a time when she *had* felt it, her body throbbing at the sight of Giuseppe's naked torso. How everything she should be feeling now, had overwhelmed her then. But that seemed such a mad thing to think of when she lay beneath a different man. One she was soon to marry.

Johannes sat up abruptly. 'Forgive me.'

Her thoughts spiralled away, and she sat up too, quickly covering herself. Had he sensed her distraction? She should speak but could find no words. She could not look at him. 'Johannes ... I—'

His closed his eyes taking several noisy breaths. 'Forgive me,' he said again. 'That should not have happened.'

So, he had not stopped because he felt her distance.

He moved to pull her into his arms. 'Not this.' He gestured at the sofa. 'I won't disrespect you like this. We can wait for God's blessing.'

But apparently, he'd had no concerns about disrespecting others in this very place. Madonnas and whores. Wives were clearly placed in the first category. Yet, did marriage not fit more closely with the second? Even though her father had paid a generous dowry to secure this match, all that was required from her was a maidenhead and, in due course, an heir. She shook her head vexed by it all. How could words spoken by a priest change what had nearly happened here into something respectable? 'I'm not sure a god's approval means quite as much to me as it does to you.' She saw how much her words shocked him.

He stood. 'We should leave now if we are to get back before dusk.'

They rode back in silence, via the shorter route.

Ten

SCHLOSS VON CLOY, VIENNA. MARCH 1722

BACK IN THE STABLE YARD, SEVERAL GROOMS WERE busy manoeuvring a gilded carriage into the coachhouse, and Katarina's heart sank. Johannes's mother had returned. Would she sense the *froideur* between them? She was his mother, of course she would.

As their horses walked beyond the coach, Katarina had her first sight of *Gräfin* Ursula von Cloy. Small. Erect. Softly plump. Her expression one of good-natured interest in all that lay around her. How did this fit with Chiara's description of her character?

Johannes called out to her. 'Mother how wonderful to see you.' He dismounted and went to her, quickly embracing her. 'How's Aunt Brigit?'

'Much better, I'm glad to report. She's a martyr to those agues of hers, poor dear.'

A groom appeared beside Katarina to help her dismount, Johannes appearing to have forgotten her entirely. She stood watching them, momentarily uncertain what to do before steeling herself and moving forward to join them.

When she arrived at Johannes's side, he seemed unaware of her until his mother spoke. 'Katarina, how delightful to meet you at last.'

Johannes turned then, smiling and with an arm quickly looped around her waist, he pulled her close. 'Yes, Katarina has been eager to meet you too haven't you, my dearest.'

He had not called her that before. 'Indeed, I have.'

Ursula grasped Katarina's hands before stepping in to kiss her cheek. She moved away, looking her over, head to toe. 'Tonight, I think we'll have a small banquet in your honour. There are so many friends and neighbours as eager to meet you as I have been.'

A banquet? Katarina's heart sank further.

Ursula seemed to read her dismay. 'You're alarmed at such a prospect? Forgive me, I should have borne in mind how very young you are and that you perhaps haven't quite experienced our level of society before. I'm sure Vienna province is somewhat different to a small Italian city in such regards. But please don't be concerned, my dear, this occasion will not be a formal one. Just a select few of our very good friends eager to welcome you here, as I said.'

Johannes looked down at Katarina with a slight frown. 'Surely you're not fearful of such an event.' He turned to his mother. 'It doesn't sound like the Katarina I know. She's a fierce little thing.'

Though Ursula's words were kind and full of reassurance, Katarina could not help feeling belittled by them. Or was she just looking to find fault because of Chiara's gossip?

She forced a carefree smile. 'I have no such concerns and look forward to meeting your friends this evening.' She knew this woman was quite aware of her age, despite her more youthful appearance. So why did she say it?

The *gräfin* smiled warmly, grasping Katarina's hands again. 'Good. I want you to enjoy it.' She moved in closer to speak softly. 'I hope you will look on me as your mother, too. You've never had one, I know. And I've never had a daughter.'

'So, what did you make of her?' Chiara asked again.

Katarina had so far avoided answering by changing the subject but now as she stood in front of the cheval mirror ready to go down to dinner, she could think of nothing further to distract her maid. 'She seemed very considerate ... and friendly.'

Chiara snorted. 'Considerate? *What*? Springing a bleedin' banquet on you the minute she gets back?'

'I don't think it's a proper banquet—'

'Not a proper banquet? Have you seen the table? It's a proper bleedin' banquet, all right.'

Katarina studied her reflection. The indigo satin gown emphasised her pale skin (a touch too pale, in truth). Chiara had dressed her hair to hang loose down her back with side sections elaborately pinned up with jewelled brights. When she touched the froth of lace edging the neckline, the newly re-set emerald and diamond ring still appeared too heavy for her small hand.

Chiara watched her scrutinize it. 'It don't suit, do it?' She made a hissing sound through her teeth. 'But you looks lovely, Madonna. You truly does.'

When she chewed her lip, it was obvious to Katarina that she was holding something back. 'What? Tell me. I know there's something.'

'Might I give you some advice, Madonna?'

Katarina nodded.

'If he don't come to you tonight, go to him—'

'Chiara! It's not your place to say such a thing.' What was it with maidservants ... and former maidservants? And he had already told her they must wait.

'Don't you get it? She'll try and part you, sure as eggs is

eggs. They've picked his wife and it ain't you. If he's had you, they can't.'

'If they tempt him away from me, how would that change anything for him? I wouldn't be his first, you know that.'

'You're his betrothed. You were pressed into his bed because of it. So scandal. That's what. Bleedin scandal. They don't like that, them sort.'

Katarina shook her head. 'Johannes chose me for himself. He will marry me despite his mother. And as far as I can see, she seems content enough with it, anyway.'

'Ha. That's what you think. Mark my words, she's about as far from content as is possible to be.'

Just then a tap on the door ended the conversation. Johannes was ready to take her down to dinner.

And it was a formal banquet. Of course it was. The polished mahogany table, long enough to hold fifty guests, was resplendent with a glittering array of crystal glasses and silverware, and at its centre down most of its length, several mirror-lined *surtout de table* trays holding elaborate floral arrangements, bright under candlelight from many tall candelabra placed amongst them.

The *gräfin* had led her guests into the dining room on Johannes's arm, with Katarina following on the arm of *Graf* von Lambsdorff, bald and corpulent with meaty, moist lips over a cascade of chins, he had not deigned to utter a word to her as they made their way down the drafty gallery from the cavernous salon where fruit punch had been served. He was an old friend and her closest neighbour Ursula had said when pairing them.

Ursula and Johannes took the head and foot of the table while Katarina was seated halfway down between the *graf* and another elderly gentleman. As the table began to fill, Katarina noticed that Johannes was now flanked by two extremely attractive young ladies, one especially so with hair the colour of buttermilk and a gown cut low to display her ample figure. She was already leaning close to Johannes who seemed engrossed in conversation with her. The other woman, dark haired and thinner, watched them intently. Were these two of those chosen by his mother and Ida as suitable wives? The fair women's bray of laughter with head thrown back was loud enough to reach Katarina where she sat, and she watched with amusement as the dark-haired companion took the opportunity to draw Johannes's attention to her.

It was then that she spotted two bejewelled women seated close to each of the young ladies who were as engrossed with their activities as she was. It was easy to see which mother was which, one fair and pillowy, the other – with grey threading her dark hair – erect and rather hatchet faced. Was not a man meant to see his wife's future appearance by looking at her mother? Johannes had seen her mother's portrait, but she had been so young then, and like all who viewed it, he had commented on the remarkable likeness between them.

She gazed along the length of the table at those seated opposite. Men of all ages, most in dress uniform as Johannes was, others in fine velvet and satin their stocks dazingly white. Women with tiaras and jewelled collars, and diamond pendants, old and young. The rustle of silks and satins as they turned from one conversation to another. The trill of their voices.

Graf von Lambsdorff, who had been talking to the toothy lady seated to his right turned and spotted the silver-haired fellow beside Katarina. 'Otto! How good to see you. I didn't know you were returned from the city.' The words were accompanied by a fine spray of spittle from those thick, purple lips.

Katarina leant back to move out of range, as the two men held forth without either showing the slightest sign of having heard the other or halting their own inconsequential torrent in order to try. Arrays of dishes were brought to the table for *le service à la française* and set out before the diners so they could serve themselves and others as they wished, servants making sure there were interesting selections near each guest. Soups. Stews. Vegetables. Boiled fish and meats. Peacock pies. Gumballs and cheese wigs (yes, they really were wigs made from cheese displayed on wooden heads). Sweetmeats and sugar sculptures. Iced creams and Jellies. Sponge-cakes made to look like boar's heads or dolphins spouting water and many other such fancies. All very different from the lighter Italian fayre she was used to.

When Katarina managed to serve herself a small portion from one dish or another, she then found it difficult to keep her plate away from the constant mist of saliva discharged during the *graf's* monologue and consequently ate very little. Glass after glass of wine, too, was poured to accompany the feast with glasses removed for washing at the sideboard fountain and cistern.

White for the fish. Red for the meats. Sweet and sticky with desserts. As her goblets were well outside the *graf's* range, she drank each one readily and gradually the whole experience did not seem quite so abhorrent. Even Johannes's obvious enjoyment of his two lovely companions seemed amusing rather than hurtful. When she saw the *gräfin's* eyes move from this trio to her sandwiched between the two old men, she had to fight the desire to laugh. Instead, she turned away and drained another glass.

Then, at last, the ladies withdrew leaving the gentlemen to their brandy and tobacco, and Ursula took Katarina's arm in hers sweeping her away to the salon where card tables awaited the men's return and a pianoforte had been brought out for the ladies to provide entertainment. For the moment though they

THE VIOLIN MAKER'S WIFE

were all seated, taking their dishes of coffee or saucers of champagne, as close to the fire as was possible, though it burnt in a grate rather lost in the enormity of the fireplace.

Ursula sat beside Katarina on an unyielding sofa. 'Forgive me, my dear.' She moved closer to speak into Katarina's ear. 'I cannot imagine what Ida was thinking when she placed you between Karl and Otto. You appeared not to be having a happy time.'

With the alcohol still fizzing in her blood, she spoke without thought. 'Well, Johannes seemed placed to have a delightful time, did he not?'

The *gräfin* tilted her head. 'It did appear so. I shall need to have words with Ida.'

Was this woman sincere or was Chiara right and Ida had simply acted on her instructions? Katarina shrugged, finding she did not much care. 'She did what she thought best, I'm sure.'

Ursula patted her hand. 'That's a good attitude to have, my dear. Now, if you'll excuse me, I must mingle.'

Katarina sat alone on the sofa holding her empty champagne glass and staring into the flames for a time before turning to survey the room. She became aware then of the scrutiny she was under, especially from the two mothers and daughters, seeing their heads together as they whispered, certain they were questioning how Johannes could possibly have chosen her over them. They would know immediately by her lack of jewellery and her gown – fine for Cremona but not in the Viennese style, of course – that it was certainly not for her fortune. Why then this nondescript slip of a girl? That no one spoke to her left her unsurprised.

All heads turned at the sound of male voices and guffaws approaching. Hair was patted, creases smoothed from skirts. Bodices lifted ... or lowered to reveal more flesh. The doors burst open allowing the tide of men to sweep in on a cloud of tobacco smoke. Some came to fetch partners for the card tables others to sit beside wives and take coffee. Many of the younger men resplendent in their gold-lace embellished uniforms gathered around the pianoforte where young ladies were already assembling clutching their sheet music. Meanwhile at the card tables, laughter and groans could be heard as couples began to win and lose. Katarina had no idea what card games were played, there seemed no sign that gambling was involved, as always seemed to be the case with the officers back home.

Katarina jumped when Johannes sat beside her, turning to him with a small gasp. He took her hand, bringing it to his lips. 'You're looking forlorn, Katarina. Mother told me you had an unfortunate place at table.'

So, he had been too engrossed to even seek her out, with eyes only for his two former flames. 'The *graf* spat over my food so it wasn't the best experience, no.'

He frowned. 'Why would—'

'He spits when he talks, and he talks a lot.'

'Well, at least he spoke to you.'

She snorted. 'Hardly. He only conversed with the man beside me. They leaned forward to speak across me.' Johannes turned away as the first notes sounded on the pianoforte. The young lady playing was hatchet face's daughter. 'Who is she?'

'Druella von Klomp.'

He said nothing more as her slight, high voice joined in with her rather plodding piano rendition of a piece Katarina did not recognise. She watched the girl's mother smile with pride and moved to whisper in Johannes's ear. 'Who was the other one?' He frowned. 'The fair one sitting with you at dinner.'

'Gesine Schneider. She'll play a little later, I'm sure. She is rather more accomplished than Druella, though I would never tell her so, of course,' he murmured.

Katarina handed him her empty glass and moved closer again to speak in his ear. 'As my wine was unsullied by the *graf*, I am now in some need of the close stool.' She stood and hurried from the room. And she would fetch her violin. Why not? If these people wished entertainment, she was more than capable of offering something of a rather higher standard than they were getting now.

After tripping on the stairs, catching her heel in her gown and hearing it tear, she quickly checked behind her, grateful no one had witnessed her down upon her knees clinging to the stone banisters before struggling back onto her feet.

In her room, she made use of the chamber pot before locating her violin in the cabinet where Chiara had placed it. When she lifted it from its case, a small voice of caution whispered, *is this entirely wise?* She had drunk far more wine than she was used to. So was wishing these people to see her ... to notice her existence when the few that had, had found her inexplicable, truly wise? She lifted her chin. 'Why not, though?' she said aloud before making her way back downstairs, this time without mishap. *Why not show them exactly who I am?*

Returned to the salon with her violin at her side concealed within the folds of her skirts, she found Gesine Schneider now seated at the keyboard. Her voice and her playing were, indeed, superior to her rival's but still showed little talent in Katarina's opinion, however, at least this time she recognised the music. She wove her way through the guests standing around the piano until she found a space large enough to allow her room to play.

And taking a deep breath, her heart hammering, Katarina lifted her violin, placing her chin upon the guard, and began to play joining in with the pianoforte. She was immediately aware that her instrument was slightly out of tune and that there was insufficient rosin on her bow, meaning that in some positions on the strings, no sound was made. How in God's name had she failed to perform a preparation ritual that was so ingrained in her that it needed no thought to undertake it every time before she played? Jesu, was she drunk ...?

Yet, inexplicably, she could not seem to stop playing. Despite the discord. Despite the missing notes. Even when Gesine halted with an angry crash of notes and turned to her in fury, she could not stop. Instead, she launched into the piece she had composed herself that had so delighted guests at the Santa Cecilia celebrations and at *Palazzo Poli*, her mind blotting out the flaws as she swayed precariously to the sound she remembered. Even the angry cries to 'stop at once' failed to reach her.

Johannes's arms closed around her, forcing her to lower her instrument and it was then she became aware of the red, angry faces and mocking grins of those surrounding her. She pulled away from him and fled the room, afraid now she was about to vomit.

As Johannes made to go after her, his mother moved in front of him, blocking his path. 'A word,' she hissed.

He followed her outside into the long gallery, grateful that Gesine had begun to play again and had drawn most eyes back to her. He must remember to thank her for it. How had this happened? Yet he knew it was his fault. He should have taken more care of Katarina, made sure she was suitably seated, at least with men who would show her some decent consideration.

'This must never happen again. Do you understand, Johannes? Never. The girl made an exhibition of herself in front of my guests—'

'I've heard her play that piece beautifully. Magically. She composed it herself. She—'

'Playing an instrument like that, displaying herself like that, will never be appropriate for your wife even when she's not inebriated with a torn gown and half her hair come loose, regardless of the amount of skill she might demonstrate.'

'I'm not talking of more skill. She's an exceptional player, Mother. I have never heard her like before.'

'If you say so, though she showed little sign of it this

evening. But, I say again, it is not suitable for a wife in Viennese society. Does she not play the pianoforte or perhaps the harpsichord – they must be a touch backward in Italy, I imagine – and surely she can sing if only a little, can she not?'

Johannes, of course, had no idea. Why would she do either when her talent lay elsewhere?

His mother stared at him. 'Well, I shall see what can be done with her. I only wish to help, you understand that, don't you?' She frowned. 'She cannot be entirely without musical talent.'

'*What?*' he replied as she turned and walked quickly away. There were others out in the gallery now, so he stifled his desire to call after her. To force her to listen to him. 'Without musical talent?' he muttered. 'What is the woman talking about?' He had intended to question her about how Katarina had come to be seated between two deaf old men in the first place, but she had not allowed him the time to do so. Something that seemed to be happening more and more now he came to think of it. Well, she need not imagine this was the end of it. He would make sure his mother was fully aware of his wishes regarding Katarina's treatment before he returned to his regiment. After all, it had been she who had requested that Katarina join them so she could have time to get to know her before their wedding in June. Yes, he would definitely speak to her.

In her chamber, Katarina made it to the bowl on the washstand just as the door flew open and Chiara rushed in to help her, holding her hair back as she vomited. When had it come down?

'Don't you worry yourself, Madonna. You've had too much wine, is all. We've all of us done it. You just need to sleep it off now.' Averting her nose, she moved the ill-used washbasin onto the floor and covered it with a towel.

Katarina shook her head, miserably. 'Well, *I've* not done it.'

Chiara appeared dubious. 'You've never been pissed enough to puke before? Really?'

'Yes, really. I've never even been drunk.' She moved away to sit on the bed holding her head in her hands. 'And I don't much care for it, so I shall certainly never do it again.'

'I've heard that one before,' the maid murmured just loud enough for Katarina to heed her before pouring a cup of water from the ewer and handed it to her. 'Drink up.'

After gulping it down and accepting another, her eyes widened. Oh, Chiara, I think I behaved quite shockingly … and made a laughingstock of myself.' While the maid helped her into her nightgown, Katarina told her all she could remember of what had occurred (some of it still quite hazy) as tears rolled down her face. She swiped them away, angrily. 'I just don't understand what got into me—'

'Drink is what got into you, Madonna. Wine somehow dulls you while at the same time tricks you into foolishness. A full belly helps, but I get you'd not eat what'd been doused in gob.' She shook her head. 'She's chose that place for you. And gawd, didn't it pay off for her. She'll have already been in his ear, of that you can be sure.'

But Ursula had apologised and blamed Ida for it. Could it be true that she had been behind it? Katarina climbed onto the featherbed and allowed Chiara to cover her with quilts.

'You'll feel better in the morning, Madonna. Take it from one who knows.' She laughed then. 'And better still the day after.'

Katarina did not hear the door between the two rooms open but woke when he moved close to her under the quilts, pulling her into his arms. 'I'm so sorry this happened to you, dear one. Sleep now. I'm here.'

In the morning she woke to a dry mouth and a raging headache (how was this better?) and an empty bed. Had she dreamt Johannes's presence? She prayed not, for it had brought her such comfort to feel his arms around her, but when it was not mentioned the next day, she understood it had been a dream.

It was a long time before she learnt the truth of it, for neither had raised it with the other for fear of a misunderstanding.

Eleven

~~∞~~

SCHLOSS VON CLOY, VIENNA. MAY 1722

THAT THEODORE FISCHER MADE LIGHT OF HER blunders time and time again still astonished Katarina, and she smiled her thanks as always, which he returned with his usual wide grin. With his mop of sandy hair constantly falling across his forehead into his eyes, he was tall and broad-shouldered sporting the wide back of a countryman. And he did indeed come from good farming stock. Katarina smiled still, watching him rake his hair back with his big fingers. He truly was the most amiable of souls. Always cheerful. Always full of under-served praise for her sad efforts on the pianoforte.

'Let's take the air for a while. The sun shines outside and this room is gloomy. The warmth will cheer us.'

Katarina thought he needed little cheering. She sighed and stood. 'I'm sorry, Theo. I really am doing my best.' It didn't help that she never knew when Ida lurked outside the morning room door listening to her painful progress ... or lack of it. She had learnt of this 'lurking' from Chiara.

Theo opened the tall casement window which gave access to the gardens via a short flight of steps, without the need to pass through the rear lobby and risk a possible encounter with Ida. 'Come, Katarina.'

She took his hand, feeling the strength of those fingers that danced so incongruously across the pianoforte's keyboard. After climbing out and down the stone steps, the scent of lilacs growing around it lifting her spirits, she followed him across a gravel path into a small beech copse where dappled sunlight filtered through leaves of the tenderest green onto the bluebell carpeted ground. Beyond this was an open meadow, yellow with buttercups, far enough away from the formal gardens that they could walk there undiscovered.

'How's Hanna?' Their first child was due any day and Katarina had questioned whether he should still come to the *schloss* for her lessons. She had embarrassed him by raising it she quickly realised, for he was in dire need of the money. When she broached it with the *gräfin*, she had made it clear he was to be paid strictly by the hour.

'She's well. Eager to have the child with us, of course.'

This was not the first time they had exchanged these words.

'I'm sure. Do pass on my good wishes.'

Katarina now understood why she had been brought to the *schloss* so long before her wedding. Ursula was moulding her to become the wife that both she and Viennese society would expect her to be. She now appreciated the scale of the place and its surrounding estate and farms, how it was run, and who was responsible for it, Ursula stressing that it would be her duty to oversee all these arrangements when Johannes became *markgraf*.

More banquets were held, and Katarina was always seated between kindly men more than ready to converse with her but found they had little common ground. The delights of Cremona and the River Po and its hinterland were of little interest against the wealth of these people's shared history and interests. And she could not talk of the violin, of course. Ursula had been firm about that, hoping her behaviour at that first dinner would be forgotten. She tried her best, but conversation often faltered. But at least she could eat in peace even though the somewhat stodgy Austrian food was not really to her Italian taste. Thankfully she was never called upon to entertain at the pianoforte but had a talent for cards that found her never short of partners.

Father Martin's instruction in Catholicism readying her for her marriage went well, though embroidery and the pianoforte were not flourishing. And everyone had agreed there was little to be gained by continuing with singing lessons. How could she not yearn still to feel wood beneath her fingers and work a thumb plane instead of a needle and embroidery silks, when she always seemed to leave blood behind on the cloth from a pricked finger?

Contemplating Chiara's continued insistence that the *gräfin* was not to be trusted, Katarina found it harder and harder to credit. Why would she have given up so much of her time, if she wished to part Katarina from her son? And she could not deny that she was woefully ignorant about the ways of polite society, or at least how it operated in Vienna. No, Ursula had shown her nothing but kindness and she was starting to believe that she really could become a mother to her as she told her often that she wished to be.

The following week, the moment Katarina stepped into the morning room and saw Theo standing beside the pianoforte, she knew his child had been born. 'Boy or Girl? she asked moving to him and taking his hands in hers, looking up and searching his face. 'Are they both well?'

'We have a daughter. Gisela for my mother. And they both thrive.'

'I'm so glad.' She pulled him close and hugged him. 'Go home. Back to them.' She gestured to the window. 'Escape through there. No one need know.'

He laughed. 'I can't do that, but neither do I wish to make you miserable with another hour of torture—'

She chuckled. 'Please don't worry about me.'

'Katarina, I see what music means to you.' He placed his big hand on his chest. 'How it affects your heart. Your passion for it, and your frustration with the pianoforte because it doesn't work for you. It is not fluid enough for you.' He tapped his bottom lip with his index finger. 'So, I wonder ... might you play your violin for me. I've never heard you play, and I'd love to accompany you.'

Katarina was about to refuse but hesitated, knowing the *gräfin* was with her sister who was unwell yet again, which meant Ida would be busy in her absence with no time to eavesdrop, surely? 'Why not.' She had been forbidden from playing in front of guests, but not her teacher. 'Wait here, I won't be long.'

She walked along corridors and through halls, climbing stairs and passing servants who offered perfunctory bows and curtsies, moving purposefully but not noticeably in a hurry. She believed she had not drawn any unwelcome attention. Not all servants could be trusted. In truth, few were allies. Inside her chamber, she draped her violin case with a shawl, finding it hard to believe that she would feel the need to conceal it in such a way, and returned to the morning room.

She had not played since that dreadful evening and tears threatened as she lifted it from its case. This time though, she applied rosin to the bow and tuned the instrument for some moments until she was satisfied. 'Do you know Monteverdi's *Maledetto sia l'aspetto*?'

Theo was now seated at the pianoforte. 'I know it a little. Don't worry, I can follow you.'

It took her a short while to find herself in the music, to abandon herself to the sensation of it moving through her so she might lose herself in it, finally. Then she no longer noticed Theo's skilled accompaniment or that after a time, he left her to play alone. When she reached the end, she lowered her instrument to her side and took a long breath before looking at him.

He shook his head slowly. 'I don't know what to say, Katarina. Why are you taking lessons from me when you have such an amazing talent? I truly don't understand why the *gräfin* insists upon it.'

She chewed her lip. 'Playing the violin in public is not a suitable activity for a wife. I think it's seen as putting on too much of a display—'

Theo snorted. 'The only display is of your talent. You bring your instrument to life. You make it speak, Katarina.'

It did occur to her then that when Gesine and the others sat at the pianoforte there was a quite blatant, though rather different form of display going on with breasts rising from bodices as they bent over the keyboard. Katarina sighed. 'I trust her to know what's best for me.' *Never mind what Chiara thinks.*

He gestured at the piano. 'Forcing these lessons on you is not especially kind though, is it? Perhaps you should be careful not to lose who you really are for *she* was whom the *hauptmann* chose to be his wife, was she not? The one who plays the violin.'

When they had said their farewells, Katarina was relieved to return her instrument to its cabinet in her bedchamber with no one any the wiser that it had ever left, unaware then, of course, that she would not see her teacher again.

Katarina never did discover just how the *gräfin* came to learn of her brief collaboration with Theo Fischer that fateful afternoon (were servants really so malign they would report hearing her play?), but when on the day after her return from the city she summoned Katarina to her private parlour, her heart fell, certain what it would be about.

Ursula sat at her little, gilded desk that looked incongruously delicate in a room full of the heavy, dark furniture so prominent in the rest of the *schloss*. 'What were you thinking, Katarina? Theodore Fischer was engaged to teach you the pianoforte not to accompany you on an instrument we have agreed is unsuitable.' She looked intently at Katarina, making no attempt to conceal her disappointment. 'Needless to say, I had to dismiss him. He—'

'No! He's not to blame. It was entirely my fault.'

Ursula clenched her jaw, looking her age and more in harsh light shining directly upon her from the large window affording views over the formal gardens. 'That's as maybe but he could have refused you. Had he done so, he would still have a position here.'

Remorse surged through her. *What have I done?* 'Please, Ursula. They've just had a child. They need the money he earns here. Please don't make him … his family suffer because of my thoughtless actions.'

The *gräfin* held her gaze. 'I have found another teacher for you who will be more suitable, I think. I'll make sure he understands how important this is for you, Katarina. You must trust I have your best interests at heart, my dear.' Something she had said many times before. She looked down at her papers again. 'You will attend him at the usual time.'

Tears pricked and she fought to control herself. 'I feel it will be a waste of time. The pianoforte is *not* the right instrument for me. I'm certain of that now.'

Ursula ignored her. 'You should know Ida has taken charge of your violin for the moment so you will not be tempted again. She thought it a kindness, and I can't say I disagree with her.'

Katarina took a step towards the desk. 'She's done what? How dare she!' Her nostrils flared, sudden rage flashing like lightening before her eyes. 'She has no right to touch my violin. It's my personal property, and what does she mean so I won't be tempted again. What, tempted to play it?' She clenched her fists. 'You will instruct her to return it at once, do you hear me!'

Ursula was on her feet then, pulling Katarina into her arms. 'No, child. No. She means you no harm with this.' She moved away searching Katarina's face now awash with tears. 'I'm only trying to help you. You know this.' She led Katarina to a sofa and sat beside her there, holding her hands. 'I know things were different for you in Cremona but here you will be my son's wife and in time a *markgräfin*. Friendship with maidservants and artisans will no longer be appropriate, you must understand that. Though I'm surprised your father ever thought they were, but that's neither here nor there.' She squeezed Katarina's hands. 'And you must not have further doubts about your commitment to God. Faith is at the heart of this family. Though Father Martin says you have done well and have certainly not expressed any such uncertainties to him, so perhaps your earlier ones were but a temporary deviation.'

How does she know these things? Jesu, Johannes must have told her. Katerina pulled away. 'Johannes chose me for his wife in Cremona. Why must I become a different person now?' Yet all Ursula had said was correct, she could not have such friends here. And Johannes had told the *gräfin* everything he knew about her ... all her confidences. It seemed it was he who did not deserve her trust not his mother.

That evening, after declining to join Ursula and her guests for dinner, pleading a headache, Katarina wrote a letter. Chiara would see it was sent with the next courier. She had taken some time deciding who should be the recipient and had eventually settled on Gianni Gabrieli for she had kept his secrets and would now ask the same of him.

She hesitated before dipping her pen, trying to decide just what to tell him. In the end, after explaining why she asked for his discretion – she had no wish for Giuseppe to know any of it – she outlined what had occurred with her violin, explaining it in the context of *Gräfin* von Cloy's desire to prepare for her role as Johannes's wife.

Finally, she asked him to come as a wedding guest and retrieve her instrument, which a loyal servant would locate, and then hold it for her for the time being. She hoped that after her marriage, she might start to have more agency within the household, so have more power to keep it safe. She closed by telling him she could not ask this of her father as he would not go against the *gräfin's* wishes.

She put down her pen and handed the letter to Chiara to read.

The maid scanned it quickly and raised her eyes to Katarina's. 'You should've told him more of what the evil witch has been doing to you—'

'She has done nothing other than try to help me. It's Ida behind this, I'm quite certain. Now, are you confident you'll be able to find it?'

'Pah, of course I shall. Don't you worry about that. Are you sure this man will come, though? It's a long way for a favour.'

'He'll come.' But would he? Chiara was right, it really was a lot to ask of a friend. But she had to trust he would, for it was her greatest fear that Ida might decide to destroy her violin. She was now entirely convinced that this woman was set against her. But why, though? Why?

Twelve

SCHLOSS VON CLOY, VIENNA. JUNE 1722

WEEKS HAD PASSED AND KATARINA'S WEDDING DAY drew ever closer, yet Johannes had still not returned from his regiment.

The new piano teacher proved to be as irascible and unpleasant as Theo had been sweet-natured and kind. His remedy for Katarina's reluctance had been to start again as though with a musical novice, making her play scales throughout the hour the lesson lasted. And then he set her a rudimentary sightreading task to be completed for their next session. Katarina was so dumbfounded she simply took the sheet from him without a word. After he left, she ripped it into several pieces and left it on top of the piano. She had composed her own pieces and could barely remember a time when she could not read music.

The next day, another summons to attend her future mother-in-law arrived while Katarina took her breakfast in the small parlour adjacent to her bedchamber.

Ida herself arrived with the message. 'The *gräfin* expected to see you at breakfast.'

Katarina blinked. 'I prefer to eat here.'

'She wishes to see you in her bedchamber.'

'Her bedchamber? How odd. Why does she wish me to come there?'

'You'll have to ask her, won't you?'

Katarina stood and rang the bell to summon Chiara. She gestured to her robe. 'Tell her I'm dressing. I shall be there directly.'

'Go as you are. She said to send you immediately.'

Katarina frowned. 'Very well.' She turned to Chiara. 'Wait in my chamber. It seems I am to go in my night attire.'

She followed Ida along the gallery to the far end of the wing where double doors led into the *gräfin's* suite of rooms. The door to her bedchamber was opposite across a square hall. Ida knocked before opening it to admit Katarina but did not follow her inside.

'Ah, there you are, my dear.'

Katarina did not answer, for she was taken aback and not a little alarmed to find there was a man in there with her. 'What is this? Has something happened?'

'No, nothing like that. Don't be concerned. 'This is Dr Müller.'

'Are you unwell, *Gräfin*?'

'No. As I said, there's no need for concern. Dr Müller is here to see you.'

Katarina moved her gaze to the trim grey bearded man. Though he smiled, she sensed he was not entirely comfortable. 'Me? I don't understand.'

Ursula nodded briskly to the doctor. 'I shall leave you to explain, Friedrich.'

When the door closed behind her, the doctor gestured to a chair. 'Please sit. May I call you Katarina?'

She sat, nodding. 'I think you'd better tell me what this is about.'

When he pulled up a chair beside her, she again sensed his

unease. He took a breath. 'You must not think there is anything unusual about this, or that it is in anyway personal. It is quite a common request from aristocratic families and from their point of view it is entirely understandable. They—'

'What is understandable?' Her heart fluttered with unease.

He sighed. The *gräfin* has asked that I examine you to ensure you are capable of bearing a child.' He looked down at his hands with their manicured nails. 'And that you are intact.'

Katarina's eyes widened and heat burnt upon her cheeks. '*What?*' Her heart began to pound unpleasantly. She was being treated like a broodmare ... no, far worse than that.

The doctor held her gaze. 'It is an intimate examination, of course, but should not be painful and it will be over very quickly.'

'Can I refuse,' she asked in a voice little more than a whisper.

He smiled ruefully. 'You can but I sense the *gräfin* is determined.'

Katarina took a long breath. *And there are other doctors.* She thought of her new piano teacher. 'What must I do?'

'Now, Katarina. Are your courses regular ...

Dr Müller was gentle and kind as he palpated and probed her body, whilst she lay back against soft pillows, staring up at a ceiling busy with centaurs, fauns, and unicorns in mythical land-scapes. What a ludicrous thing it was.

Did Johannes know she would be subjected to this indignity? This violation? Is that why he had stayed away from her bed? Or did he think she and Giuseppe had been lovers? Once again, it would be many years before she learnt the truth.

The doctor moved away. 'You did very well.'

'I had little choice.' She stood and shook out her nightgown, pulling her robe more tightly around her. 'Well, what will you report?'

He reached out to squeeze her shoulder. 'Exactly what I

expected. That you are a healthy young woman with no indication that you will be unable to bear children ... and, of course, that you will come untouched to the marriage bed.'

Other than by you.

With Chiara's help, Katarina dressed allowing her outrage free rein, lamenting aloud why she was at Schloss von Cloy at all. It had seemed the way of things and even desirable when she had set out two months before. Johannes wished to marry her, and her father had offered a generous – well, by their standards, anyway – dowery to facilitate it, but had she ever asked herself what she truly wanted?

She did not love Johannes, though she liked him well enough, or had until she knew how cavalier he was with her confidences. Had he even been complicit in that humiliating examination? It seemed naïve now to have been so flattered that he chose her, to even hope to find love with him when she clearly did not know him at all.

When days passed and Ursula still said nothing about the doctor's visit, Katarina's hopes faded that she would at least voice some sympathy for the ordeal of it. Perhaps she was simply embarrassed by its necessity? That at least made some sort of sense, and she felt a touch relieved, though could not help wondering what would have happened had she not been sound. Would she have been sent away, or would Johannes have been fetched home to confront her shame?

Then, all too soon, it was time for her piano lesson once again. In that gloomy morning room, she found *Herr* Meyer incandescent, having discovered the fate of his practice assignment.

'Perhaps you'd care to explain yourself. How dare you tear up the work I left for you?'

Surely Ursula would not think such impertinence acceptable? This had to be the tutor's interpretation of her instructions. Then she understood. It was a test. She must show herself ready to assert her position. *'Meine Dame* when you address me.'

'Meine Dame,' he muttered reluctantly. 'Well?'

'I need no practice in reading music.'

'That is not the point.'

She glared at him, eyebrows raised. Waiting.

'Meine Dame.' He cleared his throat. 'The *gräfin* wished for you to start again and that includes learning how to read music by sight.'

'Don't be absurd. How can you teach me what I already know?' She watched him draw himself up to his full height, which was by no means impressive. 'I've composed my own pieces. Have you?'

His face turned an unbecoming shade of puce. 'This is not about my accomplishments.' He tutted. *'Meine Dame.* It is about yours.' He took a long breath and gestured to the pianoforte. 'Your music is set out for you.'

She sat on the stool reluctantly. 'Hardly music, Herr Meyer.' She began to play as ploddingly as she could, hating it and hating him. When the door burst open, she cried out so startled was she, before leaping to her feet to stand gaping at the sight of Johannes.

'What in the name of God is going on in here?' He gestured at the sheet music. 'Why are you playing this?'

Herr Meyer's hands were already firmly upon his wide hips in blatant outrage. 'And who, pray, are you?' he asked, looking Johannes up and down, taking in his mud-stained uniform and jackboots.

Johannes ignored the question, waving his hand dismissively. 'Whoever *you* are, you may leave us.'

Katarina continued to stare, trying to hold back her rising pleasure at the sight of him. 'Herr Meyer is my piano teacher.'

'Johannes snorted. 'Well, he seems of little use to you if he thinks this is necessary.' He took a step towards the much smaller man. 'You're dismissed. See the steward for any remuneration outstanding.'

'I will do no such thing. The *gräfin* appointed me herself. And I say again, who are you?'

'I'm *Hauptmann* Johannes Horak and Gräfin von Cloy is my mother. Now do as I say. Leave us.'

'The gräfin shall hear of this,' he flung back over his shoulder before closing the door behind him.

Johannes gazed around the room. 'Why are you in this miserable little closet? What's been going on, Katarina?'

'Your mother has been helping me.' If she told him all that had occurred, might she sound ungrateful or even critical of the *gräfin's* actions? Or would he think she had not co-operated with sufficiently good grace? She tried to summon the disillusion she had started to feel about him but against her will, it was quickly subsumed in the joy of seeing him.

'Helping you? Has she now. Well, let's at least get out of here and find somewhere more cheerful.' With her hand held firmly in his, he led her from the room. 'I need to bathe. Come up to my bedchamber, we can talk there.'

Katarina sat on a sofa in front of a window open to air scented with summer in a room filled with sunshine, while Johannes flung off his sweat-stained, mud-spattered uniform coat and sat to remove his boots and stockings on a bed even grander than she had imagined from her glimpse through the connecting door, with its indigo and gold swags and canopies, and carved and gilded four-poster bedstead. He had just tossed his shirt onto the pile of soiled clothing at his feet, revealing the pearl-white skin of his broad chest when the door opened and his valet, Gustav, led in a small troop of footmen carrying a copper bathtub and canisters of steaming water. The tub was lined with towels before it was filled, and a Japanese lacquered screen placed around it so Johannes might strip off his breeches and make his ablutions without offending his betrothed sensibilities.

'That'll be all, Gustav. Leave us now.'

The valet nodded a bow to Katarina before closing the door behind him.

'Move that wretched thing so I can see you. Don't worry, I'm decent enough.'

Katarina moved the screen as he asked and stood looking down at him. His thick fair hair was long enough now to fall across his face, and he pushed back so their eyes met. He was much in need of a shave she noticed, the sun glittering on his stubble. How relaxed he seemed under her gaze. 'Would you like me to wash your hair?

He smiled, a fan of lines around his eyes revealed in the glare. 'Now, that *would* be a treat.'

She knelt behind him suddenly full of tenderness for him. She touched his back tentatively, shuddering slightly at the ragged, purple stripes that marred his left shoulder blade, lumpy beneath her fingertips. 'How?'

'Just glancing sabre blows. The gifts of battle.'

She filled a copper jug from the tub. 'Close your eyes.' When she was done, she handed him a towel to dry his face and he sighed contentedly.

He reached out for her hand then and brought it to his lips. 'Perhaps you can replace the screen so I may—' He chuckled half-heartedly. 'Probably best to maintain decorum for a few more days, no?'

Katarina replaced the screen without replying, wondering again about his motives.

Johannes emerged with a towel around his waist. 'I'll ring for shaving water.'

She did not look at him. 'I'll be in your parlour.'

She seated herself to wait on a sofa again placed before a

window with an aspect almost identical to that in the bedchamber. That they would be married in a few days felt unreal. Once again something that had seemed an unimaginable time in the future no longer was. She forced a smile when he breezed in dressed in an indigo satin coat that suited his fair colouring, freshly shaved with his hair trimmed back to the shorter length favoured in Vienna.

He sat beside her, grasping her hand and giving it a squeeze. 'Forgive me for keeping you waiting.'

She shrugged slightly. There seemed nothing to say.

'Now tell me all you've been up to. Mother has proved helpful to you, I trust.'

She was unsure whether he had spoken with her before coming to her in the morning room. 'Indeed.'

He raised his eyebrows. 'I should like to hear about it, Katarina.'

'I don't want to bore you if you have already talked with her.'

'I haven't seen her yet. I came to find you first.'

Well, that was something she supposed. She would be as succinct as possible. 'I can't tell you how grateful I am to her for all the time she's devoted to me.'

'I'm pleased to hear it.'

'I've learned all about the estate and its domestic arrangements and have been tutored in various pursuits suitable for a wife.' She listed them all briefly. The piano you know about but singing soon fell by the wayside.' She smiled ruefully. 'Everyone agreed there was little point as my voice would never be one that should be inflicted on others.'

He frowned, clearly puzzled. 'But your violin sings for you.'

She felt quick tears prick her eyes and turned away. 'You know what happened … why I can no longer play.'

He frowned. 'Perhaps not at the larger gatherings, but at more intimate ones in front of those with decent musical taste, where your talent will be marvelled at, surely?'

'I think it would not be approved of ... and I no longer have my instrument—'

'*What?* Where is it? What's happened?'

'I believe Ida has it.' She told him of Theo and his desire to share his happiness that day.

He shook his head in obvious disbelief while she spoke. 'None of this makes any sense to me. What was Mother thinking allowing this?'

What would he say if she told him of the doctor's examination? She realised then that she had no wish to find out. 'She meant well. She wants me to be accepted as you wife, that's all.' But did she? Not according to Chiara.

He snorted. 'You'll be accepted as my wife when that is what you are. Learning about the estate is helpful but the rest of it?' He shrugged. 'You don't need to change who you are. It's why I love you.'

If she pointed out that he had never told her that he loved her before, she understood she would be expected to say she loved him in return, and it would not be true. When she said nothing, she was relieved he appeared not to notice.

Katarina's bedchamber overflowed with maidservants, all supervised by Chiara, helping her dress in her elaborate wedding gown of peach satin – with its ostentatious quantities of lace and flounces – pinning up her hair and twittering excitedly. Katarina's mind, however, was elsewhere. 'What will I say to Gianni?'

Chiara tutted. 'He won't come, Madonna. No one's that *matto*. You'll see.' She grinned, cheekily. 'Unless he's more than a friend, of course.'

'Don't be impertinent,' Katarina replied, though returning the grin. *Unlikely, if you did but know.* Everything had changed now with her violin. Johannes had demanded it be returned to

THE VIOLIN MAKER'S WIFE

her at once, and that Ida apologise for removing it. Chiara still insisted that Ida had been carrying out the *gräfin's* instructions. Katarina sighed remembering. Nothing would divert her from that certainty. 'Well, if he does come, what can I say to him?' Her father had arrived the evening before bringing news from Cremona, though not about the luthiers' isle. Anja's letter had done that, thank goodness. Her child was thriving, Carlo was busy with orders and the Guarneris were well and prospering. No mention of Gianni. Had he planned to attend the wedding, surely Anja would have mentioned it?

'Chiara shrugged. 'Well then, maybe the wedding feast will be worth coming for?'

'I doubt that. He's Italian.' The sudden silence made them both turn. 'Ursula.' Katarina could not keep the surprise from her voice, though quickly wondered why she had been. The *gräfin* would want to ensure she looked well enough not to embarrass her, at least. She had offered her a new gown from her own dressmaker in the city, but Katarina insisted on wearing the one she had brought with her. Her father had admired it, never mind the cost of it. She would not hurt his feelings.

Gräfin von Cloy, clearly dressed in her very finest finery – which seemed to warrant jewel embellishment with an extravagance equal to that of Katarina's lace and frills – smiled benignly at her soon to be daughter-in-law, her plump cheeks dimpling. She reached out and touched one of the jewelled brights holding Katarina's hair in place. 'You look quite lovely, my dear. These add a nice touch of colour to your hair.'

'Cunt,' Chiara mouthed silently behind the *gräfin*.

Katarina fought not to react unsure, had she done so, whether it would be to laugh or scowl at Chiara's word choice. 'Thank you, Ursula. Your gown is spectacular. You quite put me in the shade.' Katarina saw immediately how this compliment pleased her. And she was literally in shadow cast by the older woman's bulk in front of the window.

'Come down to the salon when you're ready, Katarina. Your father awaits you there. The guests are assembled in the receiving hall ready for the carriages.

Katarina had gone with her father to look at the *Schloss von Cloy Chapel of Our Lady* decorated for the ceremony, the evening before. Unsurprisingly, no expense had been spared to fill the space with fragrant blooms and foliage. They had stood together before the altar with its golden monstrance, the figure of the crucified Christ life-size and bloody on the wall above, and the red sanctuary lamp burning its eternal promise. Katarina had gestured to the altar. 'I'm surprised you want this for me.' How many of the little wooden Calvinist chapel he attended, would fit inside this one?

'It's the same God, my sweet, the rest is just style.'

She had never noticed such religious tolerance in him before. Yet this was an alliance beyond his wildest dreams, there would surely be very little he would not tolerate.

Now, she stood for a moment in the doorway to the salon, studying him at one of the tall windows watching the procession of carriages making its way along the tree-lined, gravel road to the chapel. He wore his dress uniform and was still trim and straight-backed, though his hair worn tied at his neck was snowy white. 'Father.'

He turned, gazing at her for a few moments wide-eyed until a broad smile broke out upon his face. 'Katarina, dearest child. You look quite enchanting. Johannes is a lucky man.'

She was uncertain how many in the wider von Cloy family would agree. That the *markgraf* had declined to attend rather proved her point even though Chiara insisted the true reason was that he would not be parted from his latest 'bum boy,' as she so charmingly put it.

Eduard Rota held out his hand. 'Come daughter, we should keep them waiting no longer.'

Chiara and several other servants waited outside to wave

them off in the two-seater flower-garlanded open carriage taking them the short distance to the chapel. Driven by two grooms dressed in wedding finery, even the horses – a perfectly matched pair of sorrels – had been bedecked for the occasion with plaited mains and tails woven with colourful ribbons, and ostrich feather head plumes. As they made their way along the track, Katarina became aware of fast hoofbeats behind them and turned to see a coach and four rapidly gaining on them. As it drew closer her heart sank, for she recognised the Gabrieli family crest. Gianni had come.

Her father turned to look too. 'Someone's late. Horses look spent, poor beasts.'

Gianni's coach pulled up a short way behind them as Katarina was helped down from hers to stand on the chapel porch where the flower girls waited with their baskets of petals. Shaking out her skirts, she tried desperately to think what to say, watching him jump out without waiting for the steps to be lowered, grinning as he strode towards her, his magenta satin coat unbuttoned and creased. She held out her hands to him but when Giuseppe came down the steps, they fell back to her sides.

Eduard Rota moved to stand beside his daughter. While Gianni was unknown to him, he recognised the second man immediately, of course. 'What's going on? Why is Guarneri here?'

Katarina, unable to take her eyes from Giuseppe, reached blindly for her father's arm, clutching it, fearing her legs would buckle beneath her so overwhelmed was she by the sight of him. And then she understood, suddenly. He meant home and safety to her. He meant violins and music and playing, and all the lightness that brought to her heart … and her heart was full of him. It always had been. His gaze, too, was unwavering. How had this happened? Her lower lip began to tremble like a child about to weep.

Gianni looked from one to the other. 'I know you asked me

not to show him your letter. Forgive me. He had to know. You must see that.'

She was unsure whether she moved to Giuseppe or he to her, but they were in each other arms, clinging to each other. Did they both weep? It was difficult to know, wet skin on wet skin.

'Katarina, stop this at once. There's a church full of people waiting for us?' Eduard Rota hissed.

But his words went unheeded, as did the opening of the chapel door and the clip of Johannes's footsteps coming out onto the porch, so the sound of his voice startled her.

'Katarina?'

The door opened again, and Ursula joined him. 'What is this?'

Johannes turned to her, scowling. 'Go back inside, Mother.'

Ursula remained where she was. 'Who are these people and what are they doing here? Deal with it, Johannes. The guests are waiting.'

Katarina moved out of Giuseppe's arms but held tightly to his hand before turning to face Johannes. What could she say to him? There were no words.

Sunlight gleamed off him. All the gold frogging and lace on his dress uniform and the sword at his side were aglitter, while he stared intently at them, at a loss for words himself.

Katarina drew a breath. 'I didn't know until now. What can I say? I truly didn't know.'

Ursula's laugh was loud and incongruous. 'Didn't know? What is the silly girl talking about? Get rid of these people,' she said, again.

Surely the *gräfin* would be pleased if the wedding did not go ahead? Because how could it now?

'Did you come here for this, Giuseppe?' Johannes asked, quietly.

'Christ, no.' He looked down at Katarina. 'I wanted to make sure you were alright. I couldn't understand why anyone would take your violin. But when I saw you, I realised that wasn't why I'd come at all.' He placed his palm on her face. 'I came to take you home, though I didn't know it.'

Ursula took a step towards Katarina. 'You think you can choose to humiliate my son in front of our friends? A little nonentity like—'

Johannes turned on her angrily. 'I told you to go inside, Mother. This is between me and Katarina.' He opened the door to the church and placed his hand on her back ready to push her in. She clearly decided to maintain her dignity and walked inside unforced, closing the door behind her.

Katarina stepped up onto the porch to take his hands in hers. 'I truly didn't know, Johannes. I never meant to hurt you. You must believe me.'

He searched her face. 'I see truth in what you say.'

Eduard Rota seized his daughter's arm. 'You will not do this, Katarina. I forbid it.'

She shook him off. 'What choice do I have? Surely you can understand?'

Eduard's face was now puce with rage, he jabbed his finger at Katarina as he spoke. 'What I do understand, daughter, is that I have not given my permission for you to marry Giuseppe Guarneri, should that even be his intention, nor shall—'

'Of course it's my damn intention.'

Eduard ignored him, his eyes fixed on Katarina like glittering daggers. 'Now, obey me and do your duty. You have made a promise to the von Cloy family, and you *will* honour it.

Johannes turned reluctantly to the *oberst*. 'No. I shan't hold Katarina to any agreement. I won't force her to marry me.' His eyes returned to her. 'So, what now? Must I let you go?'

Katarina, nodding slowly, could scarcely bear to see his face. He looked broken and it tore her heart to know she had done this to him. Jesu, he did not deserve this.

He bowed. 'Then I wish you well.' His voice cracked

betraying the emotion his stony expression tried to conceal. Turning on his heel, he went back inside the church.

Eduard turned furiously on his daughter. 'Well, Katarina, if you're so cavalier as to turn down a von Cloy, you will not have Guarneri because if you defy me, I shall disinherit you.' He turned his gaze on Giuseppe. 'You'll get nothing, do you understand me? Everything will go to my nephew. Every last *pfennig*. Do you understand that both of you?'

Giuseppe clenched his fists. 'I want nothing from you.'

'*Really?* You want my daughter, no?' Eduard laughed, unpleasantly. 'And how will you feel about living as an artisan's wife, Katarina? Are you prepared for such a small ... such a limited life?'

'And what would my life have been here? I think I know rather more about that than you do. Playing the pianoforte to entertain my guests. Embroidering trifles to pass the hours. And all of it badly, too. This is your idea of a full life is it, Father? Well, it's—'

'Don't be obtuse. I thought better of you than this. You will give the family an heir. You will become a *markgräfin*. One day that title will be yours. Do you think it equal to that of a violin maker's wife?'

'It doesn't matter. I love Giuseppe. I shall be with him whatever that life holds.'

Giuseppe took her hand again.

Gianni gestured towards his carriage. 'Come. We should leave before they all start flooding out of the church to gawp.'

Giuseppe and Katarina both glanced at the closed doors before hurrying after him. Katarina did not look back at her father, so did not see the tears that now streaked his face.

Johannes leaned against the closed door, listening to the sound of hooves and carriage wheels moving away over gravel. His mother came to stand beside him, but he did not look at her.

'You must speak to them—'

'I shall. I don't need you to tell me.' He had to be certain his emotions were fully under control, for the blow of losing Katarina was beyond anything he had experienced before. He had not truly understood how much he loved her ... and now she was lost.

Ursula gestured towards the packed pews full of chattering Viennese high society in their competitive finery. 'The longer you leave it the worse the scandal will be.'

Johannes scowled at her. 'Why should there be scandal? I've been jilted at the altar. It's happened to many before me and will happen to many after.'

'Not to a von Cloy. Some will delight in gloating; you can be sure of that.'

'Well, I'm not a von Cloy, am I? I'm a Horak. After the man who ploughed you rather sooner than was—'

'Silence,' she hissed. 'How dare you say such a thing to me. Now speak to your guests or I shall.'

He took a long breath before striding down the aisle towards the altar.

Thirteen

VIENNA PROVINCE, JUNE 1722

IN THE CARRIAGE WITH GIUSEPPE'S ARMS TIGHT around her, Katarina watched the chapel recede as the horses trotted wearily away. Her father had remained alone on the porch, his shoulders dropped, and reading the defeat in his stance she found she could no more bear the hurt she had caused him than that inflicted upon Johannes. Two good men who loved her. When he was no longer in sight, she pressed her face against Giuseppe's chest and wept until she had no more tears to shed.

The team had now slowed to a walk. 'We must rest them properly soon. They need two days out of harness to recover before we ask them to begin the journey home.' Gianni tried to get Katarina's attention. 'Poor beasts. We ran them hard to get here, we must be kinder now.'

She turned her head, managing a small nod. He would not have the same resources to change his team that had been available for the von Cloy coach.

Giuseppe tightened his arms around her again. 'There was a village not far from here. Wasn't there a respectable looking inn?'

Gianni nodded. 'With a new thatched roof.' He frowned.' I suppose no one will come after us?'

Both men looked at Katarina. 'Why should they?' she said, her voice hoarse from weeping. 'My bridges are well and truly burnt.'

Giuseppe moved to look at her face. 'If you go back, you won't be turned away, you know that. Not by Johannes.'

Katarina had no choice, swept away by feelings so powerful it no longer mattered what carnage was left in their wake. 'I have to be with you.'

He kissed her forehead. 'Thank Christ,' he murmured.

The Forester's *Wirtshous* in Saint Gilgen had a wooden cabin behind its stables where the landlady directed them after Gianni used his not inconsiderable charm to secure privacy for them – still worried they may be pursued – though Katarina could not imagine for what purpose. She did wonder what the woman made of such a request, though she had shown no reaction other than to offer the cabin. Gianni's coachman, Angelo, would bunk with the ostlers over the stables.

Inside, it comprised a small parlour with a battered table, four mismatched chairs, and two tired sofas, with a solitary bedchamber at the rear. This housed a surprisingly large and elderly fourposter bed obviously intended for a number of occupants. The privy outhouse stood beyond the stables and would be shared with the grooms, though there were assorted chamber pots beneath the bed. The horses were released into the paddock, and with their grass diet supplemented by oats from the stables, Angelo was confident they would soon regain condition.

On the first night, Katarina urged the men to take the bed while she slept on one of the worn sofas which, though small, were more than sufficient for her slight stature. This was turned down flat by them both. And they remained quite implacable on it, damn them. So, the vast, lumpy flock mattress became hers for the three nights they remained in the cabin.

Before they parted for sleep though, Katarina had tried to explain how her time at the Schloss von Cloy had led to the loss of her violin (for she could barely allow her thoughts to probe the edges of the wound she had left behind her there, let alone speak of it). And it was strange that even after so short a time, she was able to see how the *gräfin* had manipulated her. 'Chiara was right about her, wasn't she?' She bowed her head in shame for all of it. 'When she said she wanted to be the mother I'd never had, I was lost. I lost myself to the idea of that, I suppose. So, I wanted to please her. Of course I did.' She could still hear those first siren words spoken so softly. *'I hope you can look on me as your mother. You've never had one, I know. And I've never had a daughter.'*

Giuseppe sat beside her on the sagging couch. 'It's easy to see how that would make you feel.' He was silent for a moment or two. 'It was different for me because I had Nonna Barb. And I'm sure that woman knew exactly what she was doing playing on that empty space you have.'

It was something else she had told Johannes of, that absence. It had explained her enjoyment of the Guarneri household. 'Well, she has what she wished for now.' She clenched her jaw. *Oh, Johannes.* 'Yet it made her angry.'

'Loss of face, I imagine.' Gianni sat on one of the dining chairs beside them. 'The church was full, the wedding feast ready, and she'd probably resigned herself to the marriage by then, too.'

He frowned a little. 'And as Johannes had taken charge of you. I mean he had taken you away from her influence, she must have already accepted defeat. You would become his wife.'

. . .

Katarina found sleep almost impossible that first night. The mattress was as unforgiving as her thoughts. How could she not contemplate what might have been had Giuseppe not stepped down from that coach? It frightened her to even think of it. Yet two men were now distraught who would not have been ... and the *gräfin* would be gloating. That Giuseppe and Gianni would now spend an uncomfortable night on those small sofas only added to her contrition. She had never felt so powerless ... or so full of self-disgust.

She had left the window shutters open to the moonlight for the room had felt oppressive with them fastened. The light was bright enough to allow her to observe all too starkly the difference between it and that other cabin in the woods where Johannes had kissed and desired her. Would Giuseppe come to her here? There was nothing to prevent it for Gianni would turn a blind eye. Did she wish it? This would have been her wedding night with Johannes, so she knew she should not. Though, God help her, she did. Yet another reason for shame.

The next morning, she awoke early with the sun shining into the shabby room, surprised to find she had actually slept but not, in truth, surprised to find she had done so alone. She dressed quickly, pulling on the peach satin wedding gown over her shift. In the unforgiving light she could see how creased and tear-stained it was. It looked beyond recovery even with sponge and smoothing iron. She would need fresh clothing soon but had no idea how this might be achieved.

When she opened her door quietly into the parlour in case the men still slept, she found the room deserted. The bedding they had fetched from the inn the evening before was neatly folded beneath their respective couches. How cramped and uncomfortable they must have been. She moved to the cabin door, opening it to look out at the paddock beside the stables bathed in dazzling morning light. The horses grazed contentedly, but of Giuseppe and Gianni there was no sign.

As she made her way towards the inn, the door to the kitchens opened and Giuseppe emerged beside a pretty kitchen maid carrying a large basket. When he relieved her of it as soon as the door closed behind them, she smiled her thanks, her admiration obvious. It was then he spotted Katarina and her heart swooped recognising that same admiration in his smile at seeing her. Why, though? It still seemed outlandish that he wanted her trailing her wake of destruction.

He held up the basket. 'Breakfast. I hope you're hungry. There's quite a lot of it.'

The serving girl hung back watching them with an annoyed frown before tossing her head and returning to the kitchens.

Just the thought of food made Katarina's belly grumble noisily as they walked back to the cabin together. She pressed her hand to it hoping he hadn't heard. 'I'm famished.' Yet had she any right to be? She lifted her chin. She had made her choice (what choice did she really have, anyway?) and it was time to start living with it.

He smiled, ruefully. 'So I hear.'

'Where's Gianni?' she said, to divert his attention.

'No idea. He'd gone when I woke up.'

'He must have found sleep difficult on that cramped couch, as you did, I'm sure.'

He squeezed her shoulder. 'If I did, it was because my thoughts were filled with you. How close I came to losing you and how I might never have known I had, if you see what I mean. It was blind chance I came with Gianni. How could I have been such an imbecile for so long?' He shook his head. 'What's a little discomfort compared to that.' He opened the cabin door and quickly placed the food basket down onto the table.

That summed it up exactly. The sense of fate … of pure

chance. Chance that had changed both their lives ... and Johannes's, too, forever.

'When I saw you standing on that porch yesterday, I understood everything.' He closed his eyes for a moment. 'My life would mean nothing without you in it ... my work ... nothing.' He moved to her touching her face, his fingertips a gentle feather caress. 'But I hope to God you haven't given up too much for me, Kat. I—'

She put a finger on his lips to silence him until he moved it away to kiss her ... and, *Holy God*, it set her on fire. When Giuseppe's hands moved over her body, she felt her legs would buckle beneath her and there was little doubt how it would end ... until the door flew open, and Gianni stepped inside. They broke apart, both trying to calm their breathing.

'Excuse me, I—'

Giuseppe gasped a quick breath and gestured to the table. 'That's breakfast. We should eat before it gets cold.' He began unloading wrapped platters from the basket.

Katarina ran her hand through her hair moving it back from her face. 'We wondered where you were?'

Gianni held up the bundle he carried. 'I've found some clothing for you. I didn't think you should abuse that lovely gown any longer than you had to.' He dropped his prize onto a sofa and untied its cloth wrapping. 'I asked the landlady if there was anyone in the village who might help.'

She joined him to examine the garments he had brought, lifting them, and shaking them out to see what he had found for her. Two linen shifts and woollen stockings, worn but clean. A homespun skirt and two linen bodices in the same condition. 'How did you manage this? It's so good of you.' And they looked like they would fit, too. Or would only be a touch too large.

'A woman in the village takes in washing and trades things people no longer need or are forced to sell.'

She flung her arms around him. 'I'm amazed that you

thought of it. I'm so grateful.' She gathered up the clothes and hurried to the bedchamber, pausing at the door to speak over her shoulder. 'I'll change out of this now before it comes to any further harm.' With the door closed behind her she rested against it for a few moments to collect herself – remembering the feel of Giuseppe's hands on her body and the urgency of his tongue inside her mouth – before struggling to unfasten the gown she had so recently struggled to get on.

She quickly pulled on a skirt and bodice, fastening ties and laces. A much simpler process than those on her satin gown. The outfit was, as expected, on the large side – a kerchief was needed to make the bodice a touch more modest. There was no mirror, and she had no hairbrush anyway, so had to be content with running her fingers through her hair again. She would have to do as she was. She allowed herself to smile. It would not matter to Giuseppe. He loved her. How startling ... and wonderful to be certain of it.

When she joined them at the table, they had already started on the meal, both looking shamefaced because of it. Gianni quickly chewed and swallowed. 'Forgive us. Hunger got the better of manners.'

'Nonsense. I should have thought you fools had you not.' She started on the plate of ham, soft-boiled eggs and coarse bread thick with butter they had served for her. There was no further talk until all the serving platters were empty.

Katarina leaned back in her chair, adjusting her bodice which had dropped a little. 'I'm so grateful for the clothes.' She patted her belly. 'And for the bit of extra room they give me.'

Gianni licked his fingers, noisily. 'I'm glad they suit.' He tilted his head. 'Will your father forgive you, do you think?'

Giuseppe shot him a look. 'Let's not talk about it now.'

Katarina placed her hand over his. 'It's alright. It's not something I've been able to push from my mind, anyway. I know how much I've hurt him.' *And how much more I've hurt Johannes.* She bit her lip, hard.

Giuseppe turned his hand to grasp hers. 'He loves you. He's angry, is all. Not that I want—'

'I know you don't. But if he needs to act … to feel he's punished me then so be it. In truth, he has a low opinion of Hans Rota, but he's the only family there is. He lives in Father's Vienna house rent-free because he promised Uncle Otto to take care of him. Otto knew he was unlikely to have a successful life because he expected to make his fortune without having to work for it. Hairbrained schemes. Poor investments. That sort of thing. Father says he's a dunderhead with a grasping wife and two spoilt little boys.' She pulled at her bodice again. 'So he won't want the house to go to them.' She sighed. 'But he needs time to forgive me.'

Gianni leaned in closer. 'Well, I expect your cousin and his wife will be in your father's ear now they know you've fallen from grace.'

'They weren't invited. Father wanted to keep my marriage from them for as long as possible. And I don't think he wished the *gräfin* to know I had such relatives in Vienna.'

'I'll go and see your papà. I should ask him for your hand properly.'

'Giuseppe, please don't. It would be better for me to do it.' She was afraid her father would see proof of Giuseppe's hope for financial gain.

'Then we'll go together.'

Katarina squeezed his hand knowing that there could be no reconciliation if her father accused Giuseppe of being a fortune hunter again.

Fourteen

CREMONA, JUNE 1722

AFTER THE THREE NIGHTS IN SAINT GILGEN, THEY had moved on, stopping in coaching inns along the way taking care never to overstretch the horses. Most nights had been spent with the three of them sharing a bed after Katarina had refused to allow the men to sleep on the often-filthy floors on pain of her joining them there. With Gianni in the middle, sleep seemed to find them all with ease.

'I don't desire either of you, just so you know,' he had said that first night.

'More fool you,' Giuseppe replied.

'He means you not him, Kat.'

If I wanted a man, I could do better than you.'

They had all laughed at that. Even Katarina had managed a small chuckle. That she was so racked with guilt for the pain she had left behind her, tore at Giuseppe's heart. But it would take time, he knew. And love.

Later, he wondered why he had not gone to her on those nights in Saint Gilgen when she would so soon become his wife. His feelings were complicated. That he loved and desired in a way he never imagined possible had dumbfounded him, for it had come like a bolt from the blue when he saw her standing there on the church porch. She filled a void in him he had not even been aware existed. A place he had walled up, and she had filled it with love.

But he could not shake off the idea that she had ... or would give up too much for him. Johannes Horak and the life of privilege that came with him, not to mention the rift with her father. So, should she not be allowed time to change her mind? By going to her bed, he would take that choice away from her, for he knew there could be no going back for either of them after that. He took a moment for a wry thought or two about his lack of hesitation to bed other women. Was that the difference between love and lust ... or lust and love combined? Such thoughts were uncomfortable, and he quickly pushed them away.

They arrived back in San Domenica Piazza at dusk, all bone-weary. How could Giuseppe not think of the morning Gianni had collected him? It had been a last-minute decision to go with him to Vienna, acting on a sense of unease about Kat, for he knew she could not be truly happy denied her violin.

Now he stood beside her outside his papà's shop, both watching Angelo urge the tired horses on for the last short leg of their journey home, just about able to see Gianni waving from the carriage in the fading light. After he rounded the corner, they turned back. With the shutters closed, no light showed from within.

Giuseppe rapped hard on the door. 'Papà will be up. I just need to make him hear us.' He knocked again, louder still. Then a small light approached showing through chinks in the shutters and they heard the bolts drawing back.

When the door opened Andrea – his candle guttering in the breeze – gasped at the sight of Katarina. 'Now all them boxes make sense.'

'Boxes?' They said in unison.

His papà led the way through to the storeroom where trunks and boxes had been piled high from floor to ceiling, with the stocks of wood crowded onto fewer shelves than was ideal. Giuseppe was surprised when Katarina understood this.

She gestured towards the stacks. 'We'll move it outside in the morning and I'll go through it. I won't need all this.'

He felt a familiar pang, knowing so much of what had been prepared for her new life in Vienna would be useless for the one she would have with him. 'I'll help you. I'm sorry it's—'

'Don't be sorry, there's no need.' Her hand flew to her throat. 'How though? Who has sent it so quickly?'

Andrea reached behind one of the boxes and produced her violin case and a letter.

'Johannes. Of course. Who else would it be.'

Giuseppe watched her eyes brim with tears and had to blink back his own when she handed him her violin and broke the fancy seal on the letter. She moved closer to the candle, biting her lip while she read, tears now spilling down her cheek glistening in the flickering light. 'Oh, Johannes,' she murmured, handing Giuseppe the letter.

Schloss von Cloy
June 1722

My dear Katarina

Please trust that I have no wish to cause you distress, I know you well enough to understand your decisions have not been lightly made, but in all honesty, I must tell you that my feelings for you remain unchanged (love is slow to die perhaps, if it ever does. St Paul certainly thought not) though I am being encouraged to mitigate them as I am sure you can imagine. So Chiara will pack up your trousseaux and return it immediately before anyone else can get their hands upon it. I cannot send your boxes to your father, of course, though I do hope you will soon be reconciled. Mother is working against this I'm sorry to report, but I trust your love for each other will prevail.

I know I am not without fault in this. Believe me when I say I truly wish I had done things differently. I'll never forget you, Katarina ... and what might have been ...

Yours always,
Johannes

Giuseppe sighed, handing the paper back to Kat. How much easier it would be had he stolen her away from a bastard who mistreated her. His papà had passed her a linen handkerchief and she dried her face and blew her nose, already pulling herself together. How, in Christ's name had she come to love him? *Why had she?*

Giuseppe was grateful his father and grandmother did not question her, talking instead of the goings on in the isle since he had been away, making sure to only mention people she knew. Eventually, when they had both finished all they could manage of the bread, cheese, and fruit Nonna Barb had served for them, he stood and helped Kat to her feet. 'We should get to bed.'

'Put Katarina into your chamber. The linen's fresh. You can go in with Andrea,' Nonna Barb said, her eyes on Katarina, full of concern. 'You look done-in, little chick.'

Giuseppe reached out for Katarina's hand. 'I'll take you up.' He needed some time alone with her and knew she needed it too. He did not look at his family. If they disapproved, he did not care.

When the door was closed behind them, they sat side by side on the small cot holding hands. It seemed neither of them could think what to say. When Katarina leant against him, he closed his arms around her, and their kisses said all that was needed. How easy it would have been then to move her beneath him on the bed, and it took willpower he did not know he possessed not to do it. Not to have her there and then. He knew enough of a woman's desire to know she would not resist, but he made himself move away, trying to catch his breath. 'I should let you sleep.'

'I wish you could stay,' she said, softly.

'You think I don't wish it too?' He was unsure whether he could make her understand when his head felt ready to explode trying to make sense of it himself. He took a breath. 'I want you to truly understand all you're giving up by marrying me ... the life you'll have with me. You need—'

'I won't change my mind.'

'Good.' *Thank God. Thank Christ.* He moved to kiss her chastely on the forehead. 'I'll see you in the morning.' It was the hardest thing he had ever done to walk away.

Katarina awoke with a start sensing activity already underway in the house below. Pulling on her travel-stained clothes, she berated herself for not at least finding some clean undergarments in one of her stored boxes. She thought wistfully about bathing and washing her hair, unsure how this would be achieved here. There was no bellpull in this chamber to summon servants ready to fetch a tub and hot water. Perhaps it was this sort of thing that Giuseppe wished her to understand ... and she would. She would discover all the changes she must make in the way she lived and accept them all willingly for she would spend this new life with him. And with violins.

She found him alone in the workshop which meant they felt no need to be circumspect with their greeting. They kissed for a long time until Giuseppe broke away when his papà came through from the house.

'There you are, Katarina. There's breakfast for you in the kitchen parlour.'

Giuseppe glared at his father for a moment. 'After you've eaten, we'll go through your boxes, and you can decide what you want to keep. Nonna knows where the rest can be taken if ...' He hesitated, clearly uncomfortable. 'If you wish to sell it, that is.'

'Of course we must sell it.' She frowned a little as the thought occurred to her. 'It will go towards the cost of our wedding if my father is still angry with me. Now let's get those boxes outside so you can put your storeroom to rights while I eat.'

Giuseppe grinned. 'Already out there.'

Katarina laughed as she went to join Nonna Barb in the kitchen. The old lady lifted a loaf of bread from the oven with a wooden paddle and placed it down on the table. Then she moved to pull Katarina into her arms. 'You look better, my chick. Well rested. Now we must feed you up a bit. Get some flesh on those bones.'

Katarina doubted it would be possible, however much Nonna fed her. She was not made that way. But she smiled and nodded as the old woman sliced off a hunk of the hot bread and spread it with butter and plum jam. It was delicious. She was going to enjoy Nonna's attempts to fatten her up, however futile they may be. While they were alone, it seemed a good time to raise the things she was unsure about living in this household. She could ask Anja but ... 'Nonna, if I wish to bathe.' She chewed her lip. 'How—'

The old woman smiled and patted her arm. 'In summer

Giuseppe will fill the tub outside on the terazza. In winter we bathe before the fire in here.' She pointed to the water cauldron that bubbled over the cooking fire. 'There is always water for washing.' She raised her eyebrows above shining eyes. 'In summer the river is favoured by you young ones, too ...' She nodded to herself. 'Oh yes, I remember how it was.'

After she had gone through all her boxes, aware she was taking up so much of Giuseppe's time, even though he insisted he was more than happy to give it. And he did seem to enjoy touching the lavish fabrics with their exotic patterns, appearing more reluctant than she to see them go into the pile for disposal. She rubbed his arm. 'They were never really for me, you know. They were for the woman I was supposed to become. Now I don't have to become her, do I? I can stay my real self with you.'

He stared at her intently. 'If that's true, then I'm glad.'

'You have my word it is.'

He held up some tiny garments lifted from the small box he had just opened. 'Infant's clothes.' He stroked them gently. 'They're beautifully made.'

She smiled at him. 'We shall keep those, I think.'

He returned her smile. 'Yes.'

It was late afternoon when they returned to the shop after taking the boxes of unneeded clothing to an agent in the city who dealt in such high-quality garments. They paused outside for a kiss, having already stabled the pony and secured the cart in the yard. 'I wish we could marry tomorrow—'

'Why can't we?'

'We must speak with Father Paulo first.'

She frowned.

'The priest at St Domenico's.'

'Will he make it difficult because I'm not Catholic?'

'I doubt it—'

'We could say I'm with child. He can't refuse us then, surely?'

He cupped her face. 'Let's see what he says first.'

'Cough, cough,' said a loud female voice coming up behind them. They broke apart.

'Anja,' Katarina cried, moving away from Giuseppe to embrace her friend. 'I've missed you. How is Maisel?'

'She's bonny as ever, though twice the bleedin' size she were when you last saw her. She'll be as big as you soon, she will.' Anja looked from one to the other. 'You've done the right thing, girl. Though why this numbskull didn't know he's been in love with you since he first set eyes on you, I'll never know.'

'Well, thank God, I know now, Anja, eh?'

'She was head over heels for you for such a time, she was. You nearly let her get away, then you'd of been lumbered with big Sancia. Gawd, that don't bear thinking of.'

'Sancia,' Katarina said, staring at Giuseppe. 'You've been with Sancia?'

Anja cackled, watching Giuseppe rising discomfort. 'She's been with him, more like. Couldn't shake her off like a bad smell, eh?'

Of course Sancia had moved in on Giuseppe as soon as she left Cremona. Merla had warned her of it. 'Well. I'm glad I saved you from that fate, at least.'

Anja moved closer to Katarina and touched her arm gently. 'Your father is back at the *palazzo*, Kat. He arrived last night. He—'

'You know what's happened between us?'

'I do. Gianni told me.' Seeing Katarina's frown, she touched her arm again. 'He wanted me to know in case you needed me. Don't be angry at him.'

'No, no. Of course not. I was just surprised.' She turned to

Giuseppe who had moved beside her, his arm around her waist. 'We'll go to see him in a few days. I can't let us become estranged—'

'You won't. He loves you too much for it. When he sees how it is between you two, he'll come round, I know it.' Anja said.

Katarina prayed she was right for she loved her father dearly and had always felt wrapped in his love … and his approval, too. Had she taken it for granted that she could do no wrong in his eyes? Yet how could it be wrong to want to spend her life with the man she loved? 'I do hope so, Anja.'

That night Katarina moved into the big bed with Nonna Barb in readiness for her marriage when the old lady would move out into Giuseppe's small bedchamber. When she awoke, later than she should have once again, she found the old woman had left without disturbing her. And, as on the morning before, she found Giuseppe alone in the workshop about to go into the shop after the bell had sounded. She followed him, finding an officer from her father's regiment had just come in. It was so unusual to see that uniform in this context that the sight of it startled her, setting her heart racing. *Stop,* she told herself. *It means nothing.*

She smiled, though she did not recognise the man. Then, seeing by his insignia that he was a *hauptmann,* she wondered why she did not for those of his rank would have been invited to dine. Perhaps he had only recently been posted to Cremona? 'Good morning, *Hauptmann.* How can we help you?' she said in German.

The young man paled visibly, seeming unable to speak, setting Katarina's heart to pound again. Was this …. could this be a message from her father? She felt a sudden burst of happiness. Did he wish to see her? She smiled at the captain again. 'I am Katarina Rota. Please give me my father's message.'

Giuseppe, glancing between the silent captain and a beaming Katarina, clearly could not follow what was happening. 'Can we help you, Captain?' he asked in Italian.

The officer seemed to come to himself then, clicking his heels. 'Forgive me, *Fräulein* Rota.' He looked despairingly at Giuseppe as the smile left Katarina's face like a candle snuffed. 'Might I speak with you, *Signore*?' he asked in halting Italian.

'No, you will speak to me.' Giuseppe's arm was already around her, holding her close.

'There has been an accident.'

Katarina's hand flew to her throat. 'Is he hurt? I must go to him at once.' She pulled away from Giuseppe already heading for the door.

The young captain turned despairingly to Giuseppe again. '*Signore* ...'

'Kat, wait. Let the captain say what he must.' He turned to him. 'Colonel Rota has had an accident?'

'Yes, *Signore*.' He kept his eyes fixed on Giuseppe. 'A riding accident ...'

Katarina let out a small moan. 'Oh, dear God. Is he badly hurt?' Yet, somehow, she knew the answer before he spoke it. And so, seemingly, did Giuseppe for he already held her tight in his arms again. 'Go on, lad.'

'He lost his life. I'm s—'

Katarina's shrieks made any further words redundant. She would have collapsed to the floor had Giuseppe not held her. Soon Nonna Barb and Andrea were there with them in the shop.

Later Katarina had no clear memory of what happened next, she thought perhaps she had swooned for she had flashback visions of being carried upstairs to the bedchamber feeling herself drifting in and out of consciousness, yet hearing herself crying out for him, '*Vati. Vati,*' unceasingly as though it would summon him to her as it had done as a child. Then Merla was with her, making her drink something bitter and in what seemed but the blink of an eye, she knew no more.

'When she awoke, Giuseppe was sleeping beside her. Why was he fully dressed? She looked down at herself. And why was she? They must be married now if they were together like this, so why had she no memory of it? She watched him sleep for a few moments more, his wild curls tousled on the pillow, his eyelashes so long and dark they made shadowy smudges beneath his eyes.

It was the bitter taste in her mouth that plunged her back to remembering, her heart swooping and fluttering. Would she vomit? *How can he be gone?* It seemed impossible to believe she would never see him again. That her last memory would be of him standing distraught on the church porch. She gasped a breath of sudden understanding. Now they could never be reconciled. It would be much later when she understood just what that meant.

Her gasp was enough to wake Giuseppe and she was soon held in his arms as he wiped away tears she had been unaware she shed. When, at last, she managed to speak, her voice was horse and shaky. 'Did he tell you what happened, that captain?'

'They believe his horse pulled up at the wall in a field behind the stables.'

The wall Johannes's horse had jumped that day. 'How did they find him?'

'A stable lad went out to look for him after his horse returned without him.'

She chewed her lip. 'How? I mean what happened to …?'

He stroked her face. 'His neck was broken.'

Katarina groaned.

'It would have been quick. He won't have known anything beyond the horse's refusal, throwing him. Who has not taken a tumble from a horse?'

THE VIOLIN MAKER'S WIFE

She nodded and took a shaky breath. 'He would have been angry rather than afraid, I think. I'm glad of that.' She found a small smile from somewhere. 'Damn and blast you, Sleipnir. I heard him say it many times. Damn and blast you, you brute of a horse.'

Fifteen

CREMONA, JULY 1722

TWO DAYS LATER, KATARINA RECEIVED A LETTER FROM the garrison commandant offering his condolences and informing her there would be a funeral service at *Cattedrale di Santa Maria Assunta,* followed by a burial in the barracks' cemetery. Katarina had expected his body to be interred in the family mausoleum at their home near Vienna. She knew this was what he had wished and wondered how and why it had been changed.

'Why haven't I been consulted? She asked after Giuseppe had read the letter at the breakfast table.

He reached across the table to squeeze her hand. 'He'll know the state you're in. It's a kindness, surely?

'So, why at the cathedral and not the Calvinist chapel?'

'You'll have to ask him.'

The cathedral was crowded with uniformed soldiers, which perhaps explained the venue, even though her father despised Catholicism. Had the whole regiment turned out to pay their respects? With the great bell tolling high in the soaring *Torrazzo,* the cool, gloomy interior was alive with the susurration of whispering voices rising like offerings to the vaulted ceiling collecting there with the wisps and tendrils of candle smoke.

Both dressed in deepest mourning, Katarina walked down the aisle holding tight to Giuseppe's arm hoping to still her trembling. She smelled flowers, though there were none. Not until the coffin arrived. Perhaps a recent wedding, or just the scent that had permeated the very fabric of the building over the eons it had stood? She bit her lip. Her father could never give her away at her own wedding. How could she not wonder whether, had she married Johannes, he might still live? (It was a question that would stay with her for many years, and because she could never wish it otherwise, left her guilt-ridden and fearing she would be punished for it.)

Candles were ablaze in banks beneath the brightly painted haloed saints atop the rood screen, and suspended above it, the figure of a tortured Christ looked down on the black-draped catafalque where the coffin would soon be placed.

Katarina nodded to Anja and Carlo and others from the isle as they made their way past the grey-blue pilasters, their gilded capitals aglitter, towards the front where officers were seated with places reserved for the family. When she made to enter the front row, a man quickly stood to bar her way. She knew she ought to recognise him. Short with thinning reddish hair caught in a rat's tail at his neck, dressed in rusty black stretched tight across a small round paunch. Looking on and seeming to offer him encouragement was a woman slightly taller, considerably rounder and swathed in so much black taffeta it was hard to distinguish her features beneath the wide veiled brim of her hat. 'Tell her, Hans. You tell her.' Clinging to her skirts were a pair of whey-faced little boys.

Clara nodded her recognition. 'Cousin, Hans. It's been some years since we last met. I'm sorry it must be under such tragic circumstances.'

'Tell her.' The woman said, louder this time.

Hans's face, already pink and shining with sweat, turned puce. 'Er, this is a pew for family only. You cannot sit here, I'm afraid. Forgive—'

'Hans.' The woman hissed too loudly, her voice dripping with angry spite.

Why such loathing?

Hans straightened his back. 'You must sit elsewhere.'

The boys giggled and nudged each other.

'What are you talking about?' She turned to look at Giuseppe.

He shrugged before gesturing towards the family. 'You know this lot?'

'My cousin and his wife. I told you of them.'

'Ah, them ones.'

The woman leaned forward to speak to Katarina directly. 'Dearest Uncle Eduard had no daughter, so how can Hans be your cousin, eh? How?'

She licked her lips as though tasting something sweet. *So, he did change his will. Oh, Father. I know you loved me still. I know it.*

Then a familiar voice spoke from the pew behind them. 'You will accommodate *Fräulein* Rota and her betrothed immediately or I will have you removed. Do you understand me, *Mein Herr?*' Johannes hissed close to Hans's ear.

'Johannes?' Katarina gasped. *Of course he would be here.*

He squeezed her shoulder. 'I'm so sorry. It's a tragedy ... a terrible blow for you.'

She placed her hand over his. 'It happened at the wall behind the stables. That wall.'

He nodded. 'I'm so sorry,' he said again.

Hilda leaned forward to interrupt them. 'I don't know who you are, but we're Eduard Rota's closest relatives. This woman has no right to be in this pew. He had no daughter.'

Johannes sighed. 'Keep your voice down if you please. And of course he had a daughter. What nonsense is—'

Though less than average height, the woman drew herself up to the full extent of it before interrupting. '*Gräfin* von Cloy wrote to us.'

Johannes's eyes narrowed. 'Did she now.'

'He cut her off, don't you see. She no longer existed for him. Like she'd never been born. Don't you see?'

'Nonsense, woman,' he said again.

Had Katarina seen Giuseppe at that moment, she would have understood his humiliation at Johannes's intervention, and his acceptance that though it was his place to have done it, he did not have Johannes's uniformed authority. And how this knowledge felt like a kick in his gut. Before she could see it though, the great organ boomed into life with Tallis's *Ordinal* signifying the coffin was processing into the cathedral. Hans Rota moved along the bench shooing his wife and children before him to make room for Katarina and Giuseppe, his expression brooking no argument.

Katarina patted Johannes's hand and he moved back as she stepped into her place, staring ahead towards the altar, steeling herself for what she was about to witness.

Though a Requiem Mass was new to her, she quickly felt its potency as the incense, plainsong chants, and ringing of Sanctus bells rose to join the other scents and sounds collecting in the smoky haze above. The choral music expressed her grief in ways she could never have expected, though she knew her father would not have approved. Who had authorised it? It made no sense for a Calvinist to have such a funeral. Then she stopped questioning and abandoned herself to its power. For how could she object when the service soothed her heart flensed by the sight of his flag-draped coffin strewn with white lilies?

Finally, with the casket lifted onto pallbearers' shoulders once more, she took Giuseppe's arm to lead the mourners processing out behind the coffin. When it appeared that Hilda was pushing Hans to take their place ahead of Katarina,

Giuseppe blocked their way. Again, had she glanced at his face then, she would have seen a flicker of triumph that he had been able to assert himself in this small way.

Outside, carriages waited for those attending the burial and Katarina held back this time allowing her cousin and his family to take the first one alone. She had no desire to spend even the short ride to the garrison cemetery in their company. Instead, she and Giuseppe shared the next one with two junior officers, their wives dressed in black bombazine, none of whom she knew.

The open wound of a freshly dug grave amidst the rows of crosses came as a physical blow, making Katarina gasp. *I can't see him lowered into that darkness.* Hans and his wife had placed themselves beside the commandant and the other senior officers at the graveside, where the priest now kissed the cross on his stole before placing it around his shoulders, preparing to say the committal. The more junior officers and their wives were positioned further back, and it was with them that Katarina and Giuseppe chose to stand. She glanced around, searching for her cousin's boys and spotted them some distance away removing any flowers placed on the graves and scattering them.

She held tight to Giuseppe's arm and closed her eyes. Father Tommaso's voice began its drone while the sun, beating down on her black clothing, began to scorch her skin through the fabric, adding to the torture until at last, he spoke the final Latin words, 'And let perpetual light shine upon him, in the name of the Father, and the Son and the Holy Spirit.'

'Amen,' Katarina whispered with the other mourners.

'Go in the peace of Christ.'

'Thanks be to God,' Katarina murmured the last response already turning to Giuseppe. 'I can't see him put in his grave … I can't bear it. Can we leave now?' While the regimental standard was folded, ready to give to Hans, and Hilda clutched her bunch of lilies almost trembling with eagerness to be the first to throw them onto the coffin when it was lowered into the ground, Katarina moved away.

Giuseppe made a disparaging sound through his teeth at the sight of the pair of them, before walking beside Katarina towards the coaches waiting for those invited to *Palazzo Poli* for refreshments.

'Let's walk. It's not far across the fields.' Katarina raised her black parasol, and that together with the breeze more noticeable away from the crowd, cooled her at last. Once they were out of sight, she stopped. 'I think I need to weep now. I refused to do it in front of that wretched woman.'

'Oh, Kat.' He pulled her into his arms, the parasol dropping to the ground.

'I didn't want her to think I cried over the Will,' she gasped. 'Because she would. I know she would. And she would have revelled in it.'

Giuseppe held her, rubbing her back until she was able to collect herself again and he handed her his handkerchief. 'We can just go home, you know. You don't have to do the rest of it—'

'No. I must. I don't think I have a choice.' She retrieved her parasol, and they began to walk again. When the path took them past the wing which housed her father's apartment, Giuseppe halted beside the entrance doors. 'Do you want to go in?'

Katarina hesitated for a few moments. 'I think I do. One last time.'

The young servant girl who let them in, though obviously pleased to see Katarina, appeared uneasy. Katarina dismissing it as awkwardness about mentioning her father's death, led Giuseppe through to the morning parlour where her very first violin lesson had taken place. The room looked just as it always had, and she wondered why this would surprise her. Why would his passing have any impact on his home? She took Giuseppe's hand. 'Perhaps I should see if there's anything I still want in my bedchamber before the place is cleared for new occupants.'

'There might be something of your papà's, too?'

She nodded. 'We should look.'

Giuseppe walked beside her up the marble staircase, glancing at the vast paintings of battlefields and cavalry charges and beyond to the stone balustraded landing ahead. He followed her along a wide gallery until she hesitated for a moment outside ornately carved mahogany double doors.

The last time she had been inside this room was the day she left for Vienna when she had arranged a bowl of roses on his dresser. She had wished him to find them after she had gone with a note thanking him for all he had done for her. Thanking him for his unwavering love, too, and assuring him of hers.

She took a deep breath and opened the doors. That she stopped dead meant Giuseppe collided with her. 'What in the name of God do you think you're doing?'

She heard Giuseppe gasp his surprise taking in her cousin and his wife frozen in the act of rifling through draws and cabinets whilst their boys tussled on the satin-covered feather bed, hitting each other with pillows.

'Christ.'

Katarina took a stride into the chamber. 'I asked, what you're doing in here? You've no business touching my father's things.'

Again, it was Hilda who seemed to be in charge, putting her hands on her wide, black hips. 'Everything is coming to Hans.' She gestured around the room. 'All this is ours now.' She could not suppress her glee.

Giuseppe moved around Katarina to confront the woman. 'You've seen the Will then, have you?'

She took a small step away from him. 'No ... but we've been assured of its contents.' She lifted her chin ready to assert herself again. 'What's it to you?' Her lips curled in an unpleasant smile. 'Perhaps you're eager to find out whether it's still worth your while to marry her—'

'Hold your tongue, woman!' Hans cried. 'There's no need for such talk—'

Giuseppe laughed, putting his arm around Katarina's waist, and pulling her close, his eyes on Hilda still, his face a picture of scorn.

Katarina's hand flew to her mouth, the other gesturing towards a small silver candlestick decorated with tiny white enamel flowers she had just spotted amongst a heap of objects and small paintings on the dresser, larger ones stacked willy-nilly against it as though seized in haste. It had been her mother's. So, they had already ransacked her bedchamber. And now she noticed many other pilfered items. 'How dare you steal my things. You can't just—' She pointed at a silver-backed hairbrush. 'That's mine. Then two gowns deemed too plain for Vienna. 'Those are mine. What on earth can you plan to do with them?'

Hans placed his hand on Hilda's arm when she drew breath, ready to vent her spleen on Katarina. 'We've already explained. All Uncle Eduard's belongings will come to us. This is an opportunity to select what to take back to Vienna with us now.'

'You have no right to my belongings.'

'If they're here, we do,' Hilda spat. She tilted her head staring at Katarina, scornfully. 'If these things are that important, you would have taken them with you to Vienna, now wouldn't you?'

She had been told not to pack trinkets. Things that would look tawdry beside the grand artifacts displayed at Schloss von Cloy. And, in truth, the only thing she truly cared about here was the candlestick. She had no explanation for how it had been left behind. Yet why should she explain anything to this woman? She walked to the dresser and picked it up. 'You shall not have this. It belonged to my mother.'

Hilda made to snatch it away, but Katarina held it behind her back. Jesu, they were behaving like children in the schoolroom.

'It's valuable, isn't it? That's why you want it. Now you know you'll have nothing,' she jeered before pointing at Giuseppe. 'Nothing beyond what he can give you.'

Giuseppe moved behind Katarina to take the candlestick from her fingers. 'I'm sure your, cousin has no objection to you keeping a memento of your mother?' His eyes were on Hans.

'Go ahead, of course,' Hans said, quietly.

Giuseppe reached out for Katarina's hand. 'Come. We should join *your* guests in the *palazzo's* salon.'

Katarina nodded grateful he had emphasised 'your,' and followed him from the room. 'Thank you,' she said when the door closed behind them. 'I think I was about to kick her on the shins.'

Giuseppe laughed. 'I thought as much. And though the idea of seeing it was more than tempting, I thought best not for it would be something you might regret later.'

'Oh, I would, I'm sure, but might it not have been worth it?' She stopped outside the door to her old bedchamber. 'Let's find out what havoc they've wrought in here.' Inside though little was disturbed. There were two rather worn gowns and some drab undergarments flung onto the bed and the armoire doors hung wide, but otherwise everything seemed untouched. 'I wonder why she found my clothes so desirable?'

Giuseppe snorted. 'She surely can't imagine they might fit her?'

Katarina shrugged. 'Who knows with a woman like that.' She lifted the garments from the bed.

He moved behind her, putting his arms around her and pulling her back against him. 'So, this is where you used to sleep. I often tried to picture it.'

She leaned into him, considering the carved tester bed with its fancy, floral swags before turning inside his arms to look at him. 'Did you? I can't imagine why?'

He appeared a little sheepish. 'I wanted to think of you safe and snug ... that you slept well.'

She smiled wryly, thinking of all the nights she could not sleep for rather different thoughts of him.

He bent to kiss her neck and her body responded, desire flaring in an instant, the clothing she had collected dropping to the floor when they reached for each other, losing themselves until Katarina broke away, taking some moments to catch her breath. 'We must go.'

He caressed her face. 'We must.'

She bent to pick up the clothes again before gesturing to the armoire. 'I wonder if I should take some of these old gowns—'

'Why? You have all you need for now, and then you shall have new. You'll want for nothing, I promise you.'

'I'm sorry my father—'

He grasped her shoulders. 'Don't forget you still have a choice.'

Her eyes widened. 'What can you mean? I love you, Giuseppe. You know this. What possible choice do I have?'

He sighed. 'Come. We should get to the salon.'

Giuseppe and Katarina held glasses of *Vespolina* standing close to one of the tall windows looking down onto the parterre garden from the first-floor salon, though neither had taken food from the extravagant spread set out on trestle tables, where many guests were now loading their plates. He noticed the Rota cousin and his baggage of a wife talking with the grey-haired commandant whose navy uniform now dripped with gold frogging and lace. 'He looks rather less sombre now.' He nodded towards him and watched Katarina's gaze follow his direction.

She nodded. 'Dress uniform. I hope he's enjoying more conversation with those two.'

'Looks like he's sucking lemons, so perhaps not. Can't say I'm surprised.'

Katarina pointed. 'Look at the boys.' They were sitting under one of the tables cramming food into their mouths as though it were a competition. Pieces of sausage, cheese and bright fruit cascading down the front of their black satin coats and spreading out around them on the marble floor.

'Need their arses paddled, them two.'

At last, a small group were invited into the regimental hall's anti-room where the Will would be read. Giuseppe just wanted to be done with it. Katarina looked far too pale and was clearly holding herself together by sheer courage. He wished he could spare her the ordeal, but she was determined to face it.

Hans Rota and his family sat closest to the desk where a young *avoccato* sifted through papers to prepare, glancing up at the two rascals in stained coats pinching each other and appealing loudly to their mother to clout the other, while she threatened them both with a hiding if they did not stop. Hans somehow managed to ignore this commotion, which Giuseppe thought probably explained its occurrence.

Katarina had chosen seats along a side wall, sitting beside some of Eduard Rota's closest friends and colleagues she told him. They had all greeted her warmly, offering condolences and glancing at her cousin with undisguised hostility.

'He would have rescinded it, you know that,' said a silver-haired woman who had held Katarina with, what had appeared to him, a special tenderness. 'You were his pride and joy.' She turned and stared at him for a moment before looking at Katarina again. 'He would have forgiven you. The heart loves where the heart loves. He knew that better than most.' She glanced at Hans Rota and frowned. 'Marino Grimani couldn't bring himself to read this himself, so he sent this boy instead. I believe he thought it would demonstrate his contempt for it. He knew it wasn't what Eduard wanted in his heart and tried his utmost to dissuade him from it.'

At that moment Hilda Rota turned to stare at Katarina her expression an unpleasant mix of glee and hostility. Giuseppe scowled at her. 'Why's she giving you the evil eye? You barely know her.'

It was the woman beside Kat who answered. 'She's full of bitterness and jealousy. She knows what Eduard thought of her husband and what he felt about you, Katarina. You were his princess. That's why this is such a travesty.'

Katarina patted the woman's arm. 'Giuseppe, let me introduce Lilli Schneider. Her husband, Joseph, is the regimental physician. They are ... were Father's closest friends.' She pointed across the room. 'He's there with the commandant. This is Giuseppe Guarneri, Lilli.'

Lilli leaned in to kiss his cheek. 'I know who you are, young man.' She chuckled. 'He's a pretty one, I'll give you that.'

The young *avoccato* rang a small bell to get the room's attention. *Could the lad not call for quiet in such a small space?* Giuseppe decided he was a milksop and did not change his opinion when he began to speak in a hesitant, reedy voice. The preliminaries seemed to consist of legalise about the legitimacy of the document before itemising some small bequests.

Once again, he realised how momentous his decision to go with Gianni to Vienna had been. How it had changed Katarina's life, for without it she would now be the wife of a wealthy man and likely about to inherit wealth of her own. And he would have lived a half-life without her and never known it.

'I cannot help wondering if this would have happened had I remained in Vienna,' Katarina whispered. 'Would he have returned to Cremona quite so soon?'

'You mustn't think like that,' Lilli said.

Was this something else to blame himself for? He could not bear to think Kat would take this on herself.

The *avoccato* cleared his throat. 'And now to the main beneficiaries.'

Hilda was smiling openly, and Giuseppe could understand why Kat had wanted to kick her earlier. Her father was dead, and this woman could not wait to benefit from it. Hans, though, had the decency to at least appear sombre. Giuseppe watched Katarina while the lawyer spoke, listing all that now belonged to Hans Rota, remembering how she had told them of her father's contempt for him and that he had only provided for him because of a promise made to his brother.

Katarina showed no emotion, her jaw clenched, and he understood what that must be costing her. When the reading was concluded and the *avoccato* began packing away his papers in a leather satchel, Giuseppe saw a slow smile spread across Hans's face and the unashamed triumph on his wife's, he grasped Katarina's hand. 'We should go home,' he said softly.

She stood, her back to her cousin. 'Yes, but I must say farewell to Father's friends first.'

He followed her shaking hands after she had hugged, noticing her straight back, the tilt of her chin, and the goodwill all these people felt towards her, his heart swelling with pride. He tried to imagine being in such circumstances himself and behaving so, and simply could not.

As they made their way downstairs to the *palazzo's* entrance, rounding the curve in the stairway they stopped, for the Rotas were striding into the hall towards the great doors, their children running around the circular space shrieking and aiming pretend kicks at the statuary that lined it. They both stepped back, so they were hidden on the stairs until the hall was silent.

'They must have been in our … the apartment again—'

'Do you want a last look?'

'No. I'm done here.'

Now the reality of her new life would become all too apparent, and he could not shake off his anxiety. His home would be hers. Did she truly understand how different this life would be from the one she had known before? Would she tire of it and grow to resent him because of what she had lost? Did she love him enough not to?

Second Movement

THE VIOLIN MAKER'S WIFE

Sixteen

CREMONA, JULY 1722

FOR THE SECOND TIME IN HER LIFE, KATARINA awakened to a wedding day, and it was a singular realisation. How could she not think of Johannes? She had hurt him because she did not love him. Lilli was right, the heart loves where the heart loves, but if Giuseppe had not arrived when he did, might she have come to love him? She would never know.

Nonna Barb slept beside her, tiny and frail-looking in sleep, her wrinkled cheeks hollow and whisps of white hair escaping from her nightcap. This would be the last time they shared this bed, for tonight Giuseppe would take her place. Her body tingled at the thought of it for there had been little opportunity for intimacy between them in the days leading up to this one.

'You look happy, little chick.'

She had not noticed the old woman wake. 'I am. It's my wedding day.' She giggled a little, embarrassed at the excitement so obvious in her voice.

'We'll help you get ready. Andrea will have gone with Giuseppe to the Stradivari's by now. Anja is bringing a special breakfast. We're going to spoil you, chick, you'll see.'

Anja had been to the food market as soon as it opened and

bought the finest prosciutto and hot spiced rolls dusted with icing sugar and was already in the kitchen when Katarina arrived downstairs. Just as plates were being set out on the table, Merla appeared through the garden gate carrying a covered skillet. She placed it down on a wooden board on the table, removing the lid to reveal a steaming frittata heavy with tomatoes, burrata and covered with chopped basil, its scent filling the room.

'Sit.' Nonna Barb, her hand on Katarina's shoulder, gently pushed her down onto a chair where her plate was quickly loaded with frittata and prosciutto. Bread was brought out of the oven with a dish of green olive oil placed beside it.

Katarina had not thought herself hungry, excitement bubbled too insistently, but surprised herself by clearing her plate with ease and finding room for spiced rolls besides. She watched these women sitting at the table with her, laughing together and enjoying this feast of a breakfast, washed down with dishes of strong coffee sweetened with honey from Merla's hives. And her heart swelled with affection for them and gratitude that they had done this for her. While breakfasts at the *schloss* might have been more sumptuous none had been made especially for her.

When the last morsel was eaten, the women sat back sighing their satisfaction before Nonna Barb rose to her feet. 'Now you go with Merla who'll wash your hair and attempt to make you even more beautiful, which is impossible in my opinion.'

The sounds of agreement from the others made Katarina smile. Whatever she was, it was not beautiful.

'Anja and I will press your gown and make you a crown of flowers. Now off you go, little chick.'

Katarina happily abandoned herself to Merla ministrations. A bathtub was filled for her out on the terrace shaded by a vine covered awning. Merla had strewn the water with herbs and flower petals. 'Will Giuseppe be bathed and perfumed like this for me?'

Merla laughed. 'More likely filled with wine.' She used a jug to pour water over Katarina's hair before soaping it and rinsing off. 'You have such lovely hair.'

Katarina laughed. 'It's ordinary hair, which is fitting for it matches the rest of me.' How could Merla compliment her hair when her own was a spectacular cloak of blue-black hanging to her waist.

'It's the colour of conkers and just as shiny. How can you not see it? Giuseppe does.'

'He's spoken of it?' How disconcerting to think of them talking about her. 'What else has he said?'

Merla smiled but did not answer right away, instead standing and holding out a towel for Katarina to indicate she should get out of the tub. 'He said he's besotted with you.'

'As I am with him,' she said wrapping the towel around her, suddenly finding her nakedness uncomfortable under Merla's scrutiny, thinking of such conversations with Giuseppe.

'He's always cared about you.'

She nodded. As a sort of sister, she had thought for a long time. She sat on a stool while Merla brushed her hair. 'We were friends.'

'Friendship that leads to love is best for a good marriage.'

'Johannes ... he was my friend. It didn't stop me hurting him. I—'

Merla squeezed her shoulder. 'What choice did you have?' She gave the shoulder a little shake. 'Don't think of it now, Kat.'

She turned to look up at Merla. 'I know Giuseppe thinks too much about what I've given up for him. It worries him.'

'Once you're married, he'll accept it and then forget it.' She began to brush Katarina's hair again, blotting it on a towel as she did so. 'Do you feel different today than you did when you were about to marry Johannes?'

Katarina giggled behind her hand. 'I do. So much. I can't wait to be Giuseppe's wife. I was anxious about marrying Johannes ... about being part of his family ... whether I was good enough for them.'

Merla smoothed Katarina's hair with her fingers. 'There.' She reached into her basket then and lifted out a small, corked pot. When she knelt in front of Katarina to open it, the scent of jasmine filled the air and she lifted Katarina's hand, rubbing the unguent into her skin. Katarina closed her eyes, enjoying she feel of the cool lotion and the gentle caress of Merla's fingers. 'This should overpower the scent of Giuseppe's wine-sotted body, I would think.' She sighed her pleasure.

'Indeed it should.'

Katarina sighed again. 'We should get back to Nonna Barb.'

'If you're ready.' Merla stood and went inside returning with an embroidered silk shift in palest green.

Katarina saw it was not from her trousseau. 'This is exquisite. Where did it come from?' She touched the fine embroidery depicting spring flowers around the hem and neck before pulling it on.

'I made it for you.'

Katarina hugged her. 'It's wonderful, Merla. Thank you.' She hugged her again. 'It feels wrong to wear my old gown over such a beautiful thing.'

The day slipped away until by mid-afternoon, Katarina was finally washed, polished, and dressed in her wedding gown with a crown of flowers placed upon her head. The gown, though not as fine as the peach satin she had worn the first time, was one of the loveliest from her trousseaux, mint-green silk taffeta with tiny pink flowers embroidered on the bodice.

Nonna had already left to go to San Domenico Basilica where the marriage Mass was to be said, Anja and Merla would walk with her there. The three women paused in the shade outside the shop with its shutters closed for the rest of the day, a notice on the door telling customers there was a family wedding that afternoon. The church bell was ringing, summoning the congregation.

Katarina turned to face her friends, reaching out for each of their hands. 'Thank you for everything.' Her eyes brimmed with tears.

'Don't you dare cry, you daft mare,' Anja cried. 'You'll wreck the galena around your eyes. You'll get rivers of black down your cheeks. Not a good look for a wedding.'

Katarina laughed, blinking them back. 'Come. Dr Schneider will be waiting for me.' He had said he would be honoured to give her away. Would her father have done it had he lived? The two women hooked their arms through hers and together they made the short walk to the church, Katarina's heart thudding and swooping like a bird trying to escape its cage of bones.

She closed her eyes for a moment on stepping inside, though sunlight through stained glass flooded jewel-like colours across the interior, and banks of candles illuminated every shadowed corner, it was still gloomy compared to the dazzle outside. Joseph Schneider tightened his hold on her arm and patted her hand before starting down the aisle to where she would join Giuseppe, through clouds of smoky incense, massed choral voices and violins.

She lifted her eyes to gaze at him. How fine he looked. A moss green satin coat embroidered with golden ferns along the front edges and cuffs. Black silk breeches and stockings. Gold buckled shoes. They smiled at each other when she left Joseph to move to his side before the altar. Soon they were kneeling side-by-side at prie-dieus. Standing and kneeling to the sound of

Father Paulo's Latin words broken by the tinkle of Sanctus bells once again rising in echoes to a distant shadowy ceiling.

Then it was done, and it was time for Katarina to return up the aisle on Giuseppe's arm, a wife. Later, she found she had only a hazy memory of the words of the Mass, though she had understood them, which was more than many in the congregation. They travelled in an open carriage bedecked with flowers to Antonio Stradivari's home where the wedding feast would be held. Though his house was also in Piazza San Domenico, he had offered it to them because of its much larger garden. How generous he was, for the carriage, too, belonged to him.

In that garden behind his house, tables had been arranged in a line with crystal candelabras hung from iron stands arching over them already glittering with candles. This long table was laid with porcelain plates, silver cutlery and crystal glassware sparkling under their light, and along the centre were arrangements of pink flowers and pale green foliage. Even in the still fading daylight the effect was magical.

Whilst the isle community provided the food, Antonio offered cooking facilities for those who wished to use them, though most brought platters from home. Unlike the other feasts Katarina had attended in Cremona, this time there was a planned menu with families agreeing which course they would be responsible for, while others baked bread and provided jugs of ale and wine.

Katarina's eyes widened looking at it all, overwhelmed by people's generosity. She squeezed Giuseppe's hand as they stood together holding glasses of wine surveying the gleaming table. 'They think so much of you.'

'No, this is for you. To welcome you to the isle. They want you to feel one of us.'

Once again, she blinked back tears. Could this really be so?

Soon they were called to take their places at the table surrounded by family and friends. Nonna Barb was sad that

Pietro had not come. Though Giuseppe blamed it on the short notice they had given him, Katarina could not help thinking he would have managed the journey had he truly wished to. He was making his name as a luthier in Venice now, though Andrea failed to show interest … or even a smidgin of pride. She wished they would reconcile, knowing now the price that could be exacted for such a failure.

The food here was very different to that served at the Schloss von Cloy. *Ravioli di magro, casoncelli, marubini* in broth, *polenta* and *bruscitti, altomilanese,* fried pike and carp, *risottos*. Platters heaped with vegetables, tomatoes, and breads. Dishes of olive oil. Deserts of *frittelle, turòon* and *baci di Cremona,* and *spongarda* another speciality of the city.

After the plates were cleared, several men began to play on a variety of stringed instruments – depending on their forte as makers – and the dancing began. Now darkness had fallen, the chandeliers over the tables were augmented by candles in coloured globes suspended from the trees surrounding the area set aside for dancing.

Katarina was leaving the floor on Gianni's arm when she spotted Sancia Estes. 'What's she doing here?' The girl was dressed in a flimsy gown that clung to her ample curves. In truth, she looked in danger of spilling out of it. The colour seemed to match her skin tone making her appear almost naked. Why on earth would she wish to look like that? To look so … cheap.

Gianni followed her gaze. 'Ah. It's a tradition here that anyone who hasn't been invited to a wedding might come later for the dancing providing they bring wine or ale.'

Katarina noticed there were now quite a few additional guests. 'Well, I can't say I'm pleased to see *her*.'

Gianni pulled her close. 'No. If you want my advice, keep away from her.'

'I intend to, believe me.'

After returning to the table to sit beside Giuseppe, she drained her wine glass and leaned in close to her new husband who was in avid conversation with Ricardo Amati about violin construction. Ricardo adamant that f-holes should not be altered, or C-bouts extended, Giuseppe vehemently disagreeing. She rested her head on his shoulder and ceased to listen after a while for these were arguments she had heard many times before. So, when Joseph Schneider, resplendent in his gold bedecked dress uniform, a silver sword gleaming at his side, tapped her on the shoulder and requested a dance, she accepted eagerly. And he was a good dancer, even on the rough boards placed over rather uneven ground. She wondered if he had ever danced in the open air before. When the music ended, they both clapped enthusiastically.

Joseph leaned in towards her ear. 'Your father would have been so proud of you today … to see his beautiful daughter so happy.'

'I hope he would. I know this marriage wasn't what he wanted for me—'

'More than anything, he wanted your happiness, and he would have seen it today.'

She nodded, still a little uncertain. 'I'm not sure what he would have thought of the Mass though. I did wonder, too, who had authorised a Requiem Mass for him when he was such a staunch Calvinist.'

'I did.'

Katarina gaped at him. 'I don't understand.'

'He never told you?'

'Told me what?'

'Your father was brought up a Catholic. The Rotas are a Catholic family. Teresa was the Calvinist. Eduard converted so her father would allow their marriage and agreed you would be brought up in that faith.' He cleared his throat, appearing a little sheepish. 'I took the liberty of having a quiet word with Father Paulo at San Domenico's, explaining the situation hoping it may ease any concerns he might have about performing a Catholic ceremony.'

She gave him a quick hug. 'I had no idea.' Had her father done the same with the von Cloys? She'd had some instruction from the priest there, but he had been very amenable.

Joseph patted her hand. 'It's time I returned you to your husband.'

Katarina smiled. Her husband. She tested the sound of it in her head and found she liked it very much indeed. As they approached Giuseppe, she saw he was now in deep conversation with several young luthiers and when Joseph left her with a formal bow, she watched them for a few moments before wondering away towards the trees at the end of the garden. And realising she was alone for the first time that day, she moved deeper under the branches until the voices and music faded. She took some deep breaths, enjoying the scent of cooling vegetation and earth. And she was grateful for this solitary time to think of all she had learnt from Joseph Schnyder. Looking back at the illuminated garden was like looking into a fairy tale to see the fairy realm itself. She spun around then, startled by the sound of footsteps behind her. 'Sancia!'

'Katarina.' Sancia looked her up and down in the moonlight, making this appraisal obvious. 'I'm surprised he went through with it. You know, after the Will and all—'

Katarina turned on her heel and began to walk back but Sancia lunged to grab her arm, digging her fingernails painfully into Katarina's flesh. She tried to pull away. 'Take your hands off me.'

'He asked me to marry him, you know. We were going to marry until you—'

'I don't believe you.'

'He came to my bed and said we would be married, so I gave myself to him—'

'You're lying.'

Sancia stamped her foot. 'I don't care what you believe. 'He was going to marry me, and you've stolen him from me ... you ... you bitch.' She gestured towards Katarina. 'Why, though? Why when there'll be no money now?' She tilted her head. 'And you looking like a kid.'

'Because he loves me.' Katarina tried to walk away once more, but again Sancia caught hold of her. 'Do you know about Merla?'

Her eyes were wild, and Katarina was suddenly afraid. 'What are you talking about now? More nonsense, I'm sure.'

Sancia's smile was cruel. 'She's been bedding him for years. Broke him in she did when he were just a lad and kept him begging for it ever since.'

'Merla?' Katarina whispered.

Sancia grinned. 'Think he'll give that up for this?' She gestured towards Katarina and began to laugh. 'He likes a bit of flesh. What do you think we've got in common Merla and me?'

'Well, certainly not intellect.' At last, Katarina was able to escape from her and stumbled deeper into the trees, trying to make sense of what Sancia had told her. Giuseppe had asked Sancia to marry him? Had been Merla's lover for years? How could these horrors be true? She wanted to get away, unable to face seeing either of them. And then anger surged through her in an icy spate.

She halted for a few moments trying to calm herself. Desperate now to leave the garden without being seen, she followed the wall to find a gate out into the back lane. And after some time, often stumbling over the uneven ground in deep shadow where moonlight could not penetrate, she found one and grasped the handle. It did not move. 'Damn it to hell,' she muttered, pulling again with all her strength until it gave suddenly with a rusty screech, landing her on her backside. She sat up rubbing her elbows, which had hit the ground, and scrambled to her feet.

Once out in the lane, moonlight lit her way and she was soon able to find the entrance into the nearby Guarneri back yard where she flung herself down on a bench at the wooden table, resting her head down on her folded arms. And there she wept ... and wept. But no one can weep forever and eventually she raised her head, drying her face on the hems of her petticoats, left then with an emptied out, shaky feeling after a bout of crying. Cleansed somehow, like a dusty street after a thunderstorm. She stood meaning to go to the well to fetch a cup of water when the gate opened, and she found herself face-to-face with Giuseppe carrying a candle lantern.

He halted, shocked by the sight of her. Her eyes red, her face blotched from weeping. Jesus Christ, what had he done to her? He should have given her more time before they married. More time to be certain it was what she truly wanted. *And it isn't, is it? She realises it now.* It felt like a physical blow to his gut. *This is it. She'll leave me.* He took some long breaths trying to calm himself before placing his lantern down onto the table and pulling her to him, stroked her damp hair back from her face. It was then he spotted the flower crown on the ground beside her feet. 'Oh, Kat.' He moved her away so he could see her face. 'Shall we end this here?' How could those words leave his lips? They made him shudder.

'What can you mean?' she answered, her voice hoarse from weeping.

His heart thudded. 'If we stop now, the marriage can still be annulled—'

She pulled away, clearly incredulous. 'You wish you hadn't married me?

'What?' He searched her face, confused, his heart pounding still. 'How can you say that? I love you. I want us to be married more than anything, but it's different for you. It's harder for you to—'

'Is it all true?'

Her interruption made no sense ... until it did. Sancia. 'Oh, Christ.' He sat at the table and covered his face with his hands.

She lowered herself onto the bench, watching him over the glow of the lantern. 'You were going to marry Sancia ... that fat trollop?'

His hands dropped. '*What*? No! Is that what she told you?'

'You asked her to marry you, so she allowed you into her bed.'

He barked an unpleasant laugh. 'You think Sancia Estes needs a marriage proposal to take a man to her bed?' Christ, she had just called the woman a trollop.

'Why in the name of God would you want *that* bed?'

He closed his eyes. 'I ... er. I don't know what to say.' What could he say? She was a body. A willing body. Why would he turn her down? He had no one then. When he was a blind fool. So mindless of what had nearly been lost.

Her lip curled contemptuously. 'When you could have gone to Merla's instead.'

'Oh, fuck'.

'How could you? And neither of you ever told me.'

He took a long breath. 'Look, I'm not going to deny Merla. I was a pity fuck the first time.' How could Katarina understand any of it?

'How many other Cremona boys did she take pity on, I wonder?'

He had once asked her that and she had laughed at him. 'You really think that of her?'

She stood, clutching her head. 'I don't know what I think.'

He looked up at her. 'We *can* end this you know ... if you want to. You can go back to Johannes. He'll still have you.'

She dropped down so she was sitting on the ground, her head bowed, tears flowing again. 'I love you,' she whispered. And then he was kneeling before her taking her face in his hands and kissing her until he felt her swept away by desire.

The bedchamber had been decorated with roses and lilies flooding it with their scent, though they barely noticed it in the moonlight as clothes were shed between kisses and caresses. Until standing naked together beside a garlanded bedpost, Giuseppe took a step back to look at his wife silvered by moonlight. With her hair a silken cloak around her, she was a tiny fairy princess. He cupped her face. 'I love you, Kat.' And then they were on the featherbed, their desire burgeoning and fierce until he moved over her, sensing she was ready, but when her body tensed and she cried out, he froze. 'I've hurt you. Christ. I hurt you.' He rolled away.

'What ... what's wrong?' she gasped, bewildered.

He moved up on an elbow to look down at her. 'It hurt you. I wasn't expecting it. It threw me. I'm sorry. I—'

'You didn't know it might hurt me the first time?' she said, incredulous.

His heart sank. How would he explain to her that he thought she and Johannes had been lovers. He had a bad feeling she was not going to understand ... or be happy about it. Fuck. He closed his eyes for a moment. Well, there was nothing for it. 'I thought Johannes would have taken you to his bed.'

She frowned. 'You thought I'd been with him?' Her frown deepened. 'So, you thought me guilty of immorality? A women must wait for marriage whereas a man can dive into any bed ... any trollop he wishes.'

He stroked her face, trying to smooth away the frown with his thumb. Its presence gave him a queasy feeling in the pit of his stomach. 'I don't think that way.'

'I still don't understand. You thought my maidenhead gone, yet you didn't try to bed me? It makes no sense.'

'I wanted you to be able to go back to him if you wished to. You would have only been with him still, don't you see?'

'But what difference would it make?'

'You wouldn't have to lie.'

She laughed. 'So, Johannes wouldn't have me back if I'd been sullied by you? Like a dog marking its territory.'

'No.' He fought to keep impatience out of his voice. 'If you didn't lie and got with child, he'd wonder if it was his. That's what I mean.'

She rolled towards him, pressing her body against his. 'None of this matters because I have no intention of going back to him. I love you. How many times must I tell you?'

He moved over her again, kissing her. 'Good, because I would have to kill him if you had. You do know that.'

She laughed against his lips. 'It really is dogs pissing.'

Katarina stood at the window, gazing out at the early morning. The trees had gathered the last of the darkness into their branches and terracotta pantiles glowed like small fires. She turned to gaze at Giuseppe, sleeping still, his limbs flung wide, and studied his naked form. She had never seen him like this, of course. She longed to touch him, to run her hands over his chest and down his belly until her fingers came to rest on his cock and feel its eager jump into her hand. She resisted, wanting to explore these feeling, bask in them, and enjoy their spectacular newness. They had become one in a way she could never have imagined.

Her body felt different, too, as though it had come into its own. A woman's body. She felt a little sore between her legs, her face and lips hot like sunburn from his lips and the dark stubble she could now see on his face. Yet languid from those explosions of exquisite pleasure. She moved to the bed, standing over him now her burgeoning desire competing with a wish to let him sleep when he looked so peaceful.

Her dilemma was resolved when his eyes slowly opened, and he stretched his limbs, grinning at the sight of her watching him. 'How long have you been up?' He reached for her hand and pulled her down, so she lay on top of him.

She kissed him and ran her fingers over his stubble. 'Hours,' she lied, her eyes dancing.

He felt the place on the pillow beside him where her head had rested. 'I don't think so. It's still warm.' He ran his hands over her before moving her onto her back, his kisses moving down her body smiling when she gasped as he parted her thighs and then she abandoned herself to him completely.

Later, outside at the terrace table where she had wept the night before, they ate undercooked eggs with stale bread and grapes freshly picked from the vines above them.

Giuseppe cleaned his plate with a heal of bread. 'I'm not much of a cook, I'm afraid.'

'I must learn. Nonna Barb and Anja can teach me.'

He squeezed her hand. 'I'm sorry.'

She pulled her hand away, vexed suddenly. 'This must stop now, Giuseppe. I've made my choice. I'm your wife and I'll do anything and everything that goes with that. I can learn and I shall. I—' Silenced by the sound of the gate opening behind her, she looked over her shoulder and it took her a few moments to recognise the young woman, for she was seeing her somewhere she should not be. 'Chiara? What on earth are you doing here?'

Chiara performed an exaggerated curtsy with a wide grin on

her face. 'Madonna. Himself sent me to you. I think I'm your wedding gift.'

Katarina dashed across the yard to seize Chiara in a tight hug. 'Johannes sent you here?' She grabbed Chiara's hand and pulled her over to Giuseppe who has risen to his feet. 'This is my husband.' She giggled. 'And that's the first time I've ever said that to anyone.'

Chiara bobbed a curtsy to Giuseppe and looked him up and down unashamedly, clearly appreciating what she saw. Then she noticed Katarina's half-eaten, and now congealed, dish of eggs and picked up her spoon to taste it. 'Gawd, save us. Did you cook this shit, Madonna?'

'That was me,' Giuseppe said. 'My nonna usually cooks. She'll be back soon.'

'Well, now she's got me to 'elp her, ain't she?'

What would Nonna Barb make of that? It was her kitchen. Would she resent Chiara's presence? 'I thought you were a lady's maid?' Not that they needed one of those either. And where would she sleep? There was only Pietro's old truckle bed in the room that would now be Nonna's. If they did not get on, sharing a room would be a nightmare. Katarina looked at Giuseppe who shrugged slightly. She imagined he had all the same misgivings.

'Lady's maid? Pah. I started in the kitchens like everyone else. I were bloody good, too.' Then Chiara smiled sweetly at Giuseppe. (Was she really fluttering her eyelashes?) 'My boxes is outside in the lane, *Signore*. Might you fetch 'em in for me?'

When Giuseppe had retrieved her assortment of bags and boxes, there was nothing for it but to take it all up to Nonna's new bedchamber. Katarina knew Johannes had meant well but what would Chiara do all day? The three of them stood in the entrance to the small attic room, which now seemed to be full of Chiara's luggage. The room's one saving grace was the large window – the whole attic space had originally been one long drying room for varnished instruments with a window at both gable ends – Giuseppe wove his way through to open the casement wide.

He stood there for a moment his hair blowing in the breeze. 'They're here.'

Giuseppe had not been surprised one jot that Nonna Barb and Chiara got on like a house on fire. Why had Kat ever doubted it? With Anja often there with them too, the kitchen became a place of constant chatter and laughter, and his wife was able to take a cautious place beside him and his papà in the workshop, which was where she longed to be. And, at last, Andrea seemed to accept her there. That she was now a Guarneri helped, he imagined.

So, one night in the privacy of their bed, when she had raised the possibility of trying her hand at making violins for children (and drowsy and sated, he had smiled a slow smile realising how carefully she had chosen her moment).

When he had passed this on to his papà the next morning, Andrea had found no real objection, other than that her expected failure would be a waste of good wood. 'T'will keep her content until her belly swells.' Giuseppe had nodded his agreement, as his papà expected him to, though he doubted it would be so, for his wife was set on becoming a luthier and he suspected not even motherhood would divert her for long.

Some days later, when Kat was engrossed in bending small ribs around a hot iron form, Gianni Gabrieli arrived in the workshop and stood behind her for a few moments. 'You really *do* know what you're doing, don't you?'

'I hope so.' She leaned closer to Giuseppe sitting at the workbench beside her. 'I've had a good teacher.'

Gianni tapped Giuseppe on the shoulder. 'Have you a few minutes? I've something I want you to see.'

Giuseppe glanced at Katarina. 'Will you be alright?' A foolish question seeing how expertly she worked.

She raised her eyebrows. 'Of course, my love.'

Outside the shop, Gianni turned to him. 'Will her instruments be accepted? A woman has never tried to become a luthier before.'

'We'll cross that bridge when we get to it. Now, what's this about, Gianni? I'm busy too, you know.'

'You'll see.'

They walked on in silence crossing the San Domenico concourse and turning left around the curved wall of the Rosary Chapel until Giuseppe realised they were heading towards Becharie Vecchie. 'Why are we going to your place?'

'We're not.' He halted outside the shop next door to his. 'We're going here.'

Giuseppe knew the building had belonged to an elderly luthier who had died some months before, leaving it empty ever since. 'You're going to expand? I didn't know you did enough business to need all this extra space?' Gianni wasn't really a fully committed luthier, Mia's family money left him free to pursue other interests too, which included a small winery, and much of what Andrea called pervert galivanting with Claudio Rugeri.

Gianni smiled sheepishly. 'You're right, I don't need it … but you do.' He pulled the key from his pocket and opened the door.

Giuseppe did not follow him inside. 'I can't afford this, Gianni, much as I wish I could. So, there's little point me coming in.'

'It's already yours.'

Giuseppe gaped at him. 'Are you mad?'

'It belongs to you and Kat. I can show you the deeds.'

Giuseppe narrowed his eyes. 'What the fuck is going on—'

'It's a wedding present.' Gianni tried to smile and gave up with a sigh. 'I was going to tell you it was from me.' He shrugged. 'But you'd never believe it. Mia indulges me but buying property for friends would be a step too far, even for her.'

At last, Giuseppe crossed the threshold into the gloomy boarded-up shop. The ware-counter and shelves were thick with dust but looked solid. 'Is this some sort of joke, Gianni, because if it is, it's not bloody funny—'

'It's the truth, you have my word. This place belongs to you and Katarina.' He reached into his coat and pulled out a roll of documents tied with a faded red ribbon. 'Take a look for yourself.'

Giuseppe took the papers but did not untie the ribbon. He had a sinking feeling in his gut he already knew who had bought the place. 'Tell me who paid for it?'

Gianni held his gaze. 'Johannes Horak.'

'Fuck! I knew it. Well, he can stuff it. We won't have charity from him. You tell him that.'

Gianni grabbed him by the upper arms. 'Think. This is somewhere for you and Kat to live … space for a family. You can set up your own workshop. Christ, man. Why would you turn it down?'

'Because he needs to keep out of our lives.' He closed his eyes for a moment, trying to control his wild anger. 'Katarina is my wife. I'll provide for her. Why should she be beholden to him? Why the fuck should I?'

Gianni ran his finger along the counter, studying the track it left and wiping the dust on his breeches. 'Don't tell her, then. Say I bought it, and you'll pay me rent.' He looked up and met Giuseppe's gaze. 'Horak didn't want either of you to know.'

Could that be true? 'Lie to her?' And if he did, who would the lie really be for? To prevent her knowing Johannes had helped them, or that he had accepted it? Following Gianni through to the workshop – bigger than his father's – and on around the living space spread over two upper floors, he knew he could not turn it down. Yes, he wanted that workshop where he could follow his own ideas without his papà's constant criticism. They could live here free from all the mithering that living with his family brought with it. And they would have Chiara who had shown herself to be a fine cook. This had obviously been part of Horak's plan all along, using his wealth to pull Giuseppe's strings just because he could. Confident that he would not turn him down. The fucker.

He sighed looking out over the garden that boasted its own small almond orchard and a pair of lemon trees before turning to take in the size of the drying attic with its big gable end windows. 'Will you give me your word that Katarina will never know?' *How can I be saying such a thing?* 'And I want the same from him. If he won't give it, then he can bugger off.' He tried to find some gratitude in his heart but simply could not. His face burned with shame.

'You have my word. And it was Horak who suggested I should claim to be the owner, so he's sure to agree—'

'In that case, don't tell him otherwise.' At least this way the man would not know of his humiliation. For that was what it was. He wanted this home for Katarina. A home he could never give her without this ... this fucking charity from his rival. And worst of all, he was prepared to lie to save face. He had never liked himself less.

Katarina, of course, was overjoyed by the move. Spending her days with Anja and Chiara cleaning and furnishing, until the place gleamed and pretty curtains hung beside the window shutters. The luthiers had been generous gifting them furniture, Antonio Stradivari most of all, donating a fine, carved tester bedstead and feather mattress.

Giuseppe was grateful that she did not think to ask him what rent they must pay to Gianni, so never questioned how they would afford it for such things were unknown to her. That Gianni and even Mia had been drawn into this deceit pricked his conscience, too. Kat was happy though, and that was all he could ever want. What did the circumstances matter anyway? She was happy.

Seventeen

CREMONA, JUNE 1725

Katarina stared at the ceiling cracks in dawn light from the un-shuttered window, turning shapes into faces, flowers, running dogs; all familiar yet somehow ever-changing, aware of a vague disquiet. *Something's not right.* She looked at the empty bed beside her. Giuseppe was gone but it could not be that for she knew where he was and why.

He had journeyed to Milan to see the bishop hoping to win a contract to supply Lombardy churches with violins. This had been put out to tender because the synod believed they were overpaying, and even the backwater churches were demanding instruments now. Giuseppe was confident of winning one because Cremona was the luthier centre of Lombardy and, for their quality, his were the best value. And with a little prettifying from her, they looked little different to those made in workshops with a more traditional approach to appearance. He was expected back later today.

She moved a hand over the great dome of her belly. This child was due any day now, which had made Giuseppe reluctant to leave her, though she had insisted he must. That contract would be a real feather in his cap and a boost for his workshop and now he had two apprentices, he would not find the extra work too onerous. It was time to rise for she could hear Chiara already moving around in the kitchen. Yet still, she slid her hand back and forth, humming to her child as she often did when alone. This child, some of the other wives had told her, would never come while she did men's work. How wrong they were, though it had taken a long time, she could not deny that. (And all that time she had seen Sancia Estes or da Sala as she now was, on her husband's arm carrying a boy she knew to be Giuseppe's.)

Something's not right. Her eyes flew wide. The child was not moving. She tried to remember when she had last felt it. She sat up. *Nothing.* It slept that was all. Surely this had happened before without her noticing. She was being foolish. Yet she wished Giuseppe were here to reassure her. She picked up a shawl and wrapped it around herself, before making her way down the twisting staircase to find Chiara taking the bread from the oven.

She took one look at Katarina and frowned. 'What's wrong, Madonna? You're pale as milk. Sit down, I'll cut you a slab of this.'

Katarina sat. 'I'm not hungry.'

The maid brought her a cup of water. 'Are you having pains. Is—'

'No. I ... I. She rested her head down onto her arms on the table and began to weep. *Something's not right.*

Chiara bent to put her arms around Katarina. 'Whatever is it? You must tell me, Madonna. Shall I fetch Merla?'

'Yes,' Katarina said without lifting her head. 'Get Merla. I need her. I'm afraid, Chiara. Fetch her, please.' *Wake up. Wake up. Please wake up, little one,* she said over and over to herself, so it seemed but moments before Merla bustled in through the door from the backyard.

'What's all this, Katarina? Sit up now and tell me what's the matter. Is there blood? I promise you such a thing is nothing to be scared about. It's quite normal when a child is so close.'

She sat up and fixed her eyes on the older woman. Merla would make it all right. Merla always did. 'I can't feel her move. I haven't felt her move for—' She shook her head, more tears falling. 'I can't remember when.'

Merla picked up a towel and dried Katarina's face. 'Stop this now. It means the child will soon come. They often become still before the birthing begins. It's truly nothing to get alarmed about.'

And, as though to prove Merla right, the first pain gripped her belly like the tightening of an iron band around her. She gasped and clutched herself before reaching out for Merla's hand and clutching that. 'Yes, yes. You're right. Of course you are.'

Merla squeezed her hand. 'So, stop worrying, yes?'

'What must I do, now?'

Merla laughed. 'Now you wait. Have some bread. Then do whatever feels right. Walk if you wish. Lie down and sleep if you can.'

Katarina clutched her belly again. 'How could anyone sleep through this?' Then her waters broke.

She woke with a start when Giuseppe sat beside her on the bed, and his arms were quickly around her.

'My poor, Kat. Is it very bad?'

She groaned, nodding, as another pain gripped her, hard. How had she slept? She had a vague memory of Merla giving her a bitter drink. The pain had become part of her dreams always there yet making no sense. Dark dreams of imprisonment and abandonment, calling for help, her voice echoing, weeping because she was alone. 'I was alone, Giuseppe.' The light seemed all wrong. How could shafts of evening sun be hitting the rooves across the street? It made no sense. She groaned again as another pain held her in its cruel vice. 'Oh, sweet Jesu, it hurts. It hurts.'

Giuseppe's arms tightened around her. 'I'm here now. You're not alone anymore.'

'I was dreaming.' She took some deep breaths waiting for the next assault.

'I got one, Kat. They gave me a contract.'

She smiled and gripped his arm. 'I'm so pleas—' Pain seized her again, making her pant. She was barely aware of the door opening and Giuseppe being swept away.

'Out you go now. There's nothing you can do but be in the way.'

Was that Merla's voice? No. Hands were upon her then. Horrible. Probing. Not Merla. Unkind hands.

'Wench be ready. Help me get her to the chair.'

'Chair?' *What chair?* 'Leave me be. I can't.'

The unkind hands had an unkind voice. 'Just do as you is told, lass.'

She blinked the tears from her eyes to clear her vision. 'Merla! Help me.'

It was Chiara's face that loomed now. 'It's all right, Madonna. It's just a birthing chair, nothing to be afeared of—'

'Madonna?' said the unkind voice. 'Who's you calling Madonna, girl? Ain't no Madonna here. This one's just a plain wife ready to drop a babby like all the rest.'

Somehow Katarina managed to draw a deep breath. 'Get that woman out of my house and her goddamn chair with her!' The words rushed from her on one expelled breath.

Now Anja's face appeared. 'She's Ma Nesta, the midwife. Barb sent for her.'

Katarina curled up on her side, and trying to speak, she could only make strangled animal sounds, hardly able to believe they came from her. 'Merla,' she managed to gasp at last.

'Chiara's gone downstairs for her. Ma Nesta sent her out of the room.'

Now the unkind voice had a face. A pig's face. Broad and pink with upturned nostrils. 'I won't work with that witch in the same room as I. If she be in here, I shall not be.'

'Good.' Katarina was impressed she had managed to speak. And quite emphatically, too. Though when she tried to repeat it there was nothing there but a weak groan. She closed her eyes. *Make it stop.*

Hands were on her again. Gentle hands. 'Merla.'

'You need to push now, Katarina. You must get the child out. It's time.' She gripped Katarina's arm. 'Chiara take her other arm. We'll get her up against the pillows.'

A cloth damp with cool water was dabbed on her face and neck and somehow, with their help, she managed to drag herself back until she sat upright.

'When the next pain comes you must push, Katarina.'

So, that is what she did. Soon moving down onto the floor where she could kneel and hold onto the bedframe. She pushed and panted. Pushed and panted until, at last, her child came with a rush down into Merla's hands. 'My child. Give me my child.' But Merla moved away, and Anja and Chiara helped back onto the bed, washing her and dressing her in a clean shift. 'Give me my child.'

'Merla is tending to her,' Anja said, not meeting her eyes.

'But she's all right, isn't she? Katarina grabbed at Anja's hand. 'She *is* all right?' *Oh, sweet Jesus, I haven't heard her cry?'* She looked from one to the other. 'Tell me!'

They moved away to allow Merla to come to the bedside. She held the child wrapped in a woollen shawl. 'Your daughter.' She closed her eyes for a moment. 'Katarina, you daughter has gone to God.'

'No. No. Not true. Give her to me. Give me my child.' *Not true. Not true. Not true …*

Merla placed the small bundle into Katarina's arms and turned to Chiara. 'Fetch Giuseppe.' The older woman pushed back the shawl from the child's head so Katarina could see her clearly. 'I'm so sorry. She never took a breath. The cord was around her neck. Nothing could be done for her.'

Thick dark hair. Blue eyes. Katarina stared into those beautiful unseeing eyes and felt something terrifying beginning to open inside her. Something capable of destroying her, and she fought it with all her strength as tears washed down her face. *I'm so sorry.* Merla's words echoed through her mind over and over. *I'm so sorry.* She did not hear the door open or see Giuseppe come to stand looking down at her holding their child. She did not see the tears on his face or Merla beside him holding his hand. It was only when he startled her by sitting beside her that she looked at him. 'Forgive me. I'm so sorry.'

Merla moved closer. 'You're not to blame, Kat. This happens. It's no one's fault.' She crossed herself. 'She's with God now.'

'Not purgatory?' Memories of the Schloss von Cloy priest telling her of that awful place arrived unbidden. She had imagined it as cold and swathed in grey mist. A desolate place. She could not bear to think of her child alone there.

'No, no. Not purgatory. She's with God, Katarina. I promise you.'

How could Merla be certain? *In truth, she is only here. This is all there will ever be of her. I know this.*

Giuseppe touched his daughter's cheek with his fingertips. 'She's so beautiful,' he whispered.

'I'm so sorry I couldn't keep her safe.' Her voice trembled.

He swiped away his own tears before pulling her close. 'No, Kat. Like Merla said, there's no blame in this.' His eyes moved to the cradle already there in the corner. 'Only sorrow, which we must find a way to bear.'

'Teresa.' She dragged her eyes away to look at him. 'She'll be in our hearts always.' *I should not have chosen my mother's name. A dead woman's name. She died in childbed. Now my child has died.*

Merla arrived beside the bed once more. Katarina had not been aware she had left. She spoke to Giuseppe. 'The priest is here. Shall I send him up?'

Katarina tightened her arms around her child. 'No, no. Not yet. I can't let her go yet.'

'You can still hold her. He'll pray over her—'

'Why, if she's already with God?' She rocked the child in her arms. *This is all I'll ever have of her.*

The priest was there suddenly. *How?* But the old man looked kind and spoke his prayers softly. Though she understood the Latin words, she did not register them but found his voice soothing ... and the pungent scent of the oil he used to sign a cross on Teresa's forehead. She jumped when he placed his hand gently upon her head. *Have I slept?*

'You should rest now, child, knowing your little one is safe with Our Lord.'

Giuseppe stirred and rose to his feet. 'Thank you for coming, Father. I'll see you out.'

Merla watched them go before returning to Katarina with a cup. 'Drink this now. It'll help you sleep.'

Katarina shook her head. 'Was it because I sent the midwife away? Tears fell again. *How can there be any left to shed?* 'Because I wouldn't sit in her chair?' (She would believe it in some dark corner of her mind for the rest of her life.)

'Don't ever think such a thing. You did nothing to cause this.' She patted Katarina's hand. 'I'll move her now and lay her in her cradle for a while so you can sleep.'

Katarina allowed her to lift the tiny bundle. 'I'll never hold her again, will I? What'll happen to her now?'

'There'll be a funeral. You'll have that, never fear.'

Katarina took the cup and swallowed the bitter liquid, ready for the oblivion she hoped it would bring. A funeral? Why would Merla make such a point of telling her that? *I don't want a funeral. I want my child.*

The days before the service at San Domenico's were vague, as though Katarina were not present in them. She had hoped to find comfort in the Requiem Mass, as she had at her father's, but instead felt only more of this distance as though she watched it all through the wrong end of a spyglass. The tiny coffin was unreal. How could her child be inside? It was easier to feel she had never existed, and this ritual was some sort of mad delusion. That Giuseppe stood beside her in the echoing space was just part of it. There were few mourners, though she did not acknowledge those who were there. She did not even look at them. Why should she when none of it was real?

It had started on the morning after the birth, when she awoke fuzzy and confused after Merla's medicine, and it was easier to decide it had never happened than to face such unspeakable loss. Even though her body told her that it had in blood and leaking milk, she let Merla dose her with potions and balms without allowing her mind to touch the reason why she needed them. No one spoke of the child, though when she asked Giuseppe if she must attend the Mass, he had looked so appalled she quickly claimed to have misspoken and had meant might she be excused the gathering afterwards.

Her black gown was tight so must be worn with laces loosened, the gap covered with a cape too warm for the day's heat. Sweat gathered uncomfortably beneath her breasts, tight and heavy, leaking redundant milk. The Mass washed over her, unheard. Even Giuseppe's grief did not penetrate her isolation, though he shook while he wept. Her mind was already back in her bedchamber where she could strip off her thick clothing and slip between cool sheets. Where she could find the oblivion of sleep.

. . .

Giuseppe did not tell Katarina that Merla had lied to the priest
to make sure of Christian burial for their daughter, telling him
the child had lived for some minutes after she was born which
meant she would have a soul – *She had a name yet no soul. How
could that be?* – and so must have a Requiem Mass. In truth, she
never took a breath and Merla believed she had died some time
before her birth. Katarina had worried she had not felt her move
he now knew, though he had not spoken of that either. He was
too afraid of the depth of her grief, of somehow making it
worse, for that surely lay behind her strange detachment. Yet
was never speaking of their child at all, best for her? He wished
he knew. Should he help her face their loss or leave her to come
to terms with it in her own way?

He sighed, knowing he would do nothing. His own grief was
hard enough to bear. And it was easier to throw himself into his
work, starting on the church commission, and leave Katarina to
rest in her bedchamber. And it was her bedchamber now, for he
had moved into a small room at the back of the house where he
would not disturb her.

Eighteen

CREMONA, NOVEMBER 1725

WHEN GIUSEPPE THOUGHT ABOUT IT WHICH, IN truth, he tried not to, he wondered just how it had happened. Katarina now spent all her time on household matters, never coming to the workshop. And she had stopped playing her violin. Had she played it at all since the birth? Yet, while she carried the child, he had never known her to play so much. He knew he should try to do something. That he should try to reach her in some way, but could not think how to begin, so instead retreated further into his work, despising himself for it.

So, one morning in late November, when he was about to show his younger apprentice how to make violin ribs by bending wood around a heated iron form and Katarina appeared in the doorway from the house, he froze, desperate not to do anything to make her baulk. Instinctively, he behaved as though it were nothing unusual.

'Don't be afraid of the heat, Angelo. The wood will absorb it.' She moved to take it from him and showed him how to hold it against the heated bar. 'It warms your hands nicely even through gloves on a frosty morning like this.'

Giuseppe showed no surprise. He wanted her to stay,

knowing any fuss would send her scurrying back into the house. 'I don't suppose you've time to help him with that while I get Guido marking up a scroll outline.' When she turned to look at him, he shrugged and turned away, though he wanted to cheer when she began to speak to Angelo again, running through the steps needed for forming and attaching the ribs.

When the bell sounded telling him there was a customer in the shop, he went through himself as he was the only one not in the middle of a process. 'Fuck,' he said under his breath when he saw who had come in. 'What do you want?'

Sancia smiled sweetly. 'That's not a very nice greeting, now, is it?' She looked down at the child whose hand she held. 'Say good morning to Uncle Giuseppe, Luca.'

The boy parroted his mother's words, his eyes flitting around the small shop with its shelves filled with wooden boxes of rosin, strings, pegs and peg dope, horsehair for bows, and other bits and pieces needed by players of stringed instruments. There was also a rack of assorted instruments. Violins. Violas. Cellos.

'I'm not his uncle.'

Sancia's eyes sparkled with glee. 'No. I think everyone sees that.'

The child pointed. 'Who she?'

Giuseppe spun around to see Kat standing behind him. 'Fuck,' he said under his breath for the second time.

Sancia ruffled her son's dark curls. 'Katarina, how are you? I haven't seen you since you lost your child. How ever do you get over something like that? You must be hoping to get another soon, though.' She tried to look sympathetic and failed.

Katarina turned and walked away. Giuseppe watched her go through the workshop and back into the house before returning his attention to Sancia in time to catch the triumph on her face. She really was an evil bitch. He took a breath. And there she was with his child. And the sight of him tore at his heart. 'What can I do for you, Sancia?' He was certain she'd already had more than she could ever have hoped for.

She was about to reply when the shop door opened and Gianni and Claudio walked in, laughing, though their smiles fell away seeing her. Giuseppe watched them exchange a quick glance before Claudio greeted Sancia and engaged her in conversation, asking after Luca.

'Is everything all right? Gianni said, quietly.

Giuseppe gestured towards the workshop, and they stepped inside. 'Could you wait in here? I need to find Kat.'

'She saw Sancia and the lad?'

Giuseppe nodded. 'Her first time in the workshop since we lost … since.' He took a breath. 'Damn that woman. It's almost as if she knew,' he hissed, conscious of the boys at their benches. 'Lads, Gianni's here, if you have any problems. I won't be long.' He moved into the house without looking back. Unsurprisingly, there was no sign of Kat in the kitchen parlour. Nor in the kitchen. Chiara was stirring a pot on the fire shelf and had not seen her.

He ran up the stairs, and with a perfunctory tap on the door, went into his wife's bedchamber. She was standing at the window, looking out over the street. 'Has she gone? She turned. 'Has she? I haven't seen her go.'

'I don't know. I left her with Claudio.' He moved to her slipping his arm around her waist, noticing immediately how thin she had become, and trying to remember the last time he had touched her. Christ, he had no idea what to say. 'Will you come down again. Come to the workshop. I need your help with the church violins. Please, Kat.'

She turned away from the window. 'There's no doubt about the boy is there? He's yours. It's there for everyone to see.'

He sighed. Why had they never spoken of it? Perhaps it was time for a little more honesty. 'I didn't intend to get a child off her. I—'

'*Really?* So that makes it all right then, does it?'

'No. I'm not saying that. Of course I'm not.' He was floundering. 'It didn't mean anything with her. I felt nothing for her.'

'It meant a child.'

'I love you, Kat. We love each other. But neither of us knew it then.'

She covered her face with her hands. 'It's wicked. It's wicked to wish that boy had died, and Teresa had lived. God forgive me. How can I think such an evil thing? I can't bear myself. But why should that … that creature be a mother when I am not?'

He gently eased her hands away and then pulled her close. 'You're too hard on yourself.' Her words frightened him. He needed to get her back from the dark place where she had hidden herself all these months. How had he not known? 'Teresa's gone and we'll never forget her, but there'll be others. You know there will.'

She raised her head to look at him. To trust him. 'Yes. Yes, you're right, of course you are.'

'And you must stop blaming yourself.'

She nodded. 'I know. I do know. And I'll try.' She gasped a sharp breath. 'You have my word.'

When he bent to kiss her, he felt the tension gradually leave her as she began to respond. Why in the name of Christ had they stopped touching each other? And then he had to have her. He burned to have her, and walking her backwards until she was pressed against the wall, he lifted her skirts to touch her, arousing her until he knew she burned for him, too.

There was no decision to move to the bed, they just found themselves there and clothes were frantically shed beneath the pile of quilts, for there was no fire lit in the chamber at that time of day. He moved the covers away briefly to look at her when his hands moved over her ribs, realising afresh how thin she had become.

'Oh, Kat. Look at you.'

THE VIOLIN MAKER'S WIFE

She pulled the quilts over herself again. 'I don't think you mean that as a compliment, do you? I—'

He silenced her by placing his mouth over hers and groaned when her hand closed around him. And then, finally, they found each other again.

Katarina followed him downstairs and into the workshop, hoping the sound of their lovemaking had not been overheard. Gianni sat beside Angelo helping him to carve the back of his violin where he would later glue the ribs he had now shaped. That the boys did not look up, told her they had not been as silent as they had imagined.

Gianni stood and kissed Katarina on both cheeks. 'You've two good lads here. Quick learners both of them. Not that I'm much of a teacher, but you two must be.'

'Giuseppe's the teacher. I'm just another of his pupils.' She smiled at him and then caught Gianni's eyes on her and saw his pleasure that she seemed more herself. It had not occurred to her when she had been so mired in her own pain, how worried her friends must have been for her. How had she found herself again? Sancia and her child had been the catalyst. And then Giuseppe had fetched her back with his body ... and the realisation that there really could be another child, and finding she could contemplate it without feeling she betrayed the daughter she had lost.

Nineteen

CREMONA, SEPTEMBER 1726

GIUSEPPE HANDED OVER THE CHURCH COMMISSION TO Katarina with some relief when other patrons placed orders, though he had baulked at her placing her own labels inside the instruments for the church authorities would not believe a woman could have made them and would only be confused or even angered by it.

Katarina was not surprised but had made them anyway (KATARINA GUARNERIA FECIT CREMONE ANNO 1726) and even glued one inside an instrument from time to time. When this provoked no complaints from the Milan diocese, she could only imagine they had not been noticed, though she did not tell Giuseppe. She rather thought he would have notions of it being her duty to obey him in all things (for had she not vowed such before God?) which would only lead to unnecessary arguments. And it was not the time for those.

In September, when the annual Santa Cecilia feast day came around again – this time to be hosted by the Amati – Katarina dreaded it. Though, as usual, she had not been asked to cook for it – for which the other guests should be extremely grateful she always thought – that task had once more gone to Chiara, and between them, she and Anja had done them proud yet again.

No, what she feared were the questions. Why was there still no child in her belly? Surely it was time to leave her lost daughter in the past and move on. Only hinted at gently, but implied, nonetheless.

What she could not tell them was that her need for another child had become all-consuming, so much so that lovemaking had become a trial, leaving her feigning her climax so that Giuseppe would take his own. Yet still there was no child. And each time her courses came she wept bitter tears over that dreaded pain and blood.

How could she tell her friends and neighbours such a thing? (She could not explain why she had not told Chiara or Anja and especially not Merla about it, but somehow her pride had become involved ... and Anja had five children so it seemed something she would not understand.) They would think her barren, for Giuseppe had a healthy son with that woman. She could not bear the humiliation of it. And that seemed somehow shameful.

On the day of the feast, Katarina steeled herself to enter Francesco Amati's garden on Giuseppe's arm. She had not told him of her feelings, though when she fixed a smile upon her face before he opened the gate, he gave her a curious look but did not comment. She had a reply ready for when the inevitable questions began. 'We're not thinking about that yet.'

She could not help remembering the first time she had come to one of these occasions celebrating the patron saint of musicians and luthiers. It had been the first time she really understood the close-knit nature of the luthiers' isle community. That she and Giuseppe would play their violins together later had become a tradition and practising for this had brought her back to playing again, making her realise just how much she had missed it. But first, the feast had to be negotiated. Friends soon gathered round to greet them, and cups of punch were put into their hands.

'How are you now, Katarina?' asked Maria Amati, Francesco's daughter-in-law.

At twenty-two already the mother of three and, by the look of her, well on the way to producing number four. Katarina caught her assessing her own slender shape with a slight frown.

'You look well.'

No, I don't. 'Thank you, Maria. I'm much better.' She glanced at Giuseppe's retreating back. Why had he abandoned her, damn him? Maria stroked her large belly. *Maybe she's just fat?*

'Let's hope you'll get with child again soon then. I'm sure Giuseppe must be praying for it.'

Well, that was more direct than I expected. It was then that she found sudden inspiration. *Praying.* These people were all good Catholics, were they not? 'That's in God's hands.'

When Maria nodded sympathetically, Katarina excused herself and slipped away, stifling the desire to laugh. And each time the topic was raised again, she answered in the same way, smiling and grateful for such an easy way out.

With that realisation she felt able to relax and start enjoying the evening, abandoning herself to strong punch and good food and when the time came to take to the small stage with Giuseppe, she knew she had never played better, so much so that he stepped back playing only to support her performance just as he had done that first time.

'I didn't think I'd see you shine again,' he said close to her ear so she could hear above rapturous applause as they took their bows.

Katarina laughed, remembering how he had said she glowed with a light seeming to flow from her the first time she had played on this tiny stage. Too much punch and light reflecting from the many candle lamps strung around the structure. They parted company when they left the dais, swept away by friends and then onto the dance floor, Katarina with Gianni, then Claudio and their host Francesco. She saw Giuseppe dance with Maria Amati before losing sight of him. After some time when he had still not appeared back on the floor, she went to look for him. First inside the house, thronged with women wrapping what was left of the food and loading it onto marble slabs in the still room, ready for the next day's picnic.

Men not dancing, were relaxing at tables drinking and smoking their pipes, though she quickly established that Giuseppe was not amongst them. When she asked if anyone had seen him, Ricardo Amati told her he had noticed him going towards the orchard with Merla earlier, gesturing into the darkness beneath the trees. *Merla?* What in God's name was he doing with Merla? She refused to contemplate the obvious. Not that. Never that. They had spoken of it not long after she had learned of their history, and she had accepted that liaison was finished for good.

But it was not without trepidation that she followed the path until she saw a small glow through the foliage ahead, seeming to waver as leaves trembled in the warm breeze. Was this them? Moving towards the light, she saw her husband seated on a stone bench beneath a sweet chestnut tree with Merla beside him. She stepped closer, still hidden in the shadows, until she could hear their conversation.

'You should say all this to Katarina, not to me,' Merla said.

Shadows flitted across Giuseppe's face from the flickering candle lamp on the ground in front of them. 'How? How can I say that to her?'

When a twig snapped beneath her foot and they both looked towards her startled by the sound, she backed away into deeper shadow and then retraced her steps. What might it be that he could say to Merla and not to her? The whole thing filled her with a sort of vague disquiet, and she decided it was time to leave for home, so after retrieving her violin and saying a few hurried farewells, she made her way back alone.

There was light showing in Gianni's bedchamber, and she imagined him there with Mia. Her own house, though, was in darkness with Chiara and the lads still at the feast. And Giuseppe would not be home for some time anyway as he always helped with the preparation for next day's picnic.

Sometime later, she was aware of him climbing into bed beside her and blowing out his candle, though she pretended to sleep. She would speak to Merla first. Her heart began to pound when she thought of them as the lovers they had once been. Merla was her friend, but she had that intimate history with Giuseppe. Would she betray his confidence? There was only one way to find out.

The next day dawned fair, with the sun just beginning to burn off the mist blanketing the rice fields as the cart rattled along the rutted track towards the river. Katarina sat beside Giuseppe on the driver's bench while he held the pony's reins loosely in his fingers. It knew the route as well as he did. If he had noticed how taciturn she was that morning, he had not remarked upon it. Perhaps he thought her tired and even a little hungover after the night before?

The picnic was laid out as it was each year and the fire lit for the fish the men would soon catch when the sun heated the air and insects rose over the water. Watching Giuseppe go with the others down to the sandy beach all carrying their rods, Katarina made her way over to Merla. 'I need to talk to you.' Glancing at the other women close by, she lowered her voice. 'In private.'

Merla looked up with a frown and nodded, placing the last of the linen-wrapped platters onto the trestle tables set-up in readiness. 'Very well. Shall we walk?'

Katarina gestured to the path away from the beach and led the way along it beneath the trees. When she reached a small clearing, she turned to face her friend. 'I saw you with Giuseppe last night. You said he must tell me what he'd just told you.'

Merla sighed. 'And so he should.'

'He won't though, will he? You know he won't. It's why he spoke to you.' She reached out and seized Merla's hands. 'Please tell me what it was about.' She chewed her lip. 'Is it me? I know I'd pushed him away last year, but things have been better between us ... I've tried ...' Was it because there is still no child? 'Please, Merla.'

Merla closed her eyes for a moment. 'If I tell you, you must give me your word you'll talk to him. Tell him I said you must talk to each other. Do I have your word, Kat?'

She sighed impatiently. 'I promise. Now what did he say?'

'We should sit.' Merla pointed to a mossy hillock. 'He told me how desperate you are for another child. About your despair when it doesn't happen.' She lifted Katarina's hand, giving it a soft squeeze. 'He's finding it hard to bear. He wants you to stop hoping for it.'

Katarina's eyes widened. '*What*? Stop hoping for it? He wants *me* to stop hoping for it? Doesn't he hope for it, too?'

'Of course he does, Kat.' She searched Katarina's face, her own full of sympathy. 'But he thinks you need to accept things as they are. He says you tell people another child is in God's hands when they ask. He wishes you could accept that yourself.'

Katarina leapt to her feet. '*How dare he*! What God might this be? The one who took my child?' She shook her head. 'I see it now. He just wants me to keep it all to myself. Let him take his pleasure and not burden him with my feelings.'

Merla stood too. 'Does that really sound like Giuseppe to you?'

Katarina covered her face with her hands. 'No,' she said softly before dropping them to her sides. 'I don't understand, Merla.'

'Talk to him.'

'All right. I will. When we get home tonight, I'll talk to him.'

Giuseppe turned with his hand raised ready to wave, watching Katarina sitting between Anja and Carlo on the driving bench of their pony cart and wondered why she did not turn to wave to him, his own hand falling to his side.

Gianni stood beside him. 'She doesn't seem very happy today.'

'I think she's tired after last night.' Giuseppe thought nothing of the sort. He was puzzled by her behaviour when they had been so close the evening before playing their violins together. He tried to think if he might have done something to upset her but could find nothing. 'Where's Mia?'

'Claudio's taken her home.'

What a strange relationship the three of them had. Mia appeared to have no objection to Claudio's constant presence in their lives.

Gianni grinned. 'What? What's that face about? Something odd about that, is there?'

'No. But you must admit it's … well, a bit unusual.'

Gianni shrugged still smiling. 'So, it's unusual. So what?'

Giuseppe lifted a tabletop into the wagon. It wasn't any of his business, he knew, but feeling peeved that Gianni seemed able to handle two relationships when he appeared unable to manage one, he found himself saying more than he should. 'Doesn't Mia object to Claudio … er, taking up so much of your time?' Gianni's unflagging good humour was up to the task, though.

'Why would she? She's fond of him and so are the children. We're a family together, you could say.'

Why did this irk him further? Even the luthier community seemed to have turned a blind eye to Gianni and Claudio, most folk probably echoing his papà's remarks about pervert galivanting but, like him, never making an issue of it. 'Not sure Katarina would be so tolerant.' He glanced at Gianni and realised he was staring at him, quizzically. 'What?'

'You're not happy.' He frowned a little. 'Kat's not happy. Do you want to tell me what your fight was about?'

Giuseppe put down the trestle frames he had just picked up. 'There's been no fight. As I said, I think Kat's tired, is all.'

Gianni shrugged, grinning once more. 'Come, let's get this packed up so we can both go home.'

Giuseppe nodded and dropped the heavy trestles into the wagon bed.

After securing the cart in Gianni's yard, the men walked together to the rear gates of their homes, the lane in deep shadow as dusk slid away into full dark. Candlelight shone from many of Gianni's windows. Giuseppe's, though, were all in darkness. Their bedchamber was at the front, of course, and it seemed Katarina had already retired. Had she thought to leave him a night candle? He sighed. 'I'll give you a hand to take the tables to the store in the morning.'

Gianni gave his arm a squeeze. 'No need, Claudio will do it.'

And with that, they parted company. Once inside the kitchen parlour, Giuseppe found a small candle had been left for him, though it had burnt down to little more than a stub. Kat must have gone to bed soon after arriving home. 'Deal with it now,' he murmured to himself, knowing his resolve would be gone by morning. He found a fresh candle and lit it from the guttering stump before climbing the stairs to the bedchamber. He opened the door softly, finding the room in darkness and Katarina sleeping, though there was a tension about her that made him wonder if she truly was. He took a deep breath. 'Kat?'

She quickly turned onto her back to look at him. 'Jesu. What do you want? I was asleep.'

I don't think so. 'We need to talk.'

She moved onto her side again facing away from him. 'In the morning. We'll talk in the morning.'

He set the candle down on the cabinet beside the bed and lowered himself to sit beside her. 'I think it should be now.'

She moved to raise herself higher against the pillows. 'Very well, if we must,' she said, crossly. 'And what, pray, shall we talk of?'

His nostrils flared as he tried not to rise to the mockery in her voice. 'What's wrong? You seem angry with me. Have I offended you? Tell me what I've done.'

She gave him a dirty look. 'I don't appreciate you taking our private problems to Merla rather than talking to me about them. And talking about my feelings to her ... or what you believe are my feelings. If I'd wished to talk of it to her, I would have done so. Don't you see? None of this was yours to discuss.'

'Christ! Merla told you?'

'Only after I challenged her. I saw you together on that bench last night.'

He closed his eyes for a moment. She had taken him so completely by surprise that he had no notion of what to say to her.

She seemed to take pity on him then. 'I spoke to her today. She told me what you said.'

What could he say? How could he tell her he found it hard to make love when he so dreaded her misery when her courses came? 'I wanted her advice ... I feel I'm hurting you—'

'*Hurting me?* It hurts me when you talk to Merla. When you share private things with her.'

'Oh, Kat. I didn't know how to speak to you about it. You

want a child so much and it's causing you too much pain. Don't you think we should stop?' He watched as tears began to fall wetting her face and glittering in the candlelight.

'What?' she whispered.

'At least for a time. Wouldn't it be better?'

She swiped away tears with her fingers. 'What are you saying? How do we stop? You'll move to another chamber, will you? And that'll be better? You'll take your pleasure elsewhere, perhaps, if I am such a trial to you—'

Anger flared. 'You really think so little of me?' He stood and moved away to the un-shuttered window, staring out at the darkness. How could he tell her he found little pleasure in their coupling when for her it was nothing but a means to a child? How it had ceased to feel about love. He had not heard her bare feet on the boards so was startled when her hand arrived on his back.

'Forgive me. I didn't mean it.'

He turned and closed his arms around her, bending to rub his cheek against her hair. 'I can't bear to see how much you suffer. We have to find a way to end it. Can't you see that?'

'I want a child, Giuseppe. How can I stop wanting that?'

When he took a breath to speak, she placed a finger on his lips to silence him. 'Don't talk to me of God. How can I trust in your God who took my daughter from me.'

'She was my daughter, too.' He took a shuddering breath. 'And we will have another, I truly believe it will happen.' He moved his hands to cup her face. 'When it's meant to.'

'Perhaps I need to do the opposite. Maybe I need to believe it won't. Perhaps I need to accept I will never have a child, so I expect nothing only to cramp and bleed each month. So I never hope.'

He pulled her close again. How bleak she sounded. 'Please don't do that. Can't you accept and hope too?'

She gasped. 'I really don't think I can bear to.'

. . .

Katarina lay awake long after Giuseppe had lost himself in sleep. Though their lovemaking had been especially tender – she wondered when she had stopped noticing its absence – she needed time to think through all that had been said between them. She understood she must forget about becoming a mother if she were to move forward with her life. It had not occurred to her how her distress would affect him. She truly had become so mired in her own pain once more (had she learnt nothing?) that she had not thought of his. She made an effort to remember her life before this obsession had taken hold. Then it had been all about violins, of course. And so it must be again.

In the months that followed, Katarina matched Giuseppe's hours, working again on the instruments for the church and dutifully sticking his labels beneath the f-holes before the back and front of the instrument were clamped and glued together.

She was unaware, of course, that this had been discussed outside their workshop until one Sunday when she found herself alone outside the church after Giuseppe had returned inside to retrieve his hat. Maria Amati arrived in front of her as she scanned those flooding out through the San Domenico central entrance doors for a sight of her husband.

Katarina, how are you?'

Jesu, not this wretched ninny. And, dear God, it looks like she carries yet another child. She forced a smile. 'I'm well, Maria. As are you, I see.' She could not help hoping the woman really was just stout this time and would have to acknowledge it. Unsurprisingly, such a mean-spirited wish was not to be.

The woman caressed her belly. 'Yes. Number five, if you can believe it.' She frowned suddenly, an expression of almost comically insincere compassion on her face. 'I'm so sorry you're still not blessed yourself.' She reached to pat Katarina's arm. 'You know, if you spend all you time doing men's work, your womb will shrivel and never welcome a child. I'm surprised you don't know this, Katarina.'

Christ. Does she really think I haven't heard this nonsense before? 'Why thank you for that insight, I truly didn't know. I shall certainly bear it in mind now that I do.' She knew Maria would not realise her words dripped with sarcasm. *Where the hell are you, Giuseppe?* Spotting him at last, she turned back to Maria. 'Please excuse me, I must join my husband.' As she hurried to him weaving her way between parishioners gathered in small chattering groups, it occurred to her to wonder how Maria knew about her work as a luthier.

Giuseppe was always discreet about it for the Church must trust the provenance of the instruments delivered to them. The apprentices had been told not to talk of what happened in the workshop – as many apprentices and journeymen were – for each luthier's patrons and commissions were well-guarded secrets, as were any innovations practiced in a *maestro's* workshop, unless he chose to share any of it himself.

When they walked home arm-in-arm, Katarina told Giuseppe what Maria had said. 'Surely no one from our workshop has been talking about me?' She turned to look at him when he did not reply immediately, puzzled by his expression. 'What?'

'You don't think there's any truth in what she said about '

Katarina laughed uproariously. 'The woman is an imbecile. That's nothing but an old wives' tale.' She snorted derision. 'Why do so many of them seem designed to keep women in their place? To keep us in drudgery as unpaid servants to husbands and sons.' She was pleased to see a flush of colour on his face.

'I didn't really think ... I mean, I knew it was nonsense.' He cleared his throat. 'I'll look into it. It's a bugger Maria Amati spoke of it. That means the big families know.'

'How is it anyone's business but ours? What can they do, anyway?'

'Let's hope they won't be interested.'

The following day, Giuseppe questioned the apprentices and even Chiara about talking of Katarina's work to outsiders. (As a precaution, she always sat at the end of the workbench, not easily visible from the shop.) When all denied it, there seemed nothing more to be done.

So, later that same day, when Ricardo Amati arrived, Katarina understood immediately what had brought him. Giuseppe invited the unprepossessing man – all jowls and belly – into the parlour on the first floor and Katarina followed them upstairs. As this was surely about her, she would not be excluded from the conversation.

When she followed them into the room, Ricardo turned to her with a condescending smile. 'I would prefer to talk with Giuseppe alone if you don't mind, Katarina.' He turned to Giuseppe, expectantly.

'Yes, of course. Katarina, would you …' He made a small shooing gesture.

She fought hard not to argue when Giuseppe's expression conveyed she must not. Jesu, though, it did not come easily. She lowered her eyes and softened her voice. 'Very well, might I fetch refreshments, husband?'

Now she battled not to laugh at Giuseppe's astonishment.

Ricardo raised his hands. 'Not for me.'

Katarina fled the room before Giuseppe could answer, worried he would take advantage of her pretence at wifely subservience and request a glass of wine. Well, nothing had been said about eavesdropping, so that is what she did, standing outside the door with her ear pressed against it. And it was Giuseppe's voice she heard first.

'Do sit, please.' There was a brief silence while they both did so. 'Now, what can I do for you?'

Katarina pressed her ear harder against the wood. 'I'm sorry to have to raise this with you, Giuseppe. My father and the other grandees ... er.' He cleared his throat, plainly uncomfortable with what he had been sent to say. 'Look, Giuseppe. They're old and set in their ways.' A few moments of silence again.

Katarina smiled. Her husband was not going to make it easier for him. *Good.*

'They even disapprove of your innovations, which incidentally I admire. They think everything should stay as it's always been. And, well, it's been agreed that Katarina must not be involved in making instruments.'

'I see,' Giuseppe said.

Say something. Challenge him for God's sake.

'I know it's nonsense that she has been making complete instruments. Everyone agreed that would not be possible for a woman.' He laughed. 'Christ knows what such an instrument would sound like, eh, eh?' He cleared his throat again, his laughter dying away when Giuseppe did not join in.

Say something, Giuseppe.

When he finally spoke, his voice was almost too soft for her to hear. Did he suspect she was listening?

'So, if my wife wishes to help out with a little decorative purfling or to carve a scroll from time to time, I must forbid her from doing it?'

'Er ...'

Again, his discomfort was clear, even without seeing him, she could imagine him squirming. 'The consensus seems to be that your label is a contract promising the instrument is a product of your own hands—'

'So, my apprentices are not allowed to work on an instrument for me? In that case, what is the point of them?'

Ricardo laughed again though this time awkwardly. 'No. No, of course not. That's not a problem. We all use apprentices and journeymen to help our output, particularly on less valuable commissions. That's standard practice. Always has been.'

'Then it's just help from a woman that's not permitted?'

'That's about it, really. Can't think it'll make much difference to you really, will it? My wife seems to think she might fall with child more readily if she confines herself to more womanly pursuits, too. A woman who is not content with her lot can become a thorn in the side. A shrew, even, it's said.'

By whom? Your ninny of a wife? There was a sound of boots scuffing the floorboards as the men rose to their feet and Katarina made a dash for the door into the dining room, closing it softly behind her just as she heard the other open followed by footsteps on the stairs. She moved out to wait at the top of the staircase until Giuseppe arrived below and looked up at her.

'I take it you heard all that?'

'I did indeed.'

'Ricardo had been delegated by the families—'

'So I gathered. I was waiting for you to challenge him.'

'I've no intention of challenging them—'

'Now, why doesn't that surprise me.' She turned on her heel and moved into the parlour as Giuseppe pounded up the stairs after her. She stood facing him, hands on hips.

'Fuck, Katarina! Would you do me the courtesy of allowing me to finish?'

'Fuck, Giuseppe, perhaps I won't.' She enjoyed the look of shock on his face that she had used the same word he did. 'I'm sure it's a term often used by shrews … and men, of course. Men toss it into their conversations all the time. Some men.' Not Johannes though. She had never heard any such profanity from him.

'Katarina, I'll not challenge them any more than I'll heed them. The design changes I make have long been a bone of contention with the first families. Have you noticed me change what I do?'

She frowned.

'Have you?'

'All right. No, I haven't.' She sat on the sofa and Giuseppe sat beside her. 'So, I can still make violins?'

'Of course.' He grinned. 'How can I say no when they're so good? We'll just have to be more discreet about it.'

'Well, if we're certain no one here has talked, perhaps it's as simple as putting a door between the workshop and the shop to make certain I can't be seen?'

'Hmm. Can't harm.'

'We can fit a small window so we might see who comes in.'

'I'll get Angelo on it. He can go down to the timber yard.' He took her hand and gave it a squeeze. 'Happy now?'

'Why are men so afraid of women's abilities beyond domesticity? It makes no sense.'

'Maybe they fear women might outshine them given the chance.'

Katarina laughed. 'Is that what you fear?'

He grinned. 'No one's better than me, Kat.'

'True.'

After Giuseppe had returned to the workshop, Katarina joined Chiara in the kitchen parlour where she was chopping celery, onions, and carrots to make *soffrito*, the base for the pasta sauce that would be part of their dinner. 'What did that arsehole want, Madonna?'

Katarina snorted. 'I'm no longer allowed to make violins apparently ... not that they'd be any good if I did manage to make one. Weak and feeble as I am.'

'Pah. What a load of old bollocks. Bet yours is a damn sight better than anything he does. Have you seen how him and his hulking wife is the spitting image of each other with their round, sweaty faces and ginormous bellies? Has he grown his to match hers what's always got a brat in it?'

'I don't wish to contemplate either of them.'

With the door in place, Katarina returned to the workshop where she continued to make violins and violas, though any thought of using her own labels had been well and truly abandoned. That Giuseppe was happy for her to glue his into the instruments she was completely responsible for was quite a compliment when she came to think of it, especially as he examined them all thoroughly after each process was completed, and played them, too, at the end. Usually, they were hung on the storeroom racks without comment, some eliciting a nod and infrequently a 'good work.' She kept her face expressionless on such occasions, not wishing him to know how her heart turned summersaults with joy.

Third Movement

VENICE

Twenty

CREMONA, MARCH 1728

'HE DIDN'T BOTHER COMING TO OUR WEDDING, SO
why the hell should we bother going to his?'

Katarina sighed. Jesu, it was time the brothers healed the rift
between them once and for all. 'Come on, Giuseppe. He hadn't
time to travel from Venice with the notice we gave him.' Pietro
had invited his father too, of course, but she had little hope of
changing his mind on it.

'He hasn't been back here once in all these years. Not
once—'

'This is his wedding, and we have plenty of time to get
there.'

'Not in this weather.'

Katarina tutted. Another excuse. All right, Cremona was
gripped by cold winds with snow still lying in places, but the
river traffic was operating normally. Proved by a delivery of
wood just two days before.

'What if the thaw has already started in the Cottian Alps?
The Po could be in spate at any time, the journey down would
be damn dangerous then.'

. . .

Finally, sitting beside him in the workshop one chilly morning, hard cold light from the frost-streaked window silvering his stubble, Katarina tried a different tactic. 'I've never been to Venice. I'd love to see it. You can't tell me you don't feel the same?' He could not deny it. 'Let's take some instruments with us. Show the Venetians how superior ours are.' She knew appealing to his view that no stringed instruments in the whole of Italy came close to those made in Cremona would prove an irresistible temptation if anything would.

He turned to look at her, shaking his head but with a smile. 'Very well, you've persuaded me.'

'Good. He *is* your brother and it's time you resolved things properly with him.'

'Perhaps it's time he resolved things with *me?*' He tilted his head looking at her. 'But the main reason we'll go is so that I can show off my beautiful wife.'

There was muted laughter and some friendly jeering taken up along the other benches, which grew in volume when Katarina leaned across to plant a kiss on her husband's lips.

Though fond of Gianni and Claudio, Katarina was not entirely happy they would accompany them after Gianni received a wedding invitation too. (And why take Claudio and not Mia?) She worried the men's presence would intrude on the time the brothers might spend alone together but there was nothing to be done. Gianni had been a close friend of Pietro's, and some believed the rumours about them had hastened his move, even suggesting that Venice's more relaxed attitude to such things may have influenced his choice. Gianni, though, denied there had ever been such a relationship, and Giuseppe was certain his brother had gone there for its respected luthier community.

The four set out together in Gianni's coach to make the short journey to the city docks where they would board a raft boat used to transport goods along the length of the river east into the Adriatic. They would stop at ports where goods would be unloaded and more brought onboard. Casalmaggiore. Boretto. Ferrara. And smaller quays along the way served the river's hinterland, with Chioggia in the Adriatic the last stop before entering the Venetian lagoon. Passengers, too, would come and go though some remained until they reached Venice.

The early morning was cold with snow flurries in the air and Katarina pulled her fur-lined cloak tighter around her. Gianni had thought to provide hot bricks for their feet, which she knew would be difficult to leave behind. Giuseppe looked glum although the other two men were in high spirits.

'Why are we doing this?' Giuseppe asked no one in particular.

Katarina turned to him. 'Perhaps because your brother is getting married?'

'Or because Venice will be full of glorious entertainments?' Gianni suggested.

Giuseppe snorted his derision. 'That's if we don't all drown on the way?'

Katarina sighed. 'Do you really think all these merchants risk their goods on a boat that's unsafe? You were happy to use one to go to Milan a few years back to chase that church contract. You had to go through those narrow *navigli*, too. How can this be worse?'

'That was summer.'

Katarina tutted and turned away to gaze out of the window. They had arrived at the waterfront where many vessels were tied up along the wooden wharfs including barges and rafts of various sizes. The shallow drafted rafts were the ones most favoured to navigate the Po down as far as the sea as they were less vulnerable to the shifting sandbanks of the river delta. The *Regina del Fiume* had arrived the night before bringing spruce and maple down from Pavia to supply the luthiers amongst other cargo now being unloaded on pallets, winched off inside rope nets and lowered onto the quayside where handcarts and pony carts waited to receive them.

There were already a straggle of passengers gathered by the gangway waiting for this process to finish, so they might board the boat before the loading began. Katarina could not blame them for their eagerness to get out of the icy wind.

Inside their cramped cabin Giuseppe and Katarina found a single chair and a small cot tight up against a wooden partition in the deck superstructure. This stretched most of the raft's length and housed the handful of tiny cabins, an area of benches for those without one, the greater part given over to a cargo shed, with an open poling platform at the rear to steer, keeping them out of shallow water close to the bank and to navigate sandbanks. Though the raft relied largely on the river's flow for propulsion, sails were there when needed with masts fore and aft.

'Christ,' Giuseppe said, look around the cramped space. He pointed at the cot. 'How are we both supposed to fit in that? Remind me why are we doing this again?'

She put her arms around his waist. 'Don't you find it just a tiny bit romantic?'

'No,' he said emphatically.

Katarina sighed. He was determined to be miserable. 'Why don't we go out on deck? We can take the air and watch the scenery go by.'

He sat on the bed. '*What?* You want to freeze and watch a wall of impenetrable thicket? You must be out of your mind.'

Katarina collected her warm cloak from the peg where she had hung it and left the cabin without another word. She had to admit, he had a point for the air was indeed frigid and the bank she could see through the mist that clung to the water was covered with a grey tangle of bush. She stood holding the rail, hoping for something to see that would prove her husband wrong, breathing in the mineral scent of silty water and rotting vegetation.

She had to smile when the only break in the thicket revealed the wooden Calvinist chapel she had attended with her father as a child. From the water it appeared nothing more than a wooden hut with a small porch at the front and a plain cross attached to the gable end. It looked to be without windows, though she knew they were there covered by shutters.

Footsteps alerted her, just before Claudio arrived beside her. She pointed at the little church already behind them. 'I worshiped there as a child. It looks even sorrier from the river than it did when we arrived there through the fields.'

He tilted his head watching it disappear into the mist. 'It does look a touch desolate, doesn't it?'

'I never understood how God could want to be in there when there were all those beautiful churches and basilicas in the city.'

Claudio's presence suddenly awakened a memory of a hot summer's day, flinging her back to that first luthiers' picnic. She had believed herself in love with him until she found him with Gianni and realised he harboured no such feelings for her. She wondered if Gianni had ever told him she had seen them that day? She turned to look at him. He was certainly beautiful with his sleek, dark hair tied at his neck and his perfect features: large eyes full, wide mouth. Had she thought she loved him simply because of how he looked? Probably. How young she had been. 'I was thinking about my first river picnic.'

He looked down at her. 'It's hard to believe it's the same place, seeing it now.'

'I was rather taken with you that summer, you know.'

He looked genuinely surprised. 'Were you? I thought it was always Giuseppe.'

And, with a jolt of revelation, she understood that it always had been. However much she had denied it because she knew he did not feel the same way about her. It seemed no one had then.

He turned back to the desolate bank. 'I don't know why I'm doing this.'

'You sound like Giuseppe.'

'He's just apprehensive about seeing his brother face to face. It's a long time since they've been together. Only communicating by letter.' He shrugged. 'Well, it's easier to paint a better picture of one's life, isn't it? To paper over the cracks, if you see what I mean.'

Katarina was taken aback. What 'cracks' could he mean? 'I expect it will be awkward for both of them.' She tilted her head, studying him again. 'You really didn't want to come?'

'He thinks it would be good for me to have some different … company. That Venice is a place where I can relax and be myself.' He sighed. 'That I'm quite happy as I am seems of little importance. But Gianni always knows best,' he added with a shrug.

There was irony in his voice but also a sort of loving indulgence.

'Mia tried to tell him, but I think he listens to her even less than he does to me.'

'So, he's expecting you to … enjoy time with other men when you don't wish to.'

He frowned, appearing a little shocked. 'Forgive me, Kat. I shouldn't be speaking of this to you.'

'Just don't let him force you into something you don't want.'

'He answers that by saying how do I know what I want until I've tried it?'

'Well, there is that, I suppose.' Katarina clutched the rail as the raft seemed to lurch a little. Was she imagining the bank to be passing more quickly now? 'Are we moving faster?'

'I believe we are.' He barked a laugh. 'That'll teach me to

admit dreading our destination. Now it seems I must get there sooner.' He, too, reached for the rail.

They both turned to look behind the boat and saw what looked like a shallow wave approaching. Katarina gasped. 'Well, perhaps even sooner than that—' She stopped speaking as she felt the vessel lift before it raced along riding on top of the weight of water following the wave.

Claudio seized her around the waist holding on tight with one arm while holding the rail with his other hand. 'This is meltwater. Spring must have touched the *piedmont* before it's found us here.'

Other passengers came out on deck when they realised the raft was now speeding down the river, many holding onto the rail to make their way to the stern where the captain and some of the crew were ready to pole the vessel away from the bank should it be necessary. Katarina did not think they looked overly concerned; in fact, the opposite it seemed, for many were grinning. A quicker journey was obviously advantageous.

When Giuseppe arrived beside them, he appeared more cheerful too.

Claudio moved to let Giuseppe take his place holding Katarina. 'Don't tell me you're pleased to be getting to Venice earlier than expected?'

Giuseppe tightened his arm around her. 'I'm just grateful to get off the river sooner.'

'So, you don't think there's any danger?'

Gianni joined them before he could answer. 'I've been speaking to the captain, and he tells me the bulk of the water will outpace us within an hour or two, so there will be no difficulty getting into Casalmaggiore, though the river will now flow faster all the way down to the delta.'

Twenty-One

VENICE, APRIL 1728

THE HANDFUL OF PASSENGERS WERE OUT ON DECK when the *Regina del Fiume* sailed into the Venetian lagoon between tiny islands covered in stands of laurel dotted with nesting white egrets. Beyond, rising out of the milky, teal waters, Venice shimmered, floating as though on a sea of mist, its campaniles towering above buildings burnished by the early morning sunshine.

After navigating the Cannaregio Canal, they entered the Grand Canal, passing the piazza's waterfront columns – one topped by a statue of San Marco as a winged lion, the other with San Teodoro. Behind them were the spire and belfry of *Campanile di San Marco* and the five-domed basilica itself glittering like a box of jewels beside the *Doge's Palazzo's* arcades patterned above with pink Verona marble and white Istrian stone. They poled on towards the merchant docks following the route taken by gondolas.

Once the raft was securely tied up at the wharf, the party of four made their way down the gangway together. Pietro's last letter had promised they would be met on the quayside and guided to his home on the Rio Marin, one of the smaller neigh-

244

bourhood canals. It took them all some moments to realise that it was Pietro himself who waited there to greet them, dressed in fine clothes, and sporting a luxurious black beard.

Katarina remembered him as smaller and slighter than his brother, though this seemed even more pronounced now that Giuseppe had become broader and more muscular with age. The brothers hugged after a brief hesitation while they registered the changes in each other.

Giuseppe pulled away first, to study his brother again. 'You look well, Pietro.'

'As do you. He glanced at the other three standing close by. 'So, you couldn't persuade Papà to come. I'd hoped he might have had a last-minute change of heart.' He moved to embrace Katarina. 'Kat, you look as beautiful as ever. How on earth did he manage to snag you? Didn't I hear you were to marry a German count or some such?'

Katarina laughed. 'Austrian actually.' She turned to look at Giuseppe. 'Your brother rescued me from that fate.' Conscience pricked. Johannes did not deserve that barb.

'Well. I'm glad you're part of the family.' He turned then to hug the others. 'Good to see you Gianni and you too Claudio.'

'I hope you don't mind that Claudio accompanied me—'

'Not at all, though Angiola is expecting to meet your wife.'

Well, of course she is. 'Mia is very tolerant of Gianni's whims.' Katarina wondered what Angiola Ferrari would make of Claudio's presence.

'Come.' Pietro gestured for them to follow him into the gloom of the *Calle del Forno*, a narrow passageway running between buildings many with shops at street level. Cobblers. Barbers. Coffee houses. Spice merchants. Sweetmeat and chocolatiers. 'I've a gondola waiting on the Marin.'

This narrow canal, deep in shadow and holding a whiff of effluent and rotting fish, looked to pass behind buildings for the walls above them were largely windowless. After a time, the houses beyond the *fondamenta* appeared more prosperous and the canal itself broadened out before the boatman steered them through a water gate towards a private landing stage within a courtyard. Katarina looked around, impressed by the four-story building made from golden stone inlaid with Istrian marble, with its terrace covered by a portico held up by fluted pillars, their capitals decorated with leaves and fruits. Pietro was obviously a very successful luthier.

After tying up the gondola, the boatman helped them onto the dock and left them, entering the building through a narrow tunnel. This was Pietro's boat then, and the *gondoliere* in his employ.

'Come inside. Angiola is very eager to meet you all.' Pietro offered his arm to Katarina and the three men followed behind. After climbing a wide flight of stone stairs, they entered the house via an impressive workshop illuminated by three triple-height windows. The benches were occupied by several men and boys, the walls above hung with their tools and racks holding rows of instruments in various stages of completion, many extravagantly decorated with inlays and tracery.

The luthiers from Cremona stopped to watch but it was Katarina who spoke. 'You build your instruments inside a mould? I've never seen this before.'

'You won't get the same variations that we get—'

'But why do you want such variations, Giuseppe? It leaves you with some poor instruments. We get consistency using the French mould. Patrons know exactly what they'll get.'

'Pah, poor instruments.' He shrugged. Maybe the odd one but we also turn out some ravishingly beautiful ones.'

'I thought beauty didn't interest you. Have you decided to follow Antonio at last?'

Giuseppe snorted. 'I don't mean beautiful to look at. Fuck that. I mean beautiful to play. I mean ravishing sound.'

'Well, we don't need that here, just consistency. The Church orders from us for that very reason. If a patron wants individuality, we give it to him with the decoration.'

'I ... we supply The Church in Lombardy, too—' Katarina felt heat burn her face seeing Pietro's frown. 'I mean Giuseppe does.'

The awkward moment was broken by a woman's voice calling from a doorway. 'Pietro? Why are you lingering here? I have refreshments waiting for our guests.'

Pietro whipped around with a frown and hurried to join his *fidanzata*. 'Come. Come, everyone.'

Katarina took Giuseppe's arm to follow them along a wide hall decorated with white statuary set in niches along its length and elaborate enamelled candle-sconces on the walls. The woman was taller than Pietro and perhaps a touch plump, though dressed in pale silk covered in so many frills and flounces it was difficult to tell. Katarina had noticed large eyes and full lips in the brief glimpse she had managed before they were all led away. A handsome face.

The salon's floor-to-ceiling windows offered a view across the canal where many houses had their own water gates. The room was adorned with gilded wooden furniture upholstered in bright silks and floral damask and here the statuary was finely cast bronze, and the wall candelabra were decorated with crystal pendants to match the magnificent chandelier that hung from a ceiling frescoed with colourful cherubs and mythical beasts. *Consistency must be surprisingly lucrative.*

After their cloaks were taken by a liveried footman and introductions made – Angiola kissing cheeks and patting hands and arms – they were invited to sit on sofas close to the large fireplace where a small fire had been lit for their benefit and offered wine, platters of sweetmeats, and cakes.

All the while, Katarina found it hard to take her eyes from their hostess. There was a certain heaviness to her features that matched her build though, in contrast, her voice was high and childlike, and she rarely stopped talking. Katarina found her somewhat overwhelming.

After the refreshments were cleared away, Angiola offered to show them all to their bedchambers herself. How long had she lived in this house? She seemed very much at home and confident that it was her place to do so, despite not yet being married to Pietro.

She and Giuseppe were taken up to the next floor where they had been given a bedchamber with tall windows and a view of the canal. The large four-poster bedframe with its swags of turquoise silk could not have provided a greater contrast to the tiny cot where they had spent the last few nights. And again, a small fire had been lit.

'You'll be ready for some comfort, I'm sure. I've never travelled on the river but from what Pietro tells me, there are many privations.'

After the door closed behind her, Giuseppe sat down on the matching silk quilt, patting it. 'A featherbed. What else? Angiola seems very much at home here, doesn't she?'

'I thought the same? I wonder how long they've been living together?'

'Well, Venice has a reputation for turning a blind eye to lax morals.'

Katarina moved to stand before him chuckling. 'You sound like a prim maiden-aunt.'

Giuseppe grinned. 'I sound like most of the inhabitants of Cremona.'

'What do you think of her?'

He tilted his head. 'She's a bit intimidating, don't you think?'

'I do. She's a striking woman, I'll give her that, but I can't help questioning what Pietro finds in her.' She drew a breath. 'That's unkind of me. Forget I said it.'

He shrugged. 'It is a little hard not to wonder.'

'And what will she do with Claudio?'

Before Giuseppe could speculate, there was a tap on the door followed by Gianni's head appearing around it. 'Hope I'm not interrupting?' He did not wait for an answer before coming in, closing the door behind him, and striding to the window to look out. 'You have a better room than I have—'

'He *is* my brother, Gianni.'

Gianni laughed. 'We're on the floor above—'

'We?'

'Mia was expected, so there's a nice big bed in there, but Angiola will have a truckle brought in for my friend.' He made a move back to the door. 'I'm going to get hot water for bathing before *pranzo*, so I'll leave you to it.' And with that, he was gone.'

Katarina moved to the bell rope. 'Hot water sounds just the thing, don't you think?'

'Damn me, doesn't it though.'

Katarina hesitated then and sighed. 'Though it probably makes more sense to wait until we change for dinner this evening.'

Giuseppe stood and moved to her putting an arm around her waist and pulling her close. 'Very well. We might even try out the bed at the same time ... for its comfort I mean.'

Katarina laughed. 'Of course you do.'

'I think I'll have another look at my brother's workshop before we eat.'

Katarina nodded. 'And I shall see if I can find our hostess. I'd like to know a bit more about her.'

'I doubt you'll have a problem with that. She does seem quite talkative.'

After leaving their bedchamber, they parted company on the floor below where, after asking a passing servant, Giuseppe took a narrower staircase down to the workshop and Katarina made her way back to the salon. She hesitated outside the double doors, one left slightly ajar, hearing male voices. At first, when she realised Gianni and Claudio were inside with Pietro (Gianni's plans for bathing must have been postponed, too) she decided to find a servant to ask where she might find Angiola for she would not be inside and silent. And this time she certainly had no plan to eavesdrop, though that is what she did when she heard what was being discussed.

'Don't feel too bad about it,' she heard Gianni say. 'Giuseppe's had his share of help, too.'

What?

'I thought Kat's father had cut her off with nothing?' Pietro said.

'He did, after she left Horak at the altar.'

'So, who helped him, then?'

'Gianni?' Claudio sounded unhappy. 'Gianni, it isn't our place to speak of this. Giuseppe must do it if he wishes to.'

What was he talking about?

'I'm involved too, so I can tell my part of it, surely?'

Katarina had a strong feeling she should walk away. Whatever this was, Giuseppe had kept it from her and if she heard any more, what might happen between them because of it? Something else others knew of that he had kept from her. Yet, afraid as she was, she found herself rooted to the spot.

'Christ, Gianni. How can you tell your part without Giuseppe's?'

Gianni laughed. 'His name shall not cross my lips.'

'Prick.'

Katarina was not quick enough reacting to the sound of footsteps rapidly crossing the marble tiles and had only just turned away when the door flew open and Claudio all but collided with her. He held his finger to his lips before closing the door behind him. 'Come away, now. You don't want to hear this,' he said, quietly.

'Oh, but I do,' she whispered. 'Either now or from Giuseppe as soon as I can find him.'

Claudio sighed. 'Very well, I'll tell you, but not here.' He took her elbow and guided her away down the hall, opening doors as they passed until he found a small over-furnished morning salon, and leading her inside, he gestured to one of the large ornate sofas for Katarina to sit before sitting beside her. He cleared his throat. 'What exactly did you hear?'

'I hadn't intended to listen—'

'I'm sure you hadn't.' He raised his eyebrows waiting for her reply.

She took a breath. 'I heard Gianni say that Pietro shouldn't feel so bad because Giuseppe had been helped too.'

Claudio nodded. 'I shan't tell you what Pietro said before that. It's his story to tell.'

'I wouldn't expect you to.'

'Nor will I tell you about Gianni's part—' He barked a laugh. 'Christ, I sound like a pompous arse, don't I?'

'No. You sound honourable.'

His smile was full of self-deprecation. 'Thank you. I am trying to be … unlike Gianni. He just wants to be the centre of attention.' He sighed. 'But Gianni is Gianni. I wouldn't have him any different.'

Katerina tapped his arm gently. 'Tell me how Giuseppe has been helped. Helped with what?'

Claudio took a breath. 'With your house. No, that's not quite right. The house and workshop were bought outright for him. He doesn't rent it.'

Katarina's thoughts went into freefall. 'What? What are you saying? Who in the name of God paid for it? Not Gianni, surely? Why would anyone do such a thing for him?'

'I think it was more for you,' Claudio said, softly.

Katarina tried to think who could possibly be behind such

generosity. 'Not my cousin? No, his wife would never have allowed it.'

'Johannes Horak.'

She was dumbfounded, feeling it like a physical blow and then wondering why she had not thought of him immediately. What did not make sense was that Giuseppe had accepted it from him. She took a few breaths to calm herself. 'Why didn't he tell me? How dare he not tell—'

'That was part of the agreement. You were never to know.'

She shook her head. 'I was supposed to believe we paid rent to Gianni. That he had used Mia's money? Jesu.' How ludicrous it sounded now. Why had she never questioned it?

Claudio grasped her hand. 'Kat. Don't tell Giuseppe, I beg you. Johannes didn't want Giuseppe to feel humiliated ... but especially not to be humiliated in front of you because of it. Both of you were never supposed to know. Gianni couldn't go through with it.'

She took a long breath. 'Yes, it would be worse for him if I knew about it. I can see that, I suppose.' She hesitated for a few more moments, allowing her jagged thoughts to coalesce. 'But what I can't see is how my knowing of his humiliation is worse than his lying to me. That keeping face in front of me was more important to him than deceiving me.'

'Well, you must decide what to do. But I know Giuseppe accepted Johannes's generosity because he hated how much you'd had to sacrifice because of him. He wanted you to have a home of your own rather than to live with his family.'

Katarina tilted her head back. 'And he wanted his own workshop where his father couldn't hound him about his methods and experiments.' She stood. 'I don't know what I shall do, Claudio. I need more time to think about it all. To get it straight in my mind.'

He rose and gave her a quick hug. 'I can understand that.'

'But thank you for telling me.'

. . .

After *pranzo* served in the dining room where Angiola talked so unremittingly in her little girl's voice that Katarina stopped listening after a while, allowing her mind to return to all that she had learnt earlier as she moved *caprese* around on her plate, eating very little. She noticed Giuseppe wore a rather glazed expression. In truth, they all appeared somewhat overwhelmed by Angiola's stream of words which jumped at random from one topic to another so, even with the best will in the world, it was impossible to follow her. The only one who appeared untroubled by it was Pietro who, she imagined, was accustomed to it.

It was obvious to Katarina that Giuseppe was eager to return to Pietro's workshop, their surreptitious glances at each other spoke of such a prior arrangement, so she was unsurprised when, as soon as was polite, the brothers made their excuses and left the table. After Gianni and Claudio rose too, saying they would like to explore the city and Katarina turned down Gianni's rather half-hearted invitation to join them (God forbid when she knew his purpose), she found herself alone with her hostess.

Angiola stood. 'Come. Let us move to the salon where we can make ourselves more comfortable.' Katarina followed meekly.

Angiola gestured around her. 'What do you think of it? I've made a lot of changes. It was horribly dull and old-fashioned before I got my hands on it. I particularly—'

'How long have you lived here, Angiola?' Katarina was determined to get a word in this time. She could not face another monologue.

'All my life.'

Now, that was a surprise. Katarina knew she need not ask any further questions to get more information, so she sat back on the sofa beside her future sister-in-law and waited.

'When Pietro asked my papà for his permission to marry me...' She fanned herself with a dimpled hand. 'Lord, but he is so in love with me. Well, Papà decided he could safely hand over the workshop to him – he'd been running it anyway in all but name for years – and he and my mother thought it the perfect time to retire to their house, well, Mamma's house in truth, on Capri.' She giggled. 'They off-loaded two birds with one stone as it were. So I wanted to make the house my own and Papà allowed me an unlimited budget.' She gestured again around the large, gilded space. 'And this is the result. I wished—'

'I hadn't realised Pietro worked for your father.' *And I hadn't realised this wasn't his house.* So, this was the help he had received to make such a successful career as a luthier. And it was rather more substantial than Johannes's to Giuseppe ... to her.

'Oh, yes. He came to us straight from Cremona. Papà liked some of the methods he brought with him, particularly his ideas for decoration, and they proved quite lucrative for us. It wasn't long before he ran the workshop, as I said. He became one of the family, really.' She giggled again. 'And, of course, he fell in love with me right away. But I was so young, so we had to keep it secret. It wasn't until Papà began to talk of retirement – his rheumy fingers meant he couldn't make instruments himself anymore – that Pietro thought it was time to come out openly about our feeling for each other. It was so romantic and really quite exciting. We—'

Katarina interrupted her again. It seemed the only way. 'Pietro was certainly lucky coming here and finding a new family and such a successful workshop.' Was it unfair to find it all rather calculated? The secret declaration of love to the young Angiola that only became known to her parents when the house and workshop seemed up for grabs?

'Might I ask you something, Katarina?'

She tried not to show surprise. Angiola did not seem much of a one for questions. 'Of course.'

'I wonder why Gianni brought a male friend with him rather than his wife. I hope they are not estranged. My mamma is very strict about refusing contact with people who do not honour their marriage vows. Their promises before God, you know. She will question me about it when she meets them.'

Jesu. What would this mamma think if she knew the truth about Gianni and Claudio? 'No, it's nothing like that, I assure you. Mia has remained at home to look after their children, she is loath to delegate their care to others.' She hoped Mia would forgive the lie (not that she would ever know of it). Katarina now realised she had chosen not to accompany Gianni to Venice when she knew what he would get up to here.

Angiola fanned her face with her hand again (an irritating affectation). 'Well, I must say I am relieved. I'm sure Mamma will approve.' She gave Katarina a rather pointed look. 'I must say I'm surprised you and Giuseppe have no children. You have been married for quite some time. I know you lost one—'

'That's in God's hands.' Katarina tried not to snap.

'Forgive me, of course it is. I didn't mean to pry.'

Oh, but I think you did … but then so did I. Katarina stood and crossed the room to take a closer look at the portrait hanging over the large and intricately carved marble fireplace (too big for the needs of such a room in Venice's mild climate, surely?) where the little fire still struggled in its over-sized grate. 'These must be your parents.' The woman bore an uncanny likeness to Angiola, though her features were finer. Angiola's heavier ones hailed from her papà who appeared decidedly belligerent.

'Indeed. They are a little delayed arriving for the wedding, but we expect them any day.'

Katarina moved to the window and looked down on the canal which was now a rather fetching shade of blue reflecting the colour of the sky. 'I wonder if I've made a mistake not going into the city with Gianni and Claudio. It looks the sort of afternoon to be outdoors.'

'I imagine the gondola has returned by now, so feel free to use it if you wish. Giuseppe will escort you, I'm sure.'

'Then I shall.' Katarina felt obliged to add, 'Would you care to accompany us?'

'I cannot, I fear. The seamstress is due at any moment for another fitting of my wedding gown.'

The surge of relief that refusal brought her felt horribly unkind but there was nothing to be done other than hold back the grin which threatened. And she would not ask her husband to join her, for she was not yet ready for his company. She had much to think on.

When a footman arrived to tell Angiola that the seamstress had indeed arrived, Katarina made her escape; and after again enquiring from a passing servant (they seemed to be in plentiful supply) she found a way down to the landing stage without going through the workshop.

The boat carried her to the Rialto where the *gondoliere* helped her to disembark onto the concourse beside the pungent fish market, which she quickly decided to avoid. Instead making her way into *Piazza San Marco* proper, with its roiling throng of people. The terracotta block flooring surprised her especially as it was cracked and crumbling dangerously in places, causing her to all but lose her footing. Hawkers. Acrobats and flame-eaters. Courtesans and doxies. Townspeople and visitors to the city alike, there to experience it all. The covered arcades surrounding the piazza were full of shops selling everything from cheap trinkets to Murano glassware, interspersed with goldsmiths, coffee houses, and tavernas.

When a hand came down lightly on her shoulder, she spun around to defend herself as best she could, ready to lift her skirts and administer a kick. 'Claudio! You startled me.'

'Forgive me. I followed you from the Rialto. I was on the bridge and thought it was you at the landing steps, though I wasn't certain, but I kept telling myself how many women could there be of your stature, wearing that exact shade of green. That exact gown, in fact.'

How extraordinary he should remember her gown in such detail? She felt certain Giuseppe would not. '*Really?* You noticed my gown?'

He smiled sheepishly. 'I did ... and perhaps the *gondoliere*, too.'

She laughed looking around her. 'Where's Gianni?'

'I left him in a taverna.' He looked away.

'I expect he's making new friends, is he?'

'You might call it that. Friends he pays for.' He sighed. 'And I want none of it. I shouldn't have let him persuade me to come.'

'Well, I'm glad of your company. The crowds are over-whelming.'

'If we leave the piazza by one of the calles, we should escape the worst of it. And I'm sure you're ready for a glass of wine.'

Katarina followed him down an alleyway between stone buildings, again many with shops fronting the street. And, after crossing several iron bridges over narrow canals, they arrived in a small piazza where a taverna had a few tables outside under a faded red canvas awning.

They chose one close to a small fountain and Katarina sat on the wooden bench while Claudio disappeared into the dark interior to order their wine. She held her hand to the falling trickle of cool water that dropped into its mossy basin, surveying the three and four-storey houses surrounding the square with their shuttered windows, some with balconies where limp washing hung in the hot still air, others with pots of trailing scarlet geraniums.

This peaceful neighbourhood could not offer more of a contrast to the busy heart of the city with its glittering basilicas, campaniles, gilded marble statues of horses, dukes, and saints, and those ever-present restless, seething crowds.

Claudio arrived at their table trailing a youth carrying a tray over his shoulder on an upturned palm (in imitation of the *San Marco* waiters, though lacking their studied insouciance) balancing a bottle of red wine, two glasses and a dish of green olives. With the wine poured, Claudio lifted his glass and held it out to Katarina. '*Salute.*'

They clinked glasses. '*Salute.* I was just thinking how different this feels to the centre.'

Claudio looked around, nodding. 'There is something a touch too decadent about it. Something sordid and venal underneath all the splendour. Or perhaps that's just how it feels to someone like me.' He sighed. 'Though Gianni revels in it.'

Katarina tilted her head studying him. 'I hope you don't mind me asking?' She watched him raise his eyebrows, appearing a little wary. 'I've always wondered how you and Mia get on?'

His eyes widened. 'Is that all? I wondered what was coming. Mia is … Mia is like a sister to me. That must sound an odd thing to say but, well, we both love Gianni. That's forged a kind of bond between us. You know Gianni. He's a big character. Full of life. He wants to know everything. To feel everything that it's possible to feel.' He grinned. 'So long as it's pleasurable, of course. He's kind and thoughtful, too. He'd do anything for anyone. So, he's almost overwhelming to live with, or live up to, and it seems to take the two of us to cope with him. I don't know if either of us would be enough for him alone. Does that make any sense?'

'Yes. It really does—'

'What made you ask this now?'

'Angiola asked why you were with him rather than Mia.'

'Christ. What did you say.'

Katarina told him. 'I hope Mia wouldn't mind me making her sound like a rather fanatical mother.'

Claudio laughed. 'I think she'd be happy to be described like that. She is besotted with her children, you know.'

Katarina studied her fingers. 'Aren't all mothers? Angiola asked me why we have none.'

'I'm sorry. It can't be easy to be asked over and over.'

'Indeed, it isn't.' *Especially when I have no answer or at least not one I believe.* Time to change the subject. 'Angiola told me all about Pietro's situation in that household. I must say I find them a strange couple. I don't think she's the love of his life, shall we say.'

Claudio drained his glass. 'But we can't all find that, can we. He'll make her an adequate husband, I'm sure.'

Adequate? Afterwards, she could not explain why she said what she did next. 'Before he left Cremona, there were rumours he was involved with Gianni. That there was more than friendship between them. Giuseppe was always adamant it was untrue.'

Claudio refilled his glass and topped up Katarina's. 'I'm sure he was. Adamant, I mean.'

Katarina blinked. 'Are you telling me Giuseppe was wrong?'

'I'm not telling you anything, Kat.'

She felt the alcohol fizz a little in her blood and knew she was losing control of her tongue but could not seem to do anything about it. 'Pietro is a good-looking man who could attract a ... shall we say ... a more appealing woman than Angiola. She gulped more wine and then held up her glass, surprised to see it was empty. 'Yet with Angiola comes a fine house and a busy and successful luthier's workshop. And Venice is a city of courtesans ... both male and female, so the appearance ... shall we say the desirability of his wife is perhaps not that important, is it?'

Claudio smiled, refilling her glass from a fresh bottle which she had not noticed arrive at the table. 'But is it men or is it women?' She placed her hand over his on the table.

'You're determined to turn me into a gossip, aren't you?'

She raised her hand to tap him on the arm with more force

than she had intended. 'Well, I seem to have become one, so why should you not keep me company?'

'I think we've both had too much wine, Kat.'

'Well?'

'Men. It's men.' He drew a long breath. 'Is that really so unexpected?'

Giuseppe made his way up to his bedchamber returning his cloak to the armoire after his brother had taken him out to his timber merchant on the small island of *Spinalonga* in the lagoon. The variety and quality of maple there had been a revelation. The sail out on a small pinnace had also been a revelation but of a rather different kind. He shuddered at the memory. Pietro had laughed at his discomposure, telling him the lagoon was like a mill pond. *Mill pond my arse.*

He would be glad of some time alone to mull over all he had seen in Pietro's workshop. He didn't quite know what to make of it. That he had assistants concentrating on specific parts of the process rather than turning out instruments individually felt somehow soulless ... and left their wider skills as luthiers unfulfilled. Though using the French mould meant there was little variety between instruments anyway – apart from the decoration – so he could see it made sense for each man to have his own speciality. This was a good way of making in quantity.

His method of building them around a form meant fewer completed but higher quality. More variety. And, most importantly as he had stressed many times to his brother, a chance for the spectacular. That wonder of an instrument that made him strive again and again to achieve it.

They had returned to their old argument about tool marks on finished instruments too, one little changed from those they had indulged in back in Cremona all those years before. They had both laughed uproariously when they realised neither had shifted one iota in their opinions. Pietro still using the perfection of Antonio Stradivari's work as an example, and Giuseppe insisting that subtle tool marks were an intrinsic part of what made each of his violins unique.

When he opened the door to the bedchamber he halted, astonished to see Katarina there asleep on the bed in the semi-darkness. That no candles were lit suggested she had been there for quite some time. Shame gripped him, realising yet again, he had not given her a thought all afternoon. What had she done with herself in the hours since he had last seen her? He was immediately beset by a familiar guilt that he could forget her so completely, yet however much he promised himself it would not happen again, it always did. He moved quietly to light the candles with a taper from the fire that was on the verge of going out and added more logs, hoping it was not too late to save it, for he was still chilled from his journey out onto the lagoon.

'Giuseppe?'

He turned to see her sitting up looking dishevelled, her hair having escaped its pins, hung around her like a cloak of brown silk. 'Forgive me for waking you.'

'I didn't mean to sleep for so long.' She clutched her head. 'Oh, God. I really did drink too much wine. We both did.'

He moved to sit beside her on the bed. 'I didn't see Angiola as a drinker.'

She sat up higher against the pillows, snorting. 'Jesu. Not Angiola. God forbid,' she added with obvious distaste. 'I was with Claudio.'

It took Giuseppe a moment to understand. 'I thought he'd gone into the city.'

'He had. I decided to go too, later, and we bumped into each other.' She shook her head. 'How unlikely does that sound when the place is so horribly crowded? But it happened, luckily for me.' She rubbed her forehead. 'Apart from the wine.'

'You went in alone? Was that wise, do you think?'

'Well, you weren't exactly available to accompany me, now were you?'

'True enough. Forgive me for it. I shouldn't have abandoned you like I did.' *Like I always do for anything to do with luthier business.*

She reached for his hand and grasped it. 'Giuseppe, you're freezing. What on earth have you been doing?'

He gave her a succinct account of his afternoon. 'That water was not calm whatever Pietro claimed.'

Katarina laughed. 'Ring for hot water. Bathing will warm you. I'm not sure when we're expected downstairs for dinner, so we might as well get ready now.'

Giuseppe did as she suggested, telling the servant at the door what was required before turning back to Katarina who was rifling through her gowns in the large armoire, trying to decide what to wear by holding them against herself in front of the cheval mirror.

Giuseppe tilted his head. 'That one,' he said.' The pale peach silk was his favourite. Somehow it seemed to highlight the creaminess of her skin and the rich brown of her hair.

She smiled meeting his eyes in the mirror. 'I knew which one you'd choose.'

He moved behind her, running his hands down her body 'But first we must remove this.'

'Claudio claimed to remember it, so he knew it was me at the Rialto.' She rolled her eyes. 'But it was really the *gondoliere* he recognised.'

'Wasn't Giuseppe with him?'

'No, they'd parted company by then.'

'So, where was he?'

'I'm not sure you want to know.' But she told him anyway, and what they had spoken of in the taverna.' He frowned, feeling she was holding something back but before he could press her on it, a knock on the door brought footmen with water and a copper bathtub, and maids with linen towels and soap.

THE VIOLIN MAKER'S WIFE

When the tub was placed before the fire and filled with steaming water, they were left alone once more. He gestured towards it. She always bathed first.

'No, you're the one who's cold, you must go first.'

He moved behind her and began undoing her skirt laces, bending to kiss the top of her head. 'It will warm me to wash you.'

'Well, there is that.'

Giuseppe sat on a small, ornate, and supremely uncomfortable chair in front of the window where the curtains had been closed to shut out the last of the twilight, watching a sour-faced maid pinning up sections of Katarina's hair over some strange cloth pads to make it unnaturally tall and wide. Kat did not appear too happy about the process, either. When she cried out because the woman had burnt her with the curling irons or pulled her hair too sharply, the maid harumphed and shook her head, her expression saying she was dealing with an idiot.

'Had you dried your hair correctly, Madonna, this task would have been so much easier for both of us,' she said, crossly.

'Are we done?' Katarina's tone matched hers.

The maid stood back surveying her work, her face pinched with dissatisfaction. 'I've managed all I can with what I had.'

Katarina's dismay was clear studying her reflection in the toilet table mirror. 'Then you may leave us.'

When the door had closed behind the woman, Katarina turned to him. 'My head looks deformed. Why did Angiola send her to me, her hair didn't look like this earlier.' She frowned. 'Oh, God. Is this some hideous Venetian fashion?'

Giuseppe stood behind her. The woman had smeared some sort of paste on it too, so the colour had faded into a dirty brownish grey. He reached out to touch the horror but hesitated, leaving his hand hovering, afraid the whole edifice might collapse. 'What's happened to your beautiful hair—'

'Don't worry, she'll not get her hands on it again,' she snapped. 'Fashion or no fashion.' She stood. 'We should go down. Jesu.' She clutched his arm. 'What if I'm the only one who looks like this?'

'She looked far too familiar with her pads and paste for you to worry about that.' He watched her nod, reassured.

They found an older couple already seated in the salon, the woman appearing none too pleased at their intrusion. 'Her parents.' Katarina hissed as Giuseppe closed the door behind them.

'And just who might you be?' she said, scowling.

Giuseppe was relieved to see she sported a hairstyle even more outrageous than the one inflicted upon his wife. 'Giuseppe Guarneri. My wife Katarina.'

The man stood and came to shake Giuseppe's hand, his welcoming expression starkly opposite to that of his wife. 'Lorenzo Ferrari. He gestured. 'Lucia, my wife. And you, *Signore*, are Pietro's brother.' He grasped Katarina's hand and brought it to his lips. 'So glad to meet you, my dear.' He turned back to Giuseppe. 'Pietro has told me much about you over the years.'

Giuseppe wondered why his brother had never mentioned this man in any of his letters, or anything about this house or his life here. 'Good things, I hope.' He could think of nothing else to say. But before Lorenzo could respond, his wife broke in addressing a question to Katarina.

'So, you're the one who was cut off by her papà for jilting a count at the alter?' She turned her gaze on Giuseppe. 'How disappointing for you to find your prospects so diminished now because of it.'

Flabbergasted by her shocking directness, Giuseppe forced a

smile. And it was not entirely true either, was it? His situation had improved beyond measure because of Johannes Horak's secret generosity. And again, he wondered what Kat would think if she knew how much he had deceived her. He dragged his thoughts away. It was something he tried not to dwell on, for what good would it do? He realised then by the Ferraris' expectant expressions that he had taken too long and took a breath ready to reply just as Katarina did so for him.

'There has never been anything disappointing about our marriage.' Her pointed glance told him where her thoughts were, and it took some self-control to hold back the laughter he felt bubbling in his chest. He cleared his throat. 'Good to know.'

Lorenzo, looking from one to the other, seemed to suspect what lay behind Katarina's words and smiled at them indulgently. Lucia appeared even more disgruntled but was distracted when the door opened admitting Angiola and Pietro, closely followed by Gianni and Claudio. Giuseppe edged Katarina away until they stood close to one of the great windows left uncovered to show the canal ruffled by the evening breeze, glittering in the moonlight. He used the chatter of introductions to cover his whisper. 'If it's any consolation, your hair is the least freakish.'

They both glanced at Angiola, whose creation did not quite match that of her mother but, like her, did nothing to improve her appearance. 'Not much of a comfort, in truth.'

While Gianni directed the full force of his charm on Lucia Ferrari, somehow eliciting giggles from her, Claudio joined them at the window. 'Good Lord, what is it with the hideous hair? Why would you do this?'

'I didn't,' she hissed, gesturing towards Angiola. 'She sent a maid to me. If I'd known this would be the result, I would never have let her in.' She raised her hand towards her head, and like Giuseppe earlier, hesitated to touch it. 'I shall have to wash it as soon as we return to our bedchamber.'

Then, before Claudio could reply the doors opened and a liveried footman summoned them to the dining room. Angiola led them along the gallery on Pietro's arm with her parent following. Claudio and Gianni walked behind, Gianni loud and lively. Giuseppe wondered if he had been drinking all day. Claudio was already hushing him, which did not augur well.

Katarina moved closer to him to whisper. 'Why do I find myself dreading this?'

'Let's hope we are sitting together, at least.' But that was not to be. He quickly discovered he had been placed between Angiola and her mother, while Kat would sit between Lorenzo Ferrari and Gianni. Claudio sat beyond Angiola beside Pietro.

Wine was poured and food served. *Sarde agrodolce. Risotto al nero di seppia. Fegato alla veneziana. Molèche.* Sweet *fritole,* and platters of breads, fresh fruits, and vegetables. Giuseppe watched Kat listening to the two men discussing luthier techniques, rudely talking across her. It amused him to know that she was a better and more practiced violin maker than Gianni who had too many other interests. However, at least it was a familiar topic that interested her, whereas the intricacies of what went into making and fitting a wedding gown offered neither for him.

He soon turned his attention away from the two women with their high twittering voices onto what was being said further down the table, firstly to Claudio's conversation with Pietro, and then to Gianni, whose voice rose in volume as he drained his wine glass (and not for the first time), telling Katarina about his adventures in the city after he had parted company with Claudio. By now all eyes were upon him by dint of his volume.

'Claudio was lucky to spend his afternoon with you even though the wine consumption was a little incautious from what I heard—'

'As is yours now.' Claudio leaned closer across the table. 'And might I suggest you lower your voice. You're drowning out all other conversation.'

Gianni laughed and touched the side of his nose. 'Noted, dear one.'

All three Ferrari frowned.

Gianni took a breath and began to regale Katarina once more with his tale, though with no discernible reduction in volume. 'The two I had found for us took me back to a most disreputable house in *Cannaregio*. Christ, you should have seen those tight little backsides when I peeled the—'

'Gianni!' Pietro's voice boomed. 'Not a topic for the dinner table, if you please.'

Gianni nodded, sagely. 'Quite right. Quite right.' He turned to Katarina again. 'Forgive me. What topic would you prefer?' He placed his elbow on the table and rested his chin upon his palm. 'I know. Why don't you tell me how on earth you made the varnish on that last violin look so luminous? I've never seen one quite like it before.'

'Christ.' He's doing this on purpose. I'd wager he's not really in his cups at all. He's doing it because it amuses him. The prick. He should intervene but his panicked mind went suddenly blank. Kat spoke before he could compose himself.

'Just a fluke, I'm afraid.'

But Angiola's interest had been peaked. 'Giuseppe allows you to assist in the workshop?'

Kat glanced at him her expression wary, and he was quickly aware of her quandary. 'Er, let me answer that. Katarina has something of a talent for varnishing and often helps my apprentices—'

'Oh, come on, Giuseppe. You know that's not true. Kat's a brilliant luthier in her own right and you profit from it. You know you do.'

Kat forced a laugh. 'Nonsense. What's got into you this evening, Gianni?

'Too much wine and a fanciful imagination,' Claudio said with venom.

Gianni laughed, uproariously. 'Why the deceit? Is it so shameful that Katarina is as talented at making violins as she is at playing them? How can you deny it?'

Lucia Ferrari joined in with Gianni's laughter, high pitches and giggly. 'You are a one, *Signore*. As if a woman could make an instrument. It's quite preposterous.' More giggles. She looked directly at Giuseppe then. 'But you should keep your wife away from your work. Has she no children to occupy her?'

'No, Mamma, she told me she has none, as yet.'

Katarina banged her hand down on the table, so all eyes turned to her. 'Please don't discuss me as though I'm not present—'

Lucia acted as though Katarina had not spoken. 'Well, no wonder there are no children if you dabble in men's work, however inept you might be at it. Didn't your mamma tell you this? If you're barren, then this is why. Your poor hus—'

Another hand banged down on the table, harder this time, silencing her. Lorenzo Ferrari, who had sat with an increasing look of horror on his face as his wife's words became more and more tactless, seemed to pull himself together, at last. 'Now, now my dear. That's enough of that. We mustn't distress our guests. They're here to celebrate Angiola's and Pietro's wedding. They're his family. His friends.'

Lucia had the good grace to look ashamed. 'I meant no harm, husband.'

He reached across to pat her hand. 'I know you didn't, my dear.'

Giuseppe noticed Gianni mouth 'Forgive me,' when he managed to catch Katarina's eye. He could not tell from her closed expression whether she had ... or even could.

· · ·

Two day later, when the wedding day finally arrived, Katarina was a little ashamed at the extent of her relief as it meant they would soon return to Cremona. She did not wish to think about that dinner, unnerving and nightmarish, from the grotesque hairstyles to Gianni's idiocy, to Lucia Ferrari's ignorance and cruelty. She had wept in Giuseppe's arms that night, once again submerged in the loss of their child and her heartbreaking failure to get another.

Giuseppe had been attentive since then too, admitting he had lost himself in his brother's studio and allowed her to slip from his mind. Did he think she did not know this about him? But that there were no more such sessions with Pietro made her happier than she cared to admit. Yet wasn't she content in her own company? Though the circumstances were different here. In Cremona she had her own instruments to fill her thoughts, though she never allowed Giuseppe to slip completely from her mind as he did her.

They had spent their remaining time exploring the city together. The *Basilica San Marco* with its marble façade topped with statues, its colourful columns and lunettes filled with jewel-like mosaics set against golden backgrounds. The four bronze horses. The golden lion with wings overlooking the piazza.

Inside, after genuflecting and dipping fingers in the stoop of holy water to cross themselves, they halted giving their eyes time to adjust from the dazzle of sunshine to candlelight reflected by thousands of glittering tiles, once more set in gold, with all five domes lined with these mosaics depicting saints, prophets, and biblical scenes. They were silent then. Spellbound.

Next, they visited the *Palazzo Ducale*, walking through the spacious courtyard with its statues of Mars and Neptune, and on up the *Scala d'oro* to the *Consiglio dei Dieci* and the *Scrigno* council rooms, admiring paintings by Tintoretto and Titian. Venice was certainly a city of gold. A city of splendour.

The subsequent dinners at the house had been subdued affairs with some desultory conversation. Angiola and her mother, though, had talked happily about the wedding arrangements, seemingly unaware of the demeanour of others seated at the table.

Gianni, in particular, seemed more than chastened by his earlier behaviour. He had knocked on their chamber door early on the morning after that ruined dinner before either were dressed. Giuseppe had been irritated by the hour, but Katarina wished to speak with him and insisted he be allowed in. He, too, was still in night attire and she wondered whether Claudio knew he had left their chamber.

He addressed them both. 'Can you forgive me?'

Giuseppe had shrugged crossly. 'It's Katarina you need to ask for forgiveness, not me.'

'What I said was at the expense of both of you.' He gestured at Kat, his lips forming a shadow of a smile. 'Glad you got your hair back.'

She ran her fingers through the tangles. 'Not quite, I had to go to bed with it wet.' She sighed. 'I wish I knew what got into you last night?'

'I wish I did, too.' He moved to the window and gazed out over the canal streaked with pink from the fiery early morning sky. 'You have a better view than us. We're at the back looking over outbuildings.'

He had said this the last time he was in their chamber. 'Gianni?'

He turned to face her. 'I drank too much—'

'Pah.' Giuseppe's voice dripped scorn. 'Not sufficient excuse. Not by a long chalk.'

'I know. I know.' He took a breath. 'Those people are so … so limited. And so wrong for Pietro,' he added, quietly.

'So, you decide to show your contempt by turning on my wife.' Giuseppe took a step towards him. 'Well, I hope it helped because it did very little for her. She wept—'

'Giuseppe, stop. I didn't weep because of Gianni.' She put her hand on his arm. 'Look, I understand how you feel about them. Angiola and Lucia are not our sort of people at all, are they? But Pietro has chosen them. He wants what he has here. Can't you see that?'

'Yes. But I don't want him to want it.'

Katarina saw Giuseppe frown, watching them. Claudio had arrived at the door then and shooed Gianni away, his face white with anger.

Later that day as they strolled along Grande Canal *fondamenta* beyond Piazza San Marco, where the crowds were less, it was clear her husband had pondered Gianni's words about his brother. 'I knew Gianni and Pietro have exchanged letters, but I don't understand why he feels so strongly about his marriage.'

Katarina could not help feeling some satisfaction that it was now her turn to keep secrets. 'You should ask him.'

He gave her a hard stare. 'Why do I get the feeling you know more than you're telling me.'

She smiled. 'How odd. I often feel that about you.'

She watched a range of emotions flit across his face. Uncertainty. Fear. Irritation, and finally the decision to bluster. 'What the devil are you talking about? What do you possibly imagine I can have kept secret from you?'

Katarina thought of that earlier conversation walking down the aisle on Giuseppe's arm in Our Lady Star of the Sea, (decorated with flowers in such abundance that their scent was almost unpleasant) the neighbourhood church where Pietro would marry Angiola. The secrets husbands and wives kept from each other.

As Pietro's closest relatives (indeed, the only ones attending) they had seats in the front pew otherwise occupied by the men from Cremona with Pietro's friends and the journeymen and apprentices from his workshop – all in their Sunday best – on the rows behind.

The other side of the church was overflowing with friends and relatives of the bride and her family, with her mamma in pride of place beside the aisle waiting for her daughter to process down it on her father's arm. Having seen Lucia and Angiola before they set off for the church it was clear that their gowns were remarkably similar as was their hair in all its preposterous proportions, though looking around, Katarina saw it was indeed in vogue on the Ferrari side of the church.

She was surprised that this little church – though displaying all the usual painted statues above banks of candles, and the crucified Christ suspended above the rood screen – was the chosen venue for the marriage. She could only conclude that it being their family place of worship had outweighed the need for more space or, indeed, greater prestige. Or perhaps it only seemed lesser after the glories of *Basilica San Marco*.

The Marriage Mass, of course, was the same wherever it was spoken, and Giuseppe grasped her hand, holding it tight, obviously feeling the same emotions that swept through her hearing those words again. She was a touch sad for Pietro as there seemed little doubt he had not found the deep love she had with Giuseppe, yet he seemed content enough when he kissed his new wife at the ceremony's end.

The newly married couple and her parents were returned to their house in the flower-decked gondola while the remaining guests invited for the wedding feast would make their way there on foot along the narrow Ruga Giuffa to the Rio Marin *fondamenta*. 'That is such a relief.' Katarina tightened her grip on his arm. 'Now we can go home.'

Fourth Movement

~

DEL GESÙ

Twenty-Two

CREMONA, NOVEMBER 1731.

THE FIRST TIME IT HAPPENED, GIUSEPPE THOUGHT HE must be dreaming, though he knew himself to be seated at his workbench beside his apprentices and assistants. Everything looked and felt normal. The wood he planed was solid in his hands, he could even smell its prickly scent. No one else had noticed her, yet the child was there. It had to be a dream. A vivid dream.

Yes, it had to be for he knew who she was. A girl with chocolate brown hair hanging in a silken stream down her back. A girl with the same honey-brown eyes he saw in a mirror whenever he looked at himself. His daughter Teresa. And Teresa was dead. She had died before she was born, so how in the name of God could she be here now? She could not, so it was a dream.

She smiled down at the small ragdoll she held. He thought for a moment. She would be six years old now, had she lived. 'I'm so happy to see you,' he said softly, but her eyes never moved from her doll. Could she hear him? And then everything changed.

Katarina stood in the doorway following his gaze. 'Who are you talking to.'

'I, er ... I was daydreaming.' Holy Christ, the child was still there, yet Kat could not see her.

His wife crossed the room to stand beside him, placing her hand on his forehead. 'Are you feeling quite well? You had a strange look on your face. You were smiling and you said you were happy to see someone.'

He forced a laugh. 'My imagination ran away with me.' He knew then he would never tell her for how could she believe him? She would worry, thinking he was losing his mind ... and perhaps he was for he could see her still out of the corner of his eye, sitting on the floor playing with her doll. He so wanted to look at her properly, but he knew the others were watching him now, too. He stood. I need some air, and with that, he opened the door into the shop and went out onto the street walking quickly away, his thoughts in turmoil.

He had seen Teresa as clearly as he saw any of the men and boys in the workshop. As clearly as he saw Kat. But how could such a thing be possible? He halted so suddenly that a woman walking behind him cried out. 'What are you trying to do stopping like that? *Idiota.*' She struck her forehead with the heel of her hand as she walked around him.

He understood then what he must do, for across the street was the looming mass of San Domenico's. He needed to speak with Father Sebastian, and walking into the silent church, he felt the weight of that silence in the gloomy space above him where the vaulted ceiling was lost in candle-smoke and shadow.

When he found the priest in the Rosary Chapel, it seemed a sign for the Guarneri family tomb was there and so, of course, was his daughter. Every time they visited her, they were grateful again to Merla for her decision to tell the authorities that Teresa had lived for a short time after her birth when, in truth, she was stillborn. Whatever the Church's teachings were, his daughter had a soul. He had seen that in her perfection the moment he set eyes on her.

He lowered himself into a pew and waited for the priest to finish his prayers kneeling before the small altar with its golden crucifix and flickering votive candles on either side. Father Sebastian crossed himself, lifting and kissing the cross that hung on his chest before rising to his feet. If Giuseppe's presence there surprised him, he concealed it well.

'Giuseppe. What can I do for you, my son?'

That always made him smile, for the priest was much of an age with him, though slight as a boy. Yet now it was time for him to speak he could not find the words. Perhaps the priest might think he had indeed lost his mind ... or that he blasphemed?

Father Sebastian sat beside him in the pew. Both looked at the altar rather than at each other. 'Take your time. I'm here when you're ready.'

Giuseppe nodded. He took a breath. Still, the words would not come.

With his eyes fixed on the altar, the young priest spoke again. 'There are a lot of Guarneri in here. It must be a comfort to you to know they are together.'

'My daughter,' he managed to say.

The priest turned to look at him. 'Is with her grandparents. Her great uncles.'

And then Giuseppe spoke in a rush. 'I saw her, Father. I saw Teresa.' He was barely aware that tears flooded down his face. 'She was in my workshop playing with a doll. She was so beautiful. She had Kat's hair. I spoke to her, but she didn't answer ... or look at me. I thought I was dreaming until I realised my men were real and it was no dream. No one else saw her.' He shook his head. 'Kat didn't. Kat couldn't see our daughter.' He swiped away tears with his fingers turning to look at the priest now. 'Have I lost my mind? Is that what this is?'

'No.' It was said emphatically.

Then the silence seemed to stretch. Footsteps sounded out

in the nave and Giuseppe wondered whether the priest would leave him, but he did not.

'Our Lord has smiled upon you, my son, granting such a gift to show you your daughter is safe in his care. Wrapped in his love.'

Giuseppe frowned. Surely if Teresa were sent by God, she would have glowed a bit or had angel wings or some such? She had appeared just like a normal, happy child. Like she might have done had she lived and come to play in his workshop. He cleared his throat and tried to articulate some of this to the priest. 'She didn't look like a vision. The sort that saints seem to get sent from God.' He snorted a laugh. 'And I'm certainly not one of them.'

'God's ways are beyond our knowing, Giuseppe.'

'Shall I see her again, Father?'

'If Our Lord wishes it.'

There seemed nothing more to be said. When the priest rose and returned to pray at the altar, Giuseppe dropped to his knees to give thanks and ask that he might be granted this vision again. Yet even as he prayed part of him was uncertain. Did he want to see her when no one else could, when he felt he could not look at her or speak to her because it made him seem a lunatic? He prayed then that if she came again, he might be alone. And with that, he rose and left the church.

Once outside in the sharp, icy wind, the cold struck him more intensely after the cool stillness inside the church, he found he did not want to return to the workshop, afraid Teresa might still be there. *Christ. What if she never leaves?* He turned instead into the Piazza San Domenico. He would visit his papà.

Andrea's health had been poor in recent times, with his bad chest resulting in a hospital stay the winter before. He hurried past Leonardo Rolla's house next door – a blacksmith with a prosperous forge down near the docks – not wishing the man to see him. His papà's old debt to him had been a burden on him for as long as Giuseppe could remember, and it had recently become a bone of contention once again. Rolla now demanded it be settled in full even though Andrea had repaid some of it by renting out a part of his house when his health had prevented him from working.

That Nonna Barb was overjoyed to see him, left him uncomfortably guilty for not visiting more often. He knew they slipped from his mind just as easily as Kat did when his work took over his thoughts. He pulled her to him and kissed her on the forehead. She seemed especially tiny now, though she had always been a slip of a thing. He had a sudden desire to tell her of Teresa, knowing she would accept it without question. Yet he found himself quite unable to speak of it. He took a breath. 'How is Papà?'

'Oh, don't you worry about him. He's better than he was last year, the Lord be praised, so we can't really complain now, can we?'

Giuseppe thought they had every right to complain but how typical of his nonna to see only the bright side of things. 'Is he able to work now?'

He watched the joy slip from her face momentary before she managed to restore her customary expression of cheerful good humour. 'He does his best—'

'Is Rolla still pestering him—'

'No, it's not like that, lad. Your papà owes him money. He has every right to expect it to be repaid.'

'But if he's unable to work properly, how is he supposed to do it? Isn't the rent money enough for the man?'

Nonna shook her head sadly, and then brightened again. 'He's getting stronger every day, though. Soon he'll be making instruments again. I know he will.'

Giuseppe sighed. He doubted this was true and with the winter approaching he could not see their situation improving. Though he could not offer them money again, remembering the scene it had caused last winter. 'I'd better see him.' He gestured towards the workshop. 'In there?'

She nodded, again unable to keep the worry from her face.

He opened the door and stepped inside. The room was cold. So cold he could see his breath misting before him. His papà sat at his workbench with a blanket around his shoulders, his head resting on his folded arms, snoring softly. Giuseppe questioned whether to wake him but knew he would be hurt if he did not when Nonna told him he had called by.

He placed his hand gently on his father's back. 'Papà?'

Andrea spluttered and sat up, shaking his head to clear his obvious confusion. 'Giuseppe. It's you. I, er … I wasn't sleeping, I was just resting my eyes for a moment. You know how it is?'

'I do. This trade of ours is tiring on the eyes.'

His father squared his shoulders. 'So, what can I do for you? You don't often show your face around here.' His attempt to assert himself was rather spoiled by a coughing fit.

When Giuseppe hurried to the kitchen to fetch him a cup of water, a thought occurred to him. He handed his papà the cup and as soon as he had sipped it and recovered himself, he spoke. 'I need to ask a favour of you. One of my best men is leaving to join the Amati workshop—'

'More fool him. No one rates them no more.'

Giuseppe shrugged. 'I know it, but what can you do? Anyway, I wondered if you might be free to help me out from time to time?'

Andrea frowned. 'Well, I don't know about that. I have commitments here, you know—'

'I'd pay you, Papa. I wouldn't expect you to do it out of the kindness of your heart, believe it or not.'

'When would you want me?'

'Whenever you can spare the time.'

Andrea cleared his throat but managed to avoid coughing.

'Perhaps the end of the week might be possible. I'll send a note—'

'No need. Just turn up when you can.'

In the weeks that followed, Andrea spent most of his afternoons in Giuseppe's workshop, where he settled into a routine carving scrolls (some of his finest work, intricate and delicate, though Giuseppe did not tell him so, knowing he would be rebuffed) and disparaging the young apprentices, who seemed to take it in their stride and were even willing to learn from him on occasion when he was in better humour. What he thought of Katarina working alongside them, he kept to himself after much harumphing. She told Giuseppe how he sometimes paid her grudging compliments, but he never did so in front of him.

As Christmas approached, just when he began to accept he would never see his daughter again, that it had been some sort of delusion brought on by an unbalanced mind, it happened. This time he was alone, as he had prayed for, up in the first-floor parlour lighting the candles as dusk fell. Katarina and Chiara had gone to a Christmas market in the *Piazza del Comune*. His first response was to cross himself and thank God, and beyond that, he decided not to question it anymore. 'Teresa. I'm so happy to see you again, little one.'

She neither looked nor answered. He did not know it then, but he would not hear her speak for many years and when he did, at last, it would bring him joy beyond anything he could imagine. That evening, though, he talked to her while she sat, seeming content upon the floor holding her ragdoll, though he could not tell if she heard all he told her of his life and of her mother.

When Katarina called from below, telling him to come down for they had brought pork from the hog roast and hot cider for their supper, he glanced away and looking back, she had gone.

He stood and closed his eyes, crossing himself and thanking God again for the miracle he had been granted.

After finding sleep difficult that night, he understood he must find a way to mark this miraculous occurrence in his life and, finally, just before sleep came for him, he decided upon a course of action.

The next day, he designed a new maker's label to affix inside his instruments. GIUSEPPE GUARNERIA FECIT CREMONE ANNO 1731 I.H.S

'What's this?' Katarina asked, pointing to the letters he had never included before.

'Iesus Hominem Salvator. Jesus—'

'Jesus Saviour of Man. I know what it means. But why?'

He blinked. What could he say? Not the truth, obviously. 'I think we have a lot to thank The Lord for, Kat. I want to honour him in my work.'

Katarina tilted her head studying him. He could read her scepticism but in the end all she said was 'Hmm.'

Twenty-Three

CREMONA, DECEMBER 1737

ONE CHILLY DECEMBER DAY, WHEN ANDREA ARRIVED in the workshop looking particularly pleased with himself despite the cold, Katarina glanced at Giuseppe who answered her raised eyebrows with a shrug.

He placed the nearly completed viola down onto his bench. 'Good morning, Papà. You're looking cheerful.'

'What? I'm always cheerful.'

Suppressed chuckles erupted around the room.

'What?' he said again, glancing around trying to scowl but not quite managing it.

Giuseppe tilted his head, waiting.'

'I've made another payment to Rolla.'

Giuseppe sighed. 'That must be a relief. It should get him off your back for a while.' He paused expectantly, but Andrea said nothing further. 'All right, how?'

'I finally sold to Jacopo.' I didn't need that part of the house, that's why I rented it to him.'

You rented it to him because you needed the money. If you hadn't wanted the rooms, you'd have sold to him at the outset when he offered for them. He doubted his papà would care to have that truth pointed out to him. 'Makes sense.'

'Glad you feel that way, lad. I worried you might see your inheritance dwindling, especially as you rent here.'

Giuseppe caught a flicker of something on Kat's face. Was she worried by their seeming lack of security? It had never occurred to him that she might be. But surely she would trust Gianni to be a good landlord? *Christ, what sort of twisted thinking is this?* 'We rent from a friend,' he lied.

'There are no friends when it comes to money. Do you think he wouldn't sell it out from under you if he got a good enough offer?'

'I know he wouldn't.' *Because it's not his to sell.*

'Pah. You know nothing.'

Giuseppe shrugged. What could he say?

Katarina had spent the morning baking with Chiara. It was warmer in the kitchen than in the workshop and she knew that Nonna Barb enjoyed her company now she could do little more than sit in a comfortable chair beside the cooking fire and allow herself to be plied with hot drinks and pastries fresh from the oven. Her increasing frailty had played a large part in persuading Andrea to stay with them through the winter months. He understood it would be too much for the old woman to care for him when she was in such a poor state herself.

Katarina lifted a batch of tarts from the oven and placed them on top of the range. 'Why is my pastry aways burnt around the edges?'

Chiara sniggered. 'Coz you don't do it how I tells you, Madonna.'

Katarina took a breath ready to deny it when she heard a violin playing briefly. Giuseppe had finished stringing the Tabolli commission. It sounded good. Very good. 'I do exactly what you tell me—'

'Kat.' Giuseppe called from the workshop. 'Can you come in here for a moment?'

She wiped her hands on her apron, still frowning at the tarts. 'Can't you cut off the burnt bits or something?'

'I'll try but ... some'll be a bit short on pastry.'

Katarina took off her apron and dropped it onto the table. 'Just do the best you can. They can't look any worse.'

Nonna Barb chuckled. 'They could. She's done 'em worse herself.'

All three women were laughing when Katarina opened the door to see what her husband wanted.

Giuseppe handed her the violin. She studied it, running her fingertips over the back plate where subtle tool marks were still visible beneath the glowing varnish. She turned it over. The purling was very fine, though with nothing ornate about it. Giuseppe still refused to do ornate. 'It's beautiful. The balance is perfect.'

Her husband's eyes were avid. 'Now play it.'

Katarina accepted the bow he passed to her and placed her chin on the rest. One glance around the room showed all eyes were upon her. 'What shall I play?'

Giuseppe grinned. 'Something hard.'

So, that is what she did, choosing Biber's Sonata for solo violin, her eyes widening at the instrument's tonal range before losing herself in the music. When she lowered it all those in the workshop clapped as did Chiara standing in the open doorway to the kitchen parlour.

'Well?' Giuseppe said.

She smiled handing the instrument back to him and kissing him. 'I think it's your best yet.'

'I think so too. The texture of the sound is intoxicating, Kat. The purity of tone; the sweetness in the upper register; the rich projection. Christ. It's too good for Tabolli. I can find another for him.'

'What will you do with it?'

'I'll put word out I've something exceptional for sale and see what happens. It needs to go to someone who'll know what they've got. Someone able to play it as it should be played, just like you did.'

She frowned slightly. 'Be careful this time.' The last one had gone for a high price, but the man had bought it to give it to his son and nothing could be done after money had changed hands.

'Don't worry. I'll need to know exactly what this one is for before I part with it. This is a king of violins. Money comes second.'

Katarina took a moment to be grateful that their circumstances now meant it could.

It was a bright frosty morning, with Christmas fast approaching, when Giuseppe learnt of Antonio Stradivari's death. Though dying at ninety-two could not be entirely unexpected – he could only pray his papà might live so long suffering from the same weak chest that had taken Antonio in the end – it was still sad. Sad for his family and for his friends.

After the messenger boy had left to carry on with his doleful task around the luthiers' isle, Giuseppe took a few moments to let the news sink in. Antonio and his family had been good and generous friend to both his father and himself over the years. Though his son, Francesco, had taken over much of the running of his workshop, Antonio had carried on crafting instruments. It seemed incredible to realise he had been doing so for more than seventy-five years. He would be missed by the whole luthier community. It truly was the end of an era.

Giuseppe sighed, knowing he must now tell his father and Nonna Barb – who was not far off Antonio's age herself – and dreading it. Both had known him all their lives. But first, he would tell Kat. A treacherous small voice suggested it might be easier for his papà and nonna to hear such sorrowful news from her, but he shook his head to banish it. They were his blood, and they must hear it from his lips.

Nonna had wept softly, holding a white lace handkerchief to her eyes. 'I scattered rose petals when he married Francesca Ferraboschi seventy years ago. I remember it plainly. It was a hot, sunny day. She was such a pretty woman. She'd been wed before and had two little children.'

Andrea was silent for a time before taking a breath as though to speak but having a coughing fit instead. There seemed nothing more to be said after that.

Did the old man fear he would be next? Giuseppe kissed the top of his head, his fine white hair damp from the exertion, praying it would not be so.

The funeral in San Domenico Basilica was held three days later. It was a frigid day with tiny pellets of icy snow falling from a sullen sky to sting the faces of the mourners as they made their way to the church, swathed in winter cloaks with hoods up tight against the treacherous wind. The isle turned out in force together with many townspeople and patrons of his workshop, leaving the church full to overflowing.

The candles danced and smoked in the eddying drafts while the Mass was said by Father Sebastian. A small chamber orchestra filled the intervals, many playing Antonio's instruments. His sons Francesco and Omobono – fortuitously visiting with his family from his home in Naples – were among them. Giuseppe had been asked but had declined needing to help his papà and nonna manage the walk to the church, Andrea on his arm and Nonna on Katarina's. Never mind that Kat was much the better player, though a woman would not be expected to play in church.

The service was a moving one, how could it not be when such a long and successful life had come to an end? With eulogies read by his other sons, many wept. When the family followed the coffin into the Rosary Chapel for the committal and internment, the congregation made their way outside onto the concourse once more, and back into the snow.

The Guarneri family were one of those invited to take refreshments at the Stradivari house – only doors away from Andrea's – at 2 San Domenico Piazza with its distinctive rooftop loft where Antonio liked to make his instruments. The house where he had lived and worked for nearly sixty years. Giuseppe could not help contrasting Antonio's financial situation with that of his papà. Yet Andrea was a fine luthier. It seemed simply that God had not smiled upon Andrea Guarneri in the same way he had on Antonio Stradivari.

The house was crowded with luthiers, their wives and grown-up children already part of their family businesses. Some of Antonio's most loyal patrons were also present, and it was with one of these that Giuseppe found himself in conversation after he had settled his papà and nonna in chairs close to the fire in the first-floor parlour, leaving them in the willing hands of Antonio's youngest daughters, who were happy to fetch hot wine and cakes. Then intending to find Kat helping in the kitchens, on a whim, he went up to the second floor instead. At the end of a narrow passageway, he found a ladder-like staircase leading up to that rooftop loft Antonio had used as both a varnish drying area and a workroom.

Stepping inside, he found it bright even on a dull afternoon with light flooding in from the two large windows. And it was full of Antonio's instruments in various stages of completion hanging from hooks on one wall, with his tools hung upon another and a drying rack for those newly varnished. All this he saw in one quick glance, for his attention was instantly focused upon the man who sat at Antonio's workbench holding a violin. And this was no luthier. He wore a heavy coat of fine wool, clearly tailored to fit, with a velvet collar embroidered with an intricate leaf pattern in silver thread. His dark hair was neatly tied with a black ribbon at his neck.

Hearing Giuseppe's approach he spun around and rose quickly to his feet. 'Forgive me. I had to see this place for myself.' He held up the rather unremarkable violin. 'And to see the Messiah.'

Giuseppe had heard of it but never seen it. He'd made it in 1716, and it had never left his desk.

'I shouldn't be in here, I know. I—'

'Neither should I. Like you, I wished to see it ... the workshop and the violin. He kept them private.'

The man, taller and broader than Giuseppe, held out his hand. 'Marco Bello.'

Giuseppe knew the name. He was one of Antonio's most regular patrons, an accomplished player of both violin and cello. He grasped and shook. 'Giuseppe Guarneri.'

Marco grinned. 'Del Gesù, himself. I'm honoured to meet you, *Signore*.' He nodded to himself. 'And very well met indeed, for I'd been hoping I might do so today.' He frowned. 'Not that I should be doing business on such a sad day but, well.' He shrugged.

'I don't think Antonio would object. He was a pragmatic man. Now, what can I do for you, Signor Bello?'

Marco rubbed his hands together. 'It's perishing cold in here.' He looked around the room. 'Presumably, he had some source of heat when he worked?'

Giuseppe pointed to a small wood burner, its grate full of ash.

'Ah. Shall we remain here for privacy or go downstairs for warmth?'

'I think that rather depends on your business, *Signore*.'

'Do please call me Marco.'

'Giuseppe.'

Marco cleared his throat. 'I believe you have a rather special violin for sale? I would very much like to see it … to play it if I may?'

'Just out of interest, who is your informant—'

They both turned at the sound of footsteps on the staircase, watching as Kat appeared in the doorway. 'I couldn't help overhearing you. You want to play the violin?'

Marco Bello stepped towards her, taking her hand in bringing it to his lips. 'Am I correct in assuming you are Signora Guarneri?' he asked before introducing himself.

She nodded, appraising him quite openly. 'Are you a musician, *Signore*?'

Giuseppe had to acknowledge he was a fine-looking man and was surprised by a sharp pang of jealousy seeing the way Kat looked at him.

'I am. I've had a few instruments from Stradivari over the years, which I enjoy playing.' He snorted a laugh. 'I don't buy them to look at, though one of his violins is indeed exquisitely decorated. A delicate tracery of tiny flowers and leaves on the ribs and neck.'

'Ours has an exquisite sound.'

'Ours?' He watched her intently.

'From the Guarneri workshop.'

He tilted his head, still studying her. 'I've heard rumours that you are a fine luthier yourself, *Signora*?'

'Don't believe everything you hear, Marco. Kat prettifies my purfling and ribs from time to time and brings a rather fine quality to our varnishing.' Giuseppe knew he was not believed. 'Though she did neither on the violin that interest you. No hand touched that one save my own.' He glanced at his wife, who gave a slight nod. On this occasion, he had spoken the truth. The work was all his.

Katarina smiled. 'Indeed. Perhaps you might care to join us for dinner one evening, *Signore?*'

'I should love to but, unfortunately, I must leave for Milan first thing tomorrow. Though I cannot say I look forward to it. Travelling at this time of year can never be anything other than a trial.'

Then come this evening,' Katarina said.

Giuseppe poked the fire in the dining room where they would entertain their guest, adding another log before taking a wax taper to light the candles in wall sconces and floor-standing candelabras. Dusk had come early. 'How are they, do you think?'

He did not need to say of whom he spoke. Katarina took a fine white damask cloth from the dresser drawer and spread it over the mahogany table. 'It's odd we see them as the same when Nonna must be at least twenty years older than your papà.'

'Fifteen, actually. My mamma was good bit younger than him. But I know what you mean. He seems old before his time. It's hard to see him now and believe he might live to a ripe old age like Antonio.'

She moved to him and put her arms around him. 'We're looking after him. Chiara is feeding him up, and Merla has remedies that seem to help.'

He crossed himself. 'It's in God's hands. We can't know his plan for any of us.'

She cupped his face with her palm. Still not sure what had inspired this powerful turn to religion. It had come about quite suddenly. 'Then let's leave God to his plan and do what we can for him here in our home.'

He grinned. 'And I'd better fetch the violin.

. . .

Katarina had thought of Gianni immediately when Marco Bello had shown himself so well-informed, so invited him and Mia to join them for dinner. And it transpired that Gianni and Marco were partners in a grain exporting business in Milan. Needless to say, this hardly came as a surprise. She would thank Gianni later for bringing her husband and Marco together.

The *Milanese* was the perfect guest, praising the food and wine and spending time talking to both Andrea and Nonna Barb, the latter seeming quite taken with him. Even a woman of her great age was not immune to his good looks, (and why should she be, Katarina admonished herself) which were even more impressive dressed as he was in a fine coat and breeches of damson velvet and a waistcoat richly embroidered with gold thread. She caught Giuseppe's hard stare and laughed. *Sweet Jesu, the man was jealous.*

When the table was cleared, the brandy poured, and Nonna settled into a chair beside the fire, Katarina decided to get down to business. 'Now I think it's time to show Marco the violin.'

Giuseppe quickly fetched it from the cupboard and Katarina smiled at the way he carried it, reminded of the first time she had watched him cradle an instrument in this way on that fateful day in his father's shop more years ago than she cared to remember. He handed it to Marco, who held it with equal care, moving it closer to the candle flame to examine it. 'I like the hint of tool markings.' Surprising her, he passed the instrument across the table. 'I've heard you are a talented player.'

Katarina and Giuseppe exchanged knowing glances before turning their eyes on Gianna who had the good grace to look sheepish. 'You seem to know a lot about us, *Signore*.' She rose then to the sound of Mia's laughter (that lady's fine eyes were decidedly fixed upon Marco, too) and collecting the bow, she decided to play the same sonata she had chosen in the workshop. At first, she felt Marco's eyes upon her but soon forgot her surroundings, as always, once the music filled her, only coming back to herself when the applause startled her.

'*Brava*' called Andrea. '*Brava.*'

Even Nonna had sat up higher in her chair to join in the clapping. Katarina handed the instrument and bow to Marco. 'Now it's your turn.'

Putting the violin beneath his chin, he played a short scale before lowering it again. 'How can I follow you? All I've heard of your talent has not done you justice. I already know I wish to buy this.' He turned to Giuseppe. 'It's time for you to name your price.'

'I shall, *Signore*. But first I should like to hear you play, if you don't mind.'

Marco laughed with more than a hint of self-depreciation. 'Very well. You must see if I'm worthy of it. I can understand that.'

Gianni leaned forward, draining his glass. 'He's a fine player.'

Marco lifted the violin and began to play.

And he was a fine player. But not as fine as her, Katarina recognised without any personal satisfaction. It was simply the truth. When Giuseppe asked him for 400 lira Austriaca, she gasped, then her eyes widened when he immediately accepted. *Perhaps we should have asked for more?* Though Gianni's raised eyebrows told her they had done better than he anticipated.

Giuseppe locked the violin inside a cabinet where it would remain until Marco's agent called with a bill of credit before moving quickly around the empty room extinguishing candles, but when he turned towards the fireplace, he gave a slight gasp to see Teresa there, kneeling to play in the firelight. Why was he still startled each time he saw her? She would be twelve years old now. Slender as a willow, with Kat's silken hair hanging to her waist. She kept flicking it away as she bounced a tiny ball and raced to pick up a handful of small wooden crosses before catching it again. It looked tricky but she seemed to manage it easily.

As usual, she never glanced at him, and he had the same feeling he always had, that he was seeing her somewhere else. That the surroundings she saw were not these. Yet it did not look like heaven. Or not any heaven he had read of or seen in paintings. But how did anyone truly know the landscape of paradise? Maybe it was not much different to Earth. He shrugged and sat to watch his daughter play.

And he spoke to her as he always did. Telling her of the Requiem Mass for an old friend, and how he had sold a violin for more money than he could ever have imagined, all in the course of one day. 'A sad day and a wonderful one.' But that was life, was it not? A heady … terrifying mix of both. He closed his eyes for a moment, knowing when he opened them, Teresa would be gone.

Kat was at her toilet table already in her nightgown, brushing the silken mass of her hair when he arrived in their bedchamber. He wished he could tell her of Teresa. How she grew older with the passing years so he always saw her as she would be had she lived. *How can I now, though? Too much time has passed.* She would think him even more insane because he had not told her of his *delusions* for all these years. He suppressed a small groan, wishing she could see how beautiful their daughter was now. *Am I mad?*

'What?'

'Your hair's a picture.' He took the brush from her hand and swept it down the chocolate lengths before lifting it to kiss her neck. And suddenly desire flamed, and he had to have her there and then. He pulled her to her feet and swept her up in his arms to carry her to the bed.

'What's brought this on?' She murmured between returning his kisses.

He loved this so much about her, how she always met his desire with her own. 'You brought it on. The sight of you.'

She pulled away enough to speak. 'Or the thought of 400 lira.

They laughed together and made love fiercely ... and tenderly.

Death had not yet done with Giuseppe, though. He was awoken in the early morning of the last day of the old year by a frantic knocking upon the bedchamber door.

Signore, Signore. You must come,' Chiara called.

Kat was quicker and had the door open to admit the frantic maid before he had even found his robe. She already had a calming hand on Chiara's shoulder, having taken a flickering candle from her trembling hand. 'What is it? What's happened?'

'It's Signora Nonna. You must come, Madonna.'

Dawn was barely a hint of sapphire on the horizon, seen through the open shutters in Nonna's chamber when Giuseppe arrived at her bedside. Chiara had gone in with her dish of coffee, which she liked at the same hour each morning regardless of the season and found her gone. She had slipped away in her sleep. *A kind death.* And that thought brought his tears.

Giuseppe knelt beside the bed holding her cold hand, small-boned and light as a bird. Katarina had hurried to the floor above to send a lad for the priest. Though it was too late for the last rites, he could at least pray over her. Giuseppe hoped she was still near enough to hear those words of comfort, commending her soul to God.

He brought the hand to his lips and kissed it, thinking of

how she had been a mother to him after his own – her beloved daughter – had died in childbed. Because of her, he had never missed a mother's love in his life as Kat had. Standing to kiss her forehead, his tears spilled over her cold flesh collecting in the hollows of her cheeks, so she appeared to weep for her own death. He lifted the corner of the quilt to pat her skin dry.

Barbara Franchi was interred in the family tomb in San Domenico's Rosary Chapel just thirteen days after Antonio Stradivari. Once again, the luthiers of the isle filled the church pews, though there were fewer mourners than for Antonio. No patrons or ordinary townsfolk, of course, and many of the luthier families' younger members had been left behind to man the workshops.

When they rose to follow the coffin into the side chapel – she would be but a slight burden for the pallbearers – it had been Kat who spotted Sancia Bertolli (as she now was) nudging him and gesturing with a slight movement of her head where to look. Sancia stood between her new husband Alfonso (portly, bald and thirty years her senior) and Giuseppe's now teenage son Luca. *Does he know he's mine?*

It was a shock to see his boy so grown. Sancia, newly widowed, had taken him to Milan some years before and they had only just learnt of her return to the Bertolli house on his large estate close to the river.

'Why is she here?' Kat whispered. 'How dare she intrude on your grief today.'

But Luca was Nonna's great-grandson, so it seemed right for him to be at her funeral even though she had not known him. He imagined Kat had no wish to dwell on that relationship, though. Surprisingly, Sancia had the decency not to join the family for the interment. This time the weather had been kinder. Though cold, the sun shone in a cloudless sky of sapphire blue.

All that was missing was the summer warmth. The black-clad figures seemed incongruous in such light. He stood still for a moment taking deep breaths, suddenly bereft. A beautiful day at last. A day his nonna had not lived to see.

Sancia and her family waited close beside the central entrance doors just beyond the porch, so he had little choice but to speak with them. His wife held tightly to his arm. 'Sancia. I'd heard you'd returned to Cremona.' Gianni had been their informant, of course, as he was with everything. Sancia introduced her husband who eyed them both with some distaste. Giuseppe watched Kat doing her best to throw that expression right back at him and fought a strong urge to laugh. Odd when but a moment before he had fought back tears.

'After our marriage, we came back to live on Alfonso's estate.' Her voice had become more refined. More like Kat's. Again, he battled inappropriate laughter. Then his gaze landed upon his son, who had moved out from behind his stepfather. How could he not see himself? The hair. The eyes. And already the suggestion that he would more than match his own height and build. Again, he wondered if the boy knew who he was. *Can he see himself in me?*

'You're my papà.' It was said matter-of-factly. I don't remember you, but Mamma says we have met before.' He held out his hand for Giuseppe to shake. 'I'm sorry about your nonna.'

Giuseppe, finding himself at a loss for words, took the boy's hand in his and shook it, fighting the desire to hug him. His son. Kat still clung to his other arm.

'Is there something we can do for you, Sancia,' she asked, her voice clipped and frosty.

Sancia tilted her head, making it obvious she looked Kat up and down. 'You must be sad to have no children, Katarina. I think it would be kind to allow Giuseppe to get to know his only child, don't you?'

Giuseppe felt her anger thrumming.

'Of course, Sancia. How sad that you should have taken him away from Cremona for so many years, so he could not.'

Sancia's poise deserted her for a moment, her smile faltering. 'Well, they must get to know one another now, must they not?'

'Indeed, now they have the opportunity.'

Giuseppe cleared his throat. 'You'd be welcome to visit us anytime, Luca. We no longer live on San Domenic Piazza, we—'

'I know where you live, Giuseppe. Though I had a little more than that in mind.'

Katarina tugged at his arm. 'We must get home. We have mourners coming for refreshments after the service. We mustn't linger here.'

'Yes, of course.' He returned his attention to Sancia. 'Forgive us. As I said, I'd be happy to see Luca—'

'You'd do well to spare us a moment or two more, *Signore*.' The husband had spoken at last. His voice was surprisingly high for a man of such large circumference, and heavily accented too. Not Cremonese, though Giuseppe could not place it.

'We've just lost a dearly loved family member. This is neither the time nor place—'

'It's alright, Kat.'

'Say what you must quickly then,' she snapped.

Sancia smiled sweetly, once more. 'So, as you and Katarina.' She gave Kat a lingering look full of spite. 'As you and Katarina are childless, Luca is your heir. It seems only right and proper … I believe it is right for him to become your apprentice and learn the luthier trade so he can inherit your business.' She shrugged. 'When you are no longer with us.' She giggled behind her hand. 'Which I'm sure will be many years from now – I mean look how long Antonio Stradivari lasted – so Luca should have plenty of time to learn, no?'

'*What?*' Katarina released Giuseppe's arm and took a step towards her. 'We have nephews—'

'Yes, I heard Pietro has many sons ... and daughters too, of course. How many is it now?'

Katarina narrowed her eyes.

Giuseppe decided to be circumspect. 'I've rather lost track, I'm afraid.'

Sancia was not fooled. 'What a shame they couldn't be here for a family funeral.'

'It's the middle of winter for God's sake,' Katarina all but spat. 'Who travels at this time of year?'

'Or could it be the lady of the house is with child yet again, and her dutiful husband did not wish to leave her alone so close to her time, perhaps?'

Katarina seized Giuseppe's arm again, breathing hard. 'Anyway, there is a glut of nephews to inherit the business. To keep the family name going. The legitimate family name that is.'

Giuseppe wished she had not said that for Luca's face coloured. Her words had hurt him. Christ, whoever was at fault in this, it was not him.'

Kat tugged at him again. 'We must hurry.'

As he walked away, he turned to look over his shoulder. 'Call on me soon, we'll talk further.'

'What! There's nothing to talk about.'

He waited until they were out of earshot. 'I think there is,' he said quietly.

Jesus Christ, Sancia's bastard? In truth, his father could be anyone—'

His snort of derision silenced her. 'Don't be a bloody fool.' She had long acknowledged Luca was his.

She was quiet for a time while they hurried home, though there was no real need for concern. Chiara had left with Andrea as soon as the Mass finished and would be there to welcome their guests. Gianni, Mia and Claudio would be there by now, too. All would be running smoothly.

'Very well. Of course, I know Luca is your son but—'

'Let's leave it now. We can talk later when the wake is over.' He turned to look at her. 'I wish you hadn't been unkind to him though. I saw he was hurt by what you said.'

'Jesu,' she said under her breath. 'You're right. I lost my temper. It was unforgivable to hurt the poor boy when it was Sancia I was after. Let's hope it is your character he's inherited and not hers.' She squeezed his arm. 'Will you have him as an apprentice?'

'How can I refuse if it's what he wants? But I must find out if it's his choice and not hers.'

'Send a note asking him to visit you alone.'

He snorted a laugh. 'I can't see her going along with that, can you? She'll need to be with him if only to infuriate you.'

Kat laughed. 'Then I shall ensure she does nothing of the sort.'

'*Really?*'

'That she can witness, anyway.'

That visit came sooner than expected on a morning but two days later. As luck would have it, Gianni was with them in the workshop and went out to tend to their customer as both Katarina and Giuseppe were busy. When his head appeared around the door to tell them Sancia and Luca were there to see Giuseppe, Katarina rose taking off her apron and indicating that one of the assistants should take her place at the workbench. Sancia need not be made aware of her activities there.

'Fuck,' Giuseppe said, quietly.

'I didn't realise she was quite this eager,' she whispered. 'She clearly has no understanding of bereavement.'

Andrea, feeling stronger that morning, had decided to put in a few hours carving scrolls, looked up, clearly confused. 'Who's here? What's going on?' he asked, querulously.

As all attention was on Gianni, no one replied.

Gianni knowing what lay behind this visitation, rolled his eyes. Though he had little time for Sancia, he had agreed with Giuseppe that if Luca wished to become his apprentice, then it must be allowed. 'Shall I show them in?'

Giuseppe nodded. 'I need to speak with Luca alone,' he said quietly, standing to remove his own apron just as Sancia and Luca arrived in the workshop. Giuseppe gestured to the door through to the kitchen parlour. 'Can we offer you refreshments?'

Katarina watched Luca looking around the workshop, his eyes wide with interest. 'Come.' She opened the door and led them inside. 'Chiara,' she called making her way through to the kitchen, leaving Giuseppe and Gianni to seat their guests. 'Sancia and Luca are here.'

'Gawd. That were bleedin' quick.'

Chiara knew all about it, of course. Very little escaped her attention in this household. Katarina sighed. 'Damn the woman.'

'Coffee? Cinnamon cakes?' She grinned. 'A teaspoon of arsenic for the lady?'

'Sounds good.' Making her way back to kitchen parlour, she called over her shoulder. 'Though probably not the arsenic.'

'You sure, Madonna?'

Katarina waved her arm behind her back, laughing along with her maid before opening the door and fixing a friendly smile upon her face. It took quite some effort.

When Giuseppe suggested Luca should accompany him into the workshop to have a proper look around, Sancia made as though to stand clearly intending to accompany him. Giuseppe glanced at Katarina needing her to do something about it; however, it was Gianni who rose to the occasion, turning on the full force of his charm.

'Sancia, I'm eager to hear about your new home. Mia has learnt from our servants you're refurbishing it.' He grinned, shrugging. 'How servants always know these things, I've no idea.'

Katarina watched him. Of course, it would be he who knew of it. She was reminded again that not much happened in and around Cremona that he did not hear of. She sat back with a slight smile, only half listening to Sancia's prattle about all that was being done, making sure to itemise the cost of it. Though how could she not admire Gianni's ability to listen and respond appropriately (and even sound interested) to such emptyheaded nonsense? When their eyes met for a moment, his rolled conspiratorially.

Giuseppe introduced his son as Luca Estes to the workforce, though it was obvious all were quite aware who he really was, save for Andrea whose failing eyesight prevented him from spotting such an unmistakable likeness.

He walked him around telling him briefly what each worker was doing and describing the tools they used. Luca asked questions both of him and some of the men, which proved he had listened carefully to all Giuseppe told him. And he felt proud of his quick mind. How could he not? 'Now, I'll show you our drying attic where we put the newly vanished instruments.' He decided to take him there via the outside staircase at the back of the house. This would prevent Sancia from a second attempt at joining them.

Once they were alone in the long room, flooded with cold light from the large windows, Giuseppe could question the lad privately. Luca stood in the middle staring with curiosity at the range of instruments hanging in long racks their colours ranging from cream to deepest amber and chestnut, depending on the stage in the process.

He pointed. 'Why are those so pale?'

THE VIOLIN MAKER'S WIFE

'They've been treated with a wash. It prepares them for the first coat of varnish.'

Giuseppe answered all his sensible questions, realising again that there was a genuine interest behind them. So, it was time to ask him the direct question. 'Do you wish to become my apprentice, Luca? It has to be what you want not what you mother wants for you.' He was sure he already knew the answer.

'I do, very much, if you'll have me? He hesitated for a few moments. 'What should I call you ... perhaps you'd rather it was not Papà?'

Christ, how he wished it could be Papà. 'I think best not for now. Giuseppe will do fine.'

Sancia made no attempt to conceal her triumph when Giuseppe announced he was willing to take Luca into his workshop. After Kat, her smile fixed in place once again, had shown them out through the garden to the gate into the back lane, Giuseppe and Gianni waited for her in the kitchen parlour. Now there was another issue to be discussed. 'How shall we stop Luca telling Sancia about my work?'

Gianni answered first. 'Well, he'll live here with the other lads and won't see much of her, will he?'

'We can't stop him from seeing her altogether, though. All the lads go home from time to time.'

'And we can't ask him to keep secrets from his mother ... or to lie to her.' Katarina moved to the window, looking out over the garden for a few moments before turning back to the room. 'Giuseppe, everyone suspects anyway. Many people think I'm beavering away here making poor violins for the church because I'm Godless.' Her laughter was full of scorn. 'I heard that one in the market the other day. Let's just not make an issue of it. We can instruct him that what happens in the workshop is private as we've done with all of them, and after that, it will be up to him.'

In the event, they need not have worried. Though they could not question Luca about his conversations with his mother, the fact that no new rumours surfaced in the city, suggested he had told her nothing of the quality and extent of Katarina's work.

That he had often chosen to sit beside her meant they had formed an unexpected friendship. Just as his father had, she quickly came to admire his intelligence and his instincts about the luthiers' arts. And how could he not remind her of Giuseppe when she had first known him? A lanky boy not much older than this one, though he had seemed an adult to her then.

Who could have imagined she might become so fond of this lad? This son who was not hers.

Twenty-Four

CREMONA, FEBRUARY 1740

THE WINTER THAT YEAR WAS A BRUTAL ONE, FELT more so by the Guarneris for its effects upon Andrea. The freeze had begun in late November and by early February showed no sign of releasing its grip on the city. The Po froze over in all but a single central channel barely wide enough for boats to navigate. Thick smoke-laden fog filled the air most days, and the streets were slick with ice impossible to see beneath the rime, so townspeople ventured out only when unavoidable. Footprints, cart tracks, and hoofprints were but transient proofs, hidden by constant showers of powdery snow, sometimes the only sound that of icicles, grown heavy, cracking, and crashing down to smash on hard ground.

By February, Andrea had taken to his bed where they could at least try to keep him warm, with a hearty fire burning day and night. Yet, somehow, he never seemed quite warm enough, though they wrapped blankets around his thin shoulders, his skin remained white and his lips blue. With persistent coughing fits robbing him of all appetite, he did little else now but doze.

One drear afternoon, Katarina sat on one side of his bed with Anja on the other. She came whenever she could, leaving her large collection of grandchildren in Carlo's care (a huge relief, she claimed, though Kat did not believe her for one moment, knowing how she doted on them all) often bringing bone broth or beef jelly to tempt Andrea to eat.

'I can't stay long today.'

'I'm grateful you manage it at all.'

'Angela's first is due any time now, so I'll be taken up with that once it arrives, bless it.'

'How is she?'

'Mithered for it to come into such weather as this.' She shrugged. 'God knows we can do nowt about that, silly mare.' She met Katarina's eyes across Andrea's sleeping form, propped up on a pile of white linen pillows. 'Worrying don't make no difference. We've lost a few over the years. It don't do no good to dwell. We can't know the Lord's plan.'

Lost grandchildren but never one of her own. 'Well, he had a particularly unpleasant one for me, did he not?'

'You have Luca now. Be grateful for that.'

Katarina was about to protest, asking why she should when he was not hers ... but found the words would not come. She *was* grateful for him, and not only because of the pleasure he gave Giuseppe but for herself, too. She was glad to have him in her life. 'Yes. I have Luca.' She felt her eyes begin to blur with tears and fought to pull herself together. 'Just a pity about his fucking mother,' she said in German. They both spluttered laughter though tried not to, for it was hardly seemly in a sickroom. They were silent for a time then listening to Andrea's soft snores, and Katarina felt her eyelids begin to droop in the stifling room. It was Anja who reacted to the silence first, standing and bending over Andrea. 'He ain't breathing, Kat.'

Katarina was already on her feet reaching to find a pulse in his neck. 'Jesu, I think he's gone.' Her hand flew to her throat, her eyes already blinded by tears while Anja crossed herself and began to pray. *It's a kind release from his suffering. It is. It is.* Yet none of them were ready to let him go. She dried her face with her handkerchief. 'I'll fetch Giuseppe ... and we must send someone for Father Sebastian.'

Giuseppe found his thoughts drifting back to his papà's funeral while he waited on the quay in spring sunshine for Pietro and his wife to arrive. He had lost himself in his work as much as possible since then, often still in the workshop well into the night. Katarina would come down wrapped in a heavy shawl to find him there having lost all track of time. It was odd how he only noticed the cold when he became aware of his surroundings again. Then he would start to shiver.

His brother had not made it to their father's funeral, which had been hard for him. The weather had prevented it once again and, in truth, Giuseppe had been glad, and guilty that he was. Angiola's presence would have been difficult, especially for Katarina. How many children did they have now? Ten ... or was it eleven? Why did it seem worse for her that Pietro was a *finocchio* as she repeatedly called him when they were alone, and she vented her pain. At first, he had refused to believe this about his brother until Kat had forced a reluctant Gianni to confirm it. Many such were fathers. Of course they were. But eleven? *Really?*

No, Katarina and Angiola together when his grief came close to overwhelming him, would have been hard to bear. Even now simply thinking of Andrea brought an instant mist of tears.

When Kat had dashed into the workshop that morning, white as milk, her face blotched red, there had been no need to tell him. They had all been preparing for it, though it had not been spoken of. Yet, in the event, he was not ready for it at all. His papà had looked such a small, shrunken thing against the pile of pillows. He could barely reconcile that figure with the tall, vigorous man he remembered from his youth. And he had taught him all he knew of the luthiers' arts, just as he did now for Luca.

How strange he could not remember his funeral clearly. There had been so many over the last few years, they had somehow started to merge. Yet he wanted to remember his father's. Perhaps it had been too hidden behind his veil of tears? Andrea was the last of that generation. That he and Pietro were now next in line was a sobering thought … and Katarina too, of course, which was something he could not bear to even contemplate.

Just as he thought of her in such a doleful way, she arrived at his side, having secured a porter to take their visitors' boxes to the carriage she had hired for the occasion. He looked down at her. His tiny, capable wife. 'What makes you think they'll have too much for us to carry ourselves?'

'Angiola makes me think it.'

He snorted a laugh. 'Perhaps you are being a touch unfair to her. We haven't seen her for some years—'

'Women like Angiola don't change. And she has an infant with her so that will have its own paraphernalia, too.' She frowned. 'What's its name again?'

'Georgiana.'

'Ah, yes. Quite a mouthful. Don't they all have rather elaborate names?'

Giuseppe was saved from answering by the appearance of the boat looming out of the river mist and approaching the quay. 'Here they are, at last.'

'God help us,' Katarina murmured.

It did not take long to tie up and for passengers to begin disembarking. That Angiola and Pietro were the first down the gangway – Angiola leading, her daughter in her arms – came as no surprise. He glanced at Katarina who rolled her eyes as they both watched the procession of deckhands who followed them carrying trunks and other bags and boxes.

Katarina shook her head. 'Jesu. How long are they staying?'

'A week or so, I thought.'

'Longer. Much longer. I can tell you that now.'

In the carriage, Giuseppe watched his wife make polite conversation with her sister-in-law. Angiola's nature had not changed, just as Kat had predicted – with the childlike voice being just as he remembered, talking only of herself – though in appearance there was little of the young rosy-cheeked girl they had met in Venice. She had already been a touch portly then, but now she was positively stout, with several chins and button eyes almost lost in folds of flesh. Eleven children would do that, he supposed. Kat looked like a child sitting next to her, holding Angiola's latest infant on her lap. A chubby child, it had to be said.

Pietro had hugged him long and hard when he arrived on the dock and Giuseppe knew they both battled tears. Somehow neither of them could find words quite then – so choked were they by intense emotion – seeming only able to repeat each other's names. Pietro found his voice properly for the first time inside the carriage, though it shook a little. 'I wish I could have been there. Yet it would not have been possible, even without the winter weather up here.' He glanced at his wife clearly seeking her approval. And, of course, Angiola would never have allowed me to face such a thing without her by my side—'

'Don't forget I was but days away from the birth, dearest.'

Pietro reached across the carriage to pat her dimpled hand. 'No, I hadn't forgotten, dearest.'

Katarina handed the now grizzling child back to Angiola who passed her unceremoniously to the wetnurse who unlaced her bodice and produced a pendulous breast to which the child immediately attached herself.

Angiola showed no further interest in her daughter, her eyes fixed firmly upon Giuseppe. 'Has Pietro told you we have not received a copy of his dear papà's will—'

Pietro coloured. 'Dearest, let us not bring that up now.' He glanced at Giuseppe. 'There's plenty of time for me and my brother to talk, is there not?'

'Indeed. Your right, of course, dearest.' She eyed the nursemaid coldly. 'And not in front of the servants,' she said in bad schoolgirl French.

Giuseppe watched his wife fix a smile upon her face once more, turning towards Angiola. 'And how long will we have the pleasure of your company, sister-in-law?'

'We plan on a month. It's a long way to come for less, don't you think?'

Giuseppe coughed to cover a strangled laugh, seeing Kat's nostrils flare while her smile never faltered.

When the dinner dishes were finally cleared away, Angiola rose to her feet. 'Perhaps, dear sister, we might take a dish of coffee in the salon so the men may talk over their pipes?'

Giuseppe looked away, after watching the startled affront on Kat's face and seeing her bury it (and knowing what that would have cost her). Poor Kat. This woman was a trial and no mistake, but he knew his wife was up to it. 'We don't smoke tobacco in this house. Papà's chest could not tolerate it.'

Angiola glared at him. 'Well, that's hardly an issue now, is it?'

Katarina stood. 'We see no reason to change it. Come. I'll have coffee brought to the parlour. Please follow me.'

Giuseppe poured two generous glasses of brandy before retrieving a document from the dresser drawer where he had placed it earlier, knowing his brother would need to see it. 'This is probably not quite what you were expecting, I'm afraid.'

He drained his glass, watching Pietro read the will and

glance up at him at one point with a look of incomprehension on his face.

Finally, he dropped the papers onto the table. 'So, there really is nothing left beyond what remains of the house, and the workshop?'

'And the outstanding debt. I didn't know he paid for Nonna's funeral with a loan of 600 lire from Antonio Galanti '

'Who the devil is he?'

'A dealer. Papà used him to sell instruments in the last few years, while he was still able to make some. And if I'd known about him borrowing like this, I'd have insisted on paying myself. He told me it was his duty. I assumed he had money set aside ... I can't imagine what I was thinking.'

Pietro lifted the papers again and dropped them back onto the table. 'Then he went back to this man for another loan not long before he died. How could you not know about it?'

Giuseppe refilled their glasses. 'I've tried to make sense of it. It seems he arranged this loan on 11th December. Just before he took ill.'

'But how did he think he would ever pay it back? And why is there no trace of it now?'

'It went to the blacksmith, Leonardo Rolla. Papà took the money to him—'

'So, he borrowed from one to pay off another?'

Giuseppe nodded. 'And there's still some of that debt outstanding.'

'Holy Christ. What's to be done?'

'We must sell what's left of the house and make good the debts. I don't see what other choice we have.'

Pietro nodded, sighing. 'It's sad when you think of it. He was such a fine luthier. What happened that he should end up with nothing ... less than nothing, in truth.'

Giuseppe sighed. 'Rather different to Antonio Stradivari.'

'And they both learned from the Amati.' Pietro cleared his

throat. 'Will you leave all this to your lad? 'I already have Jacopo named as my heir.'

Giuseppe hesitated. 'It's complicated. I must consider what Katarina wants ... which is difficult when ... er ... she's not fully aware of the situation. That it all belongs to her—'

Pietro shook his head. 'In law, it belongs to you as her husband.'

'It's not about the law—'

'Of course it is, Giuseppe. Angiola's property, her inheritance when she gets it, all belongs to me, and I'll decide what's done with it.'

He did not think his brother would understand that it was different for him. He had not married Kat for her fortune, he had lost it for her. So, when Johannes Horak offered him the chance for her to have a more comfortable life, how could he not see it as a way to better his own, too? Somehow, he must find out her wishes. Or should he tell her everything? Johannes did not wish it, of course ... but—

'Giuseppe. I asked you a question.'

'Forgive me, I was miles away.'

'I asked if you have any instruments that you think stand out at the moment? I wish I could have seen the one you sold just after Stradivari died ... and the others since.'

'One or two seem promising. I'll show you tomorrow.' He grinned. 'I'm always hopeful.' He stood. 'Now I think we should join our wives, don't you?' Poor Kat. He had left her too long alone with Angiola.

In the parlour, Katarina sat on a sofa beside the woman, with a glazed look in her eyes. He had heard her high-pitched voice as they approached the door. Katarina's eyes met his with a roll as he walked into the room.

'We thought you were never coming,' Angiola said, staring crossly at her husband. 'Well, aren't you going to tell me?' She glanced at Katarina. 'Oh, dear. It's not a secret, is it? Not something else she doesn't know about?'

Giuseppe's eyes flew to his brother. Fuck. Surely he hadn't told his wife about Johannes Horak?

When Katarina began to laugh, he could tell her patience had finally snapped. 'What? That there's nothing to be had but debts? She spluttered. 'That secret?' She closed her eyes for a moment or two, shaking her head, still laughing quietly then leapt suddenly to her feet. 'Oh, dear. Do please excuse me. I find myself quite overcome with tiredness.'

Giuseppe watched her go, seeing Pietro's concern and Angiola's affront. Christ, this would be a long month.

Twenty-Five

CREMONA, JULY 1743

EXCITEMENT FIZZED. ONCE AGAIN, GIUSEPPE HAD finished a breathtaking violin. This happened more and more now, so much so they had an established routine for it. Firstly, he would hand it to Luca, having come to trust his instincts completely, knowing he would notice all that made each instrument distinctive, just from the look and feel of it. Then he would play it briefly himself before asking Kat to do so. And she would make it speak ... she would make it sing.

On this occasion, he could do none of this. It was a midsummer evening with twilight fast approaching, and he was alone in his workshop. The working day for his men had long finished, and Kat was visiting Anja to meet yet another new grandchild. He hung the violin carefully on the rack above his workbench, and knowing his wife would return home before nightfall, he decided to go out to meet her.

Though he had kept his hopes about this latest instrument to himself, he would tell her of it now. Then, on impulse, he lifted it down and placed it inside a case together with a bow. He would take it with him. Perhaps she might play it outside in the soft warmth of summer twilight? He smiled at the thought and let himself out through the shop.

In the street, shadows were pooling and dusk seemed to rise from them to climb walls and flow over rooftops. Once out into the Piazza San Domenico, the great expanse of the sky became visible. Stars were already aglitter against turquoise above the church's dome, though the horizon still showed the reds and purples of sunset, the air redolent with warm stone.

He saw Kat approaching as he crossed the square in deep shadow. She, though, walked through a shaft of light turning her hair to auburn and her skin to gold. How graceful she was. How straight her back. He stopped then to catch his breath at the sight of her, his heart seeming to jump and swoop in his chest. It was then he realised this was more than a joyful response to the sight of his wife. Something was wrong with him. He dropped to his knees on the cobbles, somehow managing to clutch the violin case against himself, while barely registering the pain of his collapse down onto hard stone. He gasped for breath as darkness seemed to roll towards him while, at the same time, his surroundings were falling away, like looking through the wrong end of a spyglass. *Am I dying? Please, God, no. I'm not ready.* He fought it. Fought to bring himself back.

Then hands were upon him. Small, strong hands. On his face. On his brow.

'Giuseppe! What's happened, Giuseppe? My love, what's wrong?'

More hands joined hers as passers-by came to his aid, and he was soon helped to his feet, still feeling far away and more than a little shaken.

Once home and installed in bed with a maid sent to fetch Merla, he was ready to rationalise what had happened. He had been working too hard in the heat, that was all. It was nothing that need worry him. It was easily explained.

Later, watched by his wife with arms folded and an intransient look upon her face, he reluctantly drank the apothecary's foul concoction made from herbs and God knew what else, though he had to admit he found the two women's confidence in it reassuring, and it did make him feel more himself. Enough that soon he was able to lie back against the pillows, feeling it more likely sleep would find him than death.

He sat up, suddenly. 'The violin? Where—'

Katarina pushed him back gently, stroking the hair from his forehead. 'Luca put it in the workshop. Where on earth were you going with it?'

'I was coming to meet you.'

'With a violin?'

He closed his eyes. 'I'll explain in the morning.'

Yes, the violin was indeed spectacular, he had never quite achieved such depth and range before. So, once again, they all agreed it was his best yet. And he had never felt more powerful in his skill. It was a heady time, but all the while his collapse in the street hung there at the back of his mind like a dark stain upon his happiness and newfound self-belief.

He questioned whether it was this fear that made him notice other things that perhaps he would not have done had he not been so aware of himself ... of his human frailty. He was always tired. Was that something new? And he would notice a momentary weakness in his hands when he worked. Had he imagined it?

As summer retreated into autumn his complexion seemed to lighten more than was normal and his lips looked too pale. But it was no longer summer, so what did he expect? And when winter arrived, he had a series of sore throats that even Merla's remedies could not banish. And then he noticed the bruises on his arms and legs. Bruises he had no explanation for. 'Kat?' he pulled up the sleeve of his nightshirt and held his arm close to the candle flame. 'Look.'

She held his arm and bent over it. 'What on earth have you been doing?'

'Nothing. I've no idea what caused them.'

'Are they only on your arms?' He raised his nightshirt, and she knelt on the floor holding the candle to inspect his legs. 'Giuseppe, you must take more care. I know what you're like when you get lost in your work.'

He did not say, *I've always lost myself in my work and it's never left me with bruises before.* He could see in her eyes that she had thought the same, and how much it worried her.

'You're getting older. You must take more care, my love.'

'You're right. I must be getting clumsy in my old age.' *I'm forty-five, for Christ's sake.* They had heard the previous week of the death of Antonio's heir Francesco Stradivari at the age of seventy-two. He was a long way from old age himself, and they both knew it.

Twenty-Six

CREMONA, SEPTEMBER 1744

KATARINA LOOKED UP AT THE SOUND OF THE DOOR opening and seeing Giuseppe there leaning heavily on his cane, she dropped the violin she was working on and leapt to her feet, hurrying to him. With her arm around his wasted frame, she helped him to his stool at the workbench. The men and boys watched in silence unable to hide their pity even though they knew he hated seeing it. At Katarina's sharp glare, they looked away to resume their work. Only his son's eyes remained fixed upon him.

Kat put her hand on Giuseppe's back once he was seated. 'Are you sure you're well enough for this?'

He managed a smile, his teeth too big now in his pinched face with its hollow cheeks and sunken eyes. 'If I waited for that I'd never get down here.' He reached for her hand and squeezed it with what little strength he had. 'Show me what you're working on.'

She fetched her violin. 'It's coming on.'

He took it from her though his hands shook a little. 'It is.'

She placed it down on the bench before bringing his thin hand up to her lips.

He smiled. 'Not sure what I can do in here just now, but I like to watch. The smell of the place cheers me.' He turned to one of his men. 'Even you, Nico.' Everyone laughed, dutifully. 'Yes. It makes me even more determined to get better. I've a lot more in me yet, Kat. Violins and violas.' That grin again. 'Perhaps no cellos for a while, though.'

'Your skills are all still there, my love.' She kept her smile fixed and refused the tears that threatened. Then he began to cough.

Luca was quickly at her side and together they returned him to the bedchamber. Luca pulled off his mules and covered him with a quilt, while Katarina poured a small dose of the laudanum Merla had left for him. They had found the right dose for now. One that eased his pain without making him too drowsy.

Giuseppe reached up to grasp her hand, his eyelids already fluttering. 'We've had too many sickrooms in this house in the last few years. I'll shake this off. You have my word.'

As September slipped by, Giuseppe clung to the certainty of his recovery. Though he did not get downstairs to the workshop in the weeks that followed, he still held tight to this optimism. And Katarina was grateful for it.

She made sure he was never alone now even when he slept, sitting with him herself whenever she could, only reluctantly handing over the vigil to Luca when other duties meant she must leave him.

One afternoon as the middle of the month approached, when he seemed a little improved having been able to eat a small amount of the coddled eggs Chiara prepared for him each morning, he asked that Luca should join them as he had something he needed to say to them both. Kat's heart began to pound. Was he going to tell them he now believed he would die? She could not face hearing those words from him.

'Let's not trouble him. Let him get on with his work. I'm here with you and there's nothing to take me away from you today.

'I need to speak to you both, Kat.'

She opened the door and called downstairs, asking Chiara to see to it.

Giuseppe watched while Luca pulled up a chair, his sunken eyes glittering. Kat blinked back tears seeing how they brimmed with love for his son.

When Luca was finally settled where Giuseppe wanted him, he drew a long breath to steel himself. 'I have something to tell you. It is for Kat but as it affects you too, Luca, it seems sensible to tell you together—'

Katarina leaned closer to him, her hands resting on his quilt. 'Must you do this now. You'll tire yourself. Wait until you're feeling stronger, my love.'

'He patted her hand. 'It must be now—'

She couldn't hear it. 'Don't say it. I can't hear you say it.'

Giuseppe managed a smile. 'It's all right. It's not what you think. I'm not done for yet, you know this, Kat. No. It's about this place.' He made a slight gesture with his hand. 'Our home. Our workshop.'

Katarina gasped, taken aback. And, of course, she knew what he was about to say. 'I already know. Don't exhaust yourself telling me.'

Giuseppe's eyes widened. 'How can you?' His voice had lost what little strength it had.

'Claudio told me years ago. When we were in Venice for Pietro's wedding, I overheard them speaking about what help you and he had received.'

'But you never said anything. Why?' His voice was laboured now.

Katarina leant over him, taking his hand in hers. She would not tell him she had wanted him to save face. 'Johannes didn't wish me to know, and I was ready to respect that, just as you were.'

Luca cleared his throat. 'But what has any of this to do with me? I don't even know who this Johannes is.'

Katarina did her best to explain it. When she had done, she sighed. 'I've given it a lot of thought over the years. I believe he felt somehow responsible for my rift with my father. I—'

'I was responsible for that …'

She could see Giuseppe wished to say more but could not summon the strength to speak. 'Giuseppe, you weren't. I was the one who disobeyed him, but he would never have disinherited me permanently. I'm certain of it. His accident robbed us of the chance to reconcile. He was angry with me then … but I know how much he loved me. I think Johannes felt his mother had contributed to it as well. She encouraged my father to punish me.'

'Why though, when she never wanted him to marry you?' Luca asked.

'Anything to hurt me, I suppose.' She shrugged. 'Because he loved me? Because I left him? 'Because he had chosen someone for himself instead of accepting one of the women she had chosen for him? Who knows?'

'Well, I still don't understand why I'm here. Why do I need to know any of this?'.

'The deeds to this place are in Kat's name,' Giuseppe murmured.

'So what? I—'

'Your mother wants me to …'

Kat finished for him. 'She wishes you to be your papà's heir.'

'And I have nothing to leave you …'

The law would say otherwise. You own me and everything that's mine. 'You don't need to think of that now. You're not going anywhere, my love. We just need to get you better.' How hollow those words sounded. How empty the conviction she filled them with. She watched his eyelids close and prayed that he believed still. He must not give up. That really would mean the end. He must *not* give up.

Luca stood and quietly moved his chair back against the wall. 'May I speak with you a moment?' he whispered.

She followed him out and stood with her back against the closed door. Looking at him was like seeing Giuseppe as he had once been. Young and healthy. It made her want to weep again, and she had done too much of that. 'Sorry if that was confusing.'

'Why do you think I have any wish to be Giuseppe's heir—'

'Your mother has always wanted it; you must know that.'

He frowned. 'My mother wants it? What the hell has that to do with me? I want nothing more than to stay here with Giuseppe ... and with you.'

She pulled him into her arms. 'And you always shall. You're our best luthier next only to your father. You'll always have a place here. A home here.'

'Next best after you.'

Later, when she returned inside their bedchamber after another brief exchange outside the door, this time with Chiara about the menu for the next day, she was surprised to find Giuseppe awake and sitting up against his pillows. She hurried to him, her hand quickly on his forehead checking for fever. 'Are you in pain?'

He managed a rasping chuckle.

A foolish question. He was always in pain. And then she saw he had not taken his night draught. She lifted it and brought it to his lips. 'You need to drink this.'

He pushed it away. 'I shall,' he whispered. 'Have something

else to tell you first.' And haltingly, he manged to tell her of Teresa and how he had seen her grow up over the years. How knowing she was safe and happy had comforted him.

Katarina watched him speak, understanding this was some sort of vision created by the opium medicine that Merla made for him, and his sickness. Had it happened over such a long period of time, he would have told her of it.

'Never told you. You'd think me mad. Should have … forgive me.'

She held the medicine to his lips again and watched him swallow it. 'There's nothing to forgive, my love.' She was glad he believed this now. Glad it brought him comfort. She sat beside him, stroking his hand until she was certain he had fallen asleep.

Two days later, it was Anja who broke it to Katarina that it was time to fetch the priest. Giuseppe needed the last rites. Katarina had left her alone with him while she spent a short time in the workshop making sure everything was going smoothly, which she knew it would with Luca in charge, but still felt duty bound to show her face from time to time.

Now Luca had taken over the vigil at his father's bedside, she sat in the kitchen parlour with her old friend. 'No.' She shook her head, adamant. 'Absolutely not.'

Anja grasped her hands. 'It's not a death sentence, Kat. People recover after it's been done … sometimes.'

'Sometimes. If he's aware of it, he will think he's dying.' *But he is, isn't he? Holy Christ, he is.*

'It'll bring him comfort … and if the worst happens—'

'No—'

'If it does. *If*, Kat. If it does and he is unshriven, how would you feel then?'

. . .

Chiara sent a kitchen girl to fetch Father Sebastian.

Mesmerised, Giuseppe watched the sun sink in the sky, a ball of fiery red against soft turquoise and streaks of orange. The priest's words had comforted him ... and the feel of the cool chrism on his flesh, anointed by gentle fingers making the sign of the cross upon his skin. The Lord was with him.

He knew Kat and Luca were at his bedside, but he did not look at them. Their sorrow would be too much to bear ... but the sky was so beautiful ... and he would not see it again once night fell. He accepted it now. He thought, too, of all the instruments he would have loved to make. How many 'best yets' there might have been. He bit his lip and groaned. How could he leave his work unfinished? How could he leave his wife and son when he loved them so completely? When tears leaked, the spectacle of the sky blurred.

Kat's hands arrived upon him, smoothing back his hair from his forehead. 'It's all right, my love. Everything will be all right, you'll see.' She stood. 'I'll fetch more laudanum.'

'No,' he managed to croak. 'No more. See the sky.' Still, he could not look at her. He was afraid to. He could not leave her. The sun sank below the horizon in one last fiery blast, and he closed his eyes, allowing sleep to seek him out and pull him down into welcome oblivion.

Later he woke in darkness broken only by the small glow of a single night candle. Katarina's body was pressed close against him, and he lay still, listening to her soft breathing. *My love. My dearest love.* The heat of her felt perfect against his chill, his limbs lumpen and immovable. He moved his head slightly, so his cheek rested upon her crown, and he breathed in the familiar scent of her hair. *My love.* Tears fell and he closed his eyes. When he opened them again, he thought at first it must be dawn for the room was flooded with light, until he saw darkness still around the shutters.

And then she was there looking down upon him, her eyes full of love. She was a young woman. Tall – much taller than her mother now – and slender, with the same chocolate hair and his honey-brown eyes. 'It's all right, Papà. Don't be afraid, you can come with me now. It's time.'

'Teresa, he whispered' How wonderful to see her look at him at last. To hear her voice. He reached out to grasp her hand which was warm and strong inside his. 'Teresa.'

Katarina woke at dawn knowing he was gone, convinced she had felt him die in her sleep. The air was still and silent, the candle on its last flickerings with the early light already showing through the shutter slats. Though he was cold beside her, she prayed it was another nightmare. She had had them before, waking and finding him dead beside her. She pinched herself, hard. Jesu. This time it was no dream.

She turned on her side and pulled his still form into her arms. 'Oh, my poor love. My poor, poor, love. It's over now. No more pain.' She raised herself to look down upon him, stroking his face and his tousled, grey-streaked curls. 'You left me while I slept.' She had thought she would be ready, but she was not. She was not ready to lose him at all. Her tears washed his skin, pooling in his hollow cheeks and spilling over. She clutched him to her, watching the daylight build. Seeing the first rays of sunlight. *How long can I weep? I feel I might die of it. Good.*

Chiara found her still clinging to him when she arrived to wake them with coffee and hot-buttered rolls, and Giuseppe's eggs. She set down her tray and opened the shutters, her face already wet with tears. 'Oh, Kat.' She moved to her stroking her face and gently removing her clutching fingers from her dead husband. 'You must let him go now. It's time to let go. Let me help you.'

Kat allowed herself to be eased from the bed and gently dressed in clothes Chiara must have had already set aside, for they spoke of mourning. *Mourning this morning. Mourning each day of a life I no longer want.*

She abandoned herself to Chiara's care then, and later to Luca and others who soon arrived after learning the news. Gianni, Mia, and Claudio first, of course. The first of many.

She had not expected that grief could feel so much like fear. And this grief was like nothing she had known before. She thought at first it was not fear she felt, though she experienced the sensation that she was afraid. A fluttering in the belly, the same sudden swooping in her chest, her heart a small bird beating against the bars of its cage. But she was afraid. Of course she was. Afraid of her life without Giuseppe. Her heart swooped and thudded. Swooped and thudded. *Am I dying? Please, God, let it be so.*

At other times, it seemed there was some kind of gauze veil between her and the world. It was hard to take in what anyone said. Or perhaps, she had no wish to understand it, for it was of no consequence. How could it be? Yet she wanted others about her, fearing any moments alone. If only they would talk to one another and not to her.

Her first night without Giuseppe was so desolate she later found it hard to let her mind revisit it. She had shared Chiara's bed – never contemplating returning to the one she had shared with him – but could only doze fitfully, always waking with a jolt and remembering the horror of it. She could not even weep now for her torment was too agonising. It froze her. She could only endure.

The next evening Merla gave her a sleeping draught, which brought a night filled with confused, anxious dreams instead.

Though she could not remember them clearly the anxiety stayed with her for the rest of the day.

On the third night, against all advice, she moved back into her own bed and found comfort there (despite Giuseppe's absence aching like a phantom limb) remembering his visions of Teresa. How wonderful it seemed to her now that he had believed it so completely. She prayed then – and, yes, she had prayed many times of late to a God she had professed not to altogether believe in – but how could she not pray to see her husband again? In truth, she felt him close. Just a glimpse, one final glimpse was all she asked. When sleep took her, she dreamt of him making violins and when she woke, she thought of all his knowledge and skill now gone forever and at last found the relief of tears.

How strange that while the familiar words and music of the Requiem Mass washed over her, she had the sensation that Giuseppe stood beside her just as he had always done. She closed her eyes breathing in the smoke of incense, certain she felt the warmth of his arm close to hers. When the stringed instruments began to play, her eyes flew open. As with Stradivari, a group – Pietro amongst them – had been brought together to play Giuseppe's instruments, many patrons having lent theirs for that purpose. Vivaldi's *Largo* from *Winter* was almost unbearably sorrowful played on Marco Bello's violin, the notes soaring into the high spaces like an offering.

That Pietro had come alone was a huge relief. The thought of Angiola's company had been unthinkable. Did Pietro understand this or was it for some other reason she had remained in Venice? He had arrived the night before and she had not yet spoken with him but was glad for his sake he had managed the journey in time. Gazing at him now, she saw his face was harrowed by grief.

Her eyes moved around the church, restlessly. The stained glass casting coloured bands across the floor, and the black-clad congregation shimmered with smoke turning them oddly solid. The rose window above the altar sent a shaft of light downwards making the golden monstrance gleam so brightly that light seemed to shine out from it, dazzling her. And as she watched the vessel seemed to vanish inside the brightness with spikes and shards of light forming a dancing ring moving ever outwards until it disappeared from her vision. And the monstrance was itself again ... and she had a pounding headache. *What just happened?* It made no sense. Was she ill? Or was it some sort of sign? She clutched her forehead and Merla looked down at her with alarm.

'Are you sick?' she whispered.

'I don't know.'

The remainder of the Mass and the interment in the Rosary Chapel passed in a blur of music and chanting, Sanctus bells and song, until Giuseppe was laid to rest beside his grandparents, parents, and his child.

Finally, she walked home supported by Merla and Pietro, each taking an arm, through a blustery October wind busy ripping the last of the leaves from the sweet chestnut trees, the air seeming filled with their swirlings.

The short walk had seemed interminable but when at last they arrived at the house, Katarina was swept up to her bed by Merla without showing her face in the parlour. Pleading infirmity meant she could avoid all those gathered there to remember Giuseppe. Surely, he would understand when he had loathed such gatherings. Yet he had always done his duty, a small voice chided. *But would he, had it been my funeral?* She countered. She closed her eyes, allowing herself to relax into the feather bed and pulling the quilt up over her. It was done. The first bridge had been crossed. Now she must find a way to go on living.

Chiara brought her a glass of wine and a plate of pastries. 'Sancia's here, and Luca don't seem too happy about it.'

Katarina groaned. 'Tell him to show her the will. That should see her off.'

Chiara managed a small cackle. 'Himself would've been tickled pink to see her face when she reads it, he would. Sour enough to curdle milk.'

Alone again, Katarina closed her eyes. All was now hers … or now it was known to be so. It was no longer possible to challenge it and she would be the one to decide whose inheritance it would become. Luca. Of course it would be his. He was her husband's flesh and blood, and she loved him with all her heart. Tears pricked. She could not love him more if he were her own. But would she tell him of her decision? She despised that small voice telling her not to trust that he would keep it from his mother, for she could not bear the thought of Sancia's triumph.

The next day, Katarina made the effort to join Luca and Pietro at the breakfast table. When Luca excused himself to go to the workshop, Pietro cleared his throat as soon as the door had closed behind him.

'I shall be returning to Venice the day after tomorrow and there's something I need to raise with you before I go.' He cleared his throat again. 'I hope you can forgive me for leaving so soon. Angiola finds it difficult when I'm away, so I gave her my word it would not be for long.'

I bet you did. 'It was good of her to spare you even for so short a time.' She did not even try to hide the sarcasm in her voice.

Pietro's eyes widened. 'She hasn't been too well—'

'Neither was your brother. He died.'

Pietro gasped. 'Katarina! I loved my brother—'

'Forgive me.' She reached for his hand. 'I'm not myself. I know you loved him.' She swiped away tears. 'What did you wish to speak to me about?' He practically squirmed with indecision, and she had a sinking feeling that this was something Angiola had charged him to do.

He closed his eyes for a moment, seeming to steel himself ready to speak. 'God know it's not the time for this, but I believe it must be done face to face. I want you to give some consideration to leaving Giuseppe's ... your workshop to my son Tomas.' He held up his hand to stop her speaking. 'I know Luca is his son and that he was fond of him, but wouldn't it be preferable for the Guarneri name to continue in Cremona. My father and grandfather—'

Katarina slapped her hand hard on the table. 'Pietro! Perhaps you should have remained here yourself then if it's so important to you.' She stood. 'This property has always been mine.'

'I didn't know.'

'Yes, you did.' She tilted her head studying him. 'Angiola does too, doesn't she?'

She watched him decide to tell the truth.

'Yes.' He studied his fingers. 'I met Luca's mother yesterday. She said to anyone who would listen that you have no legal right to inherit. She's wrong of course, but I think she would be jubilant if Luca should become your heir.'

Katarina understood what he was trying to do. He hoped her dislike of Sancia might sway her to favour his son. What he did not know was that her opinion of Angiola was little better. 'I'm sorry, Pietro, I've nothing further to say.'

A few weeks later, when Katarina had somehow found a sort of routine for herself in the workshop, a delegation arrived from the luthier families. The newest apprentice, Paulo, was sent into the shop when the bell sounded. Loud voices were heard, and Luca rose to his feet just as Paulo appeared back pink-faced and rattled. 'Signor Amati and them others wants Madonna.'

Luca made to go into the shop. 'I'll deal with it.'

'No. Show them up to the parlour. We'll speak to them together.' Katarina made her way upstairs while Luca fetched the men from the shop. She stood before the fireplace; glad Chiara had instructed one of the maids to light the fire for the air held a winter chill today. She lifted her chin when the three men walked in. Ricardo Amati. Carlo Bergonzi. Francesco Stradivari. No Rugeri, she noted. Claudio had advocated for her she felt sure, for she already knew what this visit was about. *How dare they.* 'Please sit, *Signories*. May I offer you refreshments?'

They sat. Ricardo, portly as ever and just as self-important, young Francesco uncomfortable with the task. And so he should be, his grandfather had been a true friend to the Guarneris. Carlo Bergonzi, thin and haggard, all trembling wattles and bruised eye bags, looked ill. Katarina wondered why he had come.

'Nothing for us,' Ricardo said, answering for them all.

Luca came to stand beside her. 'What can we do for you, *Signories*?

Ricardo flung him a black look when Francesco spoke first. 'How are you, Signora Guarneri? I was sorry not to see you after Giuseppe's funeral. You were unwell, I believe?'

He is trying to be kind. She found a wan smile for him. 'I am as you would expect but thank you for your concern.'

Ricardo moved forward in his seat. 'Good. Good. I'm glad to hear it. Now I should tell you why we're here.' He puffed out his chest. 'It's come to our attention that you've been selling violins with a maker's label claiming them as your work. Is this correct?'

'Yes.'

He blinked. 'Have you nothing more to say?'

'No.'

'Are you really claiming you made these instruments?'

'I am.'

Luca cleared his throat. 'What's the difficulty here? Katarina uses her own label in her instruments.' He turned to her. 'And she will now add I.H.S in memory of Giuseppe.'

Ricardo glanced at his companions but neither of them seemed to have anything to say. 'Then perhaps they are instruments left unfinished by your late husband?'

Katarina wanted to scream abuse at them. She clenched her jaw and her fists. 'They are not.' *Giuseppe was sick for months. How would he have made them?*

Luca placed his fists on his hips. 'If patrons wish to commission instruments from Signora Guarneri why in God's name should she not supply them?'

'If she is selling them under a false label. Her label ... if their provenance is uncertain then we cannot permit it—'

Katarina lifted her chin. 'Well, as that is not the case there is no more to be said.'

Luca gestured to the door. 'Allow me to show you out *Signories.*'

When Carlo and Francesco began to rise, Ricardo waved his hand at them, crossly. 'We aren't finished here. He turned to look up at Katarina again. 'It is the unanimous view of the Luthier families that the violins you are selling cannot have been made by you. A woman would not have the strength ... the skill in her hands to produce instruments of the quality you claim are yours.'

Katarina closed her eyes. They would not have come like this had Giuseppe still been alive. *No, because my label would not be in those violins, his would be. No concerns about provenance then.* (That she had used her own labels while he was ill without telling him, pricked her conscience.)

'Katarina made all those instruments. You have my word. There has been no deception,' Luca spat.

Ricardo sneered an oily smile. 'You saw her make them, did you?'

'I did. I saw her start with sheets of spruce and maple and watched her turn them into fine violins, which each patron was more than happy to pay for.'

'From start to finish? *Really?* You expect us to believe that?'

'Katarina strode to the door and flung it open. 'We're done, *Signories*.'

When Carlo and Francesco trooped out, Ricardo had little choice but to follow. Luca trailed them down eager to show them out. A few moments later Katarina went down into the kitchen parlour and dropped onto a chair in front of the fire. She ached for her husband. Ached for the comfort of his arms around her.

Chiara handed her a glass of wine. What did them buggers want? Nothing good by look of 'em.'

Luca arriving on the chair opposite, accepted a glass of wine and told Chiara all that had been said. 'Ricardo Amati is a prick.'

Katarina sighed. 'Your grandfather was apprenticed to the Amati. How can one such as him be the head of that family now?'

Chiara squeezed Kat's shoulder. 'What will you do, Madonna?'

'We'll go on as we are, and when the violins are mine, they shall have my label. I'll be interested to know just what they think they can do about it, if patrons choose to buy them.'

And that is what she did, each one ending in I.H.S in memory of Giuseppe.

KATARINA GUARNERIA FECIT CREMONE ANNO 1744 I.H.S

Coda

THE CIRCLE CLOSES

Twenty-Seven

SCHLOSS VON CLOY, VIENNA. DECEMBER 1748

KATARINA WATCHED ELLA SLEEP FOR A WHILE BY THE light of a single night candle, astonished as always by how quickly it found her once her head touched the pillow. There had been lots of hugs and kisses first. A child clinging to her and calling her Mutti. How could she ever have foreseen such a thing. But it was time to tear herself away, and she crept across the polished floorboards opening the door and closing it softly behind her.

Though candles burned brightly in the gallery wall sconces, the light from the great window caught her gaze, the newly risen full moon seeming too bright. She stood looking down on the formal gardens. All low clipped hedges and gravel paths but white and amorphous now under a blanket of snow reflecting the moon casting a glittering swathe across the garden and the fields beyond.

She tightened her shawl around her, her breath misting in the frigid air but unable to move away from the beauty of it, her thoughts wandering as her eyes roamed the transformed landscape.

Had it only been October the previous year she had walked

into the shop to answer the bell and found him there? Even after more than twenty years she had recognised him instantly. His face was thinner, but his eyes were the same vibrant blue they had always been, though with deeper lines around them now. In his turquoise satin coat, a froth of lace at his throat, and his white powdered wig queued at his neck, it was as though a peacock had strayed in off the street. 'Johannes.' Her hand had flown to her throat. What ... what brings you here?'

'You,' he said, simply.

She felt breathless with the shock of it. 'I ... I was sorry to hear about your wife.' A letter had come for Gianni telling him she had died in childbed the year before.

He looked away, his eyes roaming around the cramped shop with is rows of labelled boxes the names meaningless to him. 'It's hard that Ella will never know her. Carolina would have adored her.' He pressed his lips together, his gaze finding Katarina again. 'Losing Giuseppe must have been a terrible blow.'

'It was. I ...'

'I didn't know whether to write to you. It—'

'Gianni passed on your condolences.'

She managed to pull herself together. 'You must come through to the house. Meet my stepson. Take refreshments.'

He had appeared more outlandish than ever in the shabby kitchen parlour beside Luca in his work clothes. And he had laughed at himself because of it after Chiara hugged him and called him a popinjay. 'I's a housekeeper now, so I's allowed to hug you, ain't I.

'Of course you are.'

Katarina's hand flew to her mouth. 'Johannes, are you a *markgraf* now?'

He laughed. 'No, just a *graf.* My uncle managed to get himself an heir, believe it or not. Big relief, in truth.'

They had learnt he stayed at *Palazzo Poli* where the commandant was now an old comrade from his regiment. Joining him for grand dinners there, Katarina had found herself over-whelmed by memories. Informal ones on Becharie Vecchie both at her home and Gianni's had followed. Rides out in the autumn countryside revisiting old haunts and old discussions. It felt good to laugh so freely again, as though a pall of melancholy had lifted from her.

When the time came for him to return to Vienna, he had promised to write and then he was gone as suddenly as he arrived, leaving Katrina horribly aware how much she missed his company. She was still unsure just why he had come. And she had found it difficult to step back into the ordinary routine of her life in the workshop.

When the year turned and spring arrived, Katarina had come to a horrible realisation. She no longer found pleasure in making violins. Without Giuseppe, it had become a chore. She missed the excitement they felt when a violin was nearing completion. When he had made something beyond what seemed possible, or she had finished one worthy of his praise. She had laid her violin down on the workbench knowing it would be the last. She would train the lads. Help Luca run the workshop, but she would never make another instrument.

When Johannes returned, blown in on a March wind, it felt uncanny and when he asked her to marry him within days of arriving, there was a definite sense of the world turning as it was meant to. She made the property over to Luca with the proviso that all instruments must use the Estes name. He had been more than happy to agree.

They had married in the Rosary Chapel in San Domenico Basilica with just a handful of guests (Giuseppe and Teresa were there too, their names engraved on the family tomb). After tears and clinging goodbyes with promises to visit often, they had spent the night at *Palazzo Poli*. Katarina had stood before the fireplace staring into the flames, wondering what she was doing in her nightgown waiting for this stranger who was now her husband. What could she have been thinking?

When the door from the dressing room opened and he came out to join her in his indigo silk banyan, it was his hair that caught her gaze.

He saw her staring and ran his hand over his head, smiling ruefully. 'Time has not been kind. Perhaps I should have warned you what lay beneath my wig before you married me?'

She reached up and placed her hand upon his polled hair, now grey and thinning, receding from his forehead. 'Oh Johannes, your beautiful hair.' And with that her heart filled with such tenderness for him that all doubt left her.

He retrieved her hand, kissing her palm, and it was easy then to melt into his arms before he swept her up and carried her to the bed. And when, finally, their bodies came together they knew well how to give and take pleasure from each other and had laughed at the end, both saying it had been worth the twenty-year wait.

He had raised himself on an elbow to look down at her, brushing hair from her cheek with his fingertips. 'Don't feel you have betrayed him with your pleasure.'

She frowned slightly. 'Is that what you feel?'

'No. Not at all.' He searched her face 'Would you still have left had we already made love? I've often wondered.'

She chewed her lip for a moment, though already certain of her answer. She cupped his face. 'Yes, I'm afraid I would. I think I'd loved Giuseppe since I was thirteen.' She sat up higher against the pillows. 'I do wonder why you never came to my bed, though?'

'I've asked myself the same question.'

Even in the candlelight she could see he was holding something back.

'Did you know your mother had me examined—'

'Christ.' He was silent for a few moments. 'In truth, I feared she might. I didn't want to give her ammunition … I didn't want to risk that conversation. Cowardly of me, I know. I was young. Not much of an excuse.'

'She really didn't like me, did she. *She had said she would be my mother*. Was Carolina her choice?'

He laughed. 'Absolutely not. She was a lawyer's daughter I met through an old army friend. Not remotely to my mother's taste but I was ready for her then. And Carolina knew what to expect.'

'And you loved her.'

'Yes, I loved her. She was clever and good-natured … I loved her. But I never stopped loving you.'

Katarina blinked away tears. The moon was higher in the sky now and fresh snow was coming down in large flakes all aglitter as they fell. It was almost too beautiful. She turned away, aware again of how cold she was, thinking of the blazing fire in the salon. Not that great mausoleum of a chamber in the main house. That was now draped in dust sheets awaiting a rare visit from the twenty-one-year-old *markgraf*. No, they lived in a comfortably furnished wing with its own entrance at the rear where hills rose beyond the paddocks.

She moved quickly down the wide stone staircase and along the hall to the double doors leading into the salon. Candlelight gleamed out through one door left ajar. She hesitated for a moment looking inside. Johannes played chess with his elder son Josef who appeared older than his fourteen years. Eleven-year-old Karl stood at the table watching them, all three full of light-hearted banter. Josef was so like his father with the same thick fair hair Johannes had sported once, while Karl was dark like his mother. Watching, her heart swelled with love for them all. Her family.

She had wondered all those years before if affection for Johannes could grow into love and now she knew the answer. Though it was a quieter sort of love than she had known with Giuseppe, it was enough. She slipped inside and made for the fire holding out her hands to it. 'It's snowing again. It's pretty in the moonlight. Karl rushed to the window to look out, shoving the heavy brocade curtains aside and Katarina moved to join him there. Johannes's arm soon arriving around her waist.

Josef pushed in beside his brother. 'We should take the pony sleigh out tomorrow, Father.'

'I shall drive it,' Karl yelled.

'*What?* You? You won't allow him, will you, Father? Don't let him, please.'

Johannes did not reply, for he was busy kissing his wife.

Author's Note

Cremona was part of the Duchy of Milan until the unification of Italy (1861) and remained a Spanish dominion for many years until rule passed to Austria on 10 April 1707, during the War of the Spanish Succession.

Giuseppe Guarneri's legacy rivals that of Antonio Stradivari, his close neighbour in Cremona's luthiers' isle, with around 120 Guarnerius 'del Gesù' violins still in existence, highly prized and played by virtuosos today. His astonishing creativity and daring changes in design and construction are now seen to more than compensate for his lack of interest in the details of workmanship. Though his violins are as illustrious as Stradivari's, they are favoured by players with contrasting tastes as the two have markedly different tonal qualities. The violins of 'del Gesù' maintain sweetness but possess unsurpassed depth and darkness of sound that some players prefer. Much of his posthumous fame is owed to the Italian violinist and composer Niccolò Paganini (1782 -1740), who counted the 1743 'Cannon' as his most cherished instrument – the violin I had in mind when Giuseppe goes to meet Katarina before becoming ill. Also, the renowned 'King Joseph' violin made in 1737 inspired the instrument sold to the fictional Marco Bello.

It is likely that Katarina was a skilled luthier in her own right, her maker's labels having been discovered inside violins, though the consensus at the time insisted women were incapable of the skills required to make an acceptable instrument.

That little is known of the Guarneris' lives beyond their work, gave me space for my fiction. However, Antonio Stradivari's house at 2 Piazza del Domenico did have the distinctive loft described in my novel, and Andrea Guarneri debts at the time of his death meant the remainder of number 5 was sold. Conversely, in the book, Barbara Franchi has become Giuseppe's grandmother rather than his mother, and though Katarina Rota was a child of the Austrian occupying force in Cremona, and Johannes Horak an Austrian soldier – and they did indeed marry after Giuseppe's death in 1744 – Katarina's privileged status as the daughter of the deputy commandant, and Johannes's as an Austrian aristocrat, are entirely my invention as is Giuseppe's son, Luca and the Guarneris' child, Teresa. And while Pietro Guarneri married Angiola Ferrari in Venice in 1728 and went on to have 11 children, his bisexuality is my invention. Additionally, nothing is known of Giuseppe Guarneri's death beyond the administering of the last rites.

Finally, some linguistic choices are intentionally anachronistic, and any historical errors or inconstancies are entirely mine as are liberties taken with Italian translation.

About the Author

Dodie Bishop grew up in St Annes on Lancashire's Fylde Coast – where her family have a long history – and in the New Forest in Hampshire, spending much of her life there before moving to Devon. Now living in the Blackdown Hills with her husband and an overindulged cat, she has grown-up sons in London and Sydney. With a First-Class Honours degree in English Literature, she completed a Master's in Creative Writing and is a full-time writer, following an earlier career as an independent bookseller and company director, so books are very close to her heart.

A passion for history pushed her towards writing historical fiction, starting with a planned dual time-line novel developed as part of her MA. It was only after discovering how much more she enjoyed researching and writing the historical strand that she decided to abandon the second plot. And with that found her writing genre and Still Life, the Silence and Shadows series, and The Violin Maker's Wife are the result. So much so she now calls herself a time-traveller to the 17th century.

With her love of early modern period history, Dodie is particularly drawn to Baroque art, architecture and music, and has travelled widely visiting cities across Europe. She has a particular affection for Italy and especially Tuscany. She also enjoys birdwatching and has explored the Caribbean pursuing this. Many of the places she loves around the world provide settings for her novels.

Dodie has lived with rheumatoid arthritis since her early thirties and has brought her understanding of the constraints imposed by debilitating illness into her characters' experience.

To learn more about Dodie Bishop and discover more Next Chapter authors, visit our website at www.nextchapter.pub.

Printed in Dunstable, United Kingdom

78535567R00201